## "WAS THAT ALL YOU WANTED?"

"For the time being," Jesse said slowly, suggestively, his gaze sliding over Evaleen like a caress. She tensed her shoulders and took a step backward, her hand on the glass knob of the door. "At least until we get back to the ranch," he added, "where I'm sure you'll continue your tips on how I can be a good parent."

"You'll need a lot of them."

"Oh, I don't know. Theodora seems to like me well enough."

"You do have her wrapped around your finger," Evaleen admitted. "But that's only because the child in question is a female. No matter what their ages, you show an amazing ability to mesmerize the ladies."

"How about you, Miss Murphy?" Jesse stepped closer to her and smiled, his gaze penetrating the prim shell she'd erected when she'd walked out onto the landing. "Are you mesmerized by me?"

# BOOK YOUR PLACE ON OUR WEBSITE AND MAKE THE READING CONNECTION!

We've created a customized website just for our very special readers, where you can get the inside scoop on everything that's going on with Zebra, Pinnacle and Kensington books.

When you come online, you'll have the exciting opportunity to:

- View covers of upcoming books
- Read sample chapters
- Learn about our future publishing schedule (listed by publication month *and author*)
- Find out when your favorite authors will be visiting a city near you
- Search for and order backlist books from our online catalog
- Check out author bios and background information
- Send e-mail to your favorite authors
- Meet the Kensington staff online
- Join us in weekly chats with authors, readers and other guests
- Get writing guidelines
- AND MUCH MORE!

Visit our website at
http://www.zebrabooks.com

# RAINBOW'S END

## Florence Moyer

Zebra Books
Kensington Publishing Corp.

http://www.zebrabooks.com

ZEBRA BOOKS are published by

Kensington Publishing Corp.
850 Third Avenue
New York, NY 10022

Copyright © 2000 by Florence Moyer

All rights reserved. No part of this book may be reproduced in any form or by any means without the prior written consent of the Publisher, excepting brief quotes used in reviews.

If you purchased this book without a cover you should be aware that this book is stolen property. It was reported as "unsold and destroyed" to the Publisher and neither the Author nor the Publisher has received any payment for this "stripped book."

Zebra, the Z logo and Splendor Reg. U.S. Pat. & TM Off.

First Printing: February, 2000
10  9  8  7  6  5  4  3  2  1

Printed in the United States of America

# Chapter One

*New Mexico Territory—1888*

A half hour south of the railroad stop of Raton, bouncing along in her rented buckboard, Evaleen Murphy frowned as she spotted Jesse Stockton ambling down the rutted road toward Rainbow's End ranch, less than a mile away. It had taken her only a few well-placed inquiries yesterday to find out Stockton was known about town as a gambler and a ladies' man. Never one to take anyone's word for anything, Evaleen herself had gone in search of him and discovered he'd taken a room over the saloon instead of in the respectable Harvey Hotel, where she'd stayed.

As if staying in a saloon wasn't bad enough, that very morning, an obliging customer in the general store had pointed out Jesse Stockton to Evaleen just as he embraced a woman on the second-floor landing of the saloon and descended the side stairs. She, of course, had not bothered making his acquaintance at that time, nor did she particularly wish to now. Unfortunately, meeting him was going to be inevitable.

Evaleen shuddered. Sleeping with a saloon girl the night before his father's will was read! She didn't know what was going to happen at the reading of the will they were both headed toward, but if Jesse Stockton got awarded custody of her niece the resulting custody battle would make the last one look like a church social!

Stockton either sensed or heard someone coming, for he turned and raised an arm to hail her down, his face open and welcoming. It was the first time Evaleen had come so close to the younger son of the man her sister had married, and curiosity made her take a good look. Her sister had once written that Jesse was wickedly handsome, and with a catch in her throat that made it hard to breathe, Evaleen saw that she'd been right. As far as God's natural gifts went, Jesse Stockton was one good-looking man.

But beauty is as beauty does, and Evaleen could see Stockton's handsomeness had some very rough edges. His hair was brown with a glow of red highlights in it, but it hadn't been cut in Lord only knew how long. He wore a rough buckskin jacket and trousers with old mud stains on the knees. Both articles of clothing stretched over muscles that were work hewn and rippled as he moved. He also had a reddish brown beard covering his strong jaw. Despite the fact that the man's looks quickened her heartbeat—or maybe because of it—Evaleen bristled. Mercy, didn't he own a razor? He was going to the reading of his father's will, not spending the day mending fences. Couldn't he have taken the trouble to fix up a little before he left for the reading, if only out of respect for his deceased father?

She drove closer, and their gazes met. His heavily lashed, blue-gray eyes flashed her a hypnotic look of warmth and appreciation and greeting, as if she were a long-lost lover whom he'd been yearning to see for years. His gaze enveloped her, and suddenly a flow of pleasure and heat flushed her cheeks pink. No man had ever looked at her like that. Like she was someone desirable, not a twenty-four-year-old spinster with a too-round face, drab brown hair, and work-roughened hands.

She spared her hands a critical glance. They had withstood five years of hard duty as a waitress in a Harvey Hotel restaurant, keeping her and her aunt with a roof over their heads. The good Lord willing, they would help support her niece, too. She knew she ought to be proud of them even if men did prefer lily white, rose petal-soft ones, which she could never hope to have. A regrettable fact, but true, as long as she had her responsibilities.

And having those responsibilities was better than the alternative—living off men, she reminded herself firmly. Hadn't her sister proven that to her?

"Good morning," Jesse Stockton called out when she was a few feet from him, his voice as penetrating and warm as the sip of brandy she sometimes enjoyed with her aunt after a particularly trying day. "It'll be a pleasure to ride with you and make your acquaintance, sweetheart."

*Sweetheart?* She was by no definition this man's "sweetheart," and from the smooth way the word rolled off his tongue, Evaleen guessed instantly that Jesse Stockton used it on women as he used that seductive stare—to get his way. The urge was great to teach him a lesson, and remembering with deep-seated bitterness her sister and all the men who had manipulated her, Evaleen gave in to it.

Shaking her head as she approached, she called out, "If you'd saved the money you spent on that saloon girl last night, Mr. Stockton, you could have rented a mount from the livery to get you home."

His mouth dropped open, and he reached out as if to stop her horse. Her heart hastened its already swift beat.

"Yee-hah!" she called, lightly flicking her horse's reins. The horse bolted and the buckboard lurched forward, brushing so close to Stockton she could hear his startled intake of breath.

"Goddamn!" he yelled, jerking backward to keep from getting his toes run over. Tripping from a particularly deep rut, he landed on his backside. He cursed again, a string of condemnations, this time with a great deal more volume and directed at her.

Leaving him in her dust, Evaleen couldn't help but smile. Stockton might be angry with her, but she would bet her next week's tips he'd think twice before taking another female's reaction to his charm for granted. Bobbing her chin in satisfaction that she'd made her point, she continued on to the Stockton ranch, trying to ignore the heat slowly ebbing from her body. His look had aroused it.

"Damn woman!" Whooshing out his irritation in a huge exhalation of breath, Jesse rose and dusted the seat of his pants with his hat as he stared after the retreating buckboard. Who the hell was she? And where did she get off spying on his comings and goings, or criticizing where and on what he spent his money? He could still see the blue and white feathers in the woman's hat fluttering above her head. She'd had a stuffed bluebird in the middle of the feathers! Now if that wasn't the silliest thing he'd ever seen. No woman in her right mind would want a real bird nesting on her head, so why put a dead, stuffed one up there?

He was bewildered at how incensed her reaction to him had been. Jesse guessed he could understand a lone female not offering him a ride, but to try to run him over when he'd used his best techniques on her? She had to be downright ornery by nature.

Shrugging, he decided to let it go. The ranch wasn't that much farther, and he had other things to contemplate, things more important than some pinch-faced biddy with a ramrod for a spine, such as his father's death and the reading of his will at the house today.

Jesse hadn't been home for about four months, not since the whopper of an argument he'd had with his father that had driven him away from the ranch, Rainbow's End. This hadn't been the first time he'd left; after they argued about the ranch, he always took off for a while until both their tempers cooled. Then he would always apologize, and his father would ask him back. But not this time.

This time he'd left for good.

He regretted it now. While he'd been gone, his sixty-seven-year-old father had tried to break a wild mustang that instead had broken him.

Holding back his emotions, Jesse recalled himself as a boy of ten, trailing along after his father on a horse not so far from here. He'd had a bad case of hero worship then, and it had lasted right up until he'd been about eighteen or so. He'd wanted nothing more out of life than to be just like his father and take over the running of Rainbow's End when he got old enough.

But his father'd had his heart set on his oldest son, his pride and joy, inheriting the ranch. When Patrick had stolen the payroll and run off, Jesse's father, Reynard, had declared him dead to the town, and then had turned inward. He would no longer trust Jesse. Then the arguments had started, and Jesse had lashed back. The minor rebellions had irritated Reynard. Things had snowballed after that, and it had seemed like there was no turning back the clock. All because of Patrick's breaking their father's heart.

Jesse chewed on his bottom lip, changed course abruptly, and walked directly east, limping only slightly. Before he went home, he had something to do. Calloway Nesmith, the family lawyer, would just have to delay the reading of the will for him until he got there.

A quarter mile later, Jesse reached the hill where his father had buried his mother. Now there were two gravestones, side by side, at the top, stark gray squares against the baby blue sky. His mother, alone for so long, had finally been joined by the man who had gone to his grave loving only her, even though he'd taken a second wife.

Kneeling between the graves, Jesse raised his fingertips to his mouth, and then reached down and touched his mother's grave. He hadn't been here in years. He hadn't been able to come before this, to face his mother lying isolated on this hilltop overlooking the faraway mountains. But now... He stood before his father's gravestone, staring through tear-clouded eyes at the site. According to their solicitor, his father had been so admired and respected the whole territory had turned out for his funeral. Everyone except his own sons, one of whom no one knew for sure was alive.

Except himself.

His grief heavy in his heart, Jesse reached over, touched the freshly turned dirt over his father's grave, and then grabbed a handful of it. Slowly, almost reverently, he knelt, rubbed the earth between his hands and let it sift through his fingers down onto the grass atop his mother's grave, mixing the two spirits so that in his mind, he could truly believe they were united.

"I should have been here, Ma," he whispered. "If I'd been here, I wouldn't have let him get on that horse." His heart felt like a shrunken gravestone beating heavily against his ribs. Maybe he could have done better as his father's son. But he hadn't, and now there was no reason to change.

Rising, Jesse had to work the kinks out of the old injury to his leg before he could walk. He had his brother Patrick to thank for that, too. As he rubbed the muscles and took a step and rubbed some more, he fought back the unfamiliar, hot ache of tears in his eyes. At twenty-nine, he was finally totally in control of his life, with no father to stand over him and stare disappointedly; he ought to feel a sense of freedom—but he didn't. All he felt was this overwhelming sense of grief and guilt.

If he'd stayed here, his father would still be alive. In control of his son's whole life, but alive.

Drawing in a long breath, Jesse started down the hill, making himself think about anything else but what he'd done wrong. His youth might have been his father's fault, but since he'd turned eighteen or so, his life had been of his own making. He'd known his father was controlling for a long time, and he should have dealt with it instead of fighting Reynard hand and fist. Instead of throwing his youth in the man's face.

He'd reached the half-mile point to Rainbow's End when he caught the distant sight of a phaeton riding in his direction from under the gateway arch that announced the ranch. Figuring it was Calloway, the lawyer, coming to look for him, Jesse sat where he was and wiped his eyes and forehead with his handkerchief. Only the middle of May, and it was already too warm to walk.

Resting his leg, he took a good look around, savoring the fact that he was truly home. Behind him and to the west were Raton Pass and the mountains, to his east, Stockton land, prefaced by the magnificent two-story log home and surrounding support buildings. He stared at them now with a mixture of pride and trepidation—and a single question.

Was the ranch finally, irretrievably his?

Within minutes the stocky, ruddy-cheeked Calloway Nesmith reached Jesse and leaned back, halting the black mare pulling his elegant carriage.

"Jesse. Hop on," Calloway said, shifting over. "You should have told me you needed a ride. I would have stopped by for you on my way in."

"I didn't think about it till this morning." That wasn't exactly the truth. Announcing his presence in town had occurred to Jesse; he just hadn't wanted to tell the solicitor that he was staying at the saloon. Calloway had been good friends with his father and wouldn't approve. Why ruffle feathers with the man in charge of the estate? "When I heard about Pa," he told Calloway, "I left Colorado without waiting for my pay, so I couldn't hire a mount."

Calloway nodded in understanding. Mount or no, Jesse didn't regret last night or having to walk today. Cassie Jo at the saloon had been worth it, he silently told that damnable woman with the bluebird in her hat. Pushing back the tinge of denial that passed through him, he surveyed the surrounding territory for any sign of her or her wagon. He didn't want to meet up with her again, but he was curious about who she was.

"Your pa's favorite horses are all still here," Calloway said. "Waco will get you a decent mount." Waco was an employee of Reynard's who had been around for at least eight years, from what Jesse could remember. No one knew where the man had come from, or anything else about him for that matter, except that he was a master with horses and pretty damned good at overseeing the ranch on occasion, too.

Jesse nodded with satisfaction. If Calloway thought it was okay to give him a mount, that was a good sign he'd been left something of value in the will. After that last argument, he hadn't been certain his father wouldn't completely write him out.

"So why don't you save us both some time and tell me what exactly Reynard's left me?" Jesse asked.

"Can't do that."

He studied Calloway, frowning. "Why not?"

"Uh, Jesse ..." Pause. "Because there's something I neglected to tell you in the telegram."

Jesse glanced at Calloway, but the stocky man wouldn't meet his eyes, and Jesse felt trouble crackle in the air between them. The man had heart problems, Jesse knew, and didn't like too much stress anymore. So he decided to give him a break.

"When you wired me you'd be home by yesterday," Calloway said, "I went ahead and notified the other beneficiary named in the will. We all have to be together when I read it."

"You mean Patrick's at the house?" Jesse asked, his gut tightening at the thought.

"Patrick's dead, Jesse. You know that."

"That's just what Reynard told the townspeople when my brother took off the last time for good. Dead to my father is what he meant."

Calloway shook his head. "Reynard wouldn't lie to me."

Jesse knew better. But he let the subject go. No sense in arguing. If Patrick wasn't in the will, then he didn't care what everyone believed about his brother.

They were within a few dozen feet of the house, and the two mongrels that Jesse had found in Raton and adopted distracted him as they bounded by the phaeton, howling their hellos. The dogs, one spotted brown on white, and the other, a short black mutt, looked sleek and happy. Someone had been taking care of them in the couple of weeks or so since his father had died. Probably Waco. The foreman had a soft spot for animals.

Abruptly, Jesse turned back to Calloway, unable to stand the suspense. "So who's the other beneficiary?"

"Miss Evaleen Murphy."

Jesse raised his thick eyebrows in question. He'd heard the name before, but couldn't quite place it.

"Miss Murphy is the sister of your father's second wife, Cynthia."

Murphy. He remembered now. Jesse scowled. "Why would he include Miss Murphy in his will?"

"You'll find out all too soon," Calloway said. "I just thought I'd best warn you so you wouldn't be caught by surprise."

The word surprise conjured up the image of the woman with the bluebird in her hat. Jesse groaned. No, not her... Please, not her. He knew he should go find out, but suddenly, looking at the house, he was reluctant to enter, hesitant to face his father's ghost.

Calloway pulled the brake on the phaeton. Jesse closed his eyes briefly, shutting back the grief. He couldn't show tears in front of one of the townsfolk. Why, it might get around that he actually had *feelings*. When he opened his eyes again, he took a good long look at the log home built by his father some twenty years ago now. Other than ex-Senator Dorsey's thirty-five-room stone mansion a few miles away, it was the nicest place in the whole northeast of New Mexico, with six bedrooms upstairs, and a parlor, kitchen, dining room, sitting room, and study downstairs. A veritable mansion, suitable for the empire he hoped to build.

Hopping down, Jesse took a minute to give the dogs a few fond brushes of his hand. When he looked up, he saw Calloway already stood on the porch, one arm propped against the rail, waiting. Jesse joined him, carrying his saddlebags.

Yanking open the door, he entered the house and slowly breathed in the rich scent of tobacco that lingered, the scent a part of his earliest memories of the place. Glancing around, he saw nothing much had changed, except a woman sat on the far side of the sofa in his father's study. One look at her confirmed his suspicions, feathers and all.

At his entry, Miss Murphy rose, and as with every female he met, Jesse couldn't help but give her a once-over. She was shorter than he'd figured she'd be from seeing her sitting, with such an hourglass figure he was sure she was cinched in hard at the waist by way of a corset. Mounds of breasts and hips like hers, he usually saw only in his dreams, and his eyes lingered on their curves for more seconds than he cared to count. Her hair was a plain, medium brown—not dark, not light—and was pulled back up under that hat of hers which shaded a round face. She also had clear green eyes with little laugh lines at the corners. His first thought was that except for her body, the woman was quite ordinary looking.

But then she smiled, her whole face lighting up with a cheerfulness that seemed to radiate straight from her heart, and Jesse couldn't look away.

"Mr. Stockton," she said, with a voice that for some reason made him think of a rippling brook. "I do hope you've been working on your vocabulary since we last met."

Calloway looked confused. "You've met?"

"We've made a passing acquaintance," Jesse said, unable to resist. "And I do mean passing."

"At least your disposition is improving," Miss Murphy said in those same clear, sweet tones.

"Oh." Calloway looked from Jesse to Evaleen, shook his head, and walked past them to settle in a thick armchair. "I hope you two don't mind, but I'll need a few minutes to double-check my facts before we begin. The will is quite complicated."

"Take your time, Mr. Nesmith," Miss Murphy replied, smoothing her skirt under her derriere as she resumed her seat. The action outlined her every curve, and as Jesse feasted his eyes on them, he wondered if all the padding was Evaleen or some of it was wool stuffing. *It'd be damned interesting to find out,* he thought. If she riled him enough, maybe he'd ask.

But right now, he had a different question. Walking into the study, he dropped his saddlebags on the floor inches from her feet. She jerked back her toes.

"Tell me, Miss Murphy," he asked, "did that bird in your hat peck your manners out of your brain, or do you always leave strangers stranded?"

"I never stop for stray animals, Mr. Stockton. I find they are most often vicious." Her voice remained congenial but firm. No nonsense here. Her eyes sparkling, she gave Calloway a smile. He was regarding the two of them with wide eyes as he pulled a thick, folded document from inside his coat pocket.

Jesse swore under his breath. Miss Murphy was calling *him* vicious? Still thinking of Calloway's sensibilities, Jesse controlled his baser impulses and held back the reply he wanted to give her. "I suppose you haven't heard that stopping to help people in trouble is one of the codes of the West?"

"No, I hadn't. Actually, I'm not from the West. I come from the more civilized area of east Kansas."

"But you ain't in Kansas anymore," Jesse muttered under his breath.

She heard him. "Unfortunately so, for I am forced to be here with you."

"Evaleen, honey," he said, trying to ignore the hot

shooting pains in his leg, "Hell will freeze over before you're ever *with* me."

"Goodness, gracious, I should hope so." The twinkling abruptly left her green eyes as they narrowed. "My sources in Raton told me you are a wastrel and a womanizer, Mr. Stockton, and it appears to me they have you pegged exactly. I would add that you are uncouth."

Jesse was taken aback because she'd had such a swift comeback to his sarcasm and because, for a newcomer, she'd been so well informed about his character—or at least the townsfolk's opinion of his character. But then he recalled the good Reverend Mortenson, with whom he shared a mutual dislike, and the owner of the general store, to whom he owed a gambling debt from a night of poker, and ... well ... there were probably a couple of others whose feathers he'd ruffled before he'd left home. After all, he hadn't stopped by town to say good-bye. Any one of the folks could have shared an opinion of him with the girl.

"So I've made a few mistakes." He shrugged.

"A few?"

"Can you honestly say your own character is jim-dandy? You've never done anything to be ashamed of?"

"Not a thing," she replied, smiling smugly as though she were a mile thick in moral fiber. "Have you ever considered changing your ways? Seeking the Lord's help, perhaps?"

"Are you joking, or seriously concerned?"

Miss Murphy didn't answer, but she didn't have to. There was no sign of levity on her face. Jesse couldn't recall the last time a woman had wrapped his wits so completely around her little finger. Usually he remained utterly in charge, and usually the battle was more sexual in nature than character-oriented. Right now, between this mental battle with Miss Murphy and the fact that he was still reeling from his father's death, it was just exhausting.

Easing himself down onto the sofa next to her, Jesse sprawled out his legs, knocking his knee into hers. She jumped, whipped her legs away, and trembled with righteous indignation. Grinning, he stared at her for a couple of minutes. She stared back as her fingers twittered on her lap like the squirming limbs of a trapped rabbit. Although the family resemblance was there in her face, Evaleen wasn't a thing like her sister Cynthia in disposition, that was for sure.

Seeing that Calloway was still reading, Jesse pushed himself off the sofa and walked over to his father's desk, where he lifted the lid of a leather case and pulled out a cigar, wanting something to assuage his nervousness while he waited. He might be a ladies' man and a wastrel, but that was during his off hours. On workdays, he wasn't used to being idle, and he didn't like it.

Lighting the cigar, he glanced over toward Miss Murphy. Thinking about her and why she might be there made him remember Theodora, who was technically his stepsister, he guessed. He'd been almost twenty-one when his father just up and married Miss Murphy's sister Cynthia, who'd been a pregnant widow. Jesse remembered the baby had cried a lot, and Cynthia had rarely spoken—at least to him. He'd never known what she was thinking of the people around her or of life on the ranch. By contrast, her sister Evaleen's face was much easier to read, making her an open book.

Anyway, it had been Cynthia's silence that had made her leaving so surprising. Jesse wondered if the lonely life out here had gotten to her, or if Reynard had been too boring in bed. Either way, she'd walked out on his father two years after their marriage, leaving only a note of farewell. The next word of her his father had received had been notification of her death along with guardianship papers for Theodora. That had been a couple of years ago, if Jesse remembered correctly.

Not knowing what to do with a six-year-old girl, Reynard had immediately contacted Cynthia's sister, this Evaleen Murphy who now sat on the sofa. Instead of giving advice, Miss Murphy had fought Reynard tooth and nail for custody of Theodora—and had lost. Her sister's wishes had been clear. Cynthia had wanted her daughter with the person who could give her the best life, and that was Reynard. Miss Murphy was forced to work to support an older maiden aunt confined to a wheelchair and could neither afford the child nor give her full-time attention.

The cigar in his mouth, Jesse gazed at the back of Evaleen Murphy's head speculatively, wondering what she was thinking now about all this. Was she wondering if she would get custody? It was obvious she loved the child; she'd begged Reynard to find a boarding school for Theodora in Kansas, not far from where she lived, so the two could visit as often as possible. Reynard had felt comfortable enough with the arrangement not to even bother to visit Theodora, just pay her bills. So would his father give the child to her aunt now? Jesse thought he should.

Just as he thought he should end up with the ranch.

But he knew his father enough not to count on a danged thing. Suddenly anxious to find out what exactly was going on, Jesse turned back to the lawyer.

"So, Cal, do I get the title to the ranch or not?"

# Chapter Two

While the lawyer rattled papers and assured Jesse he was almost ready to begin, Evaleen Murphy sat primly on the edge of the brown velvet sofa, her bare hands folded over one another on her lap. The only sign that the calm facade she was trying to project was false was that the bluebird perched on her hat was bobbing precariously with her jerky efforts to keep still.

She watched Stockton carry a silver ashtray from the desk and set it across from her on a small table, then slump down on a chair opposite the sofa. Smoke from his cigar crossed the short space between them in a swirling gray cloud that smelled like dirty socks. Her eyes watered. She wrinkled her nose and blinked.

Opening his mouth to address them, Calloway Nesmith took a breath and coughed until he turned red. Instead of getting the hint, Jesse continued to puff away. So rude, Evaleen thought. She had a feeling no one had taken the strap to Jesse's backside enough when he'd been a child, to teach him consideration of others.

Calloway cleared his throat, which immediately, Evaleen noted, caught Jesse's attention.

"Let's begin. In regard to the ranch, Rainbow's End, Reynard has left a statement." He rattled the paper in Jesse's direction. "This is intended for you." Lifting the paper from his lap, he began to read:

" 'Your leaving and staying away for so long, Jesse, has made me realize I need to make a last-ditch attempt to right the wrongs I have done in raising you and your brother Patrick. Patrick is lost to me, but I am desperate to find some way to reach you before you, too, waste your life away.' "

Evaleen nodded. She hadn't been overly critical of Jesse Stockton. Apparently his own father agreed with the townsfolk about his son. She began to relax. Surely, if Reynard Stockton had thought his son that bad, he wouldn't have named Jesse as Theodora's guardian.

The lawyer continued. " 'Your inability to settle down and become an upstanding citizen indicates to me that you prefer not to be burdened with responsibility. To such a man, I hesitate to leave this ranch. However, I truly believe that you love Rainbow's End and the life of a rancher as much as I did, so I am therefore giving you a chance to prove yourself worthy of receiving both.' "

Calloway stopped reading and coughed again. Evaleen looked with reproachful eyes at the cigar in Jesse's hand, but he remained either oblivious to their discomfort or uncaring. This was ridiculous. She had to have some air, and so did the attorney. But she wasn't about to lower herself to argue with Stockton about his smoking habits.

"The next part—"

"Just one moment please, Mr. Nesmith," Evaleen interrupted, rising and walking behind the desk, where she pushed back brown drapes and yanked a window open. A warm breeze gushed in, and she could see it blowing the smoke when she turned back to the two men. "There. Nothing like fresh air," she said, staring at the cigar in Jesse's hand as she resumed her seat.

Jesse looked from her to Mr. Nesmith and then down at the trail of smoke, sighed in exasperation, and snuffed the offending cigar out in the silver ashtray. "Go on, Calloway."

"The next part is going to be hard for you to accept, Jesse, so I beg you to hear it out in its entirety before you protest." Calloway wiped the beads of sweat on his forehead with his handkerchief. "Also, it might be nice if you choose not to shoot the messenger."

Evaleen cast a sideways glance at Jesse, wondering what on earth the man would find hard to accept. From what everyone in town had intimated, he never took anything seriously. His eyes were hard to read, and so her eyes took in the rest of him to see if she could tell what he was thinking by the way he held himself.

His wide hands, dusted with dark hair, rested on his thickly muscled thighs. For just a moment, she imagined those hands on her skin. They'd be callused, she thought, and demanding, like the man himself. Yet when she'd first looked at him on the road earlier, there had been something in Stockton's gaze that had made her wonder if he wouldn't know how to be gentle and loving with a woman. . . .

What was she thinking? Her cheeks and throat growing warm, Evaleen slowly fanned herself with her hand and averted her eyes, turning them back to the lawyer, who was beginning to read aloud again.

"Reynard goes on to say, 'I propose to teach you a lesson, Jesse, by temporarily signing the ranch's ownership over to . . .'" Pausing, Calloway shot Stockton a worried look.

"To whom?" Jesse asked, sitting up straight.

"You'd better read it yourself, in your father's own hand," the lawyer said, rising with an "Oomph" of exertion and walking over to Jesse. "I don't want to be accused of lying. Fifteenth line from the top."

The next few seconds passed like slow-dripping molasses for Evaleen, and the suspense made her heart pound. She glanced at Stockton's face at the same time Jesse thrust down the document with a loud curse. Startled, Evaleen watched the paper drift to the rug like a lazy feather.

Sighing, Calloway bent to pick it up. When Evaleen returned her gaze to Jesse Stockton, she was surprised to see the man's stare leveled upon her, his blue-gray eyes furious.

"What the hell kind of hold did you have over my father?" he demanded.

Shrinking back in her seat, Evaleen pressed both hands to her bosom, where her heart pounded with fear from the intensity of Stockton's reaction.

"Now, Jesse, calm down," Calloway warned, returning to his chair, the page of the will in his hand. "Reynard did this entirely on his own. He was thinking of the child's best interests."

Unable to bear seeing the pain and anger in Stockton's eyes any longer, Evaleen looked at Calloway. "Are you saying I'm the new owner of this ranch?"

"As if you didn't know!" Jesse exploded. "What was it with you and your sister and men, anyway? How on—"

"Mr. Stockton!" she said, shooting up out of her seat and then, as she realized she'd lost her composure, swallowing in surprise. She hadn't known her voice could get that loud. "I'll have you know I do not like your insinuation that I somehow had anything to do with your father leaving Rainbow's End to me—in any kind of manner, let alone what you're implying. From what I've heard, you're the one with all the experience in manipulating the opposite sex, not I."

"She didn't know, Jess," Calloway broke in before Jesse could say anything. He took out his handkerchief and mopped his forehead again. Evaleen understood his nerves. A slow trickle of perspiration had been running steadily down her back ever since Jesse had first walked into the room.

"Reynard thought this up all on his own," the lawyer added. "Now sit, both of you, so we can get on with this."

Evaleen couldn't do as he bid, because once she'd looked at Jesse to see if he was sitting, she could not let go of his stare. There was something so sad in his eyes, so compelling, that she almost felt sorry for him, despite the nastiness of his innuendo. He must have wanted the ranch very badly.

"I did say temporary ownership," Calloway said, breaking into her thoughts. "Now, the other half of this is, Jesse, that you are the temporary guardian of Reynard's ward, Theodora."

"Impossible!" Evaleen blurted out. Staring at Calloway in disbelief, she waved her hands as her heart sank and anguish knotted her throat. Good Lord, she was going to cry! She didn't want to, not right here in front of Stockton. "You can't be serious, Calloway. Surely no man in his right mind would give the guardianship of a young girl to a man like *him*."

"I do believe I resent your implication," Jesse said in retaliation for her earlier statement. Miss Murphy's eyes burned into him in reply, but he didn't care. He was too damned angry.

"Would you two please hear this out?"

Miss Murphy slumped back on her seat, and Jesse stalked to the far end of the room, wanting to distance himself from her. There he leaned back against the wall next to the window and waited.

"By temporary guardianship of Theodora, Reynard means a term of six months, during which you and Miss Murphy both will be put to a test. You, Jesse, will attempt to remake yourself into a model citizen. You will participate in the town hall meetings in Raton, go to church regularly, and refrain from any activity such as gambling or"—glancing at Evaleen, the solicitor reconsidered his words—"er, that is, you shall not associate with the female employees of the saloons. Miss Murphy, whom Reynard determined to be of exemplary character, and I will be the judges of whether or not you accomplish this."

"And what the hell does *she* have to prove to you and me?" Jesse asked.

"I was just getting to that. Miss Murphy, Reynard had wanted you to take care of Theodora, but he had his doubts about whether or not you would make a good mother."

At Evaleen's incredulous look, Calloway held up his hand. "He believed you were too tied to your work, and too young; that's why he fought you in court before. In his eyes, only a woman who is devoted to child rearing could do a good job."

"Ahhh, the lady has flaws," Jesse said.

"Spoken by the man who invented them," Evaleen snapped back. Unable to remember a time when she'd been this angry, she jerked her head around to the lawyer. "I have been tied to my work to support myself and my aunt, Mr. Nesmith, and I'm darned proud of that. Still, as hard as I work, I managed to get to see Theodora and be far more of a family to her than Reynard was. Therefore, I find it amazing that he was so worried about me being a good mother when he was such a pitiful guardian."

Calloway did not comment.

"I could fight this in court, you know," she said, sitting

up straight, clutching the reticule on her lap in her two hands.

"You could, yes, but Reynard has set it up so that if you contest this will, instead of being handed over to you, the ranch, apart from a trust for Theodora, will be sold and the proceeds used to fight you. You'd never win."

Against money? No, she wouldn't. Tears rushed to her eyes, and Evaleen blinked them back. He was right, and he knew it. She didn't have to agree.

"But hear me out, please. There's a lot more to this, especially where Theodora's immediate future is concerned. One of the conditions is, Miss Murphy, that you quit your position with the Harvey Hotel where you are currently employed and move into this house with Theodora."

"Ah, hell!" Jesse broke in.

"You will learn how to manage the ranch from Jesse. He will learn how to take care of Theodora and how to be an important part of her life from you. Reynard hoped that in doing all this, you two would learn a lot more than just facts about yourself."

"What the hell does that mean?" Jesse asked.

"It's open to interpretation."

Evaleen's gaze reverted to Jesse, who moved forward and swung himself down onto the same armchair he'd vacated earlier. He looked through Calloway, as though he thought he might be in the middle of a bad dream, which was precisely how Evaleen felt. He rose and began to pace again, resembling a cat preparing to strike at its prey. Except that Jesse limped.

Evaleen looked away, not wanting him to see that she had noticed his affliction. For a second or two, she wondered what had happened to him, and then she pushed the thought aside. She had enough to think about. Her gaze turned back to Calloway Nesmith.

Earlier, the lawyer, who was somewhere in his late fifties, had mentioned his previous heart attack. Nesmith seemed uneasy and almost fearful of Jesse. Evaleen worried that Stockton's ire might be enough to launch the man into a seizure.

"Are you all right, Mr. Nesmith?" she asked. "Can I find you some water? Please don't let this upset you."

"I'll be fine, thank you." He smiled lopsidedly at her, then returned his worried gaze to Jesse. "Jesse, please sit down."

Evaleen shot the wide-shouldered cowboy the most censuring look she could muster, the one that never failed to corral wayward children where she worked. "Yes, why don't you sit, Mr. Stockton? You're not intimidating anyone, and you're dirtying the carpet."

Jesse stopped and looked down at the dirt path he'd trampled into the plush maroon carpet. Dirt from mud he'd gotten on his boots in Colorado while doing honest work, which was more than Miss Evaleen Murphy was going to be able to do for this ranch, he was certain.

"Why the hell should I care?" he retorted. "According to Calloway, I don't own it."

"But you can win it back," Evaleen reminded him. "Please give Mr. Nesmith a chance to explain further."

"You ever been a schoolteacher, Miss Murphy? The nagging, old-maidish kind we used to throw spitballs at?"

"Are you asking to be paddled, Mr. Stockton?"

For seconds, he merely stared at her, and then his eyes changed, took on an aura of something that made Evaleen once again draw in a quick breath. She had never had a man look at her that way before. Never. It brought her to her feet because she felt too vulnerable seated.

"You really don't want me to reply to that, do you?" he asked in a velvety voice.

Continuing to stare at her, Jesse wasn't giving in. Evaleen refused to look away. For a long minute they stood almost face-to-face, and she wondered if this was the beginning of a long, long battle to come. She would do anything to protect Theodora from winding up with this man, she realized. He was absolutely ... There were no words to describe him. She had no wish to be around him. She didn't like demanding males who appeared to have all their charm wrapped up in their anatomies. Men like Jesse Stockton made her feel funny inside, kind of weak-kneed and tense, like she was forever waiting for something really alarming to happen.

Finally, just when she thought she could bear the standoff no longer, Jesse pushed his fingers back through his shaggy, reddish brown hair and scowled more deeply at her than she'd thought possible. His fury at the situation showed in every taut line of his ruggedly handsome face, but he sighed with resignation and sat down.

Up, down, up, down. He was a ball of harnessed energy. Evaleen resumed her seat as Calloway mumbled something under his breath. She found herself watching Jesse again, unable to take her gaze off the way he sat, legs spread wide, body open to her.

She swallowed before her thoughts could go reeling and turned to address Calloway. "I have questions."

"Just a minute. Let me see if there's anything else, and then I'll be happy to answer them and get your decisions."

Jesse wanted to yell and kick in walls. His father hadn't forgiven him after all. He expelled a pent-up breath. Goddamn, he could just see that self-righteous preacher Mortenson sitting in town with Reynard and plotting this one on him. They'd think it fitting revenge for the times Jesse had passed by the church on Sunday morning on his way home, hungover and red-eyed, and had grinned at the preacher's and Reynard's frowns of disapproval as they'd stood on the front steps greeting the God-fearing townsfolk.

Finally, Calloway looked up again and nodded.

"Mr. Nesmith," Evaleen said, "I understand what Reynard was intending with this, and I can't say I'm happy. First, of all, about my moving in here with Theodora, I must remind you that I have an elderly aunt confined to a wheelchair living with me. Would she be welcomed here, too?"

"Oh, hell," Jesse said, turning to look at them. "That's all I need under my feet. Two old maids and a young one."

Evaleen jumped to her feet. "And I personally think one child to care for will be quite enough in my life, thank you," she retorted crisply.

Again, their gazes did a stormy battle across the room, and neither budged until Calloway spoke.

"Jesse, if you're at all worried about the company you'd be keeping, I'm certain you'd be perfectly comfortable living in the bunkhouse."

"Oh, for God's sake," Jesse muttered in disgust. He'd be damned if he'd abandon his home. "I don't believe this. C'mon, Calloway, you've got the best interests of the kid at heart. Can't we just send her off to Kansas with Miss Murphy and bypass all this foolishness Reynard wanted? How can I do my best with the ranch if I've got three females to worry about?"

"That is the whole point Reynard is making. He wants you to learn—" Suddenly, Calloway shook his head and stood. "Never mind, Jesse. If you won't *both* go along with this, my instructions are to stick Theodora in a boarding school in the East and give the ranch to the church in Raton. All other monies and lands in the estate will go into a trust for Theodora. And don't even consider asking me to go against Reynard's wishes, Jess. I was *his* lawyer, not yours."

A long silence followed, during which Evaleen stared at Jesse and he stared back at her. Finally, Calloway asked, "So what are you going to do?"

Jesse folded his arms over his buckskin-covered chest and contemplated them both silently. He loved this land, the view of the mountains, the very earth the cattle trampled. He'd both sweated and dripped blood for Rainbow's End from the time he was old enough to fire a rifle and mend fences, and he was not giving it up without a fight.

But first, he would damn well pursue all possible avenues of escaping his father's dictates.

"What happens"—he rose and walked over to his father's cigar box, picked up another cigar, ran it under his nose to breathe in the aroma and rile Miss Murphy, and continued—"if I tell you I have no intention of following any of the stipulations, and I'm staying anyway?"

"Just like I said before," Calloway told him. "Church gets the ranch and Theodora goes to a boarding school in the East—and I will have you thrown in jail for trespassing."

Miss Murphy turned her head all the way around to gaze anxiously at Jesse, her green eyes worried. "You can't let that happen to that child. This is horrible!"

He held her gaze a second or two longer than he should have, and then he dropped the cigar back down into the box and slammed the lid shut. He began to pace again, long, even steps. The church wasn't getting his property. He wasn't living here with Miss Murphy. He'd already had enough of the woman, and their six months hadn't even started. There seemed no way out of this, either, unless . . . *she* was the one to turn the proposition down?

"You don't want to stay here with me, do you, Miss Murphy?" he asked. "Your virtue may not be safe with a ladies' man in the house."

She eyed him evenly. "I think you overestimate your

talents all around, Mr. Stockton. Still, you have a point; you can be trying. Perhaps you should consider *your* safety. If you're annoying enough, Aunt Victoria may lose her temper and brain you with a skillet."

Calloway hid a smile.

Jesse ignored her comment about her aunt, so caught was he by her previous statement. So she thought he overestimated his talents with the ladies, did she? It might be interesting to give her a demonstration of just how talented he was and then see if she still thought the same way afterward.

"I think it's time to ask for your decisions," Calloway said, interrupting Jesse's thoughts. "Miss Murphy?"

Evaleen had absolutely no desire to let Jesse Stockton get control of poor Theodora, nor did she wish to sentence the girl to the next nine years in a boarding school with no family life to speak of. But she didn't have the money for another custody fight. The last one had almost wiped out her small savings, and taking care of Aunt Victoria meant they counted pennies.

Her aunt Victoria wouldn't mind the change of scenery, she was sure, and she would be a fitting chaperon with Stockton in the house. But the thought of giving up the security of her position at the Harvey Hotel set butterflies fluttering in Evaleen's middle, though she imagined if she told her manager what was going on, she might be able to return to work as soon as she got legal, permanent custody of Theodora. The Harvey line of restaurants and hotels were very fair employers, and the more she considered taking a leave of absence instead of quitting permanently, the more she liked the idea. Calloway wouldn't have to know.

Yes, that was precisely what she'd do—arrange to get her position back the second she was free. She'd be damned if Reynard Stockton was going to dictate how she lived her life. How dare he? This certainly showed her that Cynthia had been right about his dictatorial ways. Poor Cynthia, married to the man!

"Miss Murphy?" Calloway asked.

"Of course I agree," Evaleen said smoothly.

"And you, Jesse?"

Jesse shifted his weight. Could he fake being an upstanding citizen for a few months in order to keep his ranch? Hell, yes. Once he had the deed to the place and Miss Murphy and Calloway off his back, he could go back to doing exactly what he pleased. Come to think of it, he'd get away with as much as he could during the next few months too. He had no intention of living like a saint, not with Miss Murphy wiggling around him for hours every day and reminding him he wasn't one.

But he would try to be the best damned father he could. Every kid deserved that much. As for the school-board meetings and going to church, well, how the hell hard could that be, apart from the time spent? He'd show up, agree with the others, and leave, and that would be that. Afterward, to hell with what the town thought. He had nothing to prove to anyone except himself. And all he wanted to prove to himself was that his father had been wrong about him failing as a rancher.

With a start, Jesse realized that his father probably had expected him to fail at becoming a fine citizen and lose the ranch, as a lesson. Well, there were ways around everything. Even Evaleen Murphy.

"I accept," he said grimly.

"Fine." The wrinkles on Calloway's furrowed brow seemed to lessen as he nodded. "Miss Murphy, I need to know when you can start the arrangement."

"As soon as I speak with my superior in Kansas, I'll go to Kansas City to pick up Theodora and come back here."

"Fine. Then everything's settled?"

"Except for one thing," Evaleen said. "I should hope it would be obvious, but I'm not doing anything personal for Mr. Stockton."

"Personal?" The lilt in Jesse's voice made it sound as if he was taking her statement differently than Evaleen had intended it. She kept her eyes on the lawyer as she blushed.

"Yes. I'm not hiring on as his personal maid. I'll be happy to make enough for him to eat, too, but I won't clean his room or do his laundry."

Calloway frowned as though he'd never given the matter any thought. "Jesse?"

Jesse scowled. "I promise you, Miss Murphy, you'll never have to see the likes of my underwear, on or off my body, no matter how much you might want to."

"Want to?" Her face grew pink with anger. "Want to? I assure you, Mr. Stockton, I would prefer burning in he—"

"Ahem!"

They turned. Calloway was staring at them both. "I am beginning to wonder if you can be exactly fair as far as judging Mr. Stockton, Miss Murphy."

"Oh, I'll be fair, Mr. Nesmith. I plan to keep a journal of Mr. Stockton's progress—or lack of it. You'll be able to veto my decision if you have the slightest doubt."

Calloway considered both of them for a long moment, and then, with a slight shake of his head, said, "So, Miss Murphy, if you're picking up Theodora from Kansas City, you'll probably need a letter to withdraw her from the school."

She nodded.

"I'll have one drawn up. Please stop by my office before you leave Raton." Calloway looked to Jesse as though waiting for him to protest.

"What can I say?" Jesse asked, throwing up his hands in surrender. Thinking hard, he gazed at Evaleen Murphy.

As she reached down to pick up her reticule, a satisfied smile settled over the curves of her lips. For a few seconds, Jesse was mesmerized by that smile, but then he mentally yanked himself away.

*She is gloating inwardly,* he told himself, *and thinking the matter settled, no doubt.* Jesse glanced at Calloway, who had started gathering up his papers. A mistake, his sparring with Miss Murphy. Now he'd just have to work that much harder to convince Calloway and the woman herself that he could change and he deserved the ranch.

"I'll check and see if our rigs are ready, Miss Murphy," Calloway said, interrupting his thoughts. "Will you be all right?"

For a fleeting second Evaleen looked frightened at the prospect of being alone with Stockton, but she recovered quickly, her chin bobbing upward. "Of course. Thank you."

Having no intention of bothering her, Jesse threw himself into a chair, thinking hard. This whole arrangement bothered him, but he couldn't see any way out of it. He was going to be forced to go along with this ridiculous scheme of Reynard's.

He glanced at the woman, now in the hallway in front of his father's mirror, smoothing wisps of hair under that ridiculous hat of hers. Evaleen Murphy was full of vinegar, and she could stand up for herself, he gave her that much. Did she find all the interference in her life as repulsive as he did? He wanted to ask, but he was totally unsure that she would give him anything but a sarcastic answer. It wasn't as though they were or could be friendly.

Friends. Thinking back, Jesse realized that between working on this spread and spending all his time fighting his father, he'd never tried to make any friends—he didn't count the men at the saloon—and he wasn't sure he'd know how. But maybe, considering what was at stake here, he thought it was time he started trying to make his first one—Evaleen. He had a feeling his life was about to become hell if he didn't.

# Chapter Three

Why was Jesse Stockton staring at her? Evaleen wished she had gone outside with Mr. Nesmith and checked on her own rig instead of staying in here to be picked apart by this cowboy's intense stare. Her hands began to shake under his scrutiny as she continued to fiddle with her hair, and she dropped them to her sides in exasperation. Her trepidation was absolutely ridiculous. Stockton would never want her. What did she have to worry about, really?

She glanced at him out of the corner of her eye, and she knew she was kidding herself. Jesse appealed to her senses in a way that told her he was every bit a man. It wouldn't be Stockton she'd have to worry about. It would be herself.

Through the open window, they heard the dogs howl and bark, and happy for a distraction, Evaleen walked to the door.

"What now?" Passing her, Jesse flung the door open and stood within inches of Evaleen to look outside. Her heart skipped a beat and paced furiously. She considered backing away from him, but didn't want to give him the satisfaction. What was with her anyway? She'd never reacted to any man like this before.

For some reason he didn't understand, Jesse couldn't stand being so close to Miss Murphy, so he pushed through the door and down the porch steps to look at the visitor the dogs were greeting. With foothills and mountains in the distance, and the closer, more peaceful meadowlands directly behind him, a washed-out-looking man with a straw hat was riding on horseback up the long, trampled drive, the dogs yipping at both sides of the horse and helping to kick up dust.

Jesse recognized him. Nate. He participated in an occasional Saturday night poker game for fun, but usually he just hung around the general store in town, watching the trains come and go.

While he waited for Nate to get closer, Jesse breathed in the crisp air and stared at the mountains to the west. He was either going to have to make friends with Evaleen or fight her to the hilt to make her believe he fit the stipulations to the will. That wouldn't be easy to do, considering he had no intention of letting Reynard order him around from the grave. But he had no intention of giving up this ranch, ever. Not for anyone.

He sighed. He had loved his father so much. This just wasn't right, Reynard's taking revenge on him by denying him the land he loved. What had he done that had been so wrong?

"Howdy, Jess," Nate greeted. "Heard you were back. Coming to town for the Saturday night poker game?"

Jesse began to say yes, remembered, and shot a look backward. Sure enough, Evaleen Murphy was standing on the porch, hands on hips, the bird in her hat close to chirping.

"No, Nate," he said. "I believe I'm turning over a new leaf."

Nate looked confused. But then Calloway rounded the side of the house to join them, and Nate got off his horse, never losing the piece of straw dangling between his teeth. "This came for you on the wire, Mr. Nesmith," he said, pulling a slip of paper from the pocket of his flannel shirt. "Proctor at the station said it was urgent. I figured, you bein' here with Mr. Stockton and all, and it bein' a nice ride, I'd bring it out."

Taking off his hat, Nate turned back to Evaleen, grinned, and nodded. "Mornin', ma'am. New in town, ain't ya?"

"Good morning," Evaleen said, shining her smile on Nate and winning a bashful look in return. "I'm Evaleen Murphy. I'll be moving to the area soon."

"Well, ain't that a plumb treat!" Nate said, slapping his hat against his thigh.

*Yeah, Nate? Just wait till she runs you over!* Jesse clamped his teeth together and shook his head. He needed a cigar.

"Ahem, Nate," Calloway said, drawing the man's attention back to the matter at hand. "Could I have that message?"

After handing the lawyer the paper and receiving a couple of coins for his trouble, Nate rode off with a wave and a sweeping grin at Evaleen, who gave him a pert little smile in return. Maybe, Jesse thought, he could spark a romance between the two and get the woman out of his hair on an occasional evening or Sunday afternoon. That would increase his chances for enjoying himself considerably.

The lawyer pondered his message for so long, Jesse had to force himself not to pluck it out of his fingers. Even Evaleen gave a dainty sigh of impatience from where she stood on the porch. By the time Calloway finally looked up, Jesse felt ready to explode again. "Well?"

"There's a problem."

"Ah, hell, Calloway, I already figured that out."

"This is from the headmistress of Theodora's boarding school." Calloway's ruddy face reddened even more, and his eyes got dewy. "Theodora has disappeared. A possible kidnapping, but they aren't certain. Who would steal that child? She must have run away. I just don't understand. How could this happen?"

Evaleen gasped, picked up the dark blue skirts of her traveling suit, and rushed down the porch steps right toward Jesse, stopping within a foot of him. "You son of a bounder! What did you have to do with this?"

"Not a damned thing!"

"I don't believe you," she said, shaking her fist and reaching back.

Uttering a forceful swear word he seldom used but now was driven to, Jesse caught her wrist firmly before she could hit him, forcing it down to her side. Their eyes battled for a full minute, and then her arm relaxed. Apparently, whether she believed him or not, she'd decided not to fight him—physically.

"Calloway," Jesse said, letting her arm go, "Patrick might have found out about Theodora's value and taken her."

"Patrick?" Evaleen's eyebrows lifted in question. Seconds later, she remembered what Cynthia had written her once. Patrick had been Jesse's older, ne'-er-do-well brother.

"He's dead, Miss Murphy," Calloway told her. "Jesse just refuses to believe it."

Evaleen shot a strange look at Jesse and then turned to Calloway. "Mr. Nesmith, I want to hire someone to search for Theodora immediately."

"Hire? I wouldn't know how to begin to find a man. Certainly there is no one who could do something like that in Raton." He looked to Jesse for help.

"Ah hell," Jesse said. He didn't know anyone in Raton

he could trust to hire either. His leg wasn't up to the trip, but somebody had to go. Calloway couldn't; the man might have a heart attack with the stress. Besides, despite what they all wanted to think about Patrick's being dead, Jesse suspected his brother was involved somehow. How he would have found out anything about their stepsister, he didn't know, but he wouldn't put anything past his brother—not even having someone spy on the goings-on at Rainbow's End.

If he was right, and Patrick was somehow tied up with this kidnapping, getting the child back might lead to violence, and Jesse couldn't ask anyone else to get involved in that.

"I'll go after her," he said curtly.

"You?" Evaleen scoffed, shaking her head. "Ha! I'm inclined to think you'll be more of a father to the cattle on this ranch than you'll ever be to Dorie, Mr. Stockton. If she's left in your custody, I hesitate to consider what might happen to that child."

"She's already missing, Miss Murphy." Jesse's temper was sorely tried. "What the *hell* else could happen?"

"Exactly my point," she replied without flinching. "Left in your and Mr. Nesmith's care, the child has already disappeared." Drawing in a breath, she watched his look of disbelief. If she was being unfair, she didn't care. Theodora was missing. She had every right to be furious.

Wrapping the ribbon to her traveling purse around her fingers tightly, so the discomfort would remind her not to show them how worried she really was about Theodora, she made a decision. She was strong and independent. She certainly didn't need these two men or their help.

"I'll go find her myself," she told them. Unable to resist, she added, "And since I'm leaving to find *your* charge, Mr. Stockton, you will kindly tend *my* cattle while I'm gone."

Since both men stared at her without replying, Evaleen

continued. "As soon as I've found the child and quit my position at Harvey's, I'll bring her and my aunt back here with our things. Mr. Nesmith, we will work out my reimbursement for the expenses of finding Theodora later when we set up the household accounts." Thank goodness, she told herself, she had two weeks' pay coming to her, such as it was, and a little bit left in savings.

Brushing past both men, she headed toward the rear of the house and her rig, totally aware Jesse was at her heels. Whirling around, she said impatiently, "What?"

He skidded to a stop in the dirt. "I'll go with you. You can't go against whoever took her alone."

Evaleen's green eyes glinted. "Who says? You may have a license to run Dorie's life when she returns, Mr. Stockton, but don't even consider trying to run mine. I have the advantage of being a woman. I can outthink you, outreason you, outtalk you—"

"That," he drawled, "is for sure. But I'll bet you can't outdo me on one other thing." His whole face changed suddenly, and she knew what he was talking about. So hot was the tension between them, their gazes seemed like two burning flames that met and exploded, and she abruptly closed her mouth.

*He wanted to kiss her,* she realized with crystal-sharp clarity. Just as clear was the fact that she wished he would. If he did, then she could hate him without feeling guilty, and their upcoming time together could be total war. That she could deal with. What she couldn't deal with was the fact that his lash-shaded eyes were once again evoking strange, riotous feelings within her, like lazy breezes pushing a wildfire forward.

He did want to kiss her. As Jesse stood there, he wrestled with the desire to haul the stubborn woman into his arms and kiss her until she grew weak in the knees and conceded without a battle the point of his going after Theodora—

alone. But he couldn't kiss her, and he knew why. Whatever kind of shrew she was, Evaleen Murphy was a good woman. He didn't mess with good women.

Evaleen was the first to jerk away, her reticule swinging outward as she turned from him, the bird in her hat bobbing as she stomped toward the rear of the house.

"We'll go together," he said, refusing to give up.

"We will not!" If she found Dorie, wouldn't that be one point for her if it came to a court battle for custody. She might not even need a whole lot of money to win.

She groaned under her breath as she charged toward her wagon. Who did Reynard Stockton think he was, putting her on equal terms with his irresponsible scoundrel of a son, when it was so obvious she was much more capable and qualified to be a parent than Stockton?

"Well then, I'll go myself," Jesse said from behind her. "You'll be wasting your time, because I mean to find her."

She reached her rig in front of the stables and pulled herself up onto the seat.

"I feel sorry for you, Mr. Stockton," she said. "You're offering to go after that girl for all the wrong reasons. The sooner you can get her back, the sooner you can win your ranch, right?" She grabbed the reins. "You don't know her, and you don't care about her. She's just another child—"

Limping to her side, he had one foot up on the buggy step in seconds and one hand gripping her wrist. "Don't presume to tell me my motivations for doing anything, Miss Murphy," he said, his eyes hardening. "You don't really know me."

For a second, reading the earnestness in his eyes she doubted he knew was there, Evaleen considered letting him come with her. Just as swiftly, she decided not to, because she didn't want to travel alone with him. She didn't want to chance getting to know a man capable, she was certain, of helping her to meet the same tragic end that had befallen her sister.

A shiver skipping through her, Evaleen glanced down at his fingers locked around her delicate wrist. "Fine. I don't know you. Now, if you don't mind, I'd like to be going so I can catch today's train out."

"Just be aware that in going after Theodora, you may be walking right into danger."

He was trying to scare her into letting him go with her, Evaleen realized. Enough was enough. "Mr. Stockton, your reputation has preceded you." She weighed her next words carefully. "They told me in town that you don't care who you hurt. You do what you feel like doing, say whatever gets you what you want, and you leave a world of trouble behind you when you go without looking back. So tell me, please, why I should believe you are telling the truth now, especially when you have so much to gain by going with me?"

Jesse's jaw set as he lowered himself off her rig. Stepping back, he left her enough room to drive away if she wanted. "Do what you want," he said, no longer sounding so glib. "I'll find Theodora anyway."

She'd wounded him, Evaleen saw, and suddenly she wished she hadn't. She wasn't normally a hurtful soul; there was just something about this man that pushed her to her limits. She was used to being in total control of her life, and now she had to fight him for every step she took where Theodora was concerned. She didn't like that at all. "Go ahead and look for her, Mr. Stockton, but you're wasting your time. You won't be able to find her."

"What makes you so sure?"

"You haven't seen her since she was tiny. You have no idea what she looks like." Slamming her hands down, Evaleen set the horse in motion. Passing a waving Mr.

Nesmith on her way down the drive, she raised a hand in farewell and headed back to town.

Evaleen had known Stockton would have to take the same train she did from Raton; it was the quickest way to get to Kansas City where Theodora's school was. She ignored Jesse for the most part on the trip, hard to do when each time she happened to glance his way, he tipped his black wide-brimmed hat or gave her a mocking grin. At the Maune, Kansas, stop, her home, she sneaked away as quickly as possible so he couldn't follow her. She didn't want him trailing her all over Kansas while she searched for Theodora. At least, she was fairly sure she didn't.

The trouble was, she was plagued by doubts about going after Theodora by herself. She'd always believed that people who worked together got more accomplished than those who remained alone. There was also his warning about the danger Theodora could be in. That chilled her, not for herself, but because Theodora might need protecting and she wouldn't be able to handle that. And then, where could the child be? Was she wrong to have spurned Jesse's offer of help?

How she hated needing help from someone else, especially an arrogant man like Jesse Stockton! Ever since she'd left her parents and four siblings behind in St. Louis five years ago to work for the Harvey Hotel in Maune, she'd been careful to make her own way in life without relying on anyone else for help. Especially not on men as her sister Cynthia had done. The shame Cynthia had brought to their mother and father in the close-knit Irish neighborhood where she'd grown up had been awful.

In her own attempt to atone for her sister's sins, Evaleen had taken in Aunt Victoria and had fought to gain custody of Theodora after Cynthia had died. She'd brought back

# RAINBOW'S END 45

honor to the family name. Her parents were so proud of her, and she had done it all herself, without the help of a man.

But now Theodora was at stake.

Deciding that worrying about searching with Jesse was silly until she met up with him again, Evaleen first visited the home of the Protestant minister and wife who were helping her aunt while Evaleen was out of town. When they heard Theodora was missing, they agreed to keep her aunt with them for as long as it took to find the child. The couple was elderly, and even though Evaleen was donating money to their church, she normally wouldn't dream of imposing on them for so long. She had no choice, however, for her fifty-year-old aunt was largely self-sufficient, but she needed occasional assistance and couldn't stay by herself. Taking her along to find Theodora was out of the question.

After letting her aunt know they'd be going to New Mexico soon, Evaleen visited her supervisor at the Maune Harvey Hotel and had a talk. He fully assured her that she would be welcomed back as soon as she was ready. Too tired to leave the hotel, she got a room there for the night and, the next morning, boarded the first train to Kansas City, anxious to start a true search for Theodora.

A glance around the car told her Jesse Stockton had ceased following her. Relieved, she decided to mentally debate the question of asking him for help, then settled back on her seat for the trip.

As the train chugged quietly toward Kansas City, she tried to figure out whether or not she would need Jesse's help, but all she ended up with were more questions.

Who on earth would have taken Theodora? Was this Patrick, Jesse's brother, really alive? What exactly would she be walking into when she went looking for the child? Should she beg Jesse to come with her if she met up with him? And finally, why on earth couldn't she handle Jesse Stockton?

Since she didn't have any answers to the first questions, Evaleen had nothing to do but mull over the last. Refusing to let Jesse help her find Theodora had been childish stubbornness on her part that she now regretted. It was just that each time Stockton had settled his seductive stare on her, she had grown confused and flustered, and he brimmed with so much anger that the only thing she could do was strike back. The two of them sparked off each other. Before she moved to Rainbow's End, she would have to find another way to calm the choppy waters between them, or he would make her peaceful life miserable.

A few minutes before they reached Kansas City, Evaleen thought she had the answer to her problem with Jesse. She reasoned that the primary difficulty in dealing with Stockton lay in the fact that he was so damn attractive, so very male. The trick then would be for her to stop thinking of him as a man and to start thinking of him as another person who needed her supervision and help, like Aunt Victoria or Theodora. Tell him the way things were going to be. Lay down rules and regulations for him to follow. Mold him into the type of man he probably longed to become. She could do that. She was certain she could.

She would have to, to keep Theodora and her own reputation, the two things she valued most in the world.

"Kansas City!" the conductor yelled, breaking into her thoughts.

Always concerned about her image as a Harvey Girl, Evaleen automatically reached up, smoothed her hair, and adjusted her hat, the latest bit of fashion she'd bought on her last trip to Kansas City. As her fingers worked, she thought about Stockton's derisive comments about her choice of hats. He was an odious man. Remembering it would help her keep in mind that someday she was going to marry a man sophisticated enough to appreciate a fine work of art and to want an independent wife so he could follow his own intellectual pursuits. Unlike Jesse Stockton, who would probably die during a card game or drown in his whiskey in a saloon somewhere.

Her hands dropped to the reticule in her lap, and she frowned at the mental image the last thought evoked. Such a waste of a man, too. Perhaps she could do something to help the poor soul.

Having arrived at Theodora's boarding school, Evaleen asked the driver of her hired hackney to wait in the rounded drive and headed up the front steps of a sprawling two-story building. The huge, old mansion housed not only the school itself, but scores of rooms in one wing provided quarters for pupils like Theodora, while the rooms in another wing were occupied by chaperons and teachers.

Quite the most expensive school in the area, set on the south end of ten acres of tree-studded and path-ribboned lawns, it was a beautiful place. Pleasant enough to live at, Evaleen supposed, unless you considered the school replaced a home and family life for Theodora. And then how did you measure? She couldn't believe that according to the lawyer, Stockton, should he get his way, planned to ship the child right back here. Jesse seemed to have no feeling, and Evaleen was beginning to look forward to teaching him a thing or two about love.

The door to the office of the headmistress, Miss Hurley, had a glass window and a welcoming foyer where a receptionist sat at her desk. The young woman announced Evaleen immediately, and she was invited right into the headmistress's private office.

Walking through the doorway, Evaleen stopped abruptly upon seeing Jesse Stockton sitting on the edge of Miss

Hurley's desk. As he rose and turned, her mouth dropped open.

If she hadn't spent quite a while perusing him back at the ranch, she would have doubted it was the same man. This Jesse Stockton had shaved, exposing a clean, masculine jaw. And he didn't have a lick of dirt anywhere on his nicely cut black morning coat and trousers. He still hadn't gotten a haircut, but his hair looked cleaner and thicker, and it was full of shiny waves. Evaleen was spellbound.

Suddenly, she wished he'd kissed her back at Rainbow's End when they'd both been so angry. She'd simply had no idea. . . .

What was she thinking? She was acting like a frustrated old maid. This simply would not do.

"You look surprised to see me," Jesse said smoothly.

"Not to see you, no," she answered, somehow finding her voice. "That you're still here at the school, yes. What are you up to?"

Before he could respond, Miss Hurley, a muscular, buxom woman, rose out of her chair and rounded her desk, her bosoms bouncing with her lively steps. Evaleen saw that Jesse noticed—and that he was grinning at her. She sucked in her cheeks in irritation.

"I am so very, very sorry about Theodora!" Miss Hurley said. "Mr. Stockton filled me in on everything—that he has temporary custody of the child, but that you would also be searching for her." She cast a sideways glance at Stockton that was anything but discreet. "Separately from Mr. Stockton, of course."

Not replying, Evaleen studied Miss Hurley, trying to think of what was different about her from their previous meetings. She was dressed in her usual black skirt with a red, white, and black striped shirtwaist, only for the first time, the three top buttons were undone, showing an expanse of creamy white flesh. Evaleen settled upon the woman's rapidly blinking eyes. The round, wire-rimmed glasses Miss Hurley always wore were now on her desk, and the headmistress was blinking because she was desperately trying to focus.

Evaleen hazarded a guess that the headmistress had taken off her glasses to attract Jesse. She shook her head in disgust. So it wasn't just her. Stockton apparently had a strange effect on all women, no matter how intelligent they were.

"Mr. Stockton and I have been talking about what might have happened to Theodora." Miss Hurley looked adoringly at Jesse and tittered. "Weren't we, Mr. Stockton?"

Dropping into the nearest available seat in front of Miss Hurley's desk, Evaleen frowned. "You've lost one of the students in your charge, Miss Hurley. I fail to find anything funny in that." She looked over at Jesse. "As for you, Jesse, I'm actually pleased to see you here. Now that I finished my business in Maune, we can continue our search for Theodora together."

He frowned deeply, looking wary.

"But, Miss Murphy," Miss Hurley said, "Mr. Stockton assured me you two were heading in different directions to find Theodora. He said you didn't like him."

He did, did he? Evaleen shot him a long, censuring look and then smiled at the administrator. "Really, Miss Hurley, you must excuse Mr. Stockton. He does come up with some tall tales. Stringing ladies along is part of his charm. He's been known to say interesting things to anyone in skirts. Indeed he often calls a lady sweetheart and tells her how lovely she is. He didn't ask you to dinner, did he?"

Miss Hurley looked at Jesse, her puzzlement evident. "Why, yes, he did."

"Evaleen—" Jesse's voice was threateningly low and controlled.

"He asks every lady he meets to dinner," she continued,

raising her eyebrows innocently in his direction. "If he shows up at all, he eats his fill and then usually makes some excuse to leave the table. After that"—she paused for effect, but she didn't have to. Miss Hurley was leaning forward, waiting—"after that, do you know what he does? Why, Mr. Stockton here ducks out the back door and leaves the lady to pay the bill. His last lady friend in Raton didn't even have enough to pay for her own dinner, let alone his. He eats like a horse. She had to do a whole bunch of dishes."

"Oh, my word!" Miss Hurley said.

"I think you've given the lady enough of an earful, haven't you?" Jesse sank into the chair next to Evaleen's and leaned close enough to her that she could smell the manly fragrance he'd splashed on after he'd cleaned up. She tried desperately to ignore the intoxicating pull the scent had on her equilibrium, but she couldn't. Leaning over toward him, she breathed in his lime and soap scent. . . .

"Why don't you do that bird on your hat a favor and bury it?" Jesse whispered in her ear.

Jerking up straight in her seat, her cheeks blushing, Evaleen intertwined her fingers on her lap. His lips had almost touched her ear!

"I'll have you know this hat is high fashion," she said stiffly. "Putting a stuffed bird on a hat is no different from using leather to make boots."

He shook his head slowly in disagreement.

"All that's important here," she said slowly, trying to breathe normally again, "is that we find Theodora. Don't you agree?"

"Precisely." Jesse nodded.

"I've come to find out what you know, Miss Hurley." Evaleen turned her gaze back on the headmistress, who was staring at them both. "Any details would be appreciated."

"Yes, Miss Hurley," Jesse said, folding his thick arms over his chest. "Perhaps we should fill Miss Murphy in on what we know."

He was making a point that he thought he was in charge, and for two cents, Evaleen would have cheerfully flattened him with a fist. To her everlasting satisfaction, Miss Hurley looked as if she agreed as she put on her glasses and turned her back to them to button up her shirt as inconspicuously as possible.

"From what Theodora's classmates say," the headmistress said, "she was on her way to her first class when she returned to her room for a book. She never got to the class. Because of the oddness of the situation, a complete search of the grounds was launched not thirty minutes later, but she didn't turn up, and no one saw her leave the area. It's as if she just disappeared!" Miss Hurley wrung her hands. "All of her belongings, except for a few articles of clothing, are still here."

"Did Theodora mention anything was wrong to any of the students? Had she noticed anyone following her? Had she spoken of any worries she might have had? Anything to suggest she might have run away?" Evaleen asked.

"Theodore was very happy here!" Miss Hurley protested, her ample bosom heaving with indignation. "She was perhaps a little fanciful, but she got along well."

Jesse's eyebrows narrowed. "What do you mean, fanciful?"

"She sometimes insisted she was a fairy princess, and the school was her prison. She said she was going to be rescued by a handsome prince from some evil knight."

Jesse shifted, feeling sorry for his father's ward. The poor kid must have been unhappy to dream about being rescued. But Reynard hadn't been worried about Theodora being up here, figuring she was getting a good education and would be terribly lonesome at the ranch with no females or children about. At least here, Evaleen had been visiting her.

Jesse looked at the woman next to him from a new perspective. She surely did handle a lot. An aunt, a job, and from what Miss Hurley had told him, she had still found time to visit her niece regularly.

"All your employees are accounted for?" Evaleen was asking.

"They all live on the grounds, and no one has been absent from their duties since Theodora's disappearance."

"And that's all you know?" Evaleen was asking.

Miss Hurley nodded.

Rising, Evaleen turned to him. "Are you coming, Jesse?"

"Why, Miss Murphy," he answered smoothly, his eyebrows lifting, "I thought you were just joshing about having me along before. What happened to change your mind? Did you get lonely?"

"No," she said, her bright green eyes challenging him. "I just thought you might need a firm hand and guidance while you searched for Theodora, so you don't get yourself all serious about some new lady and forget what you're supposed to be doing."

"I don't have the least intention of getting involved with any woman."

Evaleen shot a sideways look to remind him of Miss Hurley, who looked angry enough to spit a bullet right into his womanizing heart.

Jesse threw up his hands. Rising, he reached for a carpetbag he'd left along one wall and walked out of the room.

She was doing it, Evaleen thought with satisfaction. She was maintaining control of their relationship. Trying not to smile, she turned to the headmistress.

"Please have Theodora's things shipped to Reynard Stockton's address in Raton, New Mexico Territory. God willing, Theodora won't ever be returning here."

\* \* \*

As she came through the front door, Evaleen saw Jesse leaning against the front of the building, but chose not to acknowledge him. Breezing past, she walked down several steps before she realized he wasn't following. With a sigh, she turned and trudged right back up the stairs to him.

"Mr. Stockton, do you need me to personally invite you to come along, or will you please just pretend you're an adult?"

He shifted his feet and stood up straight. "I'm not sure what to do with you, Miss Murphy."

She tensed.

"I'm pleased you've come to your senses about our searching together," he said, taking a step toward her.

She stepped back reflexively.

"But there's one thing you'd better get straight," he added, closing the space between them.

The intensity of his blue-gray stare raked over her, and with heat filling her cheeks, Evaleen backed up further until the porch railing wedged into her back. Suddenly, he stood in front of her again, his hands on either side, their bodies touching. A thick, velvety heat seeped through Evaleen's midsection where his abdomen touched hers.

"What should I get straight?" she whispered softly.

"You try another stunt like the one you pulled with Miss Hurley in there, and I'll personally see that you regret it."

She swallowed and tried to tell herself that having him so close was terribly unpleasant, but it wasn't. Then she tried to tell herself he was threatening her. He was doing that, and her heart was pounding. But his threats weren't what was really frightening her.

"By stunt," she said, "I take it you're referring to my harmless tale about your womanizing?"

Staring at her, he lowered his head until she could see

the tiny flecks of gray in the blue of his eyes. Her lips fell open of their own accord, as thick and heavy as her insides had become. Whether in anger or with desire, she wanted him to kiss her. She was being as shameless as Cynthia had become, and she didn't care.

She honestly didn't care.

"What I'm referring to," he murmured, his voice low and sensual, his breath brushing across her cheek, "is your telling Miss Hurley that I would ever walk away from a lady. I've never done that...."

He *was* going to kiss her. Giddy with excitement, Evaleen took a huge breath, closed her eyes, pursed her lips, and waited, listening to her heart beating wildly.

"Until now."

# Chapter Four

"Oooooh!" Evaleen whispered on one long breath, watching as Jesse strolled down the porch steps toward the carriage, carrying his carpetbag. The nerve of that man! Every tingling inch of her still wanted his kiss. How could he just walk away like that? Hadn't he felt it, that almost magical sensation that had stretched between them and had almost pulled them together? Couldn't he have spared her just one kiss?

She balled her fists to fight the throbbing frustration within her. He was every bit the scoundrel she'd heard he was. Jesse Stockton was nothing she wanted in her life, that was for certain, and she had to totally ignore this . . . this . . . She searched for the word she wanted. "Passion," that was it. She had to ignore this passion he evoked in her. Jesse Stockton wasn't a man—he was a devil.

Her sister's face flashed in her mind, and Evaleen realized this same passion she'd experienced had been what had drawn Cynthia into the gutter. Jesse had just given her a hint of the power a man could wield over a woman when it came to . . . allure. Evaleen thought that might be the word, but she wasn't sure. She'd never had to deal with feelings like this before, and she was totally out of her league.

Yes, "allure" *was* the word, she decided, staring blankly at the hackney waiting for her. Jesse possessed an extraordinary allure that made her forget all her common sense. But now that she knew what the problem was, she could deal with it. She knew she could. Cynthia had simply given in too easily to men. Always delicate, her sister had no backbone to stand up to the kind of mental assault a rake like Jesse was capable of. But she, Evaleen, was different.

She was strong. Through her own hard work and determination, she'd won respect at work and in her community. She wasn't about to sacrifice her good reputation just for a few minutes of what might be an enjoyable experience, but nothing more. Jesse Stockton was not the type of man on whom she'd stake her whole future. From here on, she would merely guard herself against being tempted. It was that simple.

Jesse stopped by the hack, turned, and crossed his arms over his chest. Her heart thumped betrayingly in her chest as she realized he was waiting for her, and purposely, she drew herself up to her full height—which, granted, didn't make her very tall—pretending to have whalebone in her spine.

Jesse noticed and smiled devilishly in response to her stiffening posture. "It's mighty hard being passed by and left behind, isn't it, Miss Murphy?" he called.

Passed by and left . . . The pleased-as-sugar look on his face spoke volumes, and suddenly, Evaleen understood what Stockton was up to. His not kissing her had nothing to do with the fact that she had devalued his character in front of the school's headmistress, he had too much confidence in himself to care. Nor was his revenge over the ranch or the custody of Theodora.

No, his leaving her bereft seconds before, aching for his kiss, had been personal. They were in an intimate war, and it had started when she'd left him behind, sitting in the dust, instead of falling for his smile and the gibberish he spouted that made other ladies swoon.

This was just too much! She would walk away from New Mexico and Jesse Stockton in the blink of an eye if it weren't for Theodora. . . .

Theodora! Squaring her shoulders and painting a look of nonchalance on her face that belied the hurried thumping of her heart, Evaleen walked swiftly down the porch steps and toward the carriage. How could she have forgotten about that precious child, even for a few seconds? That was the last time she was letting her mind wander. For Theodora, she would put up with the Romeo rancher, but not for one moment longer than she had to.

Once she reached the carriage, she ignored Jesse and glanced up at the driver. "Please take us back to the railroad station."

When the man nodded, she shifted direction and stepped over to the still-closed door of the hack, which she eyed pointedly before turning to Jesse and raising her eyebrows. He might not want to kiss her, but he darned well was going to treat her like the lady she was.

Bowing from the waist, Jesse opened the door for her. Evaleen tensed her body as she reached for the sides of the door, but thank goodness, Jesse did not lift even one little fingertip to help her up. If he had touched her, she would have punched him right in his insufferable smirk.

Once they were seated, facing each other and riding toward the train depot, Evaleen folded her hands on top of her reticule and tried to catch his gaze, only she couldn't. He was already stretched out, his hat pulled down over his eyes and his arms crossed over his chest, almost as though he were determined to go to sleep and ignore her!

"Mr. Stockton," she said loudly.

Tilting his head back, he managed to move his hat from over his eyes without touching it. "What?"

"From your silly display of irritation on the porch a few minutes ago, I've gotten the impression you don't fully understand why I interfered with your impending affair with Miss Hurley."

"You were jealous?" he asked, his reddish brown eyebrows lifting.

"Of course not!" she snapped, but then she forced herself to calm down. Taking a deep breath, she paused for a few seconds, regaining her composure—which wasn't easy to do with Jesse's hypnotic eyes directed at her. "I interfered because I have every intention of keeping my promise to Mr. Nesmith to reform you in order to get custody of Theodora. Unless I had stepped into that little face-to-face you were setting up with the schoolmistress, I wouldn't have been fulfilling my part of the deal."

"Tell you what. Instead of you messing up my life, maybe we could just come to a mutual understanding?" Jesse asked, raising his eyebrows with a look of hope on his face.

Evaleen's heart fluttered as Jesse's gaze connected with hers. He really did have the most beautiful eyes, so heavily lashed and the shade of the sky right before it rained. If eyes really did reflect the inner self, she imagined his soul was all stormy and tumultuous.

"What kind of understanding?" she asked cautiously.

"As soon as we get Theodora back, we both do exactly as we please for the next six months. You take care of Theodora, I take care of the ranch, we both tell Calloway we're perfect, and then we go our separate ways."

"But that would be lying."

"Yeah," he agreed cheerfully. "So what?"

"For one," she said, trying not to grow frustrated, "I agreed to try to reform you into a good citizen. I *have* to make an earnest attempt. My reputation is at stake, and my good name, Mr. Stockton, is my life." She gave him a stern look to prove she meant every word. "If you are not salvageable, it won't be because I didn't try."

He rolled his eyes. "You said for one. What's number two?"

"We cannot tell Mr. Nesmith we're perfect. You aren't and will never be—"

"Gee, not even with your help?"

God save her, she almost smiled. Glaring sternly at him, she said, "I am only a woman, Mr. Stockton, not the good Lord. I cannot perform miracles."

"Now why didn't anyone ever tell my father that before he set this whole thing up?" Jesse asked sardonically.

"I don't know," Evaleen replied earnestly. "It would have saved us both a lot of trouble if he'd given me custody of Theodora and found a way to punish you other than me."

"Ain't that the truth?" Jesse had to smile.

"But I won't lie to Mr. Nesmith and say I've done something I haven't," she added, confused at what he found so amusing. "If you want the ranch, you will have to make a genuine attempt to change your ways. I will endeavor to stay beside you every step of the way, guiding you when you err."

Jesse groaned and leaned back in his seat. His father had surely picked the epitome of virtue when he'd decided on Evaleen for this job. No doubt Evaleen's sterling character had been his father's exact criterion. Seeing as how she peered at him from her lofty perch on that very virtuosity, Jesse was surprised to feel any attraction for the woman at all.

His eyes narrowing, he sat up straight, studying Evaleen

as she took a piece of graphite and a small book from her reticule and began to write. She was a woman of luscious curves, from her full breasts and hips to the tilting, tempting lips of her mouth, so of course he was attracted. That, he figured, could have been his father's whole idea. Reynard could have already figured that his son wouldn't pay any more attention to a woman's guiding hand than he had to his own father's. He therefore might have believed that his rascally offspring *would* fall into the trap of Evaleen's seductiveness, feel like her virtue was a challenge he could not ignore, and be more inclined to get to know her better by falling into step behind her on the road to morality like an obedient dog, therefore changing his whole way of life?

"Yep," Jesse breathed out. Sure as shootin', that was precisely what his father had been hoping for.

Evaleen had written down the date and a few phrases about Jesse's behavior with Miss Hurley when she suddenly felt his eyes studying her. Thinking it was her imagination, she ignored the feeling, but then the back of her neck began to prickle and she had to glance up at him.

He *was* staring at her, an intense look coming from his narrowed blue eyes. "Writing your memoirs, Miss Murphy?"

"No," she said slowly, unsure of whether or not she should tell him anything. Perhaps if she did, though, he would be more worried and less inclined to thwart her. "I'm preparing for our upcoming duel by gathering my ammunition."

"Your journal." He tilted his head to see what she was writing, but she snapped the book shut and gave him a chiding look as she put it and the pencil away.

"If you're so curious," she said, "I'll remind you that I told Mr. Nesmith I was going to write down your escapades and how I deal with them. I was merely recording the incident at the school."

"You mean what happened on the porch?"

Her mouth tightened, and she gave him an irritated look. "You know exactly which incident I am referring to."

He did know, but he couldn't resist getting her prim and proper goat riled even further. "Did you write down how I left you openmouthed with desire?"

"I beg your pardon," she said, her back straightening into that holier-than-thou posture he was beginning to find out she assumed on a regular basis—at least around him. "You did not leave me openmouthed."

"Malarkey. You could have caught flies in there when I walked away." Reaching over, he touched his fingertip first to the curve of her upper lip, then to her bottom lip, gently parting them.

A sensation of pure desire flooded through Evaleen in the split second before she came to her senses and jerked her head back, outraged. "Apparently, you assigned much more importance to what happened on the porch than I did, Mr. Stockton."

"Did I?" he asked, grinning at her.

"You were the one who brought it up!" She was so angry her face heated. "Let me get something straight with you, sir," she said, resisting an urge to wag her finger in his face. "Unlike most of the women you run across, I do not think of myself as existing merely for your personal entertainment. I am here to school you in the refined behavior you must learn to become a proper gentleman, and the sooner we set some ground rules, the sooner you can begin learning your lessons."

"*My* lessons? Wouldn't you like to know more about what I could teach you?"

What he could teach her brought the image to Evaleen's

mind of Jesse's finely formed mouth coming closer and closer to her face. Her breath caught, and she closed her eyes, trying to forget his face; but her traitorous imagination only made it all worse. Her heart began to beat faster as she thought about what his kiss would be like. His mouth would be warm against hers ... her skin tingling from when he would reach his hand around her waist and pull her to him. ...

A breeze came out of nowhere to brush against her blushing hot cheeks, and she opened her eyes in a flash. Jesse had taken off his hat and was fanning her with it.

"Miss Murphy," he said in a concerned voice. "I surely did not intend to provoke you into a faint."

"What you are provoking me into doing," she said, barely getting enough breath to speak, "is slapping you."

"Fine." He shoved his hat back on his head and then back down over his eyes. "I'm catching a nap. You don't have to shoot me in the foot to get me to quit dancing."

She was relieved, she told herself. Not having Jesse studying her meant she could think about the problem of his "allure." Always before, Evaleen had blamed her sister for her own destruction. Always before, she had thought only a female with a weak will could be seduced by a man; goodness knows, *she'd* never had any problem thwarting men's advances up to this point. But never before had Evaleen met a man like Jesse.

Having witnessed how her sister's shame had affected her parents in their community in St. Louis, Evaleen didn't *want* to be seduced. She'd been ten years younger than Cynthia, but still old enough that the taint had been unbearable. Each time she'd stepped out onto the street, she'd felt eyes upon her, watching, waiting for her to show some sign of bad blood and the same weakness for men her sister had displayed.

But she hadn't. After finishing her schooling, she'd gone

to Kansas, gotten a job at the Harvey Hotel, and worked her way up, almost to head waitress. She'd done everything right, and her folks had been proud of her. According to her mother, Cynthia was never mentioned in the old neighborhood anymore; the neighbors only asked about Evaleen. This brought great comfort to her mother and father.

And since Cynthia was dead, it was almost as though her fallen sister had never existed. Her parents and siblings seemed happier not to remember, and that made Evaleen more determined than ever not to fail her good name. She hadn't been lying to Jesse: her reputation did mean more than life to her. What it all came down to was, the sooner she told him her ground rules, the better, and she should definitely do it before they reached the train station and began searching together.

When she centered her attention back on the errant rancher, she thought he might have fallen asleep. Leaning forward, she whispered, "Mr. Stockton?"

Before she could blink, he leaned forward until they were almost nose to nose. "What?" he whispered back, his lips so close she thought she could taste the mint on his breath.

She leaned backward as far as she could. "You surely *are* provoking," she told him.

"So you've said," he reminded her, lifting his hat up so she could see his eyes again.

"You are, but unfortunately, I need your mind and your presence."

"You mean you need my body." He grinned, his eyes lighting up.

"Exactly," she said, smiling sweetly. He looked startled, and she smiled more widely. "That's why I'm allowing you to accompany me on my search. If we run into the man who took Theodora, I will need your body—preferably as a shield between myself and a bullet."

"Naw, sweetheart," he said, shaking his head. "You won't need me against a gun—or any other man, for that matter. That steel corset you've got on stiffening your spine should protect you against mere bullets."

Her teeth clenched. "You are surely the most vexing human I have ever met," she said. "No wonder your father tried even after his death to reform you."

Jesse seemed to go dark and closed-in all at once, as though she'd wounded him, and Evaleen abruptly closed her mouth. She hadn't realized Jesse had cared so much about his father's dying. Really, who would have thought—

The hack hit a rutted section of the road, and Evaleen grabbed the window's edge as they bounced. Jesse just braced himself with one leg, and with a sigh, leaned back and folded his arms across his chest, staring down at her from his superior height, his jaw jutting outward.

"I'm sorry," she said, filled with remorse. "I shouldn't have said that."

He didn't respond, and suddenly, Evaleen was sorrier that she had tried to apologize. With his "allure," Jesse could easily hold all the cards. Because they had to be together for the next six months, she dared not let herself be taken over by him, be led around by men as her sister had been. Cynthia had ended up so miserable. While Evaleen wasn't exactly happy, she was content, and she wasn't giving up that feeling of well-being for any man.

The cab had settled to just another bumpy ride, so she clasped her hands on her lap. "Mr. Stockton, if we are to continue to travel together, I believe we should return to the subject of those ground rules."

"Why do I think these are going to be entirely one-sided?"

"Because I'm the one who's thinking them up," Evaleen

said. At least he didn't seem to be hurt beyond repair by her earlier remark, which lessened her feeling of guilt.

She was about to continue when the cab lurched again. Having relaxed, Jesse slid sideways, and his knee ended up pressing against her thigh. Sucking in her breath and gritting her teeth, Evaleen shimmied sideways to gain some room, desperate to ignore the tingling in her leg left from the contact, a tingling that danced upward into her unmentionable region.

"First rule," she hissed out. "You don't touch me."

"That could get boring," he said. When he saw the fire in her dark lime eyes, he threw up his hands. "You betcha. I won't touch you even if I see you teetering on the brink of disaster."

"Fine."

"Or even if you are smack-dab in the path of stampeding horses—"

"Fine!" she said, opening her mouth to give him rule number two.

"Or even if you get down on your hands and ... needs"—his eyes glittered at his play on words—"and begged me to touch you."

She stared at him coldly. "If I ever need your touch that much, Mr. Stockton, I assure you I will have gone stark raving mad."

He smiled. "With desire, right?" His voice was so suggestive, so warm, that she couldn't help but meet his eyes. Something in his gaze told her she had spoken too soon, that someday she would regret goading him like this, but that, of course, was ridiculous. When someday came, she was counting on being safely back in Kansas with Aunt Victoria and Dorie.

"Rule number two?" Jesse asked. He had decided that he could play her game—for now. As soon as Miss Murphy had her say, he was going to give her a ground rule of his own.

"I think whoever took Theodora probably took her to exchange her for money. Do you agree?"

When he nodded, she continued. "If they knew she was worth a ranch, it means whoever has her knows her background. Since none of the school's staff is missing, that leaves only someone in Raton or the vicinity of the ranch as the possible abductor. So that's where we head in our search for her. Agreed?"

"Agreed. And may I say, a very intelligent conclusion."

"Thank you."

Her smile was radiant. If he wasn't careful, Jesse thought, he could end up really liking her. He leaned back and stretched his leg, wincing, and that was when he noticed she was scrunched up against the far door, putting physical distance between them. That was fine with him, he told himself, denying that he had sorely wanted to kiss her twice in less than twenty-four hours. She was a sourpuss old maid, a female version of his father, and he'd be a fool to want anyone like that in his life.

But he had to admit, he *had* been challenged by her avowal that she would never beg him to touch her. He might not have the finesse of a polished Easterner, but he sure as hell prided himself on his ability to make a lady of his choice feel like she was a queen when it came to matters of the bedroom. If she didn't have so much control over his ranch, why, just because she had practically challenged him, he'd be reaching over to this recalcitrant female that very second, pulling her into his arms, and showing her exactly how much she was missing in life. But he knew he couldn't, no matter what, and not only because of her power.

He wouldn't because he would bet money that Evaleen Murphy was untouched, and he didn't want to fool around with that. She might not believe it, but he respected her wanting to keep her reputation lily white. A woman had to.

"Another condition," she continued in that voice of hers, so clear and almost melodic. "If, indeed, she has been stolen away, and if we"—she paused and corrected herself—"when we get a chance to rescue Theodora, you let me approach her. We'll want to get her away carefully and quietly, without creating a scene, but after what she's been through, she's liable to start screaming if another man tries to cart her off. Besides, she knows me."

"What makes you think a man toted her off?" Jesse had to ask. "It might have been a woman."

She leveled her lime eyes directly at him. "Mr. Stockton, please. Make sense."

Since he personally thought his brother had something to do with this, Jesse didn't argue. "Anything else?"

"One last thing." To Evaleen's extreme relief, they were pulling up in front of the train depot and she'd soon be out of their cramped quarters. "You let me do the talking," she ordered. "You have a tendency to rub people the wrong way."

"Like you?" A laugh exploded out of him.

"Like Miss Hurley," she denied.

"Not so. I had Miss Hurley charmed until you came along."

"I hazard a guess she was desperate," she said icily. The hack stopped, and she rose and climbed out. Turning, she watched him do the same. "Very desperate."

"She couldn't have been too desperate," he protested. "You managed to change her mind easily enough."

"Then she wouldn't have been the right woman for you, would she?" The train whistle blew, and Evaleen watched as the hack driver handed down Jesse's carpetbag. Her own traveling bag was still at the hotel in Maune. "But as far as women go, Mr. Stockton, you might be very pleased to know that I do have a vested interest in finding you a good one."

"How's that?"

"I'll probably need some help in trying to reform you."

"If you reform me, Miss Murphy, you might find yourself very sorry." Their eyes met, the steel blue of his searching the deep lime green of hers.

"How's that?" she asked, mocking his earlier reply.

"You might find you liked me much better exactly the way I was."

As Evaleen felt him waiting for her reaction, she conceded he might have a point. Jesse Stockton as a church-attending, school board-voting favorite of the town would probably not have the same sensual allure for her of Jesse the bad boy and rake.

But she wasn't supposed to be thinking like that. Shaking her head in disgust at herself, Evaleen turned away from him and threaded through the crowd milling outside the depot, waiting for the train to leave. She trusted Jesse to follow her this time. Sure enough, he did, right on her heels. Part of her was pleased she wielded so much power over a man who had so much power of his own. But the other part wished he didn't exist, so she could just take Theodora and go live her quiet life working for Fred Harvey's chain of hotels, waiting for an older, scholarly gentleman to be her forever companion.

"If you'll hold up a second," Jesse said quietly from behind her, "I have a ground rule of my own for you."

She stopped where she was and turned. "I don't believe I'm in need of rules as badly as you, but go right ahead. Present it." She smiled at him and urged, "Please."

"You are free to make as much sport of my rakish lifestyle as you please, but leave mention of my relationship with my father out of your retorts."

So surprised was she by the vehement tone of his voice, her smile faded away. "Jesse—"

"You have no idea at all of what happened between my father and me, or how much I cared about him." He cleared his throat. For the first time since Evaleen had met him, his broad shoulders almost seemed to droop. A wave of concern flowed over her, but he was speaking once again and she couldn't express it.

"You don't know how I'll regret for the rest of my life not being there when he died. My ground rule is that you respect this if you respect nothing else about me: I would have gladly laid down my life for either of my parents."

Turning on his heel, he walked away toward the ticket counter, leaving Evaleen stunned.

As he bought his and Miss Murphy's tickets so they could head back to Raton, Jesse wondered how she was going to react to what he'd just said. He thought she would try to apologize again—if not right away, then eventually—because she was that type of woman. He'd learned a lot about her before he'd gone to Theodora's school, having taken a side trip to the Harvey Hotel in Maune where Evaleen worked and spoken to her boss.

According to the manager, Miss Murphy liked order in her life, and she liked everyone around her to be in harmony. The man had also said that Evaleen Murphy was methodical and organized, and followed his employee rules to the hilt. He'd even implied the woman would make a fine manager for any Harvey Hotel restaurant.

Well, she might manage things fine for Fred Harvey, but Jesse had no intention of letting the woman control anything where he was concerned—especially not his life. In the carriage with her rules and stipulations, she had sounded like his father, and he wasn't going to live like that ever again.

He would just have to teach Evaleen a few things, Jesse

decided. Things like the fact that rules, like hearts, were made to be broken, and that some people, like himself, delighted in breaking them.

Breaking rules, that was, not hearts, he qualified silently. Because the last thing he was going to do was get involved with Miss Murphy's heart.

Paying for his tickets, Jesse turned back to the hustling people behind him, looking for Miss Murphy. Frowning, he took in those in the crowd one by one, his eyes searching for that stupid bird hat of hers. Nothing. Miss Murphy no longer seemed to be in the depot.

Well, wasn't that just wonderful! Maybe, if he was lucky, somebody had toted her off to be with Theodora, and he could wash his hands of both of them.

# Chapter Five

Despite his wish that Evaleen Murphy would just disappear, Jesse began to grow anxious during the next ten minutes when he checked outside and around the depot and found she actually might have done just that. He might have acted nonchalant around Evaleen, but inside, he was already really worried about the child, and now to have the feisty, capable Evaleen disappear ... well, he didn't like it. He didn't like it one bit, the idea that someone might be out to kidnap an innocent child and a woman.

As he strode back inside with a frenzied step to make another sweep of the depot, his eyes narrowed.

"Mr. Stockton! I just wasted at least five good minutes looking for you," Evaleen said from behind him with a gently chiding voice. "Wherever did you go?"

He turned slowly, relief coursing through him. But he stopped himself before he let her know he'd been the least bit concerned and thought up a suitable fib. Why give her the advantage of thinking he had worried about her?

"I was doing what men do when they have leisure time to kill and an urge hits them."

"Oh, my."

Jesse had never seen a woman turn so red in the cheeks so fast. What on earth did she think he'd been doing?

"However did you find the time?" Evaleen asked, fanning her cheeks with her hand. "We were apart only for a few minutes."

"That's all it takes." Full of curiosity about what she was thinking, Jesse kept his gaze on her face. The deep rose blush tinting Evaleen's cheeks heightened the green of her eyes, and all of a sudden, Miss Murphy looked damned pretty. Why had she buried her light under that heavy cloak of propriety and properness? "Really," he added, "a few minutes, and then the fire burns out."

Her mouth dropped open. "I had thought doing it would take longer," she said weakly.

She swayed, and Jesse wondered if she were about to swoon. If it hadn't been for the ground rule she'd given him in the carriage—no touching—he would have grabbed her arm and propelled her to the nearest bench, but as it was, he was left to stand there and wait for her to drop to the floor.

But then again, if he let her get to the point where she fainted and became a spectacle, she'd never let him forget it. Sighing, he leaned close to her so they wouldn't be overheard—carefully, of course, refraining from touching her. "What in the blazes do you think I was doing?"

"I thought you had"—she lifted her lime green eyes to his—"partaken of a woman."

Partaken of a woman? What the hell was she talking . . . ? With the force of a steam engine rolling down the track, the answer hit Jesse. He threw his head back and roared with laughter. She honestly thought he'd visited a prostitute. In ten minutes tops?

"What are you laughing at?" she asked, glancing around at passersby who were raising their eyebrows at them. Reaching into her reticule, she pulled out her journal and her graphite. "I don't find your activity in the least bit amusing."

"Whoa," he said, snatching the stub out of her hand. "Don't you dare write what you're supposing. It isn't true. Believe me, it isn't. When I *partake*, I assure you I enjoy that particular pleasure for far longer than ten minutes."

"I do not wish to know the details, Mr. Stockton." Blushing again, Evaleen grabbed for her pencil. He held it higher, and she grabbed again and missed, feeling embarrassed like a schoolgirl facing the town bully. Somebody behind them laughed, and in a furious, low voice she said, "You must give me my pencil. I do believe you are going to be committing so many sins in the future that if I neglect to write them down as they happen, I will forget a great many of them. While it's still fresh in my mind, I have to write about your disappearance."

"*My* disappearance?"

"Yes." Raising her eyebrows, she gave up grabbing for her writing tool. "*I* certainly wasn't the one who was lost. I knew where I was. Unfortunately, I also know where you were."

He continued to hold the pencil out of her reach. "You cannot write your torrid little fantasies down. I am not guilty of what you're thinking."

"Then what *were* you doing? What on Earth else do men do when they have leisure time and urges?" she asked in exasperation, louder than she should have. There was more laughter as a few people stopped to openly gape. Mortified, she turned her back to them. "You'd better come up with something acceptable, Mr. Stockton, or I assure you, my first guess will go down in my journal."

"It was quite innocent, I assure you." He wasn't about

to admit he'd been searching the station for her, not now. She'd never believe him. He lowered his arm and handed her the pencil, only he didn't let go. She tried to get a better grip to pull it away, and their fingertips touched. He swore he felt sparks of fire when her cool skin slid against his, and their gazes met and held for so long he almost forgot what he was going to tell her.

"Mr. Stockton," she said; only the words sounded like they were coming from low in her throat, like a woman speaking at the height of arousal. Probably he was wrong. Probably Evaleen was just catching a cold. She couldn't be in the least bit attracted to him; she didn't have any passion in her. He'd swear to that.

"I was smoking a cigar, Miss Murphy," he lied sternly. "Nothing more, nothing less."

Closing her eyes, Evaleen begged the good Lord to deliver her from this form of hell on earth, and then she yanked the pencil out of Jesse's hand, turned, and started walking toward the rear door that led out to the arriving train. She should have known it had to be something simple, but it was that damnable look in Jesse's eyes when he'd said that line about urges and leisure time that had caused her to jump to all sorts of stupid conclusions. But mercy, come to think of it, that damnable look never seemed to leave Jesse Stockton's eyes, so how could she have been so stupid?

Once she was through the door and outside, Evaleen stopped a few feet from the tracks and stood alone amidst the crowd. Knowing Jesse would be following to torment her further, she didn't even jump when she felt his presence directly behind her. She wasn't startled, but she could feel the heat from him that started to penetrate her body and cause a slow, melting sensation in the pit of her stomach, heavy and low and wanting.

"Just for your continuing education," Jesse said, his

voice low and masculine next to her ear, "it takes longer than ten minutes to get the most of that particular pleasure. To do it right, a man has to wait until he's just about ready to die for it, he needs it so badly. Then he's got to take his time with it and draw on it slowly to make it last."

Little tendrils of pleasure curled through Evaleen as he spoke. He was playing her like a violin, and she didn't know how to stop him. Turning, she stared up into his eyes. "You mean smoking a cigar, don't you?" she asked softly, almost hopefully.

"What do you think?" he asked, only he said it in such a manner that she had no doubt he meant making love to a woman. Her body felt like it was blossoming, and he hadn't even touched her.

She shook her head to clear it. He was just trying to seduce her, and she couldn't allow herself to submit to his pressure. Her sister's downfall had started exactly like this, Cynthia had told her, with some man who wouldn't care about her past tomorrow sweet-talking her. She must keep reminding herself of that.

Dealing with Jesse Stockton for six long months was going to be nothing but—dare she think it?—hell. But what choice did she have? It was either that, or agree to his plan to lie to Calloway Nesmith, which she could never do.

Her sigh, heartfelt, came from the inner depths of her being. "If we could drop the entire subject, Mr. Stockton, I would be much obliged. There is Dorie to find, if you would just try to put your mind to the important things in life for a moment."

He nodded slowly. "I will," he said sincerely. "I promise."

"While we were separated," she said evenly, not wishing to invite more comment from him, "I visited the ticket manager who was just going off duty. He's seen a few little girls in the past two weeks, and two of them fit Dorie's description. As far as he can remember, both boarded the west-bound train out of here. I think it would be wise to head out as soon as possible, with a brief side trip to my house so I can arrange to ship my things to the ranch."

Nodding agreement, Jesse managed to swing his concentration off the way Evaleen's bosom was rising and falling as she struggled for control and back to their search for Theodora. He had been laying the honey on a little thick in dealing with Evaleen, but he was beginning to find that a whole lot sweeter than the bee stings they'd been giving each other. He hadn't thought her capable of it, but she responded to a little attention just like any other woman, and since he had to travel with her, keeping her off guard like this would be a whole lot more pleasant than being at each other's throats.

For now, Evaleen was right. The important thing was finding the child. They could fight their own private war later.

Evaleen found no comfort in the fact that Jesse had chosen to change his behavior for the short train ride to Maune. He was too willing to follow her direction. That made her wonder if he was too busy plotting some new scheme to get control over her to give her trouble now.

It wasn't until they were a mile or so from her home, a small wooden house with a glorified attic where she slept, that Evaleen realized something. Jesse was coming with her to her house. He'd be coming inside with her with no chaperon in sight. Was that what he was so busy contemplating?

She couldn't worry about it, she told herself as she sat in another hired cab, squeezed against one side just to avoid Jesse's touch. There were bound to be times on the ranch when she and Jesse would be alone. If she didn't trust him to keep his hands off her, and she valued her reputation, she would just have to walk away from this deal. . . .

But no, she couldn't do that either. She remembered too well the last time she'd visited Dorie at school. The child had stared at her with her big blue eyes and begged Evaleen to take her home. She was lonely. She wanted someone to love her. She wanted a mother, not a schoolteacher, to tuck her in at night.

Theodora was only eight years old.

Evaleen blinked back the heavy heat of tears behind her eyes. She should have taken the child and just run off with her then. As she'd pulled away and watched Dorie run a few dozen feet behind her hackney, her heart had broken and she'd considered doing just that. But there were others' feelings to consider in this matter. There always were. One did not live in a vacuum. Reynard would have come after her with the law, and she had to worry about her aunt Victoria and the money she earned for them to live on.

"That's the second sigh from you in less then five minutes," Jesse said.

"I'm worried about Theodora," she admitted, wanting very badly to talk to someone about it. "All she ever wanted was to be part of a family, you know."

Understanding that, Jesse nodded slowly.

"I tried to give her that, at least, but I failed miserably." She gripped the soft velvet of her reticule. "And now she's missing."

Seconds passed, and then Jesse covered her gloved hand with his and squeezed it gently for a few seconds. "We all failed her, Miss Murphy. But once we get her back, that's going to change."

Evaleen gazed at him for a minute and then gave him a nod of agreement and a subdued smile. She hadn't really expected this kind of understanding from Jesse, but it was nice to see. At least she knew they were in complete agreement that whatever their futures turned out to be, Dorie deserved much better than the hand she'd been dealt.

Her smile warmed him thoroughly. Jesse shifted and looked away from Evaleen, out the tiny hole of a window, watching the scenery of the prairie town go by. He thought he might have made her feel better and that made him as confused as she'd looked. Women had always just wanted him for his teasing banter—and his finesse in bed—but not for anything faintly resembling emotional support. He found he actually liked making Miss Murphy feel better, but it would be stupid to get used to doing it. She'd already made her position quite clear; she wished he didn't exist. And he wasn't that fond of the idea that she was going to be his personal keeper for the next six months, either.

The carriage stopped in front of a white, cracker box of a house, with a picket fence around it—of course. Jesse saw right away the place had a hominess to it that said people lived there and were happy. It wasn't a shell of a house like his own home, it was a cottage with flowerpots, a porch swing, and lace curtains in the window that would float with a breeze. A house where Evaleen lived.

"I don't want to hear a word from you about my home," Evaleen warned him as she opened the door.

Jesse continued to stare through the coach window at the property. Evaleen needn't have worried. There was no way he would criticize the size of the house, or the fact that it badly needed a good coat of paint and a nail or two on a railing hanging just a bit crooked. Jesse sensed it held happiness. He wasn't quite sure why he knew that, but he knew enough to leave happiness alone when he saw it. Only once again, he felt like an outsider who had no business intruding and bringing disharmony to such a peaceful place.

He stepped out of the hackney as Evaleen, already disembarked, asked the driver to wait, calling the man Mr. O'Henry. Apparently, Jesse thought, they were at least acquaintances. He eyed the burly man with the cropped haircut for any signs that he might be a beau of Evaleen's, but no, there wasn't that much familiarity between them. Evaleen told Mr. O'Henry that she would be talking to a neighbor, checking the house, and then loading a few things onto the cab. When the driver agreed, Evaleen turned back to Jesse.

Her tongue rested on the tip of her bottom lip as she seemed to consider what to say to him. She looked so appealing that way Jesse got an overpowering urge to just lean down and kiss her, but then he glanced at the house again and decided to leave her alone—walk away, at least mentally—something he would never have done with any other woman who sent out such instinctive signals to him that she was longing to be held and caressed.

"I want you to wait outside with the driver while I arrange things," she told him.

"Yeah. Sure." He didn't tell her he'd had no plans to go inside anyway.

She stared back at him as if she didn't believe it would be so easy. "I mean it. Stay out here."

"I wouldn't go into that house if you promised there was a chorus line of cancan dancers waiting to grant my every pleasure in there."

"I'm not asking you for the impossible," she said, the corners of her lips edging upward. Quickly, she forced them back down again.

"Whoa! Careful there, Miss Murphy. You may not have realized it, but you almost smiled."

"Maybe it's because I'm home again, if only for a few minutes." Turning, she began walking up the stone walk to the front porch. "I am serious, Mr. Stockton. Don't you come in."

"Not even if you beg me to," he called after her. The sentimental look on her face told him her home meant everything to Evaleen. Interestingly enough, it seemed that he and Miss Murphy, whether she liked it or not, had something in common. He, too, understood the desire to possess something all your own, and to have others acknowledge it and respect you for having worked hard enough to obtain it. That something he wanted to possess was Rainbow's End—had always been. It had damned near killed him when he'd left after the fight with his father, thinking he'd never return there—never have a home again.

He gazed around the long, dusty side street, with its assorted scattered small houses for the span of a block. Beyond it, Jesse knew, lay unrelentingly flat, boring landscape. After years of living next to the splendor of majestic mountains on ranchland, he felt penned in and eager to leave.

Movement in his peripheral vision caught his attention. One of Evaleen's neighbors was staring through her front curtains at him, watching every move he made. Smiling, he lifted his hat to the woman. The two curtain halves dropped into place, but out of the corner of his eyes he could see the lace moving again as the woman sneaked another look.

He could go inside with Evaleen and give her neighbor something to gossip about, he supposed. But Evaleen might want to move back here when their "misery" was all over, since she considered Maune, and this house, her home. No matter how irritating she was, he wasn't going to wreck that for her.

Evaleen appeared in the front door. She'd changed clothes and gotten rid of that hat of hers, thank God. The adornment on her new hat consisted only of a single dark green feather, which matched her new hunter green outfit perfectly. This traveling suit fit her even better than the last one had, cut close with lines that emphasized her full breasts. Intent on perusing her, Jesse also noticed one other thing.

She was frowning.

"You look very nice, Miss Murphy," he said, just as she was opening her mouth to speak. He watched her lips fall open in surprise. It took her less than a few seconds to recover, and when she did, her frown came back.

"Mr. Stockton, I need to speak with you, privately, on a matter of grave importance."

She was being formal, but that could be because of her nosy neighbor and the driver watching them.

"Certainly." He walked a few feet closer to the porch and then stopped. "You'll have to come to me if you don't want me to go inside, Miss Murphy."

"Oh, for heaven's sake," she said as though she'd just remembered how she'd threatened him earlier. She shot a quick look at Mr. O'Henry, who was watching the scene unfold with great interest, and then settled her solemn gaze back on Jesse. "Would you please just forget what I said earlier and enter the house, please? There's something you need to see."

"Is there a line of cancan dancers in there after all?"

"No, of course not." She took a deep breath, glanced at O'Henry once more, and then tried again. "Please, I'm *inviting* you inside."

"Tempting as that sounds, I can't go," Jesse said. "Unless you'd like to find someone else to accompany us?"

"No!" she said sharply. "This is a private matter."

He took another step forward, purposely shifting only his eyes to the right toward her neighbor's house as obviously as he could without making a big deal of it. "Your reputation," he whispered. "Remember?"

"Oh, for goodness sakes!" Exasperated, Evaleen charged through the door and down the porch steps. Grabbing his hand, she pulled on his arm, but he refused to budge—for her own good.

"What is so all-fired important that you want me to see?" he asked, glancing at the driver, who was grinning from ear to ear at the show. Evaleen was going to hate herself for acting like this when she returned and faced the piper in this town.

"My bed," she said without thinking, pulling on his hand again. Realizing the implications of what she'd said, her face went red with irritation and she pulled harder. She tried to draw a full breath, but couldn't. "This damned corset," she muttered. Standing so close to her, Jesse heard.

"You want me to see your corset in bed?" he asked with mock chagrin in his voice. "I can't do that, Miss Murphy. Think of *my* reputation."

Evaleen stopped short, dropped his hand, and stared at him. A few feet away, the driver let loose a belly laugh, but Jesse wasn't about to let her see he was anything but serious. Stepping back, he met her appalled glare with a glare of his own, thinking how absolutely fascinating she was.

She also stepped back from him. Shaking her head, she clasped her hands together as though she were praying for help. Spreading her hands wide, she said, "Some Irish ancestor of mine must have put a curse on me, that I ended up having to contend with the likes of you."

"What did I do?" he asked, throwing his own hands up in a perfect imitation of her and looking backward at the driver, who grinned, but had absolutely no suggestions to offer him. "Women!" Jesse exclaimed in O'Henry's direction. "First they say 'Don't you dare,' and then they damn you when you don't."

"All right, Mr. Stockton." Evaleen's eyes were full of green ice as she spoke, keeping her voice low. "I don't need this. I truly don't need to deal with the likes of you now. I will merely give up everything in my life and go into hiding and let you explain to Calloway Nesmith why I've run off. And if you lack an explanation as to why I would rather starve on the streets than deal with you, you can always tell him it was because you refused to come to my bedroom!"

"I knew you'd end up begging," Jesse said.

"Oooh!" Evaleen muttered, whirling around and stomping into the house, giving the door a hearty slam behind her.

Jesse stood there, absolutely positive Evaleen was testing him. She had to be. The second he followed his inclinations and her into that bedroom, she'd scream bloody murder and he'd be put in jail.

But then again, why the change of heart just because she'd come back to her home? Evaleen wasn't the devious type. Frowning, he stared at the door. She'd said she would go into hiding. But she wouldn't just drop the search for Theodora over something as simple as being irritated with him, unless ...

Unless she'd found Theodora.

Jesse raced up the steps and rattled the doorknob. Locked. He cursed, kicked the door, and swore again. She was the most damnable woman he'd ever met! Why hadn't she just used some logic and said, "Please come inside. Theodora is here." No, she was so damned worried about avoiding gossip that she had to cloak her words just so the neighbor and the driver wouldn't learn what was going on. Jesse didn't understand why she cared that much. He just purely didn't understand the woman.

Striding around to the back door, he tried that, but of course, she'd been away from the house and it was locked. Cursing, he returned to the front of the place and stood there, scowling, sorely tempted to yell her name. But that would bring out the neighbors and result in another black mark against him in her journal.

"Relax, sir," Mr. O'Henry called. "She won't be in there forever."

"Miss Murphy," Jesse said, still scowling, "is totally capable of surviving holed up for months if she wants to. She could wear down a charging bull with her stubbornness."

"I predict she'll be out within the next fifteen minutes, maybe even less," the coachman said.

"Don't tell me. You're Irish too, and you have the second sight?"

O'Henry shook his head and spit some tobacco on the ground. "Nope. Well, mebbe I'm Irish. But I've only got me two eyes." When Jesse didn't laugh, he shrugged and continued. "You have to understand that everyone goes to the Harvey Hotel restaurant to eat 'cause the food's so good, so practically everyone in town knows Miss Murphy."

"And?" Jesse asked impatiently.

"And Miss Murphy is respected in Maune just 'cause she's one of them Harvey Girls, and everyone knows she doesn't have a dishonest bone in her body."

"So?"

"So she hasn't paid me yet. That has to mean she isn't done with the coach, so she'll be back out."

Tipping his Stetson back out of his eyes, Jesse nodded slowly at him. "I believe you might be right about that."

Mr. O'Henry grinned, and, together, they waited.

# Chapter Six

Where her reputation was concerned, Jesse Stockton was going to drive her to the brink of disaster in Maune, which would make it very difficult for her to return. Bristling with anger, Evaleen charged up the stairs to the attic, where short minutes before she had found Theodora asleep on her bed under the twin eaves.

So much for trying to bring Jesse up here quietly so the neighbors wouldn't know a child had been living in her home alone for almost three days after having run away from the school. What irked her now was that she knew she'd handled the discovery the wrong way with Stockton, who was highly suspicious of her. If she'd just brought the child outside to him, Evaleen knew the gossip about her runaway niece would have died down far more quickly than that about the scene she'd just had with Jesse. Her face was still red over what she'd accidentally said to him. But she wasn't used to having her authority questioned, not at home or at work, and she had lost her composure. It couldn't be helped now.

Sighing as she entered the attic, she glanced around it for Theodora. The girl was gone. Whipping around, Evaleen started back down the stairs and began to search the other small rooms, not wanting to call out Theodora's name in case Jesse was outside with his ear to the keyhole. She'd only been half-kidding when she'd mentioned running away and going into hiding. She was tempted to do so and let them all look for Theodora until she turned twenty-one. But then she thought of the longing in Jesse's eyes when it came to his getting the ranch, and she knew she couldn't be so childish.

Darn it.

Coming out of her aunt's room, Evaleen finally spotted the child on the stairwell holding a slice of bread and jam.

"I was hungry," Theodora said, grinning.

"I'll bet you were." Evaleen was once again taken aback by how much Dorie resembled Cynthia, especially in the shape of her face, the intensity of her eyes, and her little bow-shaped mouth. "Where did you get the bread?"

"I bought it after I got off the train." Theodora's eyelashes fluttered, and with a clenching of her heart, Evaleen was reminded that the little girl was utterly alone. That strengthened her determination. She'd change Jesse Stockton, become Dorie's mother for all purposes, and then she would give the child the best life she could.

For a few seconds as she watched the girl eat, Evaleen wondered if someday she would have a child of her own. Probably not. Marriage, yes. Her ideal mate would be older, learned, and worldly enough to let her continue to work should she want to, a professor at a university or something of that sort. It would be a marriage of convenience and companionship, nothing more—which would rule out children.

Crossing her arms over her chest, she remained lost in thought. She'd planned to start looking for this perfect spouse when she was somewhere in her early thirties. But now, having these overwhelming thoughts of being touched led her to believe she'd be better off if she started looking right after this custody issue was settled and she was free of Jesse forever. Once married, she wouldn't pine for someone else. Not that she'd pine for Jesse, the arrogant scoundrel . . .

Anyway, if she wasn't destined to have children, then she guessed she'd better enjoy mothering Theodora.

"Did you open anything else besides the jam jar?" Evaleen asked her.

Theodora nodded solemnly, finishing her snack. "Peaches and beets."

Evaleen made a face. "We should get you a proper meal soon then. First, though, please come upstairs with me. We have to talk."

Theodora folded the napkin and carried it back to the kitchen. Returning, she glanced at the front door, and then obediently climbed the stairs.

Following her up, Evaleen studied the little girl who was now about to be under her care. Theodora was wearing one of the two dresses she had taken with her from the school, and she had tied her brown hair back with one of Evaleen's ribbons. For the first time, Evaleen thought she caught a hint of an auburn glow to the locks, but she quickly shook her head. That would be Jesse's hair, she reminded herself sternly. Any resemblance was strictly in her imagination.

Apart perhaps from decent meals, the child hadn't seemed to suffer much from being on her own for a few days, except in spirit. Theodora had been tremendously relieved to see her when she'd woken the child earlier. The girl had claimed she'd left the school because an evil knight had been visiting her there and she'd been frightened. What Evaleen surmised was that Theodora had been so lonely she had indulged in fantasies and had thereby frightened herself. It was high time the child was out of that school, so perhaps, Evaleen thought, everything with the Stocktons had happened for the best. Theodora now had a chance to live in a real family situation.

But how to tell her? Standing near her dresser, which she would soon have to start emptying, Evaleen ran her palms over her face and closed her eyes, praying for guidance. Whether she was furious with Jesse or not, she would still have to go through with the terms of the will. She simply could not take the child and her aunt into hiding. They'd all be too obvious, and she had a feeling Jesse would go to the ends of the earth to find them anyway.

Merciful Lord, but she wished everything were different. She felt woefully inadequate when it came to telling Theodora the only father she'd ever known had died. Not only that, but she had to somehow explain that everything in the girl's life was about to change—that she, Evaleen, loved her but did not have the wherewithal to take care of her unless they went to stay at Rainbow's End. And that Theodora also had Jesse, who didn't love anyone but himself but who had the means to let her live like the princess Dorie was pretending she was.

The warm touch of fingers on her cheek pulled Evaleen from her thoughts, and for a brief second, she imagined it was Jesse's touch against her skin. But then she knew it had to be Theodora. The fingers were too small to be a man's; also, Evaleen would have heard Jesse coming up the stairs.

The tiniest twinge of disappointment ran through her at the realization it wasn't Jesse, and was followed closely by anger. She didn't want to be attracted to him. She was cut from a different cloth than other women, and she could handle these urges. Keep them in their place. She wouldn't succumb.

"Aunt Evaleen?" Theodora's curious blue eyes stared up at her from inches away. When she nodded, Theodora asked, "Who was that man you were fighting with? I watched you through the window."

Evaleen was tempted to tell her that Jesse was *her* very own evil knight, but that would only add to the child's fantasy life, and right now, both of them had to deal in reality.

"That was Jesse, your guardian's younger son," she told Theodora. With mounting trepidation, she walked over to sit on the bed and patted the mattress beside her. Theodora sat down and smoothed the blue calico of her skirt like the little lady she was.

"I have something terrible to tell you," Evaleen started, but clamped her lips shut as Theodora's blue eyes crinkled and the sides of her mouth turned down. "Oh, honey, please don't cry. I'm not very good at this sort of thing, and if you cry, I'll start crying, too."

Tears brimmed at the corners of Theodora's eyes, and Evaleen damned her lack of experience at motherhood. She had the desire to be Theodora's mother, but in a way, Reynard had been right. She was woefully unprepared for the reality of this situation.

Just as Reynard had been, she reminded herself. Otherwise, he would have found some way to keep the poor child with him, which was what she would have done. Feeling better about herself, she rose, got a handkerchief, and came back to give it to Theodora.

"Is that evil knight coming to take me away to live with him?" Theodora asked.

Oh posh. She had to nip this in the bud before Theodora ran away from her. "Dorie, there is no evil knight. I know you were lonely at school, and you dreamed up a lot of interesting friends, but—"

Theodora rose to her feet and shook her head, anger sparking in her heavily lashed eyes. "There *is* an evil knight," she insisted. "I did not dream him up. He really came, and he scared me."

There was a heavy thud of boots on the stairwell. Theodora gasped with fright and hugged Evaleen, trying to hide behind her. Evaleen, though, had already figured out who it was, and turned toward the entryway. Just as she'd thought, Jesse stood there.

"Jesse, I really don't have time to deal with you right now," she told him quietly.

"How do you know Theodora didn't see an evil knight, Miss Murphy?" he asked, completely changing the subject as he tilted his black hat back a bit.

"Because evil knights are fairy tales, not real life." How exasperating he could be! He wasn't taking off his hat. No manners at all. Rising, she walked over to him, flipped the black hat off his head, and held it out to him, her eyebrows raised.

He reached out. Instead of just taking his hat by the brim, he covered one of her hands with his own and rubbed her knuckles, the warmth of his fingers giving her goosebumps up and down her arms and arousing the nipples of her breasts. As he took his hat from her, Jesse purposely gazed down at those hardened tips and raised his eyebrows in return—and then he grinned.

To Evaleen's chagrin, out of the corner of her vision she saw an unsuspecting Theodora smiling at him. Evaleen's eyes narrowed with suspicion as she studied the girl, looked back at Jesse, and asked again, "How on earth did you get into this house?"

Jesse winked at Theodora. "I believe a fairy must have waved a magic wand."

Theodora smiled wider, and Jesse smiled encouragingly at her. "Hello, Theodora. I'm Jesse," he said.

Evaleen narrowed her eyes at her niece, remembering Theodora's last glance over her shoulder at the front door when the child had started up the stairs. Probably Theodora had unlocked the door while Evaleen was in one of the other rooms looking for her. One more look at the way Theodora was staring up at Jesse in awe confirmed it in her mind.

*Just what I need,* she thought. *Another female enamored with the man.* "I don't know why your head isn't swelled to the size of a watermelon," she told him crossly.

"I'd be too ugly to be Theodora's Prince Charming?"

Now Theodora was positively beaming. "Look, Jesse," Evaleen said, frowning at him with her hands on her hips, "it's bad enough that Dorie's making up stories about an evil knight talking to her. We don't need to encourage such imaginings."

"Why not?" Jesse asked. "What's wrong with staring at clouds and seeing animals, or looking at rainbows and thinking about the pots of gold at the end of them?"

"Or wishing for knights in shining armor to ride up and carry you away to a castle where you'll be taken care of?" she added. "My sister thought that way, and it did her no good at all."

"Are you sure you want to discuss this in front of the child?" Jesse asked, cocking one eyebrow.

"She should know and remember what her mother went through so she doesn't follow in her footsteps."

"Is that why you're so stiff-backed?" Jesse asked. "Because you want to avoid your sister's fate?"

The words hurt. "If I'm stiff-backed, as you say, it's because I haven't had time to be otherwise. Fanciful dreamers don't get dinner on the table or keep families together.

And now I have two people to look after. I can't afford dreams."

"Life isn't worth living without dreams, Miss Murphy," Jesse said, wishing he hadn't brought that sad look to Evaleen's face. But it was true nonetheless. The last time he'd been away from the ranch, thinking he would never go back, life had been dull, meaningless, and full of work. Tumbling sweet young things in bed hadn't filled the void. Nothing had, until he'd gotten a second chance at his dream—having Rainbow's End for his own. He wasn't about to give up that dream ever again, not for anything.

Evaleen turned away from the man in front of her. No matter how interested she was in finding out how Jesse's lips would feel on hers or how his hands would feel sliding down her body, she could not afford to indulge in dreams. She had responsibility for her aunt and Theodora to think about, and she couldn't afford to take risks, no matter how much her body ached for Jesse's touch or her heart for a family of her own and someone to love her.

"I paid the hack driver and sent him on," Jesse told her. "You ruined his faith in you when you didn't come back out."

Her mouth dropped open, and she snapped it shut. When she'd gone outside earlier, Jesse had rattled her so badly she'd forgotten that she was going to pay Mr. O'Henry and tell him to return for them later. Originally she'd assumed she'd take no more than twenty minutes to get her necessaries packed and then arrange for her neighbor to watch her house for the next six months, but finding Theodora had changed things. She still had to explain to her niece about Reynard's dying.

"I take it since you haven't disappeared, you're planning on returning to the ranch with me?" Jesse asked.

"Do I really have a choice?" Evaleen asked him, but then she didn't wait for an answer. Turning, she glanced down at Theodora, considering if the time were right to let her know about the man who had been her guardian. But Jesse was already going around her to Dorie's side, where he hunkered down next to her.

"So what did this evil knight look like?" Jesse asked.

The news of Reynard's passing would have to wait. Going to pull out a dresser drawer, Evaleen grabbed an armload of chemises to carry over to her carpetbag.

"He had hair like yours, only darker, and blue eyes just like yours, and he was tall like you, only not so tall."

Stuffing the chemises into her bag haphazardly, Evaleen met Jesse's eyes. "Quite a description," she said, her voice mirroring her dismay that he was pursuing this.

It was, Jesse thought, ignoring Miss Priss's anger. Theodora's evil knight could have been him. . . .

Or it could have been his brother, who resembled him. This about cinched Jesse's suspicions that Patrick existed, had returned, and was up to something. After all this time, who else would bother the child?

Bent at the knee as it was, his leg was beginning to protest. Grabbing onto the bedpost, Jesse hauled himself up, settled on the bed, and smiled encouragingly at Theodora. She could have been his little sister in looks, but he knew there was no chance of that. Cynthia had been a pregnant widow when Reynard had met her and there had never been any talk at all of Reynard being Theodora's father, except in name only.

"So tell me, Theodora, what did this evil knight say to get you all lathered up?"

"I'm not a horse," Theodora said seriously.

"No, that's true. Right now, you're more like a pony," he said seriously, and Theodora let out a giggle.

Evaleen pursed her lips so she wouldn't smile herself, and made another trip to the dresser to pull out her skirts. Let him talk to her for now. In the time to come, he'd be too busy working the ranch to have much influence on Theodora, and Evaleen would have ample opportunity to teach the child the value of hard work and seeking goals. When he saw how well her theory was working with Theodora, maybe, just maybe, he would start to believe in her values and understand that they really were the best thing for the girl and acknowledge that she wasn't out to do her niece irrevocable harm.

After all, she lived by those values, and she wasn't such a bad person.

"The man said he was going to take me far away, where bad people couldn't find me for a while, but then Miss Hurley was calling for me in the hallway, and he left the window."

Pausing in the middle of stuffing the last skirt in her bag, Evaleen frowned. "You were in your own room at school?"

Theodora nodded. "It was nighttime, and everyone was supposed to be asleep. But he called my name, and when I went to the window there he was. I was scared."

Jesse shared a long look with Evaleen. Finally, she shook her head and said to Theodora, "There you go, Dorie. It was nighttime, and everyone was asleep. You probably just had a bad dream."

"Did Miss Hurley see the man?" Jesse asked.

Theodora shook her head, sending gleaming reddish brown waves over her shoulders. "I shut the window and hopped back into my bed before she got into the room, because we aren't supposed to be out of our beds late."

"Did the evil knight come back again?" Jesse asked.

"I don't know. When I woke up the next day, I got out Aunt Evaleen's last letter with her address on it and took my money and came here on the train. I got into the house through the coal chute."

Evaleen shook her head in disapproval, but Jesse was

grinning again, his eyes intent on the child. "Sounds like fun. Do you think I could slide down it?"

Theodora giggled. "You're too big. You'd get stuck. Then you'd have to take a bath."

"Misery!"

The two of them collapsed into laughter. Standing aside and looking on, Evaleen smiled, but she couldn't laugh like that. She just couldn't let herself go to that extent, and she felt almost ... left out.

Shrugging off the feeling as nonsensical, she admitted one thing about the man as she finished packing, put her carpetbag on the floor, and studied him. If she could bottle and sell his charm with females to the male gender, she'd be rich.

Jesse saw she was watching him and gazed back at her intently as he and Theodora played cat's cradle with string Jesse just happened to have. He bobbed his chin toward the door as though he wanted to speak with her privately, and she nodded agreement, walking out of the room onto the small stair-top landing. Telling Theodora to stay where she was, Jesse followed her out and closed the door to the bedroom.

"I think we ought to check back at the school with Miss Hurley about this evil knight Theodora saw," Jesse told her. His blue-gray gaze was riveted on her, and he was truly, honestly, asking her opinion without any hint of mockery or animosity in his voice. If they could continue like this, she might even enjoy the next six months around Jesse. Dare she hope?

"I think going back to the school would be a waste of time," Evaleen said, determined to tell him her true feelings even though she knew it would cause trouble. "Theodora started her fairy-tale fantasies a while ago after she read some storybook at school. My guess is she got lonely and wanted some attention."

"You don't find the appearance and threats of this visitor of Theodora's strange, coming as they do right on the heels of Reynard's death and our custody problems?"

She shook her head. "You have a lot to learn about children, Jesse." She realized immediately that she had used his first name again, but Theodora had been spouting it since he'd come into the room, and somehow, it just seemed natural to do so now. "They have wonderful imaginations."

She couldn't tell if Jesse was considering what she'd said or not. His face was carefully masked.

"Was that all you wanted?" she asked.

"For the time being," he said slowly, suggestively, his gaze sliding down over her like a caress. She tensed her shoulders and took a step backward, her hand on the glass knob of the door. "At least until we get back to the ranch," he added, "where I'm sure you'll continue your tips on how I can be a good parent."

"You'll need a lot of them," she said.

"Oh, I don't know. Theodora seems to like me well enough."

"You do have her wrapped around your finger," she admitted. "But that's only because the child in question is a female. No matter what their ages, you show an amazing ability to mesmerize the ladies."

"How about you, Miss Murphy?" He stepped closer to her and smiled, his eyes penetrating the shell she'd erected when she'd walked out here onto the landing. "Are you mesmerized by me?"

Couldn't he tell? She took a deep breath, and was suddenly aware of how his gaze went right to her expanding bosom. Before she got flustered and let him do something she'd be sorry for later, she opened the door to the room so Theodora would be a witness to the rest of the conversation. She hoped that would make him behave.

He glanced at Theodora and back at her. Then that damnable smirk returned to his face. "I think you just gave me your answer," he said.

Before she could reply, he walked past her and back into the bedroom, leaving her with an unmistakable urge to do something very unladylike, like find a flowerpot and break it over his condescending head.

Watching Evaleen organize, Jesse found himself in awe of her. Within three hours, she had packed more things, made final arrangements for her house to be looked after, and they'd eaten at the Harvey Hotel restaurant. Evaleen had purchased some items Theodora would need to last her until her belongings arrived from the school in Raton, something he would never have thought of. They had picked up Evaleen's aunt Victoria, a small, brown-haired woman of fifty or so, who had barely uttered more than a hello before fixing her steely-eyed stare on him and watching every move he made. Luckily, the talkative Theodora had kept up the conversation. And lastly, the well-organized Evaleen had reminded him he might want to send a telegram to Calloway Nesmith informing him that Theodora was safe.

During the entire time Evaleen was doing all this, Jesse noticed that she did not do one thing for herself. Everything was concerned with other people, something she seemed to concentrate on. He had to wonder that she never seemed to have any personal needs or desires. Even he had stopped to buy some cigars at the counter at the Harvey Hotel restaurant, to Evaleen's obvious disgust.

Why he even cared that she knocked herself out for everyone, he didn't know. If Evaleen had her way, she'd be rid of him and fast. Even as well as they were cooperating with each other now, he wasn't fool enough to think the harmony could last. Not when they returned to the ranch and he resumed life as usual, which only meant living the way a man should live.

He would have to find a way around her, he thought, gazing out the window of the train as the four of them sped toward Raton that night at the breakneck speed of twenty-five miles per hour. He half-listened as Evaleen complained to her aunt that she could no longer take advantage of the Harvey employees' benefit of traveling anywhere on the railroad lines free of charge, since she'd been forced to leave her position at the Harvey Hotel. When Victoria scowled at Jesse as though he were to blame, he knew he was in for trouble. He had a feeling Victoria was what Evaleen would be in thirty years—a grown-old version of her niece, with double the experience of making a man's life miserable.

Theodora was reading a book her aunt had gotten her while they'd shopped, so at least he didn't have to listen to three females talking at once. He supposed he liked the child well enough, and he felt empathy for her because of her loneliness. But Theodora had latched onto him so fiercely she was now calling him the handsome prince who had come to rescue her, making him feel somewhat stifled. She trailed him all over the place, including to the telegraph station when he'd wired Calloway, and he could tell Evaleen didn't like Theodora's hero worship one bit. Which would mean even more to contend with later.

But then again, if Theodora did everything he asked her to immediately, Calloway would think he was doing a great job at fatherhood. It might work out for the best.

Leaning back in his seat, he pulled his hat down over his eyes. It was the only way he had of shutting out the world. Come to think of it, why shouldn't the lawyer believe he was being a great father? He guessed he wasn't doing so badly with the young lady. And as long as he kept Evaleen off her guard by continuing to use his charms on her, he imagined even she would be manageable enough. After all, the girls in Raton didn't call him The Best in the West for nothing.

# Chapter Seven

By the time they'd been back at Rainbow's End a few days, there had been no further sign of Theodora's evil knight, and Evaleen became certain he had been a figment of the child's imagination. So both she and Victoria ignored Jesse's order that they keep the child with them at all times, just in case the man came back.

Jesse, because he was so busy with the ranch, hadn't thus far noticed his ward wasn't being watched every second of the day. That had proven to be the only thing she'd made a decision on which had gone smoothly, Evaleen thought as she got ready for bed that Saturday evening. Jesse was determined to make everything either of them wanted to do at Rainbow's End into an argument.

Blowing out the lamp, she pulled back her coverlet and got into bed. First of all had been the problem of where they would all sleep. Because of her wheelchair, Aunt Victoria really required having a ground-floor bedroom, the same one Jesse wanted. Since Evaleen did not feel comfortable having him on the second floor with her, albeit in separate bedrooms, she had asked him to move to the bunkhouse.

He'd refused. As a compromise, he'd offered to carry Victoria upstairs each night so he could keep the sole downstairs bedroom. Evaleen had explained, quite patiently, that there would be nights when Jesse would not be there, and besides, Victoria was really quite self-sufficient as long as she had easy access to her belongings, which she would not have with an upstairs bedroom. To take that self-sufficiency away from the fifty-year-old woman would be a crime. She'd compromised with offering to let him sleep in the study.

He'd just looked at her. But finally, he'd given Victoria the downstairs bedroom, with a stipulation. He had to have the study free to entertain male acquaintances he might have over for card games, since his trips to town for entertainment had been forbidden. He certainly was not going to put a bed and dresser in there, and neither was she. And he was sleeping in *his* house. So he guessed they would both have to occupy the second floor.

Grudgingly, Evaleen had caved in, on the condition that they sleep at opposite ends of the hall. She'd ended up in the bedroom right next to the staircase. The problem with that was, when Jesse came up to bed, she could hear footsteps all the way up the stairs.

As she had seconds ago, she thought, when he'd paused at the top landing for a few seconds and then had headed past her door and down the hall to his own room.

Rolling over, Evaleen pressed her body against the mattress to numb the yearning and desire that had been all too prevalent in her since Jesse had begun to be civil back in Kansas City. As her body began to relax in the comfort of the feather bed, she wondered what it would be like if she were married to a man. *Not Jesse,* she told herself sternly, *just any man.* She'd be lying in bed and would hear him come up the stairs, and she'd know he was coming to her. To this bed. To do what married people did. Or what unmarried people, like Cynthia, sometimes did.

Evaleen wasn't sure of the technicalities of what her sister had referred to as *the act.* All her mother would say was that when Evaleen got married, she should put up with what the man wanted from her when they were in bed; it would be her duty as a good wife. Between that and Cynthia's telling her that what happened between a man and a woman had nothing to do with *duty,* and everything to do with touching and kissing, Evaleen had become so confused she was afraid to get involved with any man, lest she let things go too far by accident.

Since her mother was an upstanding woman, Evaleen wanted to believe she had given her correct advice, but her mother's referral to duty sounded almost painful. On the other hand, Cynthia couldn't hold her head up when she'd come home to visit in the neighborhood, so bad was her shame, yet she made relations between a man and a woman sound like something mystical, magical, wonderful.

So what all that meant was, if the footsteps she'd heard just now walking past the door had belonged to a theoretical husband, she wasn't supposed to look forward to him coming to her bed. At least, that was what she thought it meant.

But she had no husband. The footsteps belonged to Jesse Stockton, a ladies' man from whom "allure" emanated like he'd originated it, and she couldn't help but be fascinated with the fantasy of him entering her room. Evaleen tossed her head in the opposite direction. What she didn't understand was how Jesse could stir such feelings in her, but none in Cynthia, who at the time she'd known him had written that he was handsome, but hardly unique. And from what she'd learned later, Cynthia would have had the experience to know.

Evaleen balled her fist in frustration. She didn't understand why she had to be put to this kind of test, now, with a man who would never care about her the way she needed a man to. Even knowing that, she couldn't stop thinking about Jesse. It almost made her wish he would go back to being an insufferable bounder.

Jesse sat on the edge of his bed and pulled off his boots, being careful not to jar his bad knee, achy as it already was from the long day. He'd been out with Waco looking over the barbed wire fences around the ranch and seeing what needed fixing so he could get time away from Evaleen. But Waco had mentioned it might be a good idea to teach Evaleen how to ride so she'd have more freedom, which had started him thinking about the woman all over again.

When he'd returned, he'd gone into the kitchen, supposing he'd have to make his own dinner because he was late the second night in a row, and Evaleen had warned him she was only doing the dishes once. But no. She'd left him a plate anyway filled with roast beef and fresh bread so he could make a sandwich. She was a woman of contradictions, and he couldn't figure her out. One second he would swear she sensed this desire between them, but the next would bring only her confused stare, like she wished she didn't have to deal with him.

Still in his jeans, Jesse lay back on the bed against the pillows. After a week of living in the same house with Evaleen, knowing she was just a few feet from his bedroom, his body was lusting for her. That's all there was to it; he was aching to get her naked and soft next to him. But what to do about it?

He had to get to town, to one of Nicholson's doves. That

was probably his real trouble. He was just having some sort of fantasy thing about Evaleen, and he needed his fantasy fulfilled. Having done without a woman for well over two weeks now, he had the feeling that any woman with fleshy hips and nicely rounded breasts would do. His body seemed to agree with him, so he rose to his feet to pull his boots back on.

All he had to do was to wait until everyone was asleep. It was Saturday night. Cassie Jo would welcome him at the saloon, as would its owner, Nicholson, and all the rest of the men who by now were probably sure they wouldn't see him again until the next church social. Well, he'd just show them. He was his own man, and he wasn't going to let a set of skirts dictate anything to him.

Restless, Evaleen sensed footsteps again in the hall an hour after she'd first heard Jesse's. Frowning, she rose from her bed and padded across the rug to press her ear against the door. The steps were too heavy to be Theodora's so the person going downstairs had to be Jesse, with his boots on, she'd listened to his steps long enough now to tell the difference. At this hour, boots would mean he was headed off somewhere. She would bet this ranch on it.

Fuming, she yanked on good, serviceable clothing—a black skirt and shirt that had been her waitress uniform—and then pulled her slippers on because they were faster to don than shoes. She would have to get to Jesse now; after he rode out would be too late. Having grown up in the city, and poor, there had never been any reason for her to learn to ride. She'd only learned to drive a buggy to run an occasional errand for the Harvey House. She didn't even know how to hitch one up. With no transportation, she wasn't about to walk the three miles to Raton at near eleven o'clock at night to yank him out of a saloon.

Leaving her room, she flew down the stairs and out the back door. Whether Jesse liked it or not, he was staying and following the terms of the will. She just wasn't certain how she was going to bring the miracle about.

Jesse was leading his mount, a feisty mare named Nowhere, from the stable when she located him. Since he was headed right in her direction, his head lowered, Evaleen just waited where she was, hands on her hips, waiting for him to notice her.

He was almost in front of her when he stopped and met her eyes. The moment of silence that followed was so full of danger, Evaleen felt she was in one of those showdowns she'd read about in the dime novels. Only instead of guns, he was holding the reins of his horse—his freedom—in his hand, and she was holding her righteous indignation—her only defense—in her heart.

"For mercy's sake, Jesse, can't you control yourself for six months?"

Jesse glanced around the moonlit yard to make sure they were alone, then slowly shook his head. "No. If you knew anything about men, sweetheart, you'd know we can't go for long without what we need."

"That's so much stuff and nonsense. Women seem to manage." *Aside from Cynthia, that is.* She shook off that thought.

He let go of the reins and stepped forward. "If you would let yourself feel passion, Evaleen, instead of the starch in your pantaloons, maybe you would realize that people have *needs*. I'm no different—and neither are you." He took her in from head to toe with a long, searching look that made her shiver. "I want a fleshy, feminine body next to me in bed tonight. I need a warm, sweet woman who'll smile at me." He looked at her beguilingly. "If *you* would volunteer, I'd stay here."

Evaleen felt like Eve must have in the Garden of Eden. Tempted. Would the feelings that started whenever Jesse came so close to her cascade to an unbearable level if they were side by side in bed?

Why was she even asking?

"Sorry, Jesse," she said, softly. "I'm not feeling warm and sweet, and I'm definitely not in the mood to smile."

To her surprise, he didn't smirk. "I could make you warm and sweet. Would you come to bed with me if I don't ask you to smile?"

This was getting absolutely ridiculous. "Perhaps I should go back to calling you Mr. Stockton," she said. "You are assuming a whole lot more about our relationship than you should."

"I'm not assuming anything, sweetheart. You and I want each other. The only thing I'm not sure about yet is if we're going to end up doing anything about it."

She couldn't deny what Jesse said, because he was right. Physically, her body was already responding to him while he was just standing there. Her breasts were aching for his touch, and deep within her, her womanly parts were clenching so hard she was throbbing. She sighed, disappointed in herself, knowing she was supposed to set an example for the errant cowboy. But how could she, when she was reacting like this to him?

"Do what you want, Jesse. Just be aware that your trip is going to be written up in my journal."

Turning to go back to bed, she'd gone only a few feet when his fingers wrapped gently around her upper arm. Using both hands, he twirled her around and pulled her into his arms, clutching her to him as if he were holding something precious. His mouth lowered, and his lips brushed hers in the gentlest of kisses.

A rapturous sense of contentment flooded Evaleen, catching her unaware and stealing away any reason she could call on to protest. Gradually as he continued to kiss her, her hands crept up the ripple of muscles to his broad shoulders. She wrapped her arms around his neck, unwilling to let him pull his mouth away, experimentally touching her tongue to his. His lower body bucked and hardened, and he moved his hips slowly against her.

Evaleen had never felt this way before. Even knowing that she was flirting with danger, that this was the same thing that had corrupted Cynthia, Evaleen could not draw back. She'd never known this strong a need to be held before, not by any man. Running her fingers down Jesse's arms, she continued to kiss him, clutching at the flannel of his shirt almost desperately.

He pulled his mouth away from hers. "Now do you see what I'm talking about?" he asked, his voice raspy. "Do you really want me to keep doing this to you until you finally give in to me, Evaleen? Because you will, you know, and what with me being the kind of man you despise, you'll regret it."

His words were a splash of cold water on her flushed face, and she backed out of his arms. He let her go without a struggle.

"You have a point," she told him. "I guess, under the circumstances, I would be a hypocrite if I wrote you up."

His mouth set in a line and his jaw firm, he stared at her. There was a "but," he could hear it in her voice.

"But you're going to have to try harder than you've been doing with Reynard's other goals for you, Jesse." Swallowing, Evaleen pressed her lips together. "And I, in return, will try harder to make things a little easier for you around here."

He felt cocky with success. "That means you are volunteering to keep me here tonight?"

"Not that easy," she said hurriedly. But she smiled at him then. He had been right. He could have used his allure to draw her right into his bed, and then she would have ended up hating him for her own inability to resist. "You have more scruples than your father gave you credit for, Jess. He was too hard on you."

"Thank you." A single, small chuckle sounded deep in his throat. "Too bad you weren't around before he died to convince him of that, Evaleen. You might have saved us both a whole lot of trouble in the weeks to come."

"Are we going to have trouble?" she asked, with an edge of sorrow in her voice.

"Yeah. I think we are. But it won't be the kind you might envision." Abruptly, he grabbed the reins of his horse and strode away from her, and Evaleen was left to stand there, staring after him. She regretted that she wouldn't be the woman he would be with tonight, but she couldn't be, and they both knew that. Deep inside, that hurt, and she didn't even understand why.

Jesse swore under his breath. Cassie Jo was seated on the red satin-covered bed in all her frazzled blond glory, studying him as though he'd suddenly sprouted spots.

He'd arrived in her room above Nicholson's bar all ready to lose himself in a woman's warmth. He'd even gotten to the point where they'd been rolling naked on the bed and he'd been kissing the soft skin of her neck. But then his mind had taken over, and he'd grown cold inside. He'd pulled away from the delectable, fleshy woman and risen from the bed.

He might have gone frigid inside, but not on the outside, which was why Cassie Jo was studying him. She was puzzled over why, when he was so hard with desire, he wouldn't take advantage of his golden opportunity, as he used to call her. Even he was beginning to think he was loco. He had what amounted to Evaleen's permission, if not her blessing, but he couldn't bury himself inside Cassie Jo and gain the relief he sought. It was like Evaleen was standing to one side of the bed, begging him not to do this, begging him to come back home where he belonged.

He shouldn't have kissed Evaleen's sassy little mouth. That had been stupid. Now her wildflower scent, her touch on his arms and shoulders, and her soft voice hung in his mind like a song that wouldn't go away.

"Don't worry, honey. All men go through this from time to time," Cassie Jo said, reaching for her lacy wrapper at the foot of the bed. "I just never thought you'd be one of them. And I've never seen such a hard case of impotence," she added, eyeing the bulge in his trousers.

"Was that supposed to be funny?" he asked, puffing on the cigar she'd offered him when he'd pulled his pants back on and it was obvious he wasn't coming back to bed to finish what he'd started.

"You paid me. I promise I won't spoil your reputation."

His reputation wasn't currently what was bothering Jesse. It was the ache in his loins that he knew would make him very, very irritable in the days to come if he didn't get it relieved. It was also the fact that he was beginning to suspect Evaleen might have to be the one to finally assuage his desire.

That was what worried him most. He'd walked away from her earlier for a couple of reasons. Foremost, he didn't want to make love to Evaleen because he had a feeling that their being together wouldn't be as simple as a roll in the hay. He didn't want to tangle up his emotions to the point where he cared about her. She just wanted the child, not him, and when she had Theodora free and clear, she'd be leaving the territory. Such was the way it went for him; no one in his life seemed to know the word forever. He'd be a fool to think Evaleen would.

The second reason he'd walked away was much simpler. He'd known he could seduce her right into bed, and then she would hate him. And whatever his father had thought about him, Jesse was not in the habit of ruining decent women. Even Evaleen had recognized that. He just hoped like hell he didn't end up disappointing her if his need for her got too strong. No one had ever forced him into sainthood before.

Jesse hadn't been as late as she'd expected he'd be, Evaleen thought the next morning as she went around the table filling first her own, and then Victoria's coffee cup. But then, as Jesse had teased her at the train station in Kansas City, she would have no idea of how long something like that would take.

Bending low as she filled Jesse's cup, she breathed in his scent. He smelled fresh, like soap, which meant he'd scrubbed away any scent of the woman he'd gone to see. She appreciated that, she truly did. Now she could pretend the night before had never happened, and forget that he'd gone against the will. She could lie to Calloway with the impunity of having lied to herself.

Unfortunately, controlling Jesse wasn't her only problem. She glanced at her aunt Victoria, who was busy reading a book. Victoria had petite, almost miniature features and the same plain brown hair Evaleen had—that seemed to run along her father's bloodlines—only hers had streaks of silver in it. Being in a wheelchair and looking delicate led people to believe Victoria could be ordered about like a meek little mouse, but that was far from the truth. She'd slapped Jesse's hand for stealing one of her batch of cookies before she was ready to hand any out. Part of that was feistiness, but most of it was Victoria's dislike of Jesse, which had been immediate.

What had surprised Evaleen was that the older woman had refused to discuss her reasons for it. Victoria and Evaleen were the greatest of confidantes about everything—except Jesse. With Victoria shooting her niece disapproving looks every time she went near him, Evaleen was beginning to realize she was going to have difficulty working with him and keeping her family intact at the same time.

Since Victoria was intent on her book, Evaleen dared to cast another look at the man in question. Bent close to her niece, Jesse was listening to Dorie whisper in his ear. This morning he wore a brownish red shirt that matched his hair color and hugged his shoulders as she'd done the night before. The memory brought a niggling doubt back into Evaleen's mind. Should he try to persuade her to his way of thinking in a similar fashion in the future, was she going to be able to resist him again? Firmly, she pushed her doubt away. Somehow, with the good Lord's help, she could find a way around Jesse Stockton and temptation.

When she scooped eggs onto his plate she looked at Jesse again, and found his blue-gray stare fastened on her. Why, she didn't know, but it made her feel off-kilter, and she knew she had to get control.

"Do you feel any better this morning?" she asked sweetly.

Usually when she asked that question, it was directed at her aunt. With her attention drawn, the other woman looked at Evaleen.

"Oh, me, my memory must be fading. I don't recall mentioning feeling poorly last night."

"You didn't, Miss Murphy," Jesse said, putting down his fork to reach for a biscuit from the basketful on the table.

"I believe Evaleen was referring to me. I had a needlesome ache I couldn't get rid of."

Evaleen gasped, and Victoria peered over her wire spectacles at her. Then she turned her scrutiny on Jesse, who merely smiled innocently.

"You do have quite a limp," Victoria said finally as they both watched Theodora leave the kitchen. "A recent injury?"

Jesse's face closed off in a flash, and at first, Evaleen thought he might not answer. But then his deep voice rumbled through the kitchen.

"It happened long ago. My brother tried to kill me."

His brother ... Evaleen sank into Theodora's vacant chair. Jesse had an alarming ability to throw her for a loop. "You're serious, aren't you?" she asked weakly.

"You seem awfully upset at the idea. And here I'd thought my dying would be a blessing to you," Jesse said, grinning as he wondered about the strength of her reaction.

Evaleen shook her head, her lips forming the tiniest of smiles. "You aren't *that* disreputable—not bad enough that I want to see you dead anyway."

"How comforting," he said, his eyes twinkling as he gazed at her. "Don't worry yourself. It's been a long, long time since Patrick has tried something with me. This happened when we were very young children."

But Evaleen wasn't so accepting. She thought there had to be a whole lot more to it from the way his face had been shadowed before he'd answered, and from the fact that he still limped some twenty years after whatever it had been that had caused his injury.

When Jesse looked up at her, she knew that she was right. His grim look made her think that boys or not, he'd never forgiven his brother for what had happened to his leg. She decided to put off any discussion of that until another time; right now they all had something more pressing on the agenda. But before she could open her mouth, Jesse spoke.

"I'm going to check fences again today. Do you want to come along with me, Evaleen?"

"I don't know how to ride," she told him. She would have added that she would find looking at fences all day boring, but Jesse's gaze held hers so long and caused such sweet feelings inside her, she almost wished she could go and spend the time with him. But that was only asking for more trouble.

"Waco and I were discussing teaching you."

"No, thank you," she said quickly. He opened his mouth as if to protest, but then he shrugged as though he didn't care in the least. That left her free to tackle the next topic she needed to have out with him.

"Theodora," she said, calling into the other room through the open door, "Jesse is taking you to school today."

"He is?"

"I am?" Jesse put in at the same time Theodora spoke.

"That's right," Evaleen said in answer to both questions. "Theodora, please go upstairs and get your slate so you two can leave." The child disappeared, and she turned back to Jesse. "You need to go so you can speak with the schoolmarm and get an idea of how far along Theodora is in her studies."

"But you've already talked to her," Jesse protested.

"I made an effort to see her teacher because I love the child, and I'm interested in her welfare. But I am not her guardian, Jesse. Miss Worrell wants to talk to *all* the parents—namely you."

"Then have her come here."

Evaleen recognized the ploy for what it was. If they set a time for Miss Worrell to come, Jesse would know and could arrange to be somewhere else on some "emergency." But Reynard had decreed that it was up to her to make sure he understood what a responsibility being a father was. She couldn't let him get out of this.

"Keeping track of their children's education is something parents do, Jesse. If you don't want to do it, just go to Mr. Nesmith right now and tell him you give up and you don't want this ranch." She knew she was being rigid, but her tone also reflected her resolution of the night before to make sure Jesse didn't walk all over her. To remember he was just a man, and she had something he wanted, and therefore, that meant she had the power.

He stood, and her gaze swept over him, her eyes lingering on his mouth for the briefest of seconds. If only she could forget that he had something she wanted, too....

Theodora. He had control of Theodora, and that was what she wanted. Not him.

Jesse's eyes hardened. "I'll take her to school."

"Good." Walking over to the counter, she picked up a list she'd made out early that morning when she couldn't sleep. "I realized you might not have a whole lot of experience in these matters, so to try to help you, I made up a list of things you can ask Miss Worrell. Things about what Theodora needs to work on and what you can do to help her."

"What I can do . . . ?" He stared at her as though she were speaking Greek to him.

"Yes. You need to start spending time every evening helping Theodora with her schoolwork so you show her that you care about her achievements."

"My father never did that."

"Fathers usually don't. That's usually the realm of the mother," she agreed amiably, then added, "But for right now, unless you have plans of bringing a suitable wife through the door who can take over the task of mothering

Theodora for you until the six months are over, you're going to have to learn how to be both father and mother."

Reaching forward, Jesse took the list out of her hand and stalked out of the room, a grimace on his face.

"Bravo," Victoria warbled, clapping her hands softly.

Evaleen jumped, having forgotten her aunt was in the room. Surprised at the other woman's voicing her opinion after a whole week, she smiled apprehensively. She was glad her aunt approved of what she had done; she just wished she hadn't had to boss Jesse around like that.

"I was beginning to fear Jesse was going to overwhelm you," Victoria told her. "But I should have known better. You, my dear girl, are made of steel where men are concerned. That's very fortunate."

Evaleen's smile slowly faded as she turned back to clean up the table. She didn't know if she agreed with her aunt about her formidability being good. It might enable her to win Theodora, and that would be fine, but in the process of alienating Jesse so he'd respect her enough to let her mold him into a fine citizen, would she lose a chance at love?

She shook her head hard. Now there she was, getting all fanciful. Love was not in the cards for her. A good marriage was, and she would make one, just as she did everything else. With planning, and lots of forethought. She couldn't allow her heart to rule her head. She would just turn out like Cynthia if she did, and she could never let that happen. Never.

She wanted people to like her.

# Chapter Eight

Curious as to how Jesse had gotten along with the schoolmarm, Evaleen picked her niece up from school that afternoon. From the looks of Theodora's set chin and pout as the child walked slowly from the schoolhouse down the well-trodden path to where Evaleen was waiting, she was glad she had. Something was wrong. Dorie should have been bubbling over with excitement about having her precious handsome knight bring her to school and about how she had shown him off to her friends. Should have been, but wasn't.

Theodora's pout deepened as she got up on the buggy and quietly said hello to Evaleen.

"Your face is going to freeze like that," Evaleen said.

The pout disappeared. "Will not. It's almost summer. It's too warm."

She had to smile at Theodora's logic. "So what's wrong?" she asked, clicking the horse into a stroll back toward Rainbow's End. "Trouble at school?"

Theodora shook her head.

"Trouble with Jesse?"

"He asked Miss Worrell to go to dinner with him, and she said yes," Theodora wailed. "That's not fair. He's supposed to be *my* prince. I asked him before, and he said he would. He's even been calling me his princess."

Evaleen felt a wave of exasperation. Jesse had turned a simple meeting with the schoolteacher into the possibility of another conquest. Not only that, but she'd told him encouraging Theodora's fantasies was a bad idea—and he had refused to listen. *Now look at Theodora!* She fumed at an imaginary image of Jesse. *She has tears in her eyes.*

"Theodora, dear, please don't give Jesse another thought," she told her niece. "There will be other princes who will come along for you when you get a little older, I promise."

"But none ever came for you," Theodora pointed out, a wail in her voice.

Evaleen briefly closed her eyes, swallowing back the hurt that galloped through her like an out-of-control horse. Theodora was not trying to hurt her with her bluntness, she reminded herself. The young girl was only concerned that *she* would not get her prince, since life obviously left some people out of the dole.

"I turned mine down," Evaleen lied, "so I could take care of you and Aunt Victoria instead."

"Oh," Theodora said, seeming to accept her explanation. Evaleen allowed herself a sigh of relief; then Theodora came up with a new problem. "But Jesse promised to protect me from the evil knight. Now he'll be too busy courting Miss Worrell."

"Honey, you have to stop pretending about the fairy tales. People aren't going to pay any attention to you when you have real trouble."

"But the evil knight is here," Theodora protested. "He's

keeping his eye on me. I saw him today during recess. He was coming out of Grover's General Store down the road."

"I'll tell Jesse." My, oh my, was she going to tell Jesse! He was going to have to sit Theodora down and have a long talk with her so she'd stop making up stories. Until he got the opportunity, Evaleen decided to humor Theodora to make her feel more protected. "For now, until Jesse takes care of this, just stick close to the house and make sure you don't go off anywhere on your own. Can you do that for me?"

Theodora nodded grimly and swiped her tears away with her sleeve.

"That's a good girl." Ordinarily, Evaleen might have punished the child for continuing to make up stories after she'd been told not to, but Theodora had been through so much lately, what with hearing about Reynard and being afraid she wasn't going to have a real home, Evaleen couldn't bear to make her any more unhappy. Theodora had run away from school once, and they still weren't sure why. Evaleen thought this evil-knight thing and the running away had to be a desperate bid for attention, and somehow, she was going to make sure she and Jesse—especially Jesse—gave the child all the right kind.

As he ate from the plate of carrots, roast beef, and potatoes Evaleen had handed him minutes before when he'd walked in, Jesse could imagine any number of reasons why she would remain standing at the far end of the kitchen. Her arms were folded over her bosom—hiding his view, damn it all!—and her foot was tapping faster than his heart was beating, even while thinking of her breasts. That he'd done something wrong was obvious. What that something was, was not. He started listing the possibilities.

He'd been late to dinner again. Naw. She had to realize

that ranching would involve a lot of catch-as-catch-can meals. Besides, if she was angry about that, why would she have served him a plate of food when it was much easier to dump it over his head?

Maybe she'd found out about his asking Miss Worrell to dinner the next evening to talk about Theodora, since the teacher hadn't had the time before class started. Theodora had refused to say good-bye to him after witnessing the invitation, so Jesse could only assume the child had been upset about it for some reason. If so, who else would Theodora go to but Evaleen, her aunt, to talk about why?

Then again, maybe Evaleen was vexed because he hadn't been able to come home early to spend time with Theodora. But she couldn't know he'd talked to the child all the way to school, about one day taking her to see castles in England and maybe even getting a glimpse of a real-life queen if they could get close enough. He'd always wanted to go over the Atlantic Ocean to England, and if he could make this ranch succeed like he wanted to, he might have the funds in a few years. In fact, he was counting on it.

Lifting his head, he eyed Evaleen, whose beautiful lips were drawn into a fine line. He'd go, that was, if *she* didn't mess everything up.

Having polished off his roast beef and potatoes, he began eating his carrots. She hadn't moved from her spot. In the other room, he could hear Theodora laughing at something Victoria was saying. The old woman didn't like him much, he knew. Maybe that was what Evaleen wanted to talk to him about. It had to be something; she still hadn't moved from that spot.

He finished the carrots and sipped some of the steaming coffee from his cup. As ready as he would ever be, he turned his chair purposely in her direction, sat back, and regarded her patiently. "What did I do now?"

The toe stopped tapping. "You greatly upset Theodora by making a date with Miss Worrell."

His mouth lifted in a half-smile. "I greatly upset Theodora, or I greatly upset *you?*"

That was all it took. "Oh, I'm upset all right, Jesse Stockton," she said in a low, brisk voice. "You have some nerve, encouraging that child with her fantasies about handsome princes and ladies in castles. You let her believe she's a little princess."

"Well, she is," he said, spreading his hands wide in disbelief that all this was as terrible as she was making it out to be. "I thought that was what I was supposed to do with a kid. Encourage them and make them feel good."

"I told you the fantasy thing was too much for her, that she had to deal with reality, but did you listen? No. Jesse Stockton is always right. You know everything. Well, now"—she paused and took a deep breath—"now Theodora was all upset because now you've found another princess."

He squinted, trying to understand who she meant. "Oh. Miss Worrell. So what's the harm? I'll just explain to her that I'm just going out with the lady to hear about what she's doing in school because Miss Worrell didn't have time this morning to tell me."

"You can't lie to her," Evaleen protested.

"Who says it's a lie?" His eyebrows lifted. "You?"

Evaleen's foot resumed its tapping. "Jesse. You're really trying to make me believe a ladies' man like you is going out with an eligible young woman like Miss Worrell only to discuss Theodora's schoolwork?"

"Exactly," he said smugly, figuring that would shut her up while she figured out if he was telling the truth or not. It was a way he could get to town and relax for an evening without her saying a damned word to stop him, and without her writing him up in that little book of hers, either.

"Ah, hmmm." She paused for a few seconds, thinking. "Assuming I believe that—"

*She said it like she doesn't,* Jesse thought.

"—and you straighten it out with Theodora, *and* you tell her that she has to stop living in a fantasy land and that you can't be her prince, even though you like her very much"—she drew a breath— "*then* I might be able to let this go. You have to make her understand, though, that she can't go around telling people she's seeing an evil knight."

He frowned. "She saw him again?"

"Today during recess, she saw him come out of Grover's General Store down the road."

"When do they have recess?"

"I don't know...." She broke off in midsentence when he lurched from his chair and headed into the other room where Theodora was. "You can't take this seriously, Jess," she protested, following him. "It's just her bid for attention, the poor thing...."

But her protests hit deaf ears, for Jesse was already sitting down next to the child, who was reading from a picture book while Victoria sat next to her, sewing. Victoria peered over her wire-rims at him, not missing a word or a stitch.

"Tell me about the evil knight you saw today, Theodora," Jesse urged.

Theodora's eyes went immediately to Evaleen. "I can't. Aunt Evaleen told me the knight doesn't exist. I can't spread stories, because people won't respect me if I keep it up."

"Your aunt is turning you into a miniature copy of herself, and that's not necessarily good," Jesse said.

Evaleen was angry. He'd gone too far now, directly undermining her. "Mr. Stockton, I wish to speak with you in the kitchen!" she said as icily as she could.

"I'll take care of you later," Jesse replied, scowling back

at her before he returned his attention to his ward. "Theodora, your aunt doesn't understand about evil knights and castles—"

"And princesses?"

"Especially princesses, and the princes who love them, sweep them away, and take care of them forever."

Once again hurt swept over Evaleen, a hurt made all the worse because Jesse was saying this on purpose to make her look uncaring. She blinked furiously, determined not to cry. She couldn't afford to be a dreamer and indulge in fantasies. She had responsibilities to other people, something he obviously couldn't understand.

She swallowed hard. "Mr. Stockton—now!"

"In a minute," Jesse said without glancing back at her. "Theodora, don't worry. I'm still your prince, just not your real, forever prince. I'm too old. But I'll stand in for now until the real one comes along when you get older."

"Whose real prince are you?"

Jesse looked up at Evaleen. Swallowing, she held her head high, waiting for his next acerbic comment, determined not to show she cared.

But it didn't come. "I don't know yet," he told Theodora quietly. "But don't worry, I'm not Miss Worrell's real prince either. She talks too squeaky for my tastes." He mimicked the teacher for a minute, and Theodora began to laugh.

Evaleen watched, and wished she didn't want so desperately to laugh along with Theodora. She also wished she didn't have so many responsibilities and that she could let herself relax around Jesse the way Theodora could. Sometimes he could be so charming, so funny, and she liked him despite everything.

"Like I said, Dorie, I may not be your forever prince, but I *am* the one who's going to protect you until the real one finds you. So right now, I need to know all about this evil knight, and how often you've seen him since you've come to Rainbow's End. Tell me everything."

Evaleen walked back into the kitchen, miserable. She was failing to change Jesse; she was certain he had more in mind for Miss Worrell than a simple discussion over schoolroom antics, like maybe creating his own with the teacher. She was failing to help him be a parent to Theodora, or he wouldn't be in there now, fueling the fire of her fantasies. She wanted to tell him that. She knew she ought to.

Only when he came into the kitchen and closed the door behind him, he stared at her so hard he sent a chill through her. He believed someone was after Theodora. She could see that immediately.

"The reality of life is very cruel," Jesse said bluntly before she could say a word. "The reality of that child's life is that there is a man following her around, the same one who caused *this*." He stuck out his bad leg. "Broken and cracked in three places. It never healed right because I had to crawl back from where my brother left me when I realized he wasn't going to tell our parents where I was."

With a small whoosh of breath, all Evaleen's fight drained out of her. In its place was left compassion, thick as honey, and just as sweet to Jesse. He hadn't been sure she was capable of showing it, or that she even knew what it was.

But he'd been wrong. Evaleen's eyes softened with caring, her lips went fuller with it, and her shoulders rid themselves of all their stiff resolve. She felt something for him. She was perhaps the first person who ever had, apart from his mother so long ago, and it moved something deep within him.

"Surely your brother—" she started.

"Surely Patrick what? Meant to tell my parents, but forgot? Hadn't really seen me fall? Hell, Evie, he pushed me off the cliff. Or perhaps surely Patrick isn't now following Theodora around, up to something damned sinister, because he's really dead and I refuse to believe it?" He walked right up to her, forcing her back against the broom closet as he put his hands on either side of her.

"Believe me when I tell you that Reynard could well have lied to the people of this town when he said Patrick was dead, Evie. I never saw this so-called report of his death; my own father refused to show me."

"Why?" she asked breathlessly.

He shrugged. "Maybe he wanted Patrick to be dead to me, too. But I'm not trusting it. I don't want to take any chances that he might get a grip on Theodora just to get what I have now. From what the child is telling me, the description fits."

"But Jesse," she protested, "I've been through this before. She's only a child who's been very lonely. I really believe she's merely looking for attention."

"And I've been through this before, too, with Patrick. I told my parents he was planning on hurting me. My father never believed me, just like you don't believe Theodora. And now I'm crippled for life." He backed up, away from her, as though her closeness had suddenly become more than he could handle.

Evaleen stared down at his leg, wanting to deny what he'd said about being crippled, since he did get around a whole lot better than her aunt did. But knowing Jesse was the one living with the pain in his leg, she couldn't. To a man, not having the full use of his leg, not being able to move as quickly and easily as a competitor or an attacker, could be as crippling as being in a chair was to a woman.

"We're talking about the same son of a bitch here," Jesse continued. "Patrick. My brother may damn well be Theodora's evil knight. I wasn't believed, and I suffered.

When are you finally going to believe the child? After it's too late?" His voice softened. "Evie, she's just a little girl. She needs to stay that way for a while. Young and innocent."

Evaleen sucked in a breath and stared into the depths of his blue eyes, remembering her own carefree days. "I know."

Jesse paced a couple of steps toward the table and back. "I think I'll start escorting you to the school, or have Waco go with you. Promise me you won't take Theodora away from the ranch without a man with you."

His voice and his eyes were so intense that even though she still didn't believe an evil knight existed, she had to agree to his wishes. "I promise."

"Yeah. Good." They heard Theodora laugh, and Jesse's eyes flashed toward the door. "Tomorrow when I'm in town with Miss Worrell, I'll check around and see if I can find out what Patrick's up to."

"Miss Worrell," she echoed softly. "Yes. If you have time."

His gaze swept down until it rested on her bosom, and he gave her an insolent smirk. "Jealous?"

"Of course not. I'm only trying to save you from your own baser instincts."

"And who's going to save you?" he asked.

"I do believe this conversation is at an end." She started toward the living room, but Jesse caught her midway there, his fingers wrapping around her wrist in a warm caress, so gentle. No matter how irritated he was, he never, ever hurt her when he touched her.

Their eyes caught and held, and they were so close she could feel the rasping of Jesse's breath against her skin. She became very aware of the rapid beating of her heart as he leaned down and kissed her and, at the same time, pulled her to him. Both his arms went around her waist and the heat of his hands warmed her back right through the cotton of her calico dress.

He continued to kiss her, and she found herself kissing him back. His lips felt so warm against her own sensitive mouth, that when she felt the muscles of his shoulders contracting to pull away from her, she reached up and circled his neck with her arms to make him continue the kiss. Was there anything more glorious than this feeling? If so, she certainly had never felt it.

He parted her lips. When his tongue touched hers, it set off sensations that made her think of nakedness, of her round, full breasts pressed against his bare chest, of his manhood pressing intimately against her belly. Of how it would feel if they were breathless together in bed and he was staring at her bare body, her breasts pushing against his mouth ...

Caught in a tornado headed toward her personal destruction, she yanked away from him. Breathing hard, for a few seconds they just stared at each other, as though neither believed what had just happened occurred.

"Why did you kiss me back, Evaleen?" Jesse asked her, in a voice that seemed to come from deep inside him.

She sucked in a breath. "To give you something to think about when you see Miss Worrell," she said in a whisper. "Why did you kiss me to begin with?"

He grinned at her widely. "To give you something to think about while I'm seeing Miss Worrell."

She licked her dry lips, then finally smiled back. But remembering the situation they were in, her smile disappeared as swiftly as it had come. "We can't do this anymore, Jesse."

"Yeah," he said, his voice reserved. "I know."

Resolutely, she set off once more toward the door, but Jesse stopped her again. "By the way, Evaleen, one of the mares is about to foal. If it happens during the night, should I get you out of bed so you can watch? I promise to be really quiet so we don't wake Theodora."

"No!" Jesse come into her room in the middle of the night? The way she was feeling right now, Evaleen didn't even want to chance it. "No," she said again, this time more controlled. "I'll see the foal after it's born."

He gave her a long look. "You don't know what you'll be missing out on, but suit yourself." Turning, he strode from the kitchen through the back door. Out of the corner of her eyes, Evaleen caught sight of the other door, the one between the kitchen and the parlor, closing. All at once, her rapidly beating heart stopped.

Hoping Theodora had not just witnessed the whole kiss, which might send the poor thing back into total confusion, Evaleen rushed to the door and opened it. Theodora still sat on the sofa, playing happily with a rag doll Victoria had made for her. Victoria, however, sat in her chair a few feet from the door, her mouth set in a grim line as she stared at Evaleen.

Evaleen opened her mouth to explain, but then closed it. What could she say? She didn't even understand the relationship between Jesse and herself. How could she explain it to someone else?

Without a word, Victoria backed up her chair and turned it to wheel around the other chairs. In less than a minute, the other woman had retreated to her room, leaving Evaleen standing guiltily alone.

Late the next afternoon, Evaleen stood at the front door, watching Jesse ride off on Nowhere to meet with Miss Worrell. He thought he was about to participate in an evening of pleasure, but she wasn't about to let him stray away from what was right and good. She had to reform him, change him. She had to.

Turning, she walked back to where her aunt was playing a card game with her niece. "Are you sure you don't mind watching Theodora?" she asked Victoria.

"We'll be fine. Theodora will lock the doors after you leave, and you've alerted Waco that we're here alone?"

Evaleen nodded.

"Then go do what you have to do." Victoria waved her on without a good-bye.

Evaleen hung back. Her aunt had been like this since the night before, even while Evaleen had helped her into bed and out of bed this morning. Resigned. Brusque. Refusing to discuss anything at all beyond the simple matters of getting through the day. Evaleen thought Victoria was waiting for an apology for her kissing Jesse, but she wasn't about to apologize. She hadn't done anything wrong. She was nothing like Cynthia, not at all.

At the same time Evaleen grabbed her reticule and headed out the kitchen door to the buggy Waco was hitching up for her, she hoped to the heavens she wasn't just fooling herself and that she was setting out to make sure Jesse stayed on the straight and narrow for all the right reasons.

---

Jesse studied Miss Worrell as they sat in the Raton Harvey Hotel dining room in the small, red building next to the Santa Fe Railway depot. Around them were mostly cowboys and railroad workers, but there were also a few customers who were just plain citizens of Raton and the surrounding area.

From what Miss Worrell had told him, she was one of two teachers in an oversized schoolhouse. Somewhere over twenty, the lady was tall, slim, and had a wide-set mouth that made for an interesting smile. Even though her hair was drawn back into a no-nonsense low bun, dark brunette bangs fringed her forehead softly, and two curled tendrils hung down around her temples. She wore a walking suit of soft brown with a deep blue scarf around her neck, pinned in place with a cameo and tucked into her basque.

She wasn't his type, and she wasn't giving him any indication that such an invitation would be welcome, but Jesse knew he was going to ask to see her again, for one very specific reason.

Evaleen Murphy. Hang what he'd told her, his kissing her had had nothing to do with Miss Worrell, and everything to do with the reality that he wanted to get control of Evie, because he fully suspected that if he didn't, Evaleen was about to get control of him. But that didn't bother him half as much as when she'd kissed him back last night with every bit of the sweetness and yearning she'd been burying beneath her strict exterior. He was getting far too involved physically with a lady who could destroy him. He couldn't afford to do that, and he hoped like all get out that Miss Worrell would prove to be the very distraction he needed, since Cassie Jo so obviously didn't meet his needs any longer. Maybe it was time he thought about settling down with a good woman after all.

"And Theodora's been eating worms during class."

Jesse jerked his head up. Slowly, a grin spread across his face. "I guess I haven't been paying attention to you, have I?" he admitted.

"I do sense your mind is elsewhere." Miss Worrell sipped from her teacup with one finger held in the air. "You've gotten the main idea of what I've been saying, though. Theodora is much farther along than the other children her age, so I'm going to let her skip a grade if that's all right with you. I don't want her to be bored in class. And I'm going to find some challenging exercises to send home with her."

"That's fine. Will she need a lot of help with them?"

"Nothing Miss Murphy won't be able to guide her with."

"Well, you see, that's a problem." Jesse was careful to look away from the lady, as though he were hesitant to admit this to anyone. "The child is legally under my guardianship, and Miss Murphy seems to think I should be the one doing the extra work with her. But I'm certain you understand a man's duties. Running a ranch sometimes keeps him away far into the evening. I'm afraid the poor, motherless Theodora isn't going to get all the help she needs."

Miss Worrell sat back and smiled fully. "Why, I'll be happy to stop by on a regular basis to check on her, Mr. Stockton."

"And I'll be more than happy to make it worth your time," he said in a charming voice that shadowed a double meaning to his words. He picked up his coffee cup.

Miss Worrell assessed him briefly, leaned forward, and said softly, "Mr. Stockton, are the rumors I've been hearing about you true? Are you The Best in the West?"

Caught totally by surprise, Jesse almost sputtered out coffee. Regaining control, he put the cup down and carefully surveyed her.

So she wasn't quite as innocent and unassuming as she'd first appeared. He grinned slowly, suddenly more amused than shocked. He hadn't pegged Miss Worrell for the type who would try to get a little fun out of life with a man.

"My reputation is probably exaggerated," he told her. "But who am I to judge?"

She smiled.

He frowned. "And if you heard any rumors from Miss Murphy, they are definitely *untrue.*"

"I see." Her gaze swept over his chest, and she glanced around the area to make certain no one was paying any attention to them before she reached out and undid the top button of his shirt. Their eyes met. "There. Now you look more comfortable."

Jesse knew Evaleen would pitch a fit right there in the middle of the dining room if she'd seen that. However, Maggie Worrell's action hadn't moved him in the least, which made him wonder if he were being entirely fair to Miss Worrell, giving her the impression that there could be something between them, when he wasn't at all sure there could be.

Inwardly, he grimaced. If he couldn't get lustful for Cassie Jo at Nicholson's, or for a woman like Miss Worrell who was respectable and was issuing an out-and-out invitation, he was worried that he might not be able to get randy for any woman—except Evaleen.

"I think I would like visiting with Theodora at your ranch very much," Miss Worrell said.

He didn't bother telling her it wasn't his ranch. He supposed Evaleen could order the schoolteacher off the property in the blink of an eye and be perfectly within her rights to do so, but somehow, he didn't think she would. It would make her appear too jealous.

"Let's say you come after school, twice a week?" he suggested. "I think we could have a real good time together." And make Evaleen think about what she was asking for next time she came up with a ridiculous idea like his playing mama to the kid.

"I think I will really enjoy spending time with you," she said, her fingers creeping up his sleeve.

"And Theodora."

"Of course," she said. Her voice sounded innocent, but her eyes weren't. All at once Jesse realized that in this case, the cure might be worse than the poison.

Aw, well, he'd never met a woman he couldn't handle or outwit. He could disappear when Miss Worrell was due to come, leave her some money or a gift, and therefore avoid having to pay for the lessons in the manner she seemed to be suggesting.

"Monday and Thursday, at five?"

That agreed upon, Jesse sat back to enjoy the rest of his coffee. Evaleen's domain was going to be interfered with, sure, but he'd arranged to have his charge tutored, so she wouldn't be lacking in education after the change from the boarding school. He believed a judge would agree that a man couldn't be expected to take time away from his livelihood to work with a child. He'd find some other way of spending time with Theodora, like riding with her once a week.

Evaleen would just have to cope with his decision. Thinking about that, Jesse's treacherous mind took things a couple of steps farther, remembering how she'd pressed her breasts against him when she'd kissed him and picturing those breasts bared to him.

His body reacted to the thought, and he took a deep breath. Damn. Dinner was over; and he was supposed to walk Miss Worrell back to her home. He had to postpone it.

"I want dessert," he blurted out.

"Fine." She smiled. "I'm ready to go too."

# Chapter Nine

After making his excuses, Jesse left Miss Worrell at her small quarters next to the schoolhouse and walked toward where he'd left his mount tethered in front of Nicholson's Saloon. A detour inside before he went back to Rainbow's End was a certainty because he wanted to ask around about Patrick—or this person following Theodora who looked so much like his brother. But what else he was going to do while he was there, he wasn't sure yet.

He could try Cassie Jo again, but the idea really held no appeal. Evaleen had gotten under his skin, and it looked very much as if he was going to end up celibate until the six months were over and she was no longer around to distract him.

Not happy about that at all, Jesse felt rebellious. Why the hell did he like the little dictator anyway, apart from that sweet little figure of hers? Just as soon as he asked himself that, he knew. No matter how irritating she was, Evaleen didn't have a selfish bone in her body. Everything she did was for Victoria or Theodora, two people who didn't have anybody else to care about them. She didn't have to help them, but she did, throwing all her energy into making the three of them into a family. And from what he'd seen, nobody was reciprocating. Nobody was doing squat for Evaleen.

He pushed the frustrating woman out of his mind and tried to think of one reason he shouldn't go ahead and have a drink while he was at Nicholson's. Even his father had indulged from time to time. In a way, he *had* to go there. How else could he convince the people of the town he was one of them unless he did what they did—drink and play cards? And he wanted to be one of them, to fit in. He was getting kind of tired of going through life alone.

Walking into the dark saloon with the low ceiling and the long, gleaming wood bar that Nicholson had ordered from back East, specially made, Jesse absorbed the atmosphere like he was coming home. Somebody was playing the piano. The smoke was thick, and Jesse breathed in deeply, relishing the sounds and the familiarity of the strictly male smells—liquor, leather, and cigars. He was comfortable here, always had been, and he began to relax.

After speaking with Nicholson about whether he'd seen Patrick and getting the same hogwash about his brother's being dead, then asking around about arranging a card game late on Saturday, Jesse walked over to Vince Grover, the owner of the general store, and asked him about a stranger resembling him, not wanting to alert him to the fact that his brother might be around. No help there either. Grover had just returned from out of town, but his wife had mentioned no one out of the ordinary.

Returning to where he'd left his glass, Jesse picked up his drink and leaned back against the bar. As he downed a whiskey straight, he stared around the saloon, nodding at Cassie Jo, who was busy with another customer, Nate, and a few other men he knew by sight who were also enjoying some leisure time before they headed home. Something in the back of his mind told him he ought to get back to Rainbow's End. He even took his watch out of his vest pocket and checked the time, thinking about dinner. But then he told himself the women were safe enough with Waco watching out for them. He was just letting Evaleen become his conscience, and that was ridiculous.

Turning, he bent forward, propped the foot of his bad leg on the footrest, and leaned his forearms on the cushion that ran the length of the bar, stretching his muscles. Nicholson came and served him another whiskey, and flipped his change on the counter.

"Card game's set for this Saturday night, ten o'clock," the bar owner said. "What do you think? Can you make it?"

"Sounds good," Jesse said, nodding. "All I have to do is get past—"

Nicholson's eyebrows shot up almost to his hairline as he spotted something behind Jesse. Thinking Patrick had returned to make his final move, Jesse whirled around and drew his gun in one swift low move, grimacing as his knee strained and protested. When he saw it was Evaleen who was entering the saloon, he cursed loudly to make sure she heard and put his gun back in his holster.

"I'll thank you not to swear at me," Evaleen called, barely glancing up as she threaded her way through the tables toward him, journal in hand, writing away.

"Apparently you've got your nose buried so far in that book you don't know you're in a saloon," Jesse told her. "Swearing is allowed here."

"I know perfectly well where I am—and, more importantly, where *you* are," she said, arriving at his side. Around them, the evening drinkers made mocking noises and hooted. A couple deep in the crowd even swore. Evaleen did not comment. She was too busy writing.

"You're going to run out of pages soon," Jesse said irritably. Hell, he'd just begun relaxing, and *she* had to go and show up. All his muscles were tightening up again. What was it about this woman?

"If I do," Evaleen said, "I'll buy another journal."

Behind her, someone muttered, "What the hell is a woman doing in here, Nicholson? Get her out."

A chorus of "Yeah" followed the order. Evaleen stopped writing and glanced behind her. "Seems you have a rowdy group tonight, Mr. Nicholson."

Nicholson frowned so hard his dark eyebrows almost blended. "Miss Murphy," he said, "I'm sorry, but women aren't allowed in this here establishment. I'm sure you're aware of that because there's a sign posted big as day right next to the door, and it seems just about reasonable that if you can write, you can read."

"I'm here to get Mr. Stockton to come back home where he belongs. He is supposed to be spending his evenings paying attention to a child"—she cocked one eyebrow—"not to a whiskey bottle."

"Mr. Stockton should take the little lady home and pay some attention to *her*," somebody called out. "Then maybe she'd stay the hell outta here."

Jesse turned back to his glass. He wouldn't have minded going home, had it been his own decision. But damn it all, this was just too much like Reynard trying to tell him exactly what to do all the time. Despite his liking for Evaleen, the old, inner hurt at not being respected when he made his own decisions chafed at him. The last thing he was going to do was leave now, just because she wanted him to. He was going to teach her to respect him.

"I'm not going anywhere," he told her.

"Fine." She resumed writing in her notes. For a few

seconds Jesse watched her write, his eyes on the lace edging her long white sleeves. Even with her domineering ways, Evaleen had a femininity about her he couldn't help but notice.

"Miss Murphy, you have to leave," Nicholson said, and then shot a beseeching look at Jesse.

He spread his palms out helplessly. "Don't look at me. I can't seem to control her."

"Oh, stop your fussing, you two," Evaleen said sweetly, her hand pausing as she looked from Jesse to Nicholson. "I'll go in a minute. I just have a few more notes to make about this place for the Ladies' Temperance Union I'll be organizing within the next few days. You have heard of them, haven't you?"

"Jess, for God's sake, you'd better get her out of here before the men figure out exactly what she means. Those women go into bars with *hatchets.*" Nicholson laid his hand lovingly on his shining bar top, looking worried.

"Yeah, get her out of here. She's putting a cramp in my enjoyment of the evening," Grover called out from a table nearby.

"Do you mean in your enjoyment of the *lady* of the evening I saw you with when I was looking in through the window?" Evaleen retorted, jotting another note down. "I haven't met Mrs. Grover, but I wonder if she'll be interested in joining my branch of the union—"

"Dammit, Nicholson!" Grover swore. "Do something about her before I carry her outta here myself."

"Jess," Nicholson pleaded, "she's your woman."

"She's not my woman!" Jesse said.

"I am *not* Mr. Stockton's woman!" Evaleen said at the same time, in a voice filled with a denial that carried clean out of the swinging doors to the saloon, Jesse was sure. "I am merely supposed to be remolding Mr. Stockton's character."

"All right, all right," Jesse said, fully aware that no one in the saloon was still laughing. They were all seeing Evaleen as a threat to their peaceful existence, and they didn't have any reason to put up with that. If he didn't get her out of there, he could only surmise general chaos would erupt, and then he'd have to save her. Besides, no one knew the true details of what was going on between him and Evaleen yet, and he wanted to be the one to tell them, just to make certain the truth got slanted in his direction.

Downing the rest of his whiskey, he turned slowly. "We're leaving," he told her, taking her arm and spiriting her out of the saloon. As they went through the swinging doors, he heard Nicholson call out that he needed to speak to him before he left town.

"If you return, don't you stay there," Evaleen warned. "I'll go right back in after you."

"If you do, I'll carry you out over my shoulder," he promised. For a few seconds, their eyes locked in battle, but then Jesse left her at the buggy to find out what Nicholson wanted. The owner of the bar pulled him far enough away from the door so that Evaleen couldn't hear them, and they were joined by Nate.

"That little lady's sure got you hogtied, Jess," Nate said, pitching his cigar on the floor and stomping it out with his boot. "You might as well be married."

"Don't even think that," Jesse muttered sourly. Too late, he recalled his idea of matching Nate up with Evaleen to get her out of his hair. When had he abandoned that? The first time he'd pulled her into his arms and kissed her?

"We were worried," Nicholson told him. "Does her showing up to get you home mean you can't make it for Saturday night's poker game?"

"Oh, I'll be here all right," Jesse promised, "but maybe

it's better we hold it someplace where she'd never dream of looking. Let me know what you figure out."

The other men were shaking their heads doubtfully as he walked out to return to Evaleen, but Jesse was certain he was going to win this war. Come hell or high water, he was not giving up his entire life to the dictates of a woman, no matter how taken he was with her. There had to be a way around this will of Reynard's—there had to be—and Jesse was determined to find it.


Although she knew she had done the right thing by following Jesse to Raton and pulling him out of the saloon, Evaleen almost regretted her decision when she saw the grim set of Jesse's mouth as he walked out of Nicholson's saloon. His friends had laughed at him, because of her. She hadn't wanted that. She knew how much it meant to people to have their friends' respect.

Jesse climbed on his horse without helping her onto the buggy, and with an oomph, she pulled herself up onto the seat. So what if he hated her now? She'd done what she was supposed to do according to the will. Jesse wouldn't be spending the night or evening with one of those women inside whom she'd seen staring moonfaced at him even as they sat on other men's laps. And if Jesse looked over his shoulder every time he stopped in a saloon now, or any time he looked at one of those women, so much the better.

His silent disdain was the price she would have to pay. All she wanted out of this six months, Evaleen swore silently, was custody of Theodora. She didn't need Jesse in her life, or the feelings he evoked inside her whenever he turned that hypnotic stare of his her way. Even though every passing day it was getting harder and harder to be near him and not give in to the desire she was feeling, she had to remember what had happened when her sister had let lust rule her life.

Suicide.

After that night, just as Victoria was doing, Jesse quit speaking to her at all unless he had to. He spoke only once when he didn't have to, and that was to ask her if she wanted to learn how to milk the cows. Since she hadn't wanted to spend any more time than she had to with the now dour man, she'd refused.

Since Evaleen was predominantly isolated on the ranch, that meant for the next two days she spoke to no one at all except Theodora. That was hard. She was used to the joking and laughter she'd shared through the years of working with the other Harvey girls, and she thought sometimes she would go crazy with all that quiet.

Worst of all, she missed her banter with Jesse, and the way he'd looked at her when he thought she wasn't paying attention, his eyes all warm and crinkly at the sides.

But then on Thursday, late in the afternoon, a visitor knocked on the door. Miss Worrell. For one precious second, Evaleen supposed that Theodora's schoolmarm was making a social call. Delighted at the idea of company, she asked her in, and then the teacher told her the reason she'd come: Jesse had asked her to help Theodora with her studies twice a week. Evaleen had no recourse but to call Theodora down and set the two up at the parlor table, where they had worked for about an hour. Afterward, once the teacher had learned that Jesse wasn't home yet and wasn't expected till later, she'd left.

As Evaleen paced the floor in what everyone now termed Jesse's study, waiting for him to return, her insides clenched. Jesse had turned what should have been a simple visit with his ward's teacher into an advantage for himself. Was he under the mistaken impression that he could hire someone to take care of his responsibilities with Theodora? Or was it merely his way of trying to make her stop dictating his life to him, to show her that if she interfered, the consequences could be other than what she expected?

Or was he merely trying to make her jealous?

Jesse pushed open the door to the study, saw her, and paused in the doorway. He stared at her for a moment and then shook his head, looking anything but pleased to see her there.

"I came in here to smoke a cigar and get some peace and quiet," he told her, shutting the door behind him. "I can't drink. I can't go to town to the saloon. If you're going to insist on me following Reynard's ridiculous decrees to the letter, you're going to have to allow me privacy in my own study, or I will go positively crazy."

"I'll leave in a minute," she said, crossing her arms over her breasts. She didn't know how he managed it, but whenever he looked at her, his eyes seemed to be taking in the sight of her whole body, and it made her feel all trembly inside. "First we must have a discussion."

"What have I done to put a bee in your bonnet now, Miss Murphy?" He smiled sourly. "Although a bee would be a big improvement over the bird, I think."

"Don't worry. That hat is in storage until I leave here," she said stiffly. The hat was a big sore point. "I don't choose to suffer your obnoxious jokes any more than I have to while I'm here."

Crossing the room, Jesse parted the curtains and pulled open the window, keeping his back to her as he stared out into the moonlit yard. "If my inability to be humorous is what you've come to discuss, I must say there hasn't been a whole lot I find funny around here lately."

Because of her. His tone stung, and added to Evaleen's

feeling of being a pariah in what was supposed to be her home. If only she didn't have such a reputation to uphold, if only her name and her word didn't mean everything to her, if only ... She would show him that she wasn't the female curmudgeon he thought she was.

She blinked away tears stemming from her loneliness, and the futility of her desire for Jesse. His back was to her. She stared at his broad shoulders and at his brown hair, so shaggy against his collar it begged her to run her fingers through it. Her lips parted as her breathing quickened, and all the anger she'd had inside her when he'd entered the room flowed out of her. "Jess?"

The way she said his name, tenderly and sweetly, made Jesse turn. When he did, he saw that her eyes were luminous, and that her face held a lost look. He wanted to go to her, pull her into his arms, make her forget all about this stupid will and the conditions. But knowing that she was a good woman, he held back.

"Sometimes I hate being the responsible one," she said softly. "Sometimes I want to forget about the past and live for the moment—just as you do. But I don't know how. I never learned."

Calling himself every kind of a fool for falling for this, Jesse strode to her, and without a single word that might cause her to argue, he pulled her into his arms, lowered his mouth to hers, and kissed her full, moist lips.

She made a small noise deep in her throat, and then Jesse felt her press against him as hard as she could, almost as if she were trying to lose herself in his body. He could feel her breasts, two soft mounds of flesh, against his chest. More than his body reacted then—his mind became lost in the kiss.

When Jesse's tongue entered her mouth, Evaleen stroked it tentatively at first with her own, and then harder. In seconds their tongues were pressing together as their bodies were. She rubbed against him, wishing for more than he was giving her, unable to think beyond the exquisite sensation that was melting her lower regions and making her dizzy with longing.

When he felt her sway, Jesse slipped his arm around her and backed her to the sofa, lowering her down on one end against cushions that had shown up one day after she'd moved in. Maybe, Jesse thought almost wistfully, this would put an end to the tension between them, he didn't know. What he was certain of was that he wanted her badly, and she wasn't pushing him away. Everything about her said she wanted him. He would just go slowly, just in case he was wrong.

Slipping open the buttons on the front of her blouse, his breath caught at the sight of her quavering breasts pushed above her corset and bound by her tight chemise, making the most tantalizing cleavage he'd ever seen. Unable to resist, he pressed his face into their bountiful softness and began to lick her skin.

A long, breathy moan escaped her lips. Her arms slipped around him and she pulled at him until he lowered himself fully on top of her. She clenched his hair as he continued to kiss and lick her bosom. Almost desperate to get a real taste of her now, he lifted her breast until her nipple was free of the corset and licked it through her chemise until it peaked. Then he sucked that right through the lace. She moaned again, this time louder, and he moved his mouth up to cover hers.

The image of her on top of him, naked so he could watch those beautiful large breasts of hers bobbing and moving while she rode him, his manhood sheathed with her heat, drove him on. He lifted her and started untying her corset, loosening it at the same time his mouth moved over hers. Then her breasts swung free under the chemise, unbound and straining against the material.

"You're so beautiful," he muttered, lowering his face between her breasts.

Barely registering his words, dazed with the strength of desire such as she'd never felt before, Evaleen pushed her breasts against his cheeks, reveling in every tingle that cascaded through her as her skin brushed his shadowy beard. This was what *it* felt like. Soon he would take off the rest of her clothing, and then his own, and she wouldn't have to think about anything, just feel. . . . Jesse thought she was beautiful.

But she wasn't. Some inner sense reminded her of that. She was only a round-faced spinster with work-roughened hands who had something Jesse Stockton wanted, just as he had something she wanted. He was just uttering words because that was what lovemaking was. Pretty words and empty promises. Cynthia had told her that often enough.

Even though she blinked hard, her eyes filled with tears. With a mighty breath, she shoved against him. He didn't move at first, but then she said his name, a little sharply, and he lifted his head, looking bewildered.

"I'm not beautiful, Jesse."

Jesse frowned, not understanding what had changed. He would swear she was feeling what he was—this need to be together, caught up in ecstasy.

"Evie, are you sure?"

"Of course I'm sure I'm not beautiful," she repeated in a low voice, pushing against him. "And I'm not my sister. I'm sorry, I shouldn't have let things get this far. They won't in the future, I assure you."

Jesse pushed himself off her and up, not bothering to hide the bulge in his pants from her. Modesty be damned. Nor did he bother turning away as she rose and used her fingers to stuff her breasts back down inside the confines of her clothing. In the state he was in, the sight of her doing that was almost as erotic as making love.

"You're lucky you were with me," he said, shoving his hand back through his hair and wishing the room had more air in it. "Another man might not have been so willing to stop."

"I know that." She glanced at him for a second and then resumed tying and rearranging her disheveled attire. "Thank you, Jesse. I couldn't have gone through with that anyway. It wouldn't have been right."

She could have gone through with it, he knew from experience, but he had to agree with her last sentence. No, their lovemaking wouldn't have been right. Every resolution he'd had not to ruin a respectable woman had totally slipped his mind when Evaleen had said his name. "I'm glad you stopped us," he said.

She stared at him in surprise. With her hair all tumbled from its bun, her lips full from his kisses, and her cheeks red from the brush of his whiskers, she never looked more beautiful. His body and his instincts told him to kiss her again, strip off her clothes and his, and just take her right there. No more waiting.

Cursing under his breath, Jesse sat down, closed his eyes, and leaned back against the pillows.

"Do me a favor, Evaleen," he said, his voice almost a growl. "Get out of here before I forget what a gentleman I really am and give you what you've been begging for."

She fled. Once he heard the door shut and he was alone, he opened his eyes and cursed himself for wanting what he was never going to have.

Evaleen.

Throwing herself on her bed, Evaleen burst into tears. She couldn't be like Cynthia. She couldn't give in to Jesse's allure against her own moral judgment. If she let temptation drag her under, he would think her easy and leave her the first time another woman beckoned with an outstretched pinky, and she would be left alone to suffer the consequences.

Clutching her pillow to her bosom, she tried to forget the ecstasy she'd felt when Jesse's mouth had been against her flesh. Even now in her lower regions, she was wet and oozing like honey because of his kisses. She wanted him. She wanted him inside her, and she wanted to push and thrust against him until this burning heat inside her cooled.

This couldn't be normal, this yearning for that kind of connection with a man. She and Cynthia must have a curse upon them. But she wasn't exactly like Cynthia, she told herself. The only man she wanted was Jesse. Just Jesse—a bounder, a ladies' man—someone who would never make her happy. No more. No less.

The next morning at breakfast, Evaleen avoided Jesse's eyes as the kitchen cleared, leaving only the two of them. She'd served everyone breakfast silently, but now that Victoria was in her room and Theodora was outside playing until she'd be taken to school, Evaleen was ready to speak her piece. She didn't really want to say anything to him, she thought tiredly, but it was her duty. She had to.

"Do you truly think hiring Miss Worrell to tutor Theodora is going to relieve you of your responsibility to help the child yourself?"

He gave her a tight smile. "Are you worried about how I'm going to pay her?"

Knowing exactly what he was referring to, she splashed coffee into his cup, not caring that a few drops flew over the sides and he had to snatch his fingers out of the way to keep from being burned.

He gave her a lazy look. "I take it you don't want to discuss what happened last night?"

"Nothing happened last night." Evaleen's chest expanded and rose as she held her breath and her tongue. "Why do you insist on riling me like this?"

"To watch you take deep breaths?" Jesse asked. "Do you know your figure would make any man yearn for home and a rug in front of a fireplace with you?"

The air rushed out of Evaleen's lungs as she flashed on the image he presented. "Please don't say things like that to me," she said softly. "I made a mistake yesterday in the study, and I'm sorry. There's no need to punish me for it."

"Maybe," Jesse said slowly, "we should try to clear the air between us."

"How do you mean?" she asked, putting the coffeepot back on the cast-iron stove.

"Admit how attracted we are to each other, act like reasonable adults, and come to an understanding."

"The only thing I want to understand right now," she said firmly, "is how Miss Worrell took over the responsibility of aiding Theodora with her studies." She couldn't face talking to Jesse about a relationship they could never have, no matter how much she wanted to.

Jesse decided Evaleen wanted to pretend everything was back to normal, even though it could never be. For now, he guessed he could let her have her way. "Miss Worrell. All right." After wiping up the spilled coffee around his cup, he took a sip. "I thought since you were worried about Theodora's studies, I would just ask her teacher to fill in where I can't."

"But I told you, monitoring a child's schoolwork is something a parent does!"

"Correction, Evie, it's something a *mother* does. A father might stand by and nod in approval every once in a while, but he's got more important things to worry about—like making sure the family gets enough to eat. Besides, it's only for a couple more weeks until school ends. Then you won't have to think about Miss Worrell until next September."

That wasn't the point. Evaleen sighed again. "I'm beginning to believe I'll never make you see what Reynard was getting at in the will."

"Maybe I understand better than you know." Standing, he faced her, and she stopped gathering the breakfast dishes to look at him. "I've already eked out time to spend with Theodora tomorrow. We're going riding together so I can show her the ranch."

"That's wonderful," she breathed, totally surprised.

Jesse purposely gave her a slow once-over from her black polished shoes to her breasts, where his eyes lingered, letting her know he remembered what she looked like underneath the starched white linen blouse she was wearing. He grinned enticingly and asked, "Want to come with us?"

Did she? Her heart was torn between spending time with this man who was slowly driving her crazy as he tugged on the strings of her desire and letting Theodora have the time alone with him that the child deserved. With both of them gone and only her aunt's disapproving presence to keep her company, tomorrow was looking dismal and boring. But she had to think of the child first. Besides, she had never learned to ride like Theodora had in her fancy boarding school.

"No," she said reluctantly. "Theodora needs time alone with you."

"Suit yourself. How are you with numbers?"

Her eyebrows rose.

"I have some work to do on the ledgers right now. You

can pull up a chair next to me in the study and help if you want."

Her breath caught. She had wanted to get to the ledgers eventually, just to see where the ranch stood financially. But she didn't think she could bear sitting next to Jesse right now, not in the study, where they'd been so intimate that her heart pounded at the memory. She had to keep farther away from him than that or she would never last.

"No, thank you." Without a word of explanation, she fled the room, shutting the door behind her.

Jesse stared at the door. He'd gotten her so flustered that she'd forgotten how angry she'd been about Miss Worrell. Since last night, she'd seemed so determined to avoid him, he'd known she wouldn't want to help him reconcile the ranch's ledgers. It was working. He was finally going to start getting his way, and she wouldn't even be able to write him up for it.

But almost as good as that, or maybe even better, was the thought that she was starting to feel something for him, and that could well influence her decision to speak against him at the end of the six months. He was going to get his ranch, she was going to get Theodora, and then they would never have to see each other again.

Why the hell did that thought suddenly bother him so much?

Walking to his father's desk in the study, he sat in the oversized leather chair and pulled the ledger he needed out of the top drawer, but he quickly found he couldn't concentrate. Rising, he went to sit on the brown velvet sofa where he'd been with Evaleen, thinking about the craving he'd developed for her.

He wanted her like he'd never wanted any other woman. Yes, her body was luscious, but it was more than that. Evaleen had made his house into a home again. For the first time in a long time, he felt as though there was a warmth within the walls, and Evaleen had been responsible for that. It meant a lot to him, much more than she would ever realize.

But craving or not, having Evaleen in his life permanently would be a disaster. She was not a person who would let him be in charge. She was like his father had been, having to have things her own way, unable to compromise, and he couldn't go back to having someone else rule his life, no matter how tempting a morsel she was in bed. He just couldn't.

And he wouldn't have to, he thought, staring at his father's desk, slowly smiling. Luckily, he'd stumbled across an ace in the hole. Shortly, he was going to play that ace and get his life back, and there wouldn't be a damned thing Evaleen could do about it.

# Chapter Ten

After giving him a list of carpentry work that needed to be done on the house, Evaleen avoided Jesse all that Friday morning, because every time she came across him, he gave her a pleased grin as wide as her skirts. Early that afternoon, Jesse finally left the house, and she breathed a sigh of relief. But not fifteen minutes later, Calloway Nesmith showed up to ask Evaleen how Jesse was making out.

Feeling on the spot, she told him only that Jesse was making an effort to be pleasant, which was true, and that she was pleased with the way he was handling Theodora, which wasn't. But the fear that Jesse might tell the lawyer about what had happened between them tied her tongue beyond that.

To Evaleen's surprise, the lawyer and her aunt Victoria went into Jesse's study and spent most of the afternoon talking. When Nesmith came out, he gave her the strangest look, which produced a new set of worries for Evaleen to contemplate. Her aunt could have told him about Jesse kissing her in the kitchen, but Victoria couldn't possibly know about what she'd done in the study, could she?

Nervous, Evaleen considered going to Jesse with the possibility that they might have a problem to handle. But she couldn't. She was too embarrassed to bring it all up again. Besides, if the lawyer was upset enough, he would have confronted her about the incident—or incidents—right then, wouldn't he?

She thought yes, he would have, but she also knew there was no way she could be certain. All she could do was wait and hope that her foolish desire for Jesse hadn't ruined her chances to get custody of Theodora.


The secret somewhere Nicholson picked for the big poker game turned out to be Thurgood's Mortuary, and as Jesse dealt cards in the back room onto the top of a casket, he thought about how good it felt to be back to one of his normal activities—even if the place was spooky. Lord, he'd almost forgotten how much he loved Saturday nights.

Shuffling the cards, Jesse looked at the faces of Seth Thurgood, Lucky Morgan, Nicholson, Nate, and Jonathan Freeman, a brawny black man who had won the town over when he'd saved the mayor's daughter from drowning. This Saturday night was really special because tonight he was going to have himself a whopper of a good time and then he was going to go back home and break it to Evaleen that her reign was over. He was going to play his full hand of cards tonight in all respects, and let the chips fall where they may.

"I can't believe Stockton has arrived at the state where he's gotta hide out in a mortuary to play poker," Lucky Morgan said, holding up one finger. Jesse, as dealer, slid him a card across the coffin. It landed on a ruby which looked real. No one knew. Thurgood wouldn't say.

"Let's just hope we don't disturb the residents," Jesse said, knocking on the coffin. Everyone jumped, and then laughed.

"Careful," Nate said, "you might wake somebody up."

"Naw, there's no one in there," Thurgood told him. "My wife told me if we insisted on meeting here, we had to play on top of an empty coffin, not in her parlor."

Jesse grinned.

"After seeing what Miss Murphy's capable of in the saloon, I'm surprised you got away from her tonight," Nicholson said. "When is she going to get you into church?"

"Never." Jesse puffed on his cigar. "But she has been trying."

The men shared long looks, each knowing that hell would have to freeze over before anyone ever succeeded in getting Jesse Stockton into church for a Sunday morning service. Still in the air was the unspoken question about what exactly the Murphy women were doing on the ranch anyway. Jesse knew there had been rumors, but what exactly everyone knew, he wasn't certain.

"How have ya been escaping going on Sundays in the first place, I'd love to know?" Seth Thurgood asked. "If I ever told my wife I wasn't going to church, she'd burn me in hell's fires by nightfall."

"For one, I'm not married to this woman—"

*"Yet!"* Nate interrupted, bringing a round of howling laughter from everyone except Jesse, who scowled at them and picked up his shot glass to down a quick tranquilizer of whiskey at the mere thought of losing all his freedom forever to a woman he couldn't control.

"As I was saying," he continued, "I'm not married to Miss Murphy, so she can't come inside my room. And for two, since I make it a point to warn her on Saturday night that Sunday is my one morning to sleep in late, I just keep snoring all morning. She can't wake me up with all her knocking, and the cowhands refuse to help her, so she gives up after about ten minutes. She's there to watch my little ward anyway, not me—no matter what she thinks.

"But what the hell," he added, suddenly feeling a little disloyal in talking about Evaleen this way. He discarded two cards himself and picked up two more from the deck. "Let's not talk about her anymore, huh, boys? I'm trying to relax here."

"So how is the kid behaving?" Nate asked, chewing on a straw again. As with his ready supply of petty cash, no one ever asked him where he got the straw. Jesse could only hope it was fresh, for Nate's sake.

"Real good, Nate." He glanced around the table. No one else wanted more cards, so he put the deck down. "Theodora isn't that bad. She talks a lot, and follows me around when I'm not taking care of the ranch, but mostly I have to contend with Miss Murphy and her aunt," he said.

Too late he recalled that he didn't want to talk about her. Hell, how could he not talk about the woman? She was almost in his every waking thought and would probably continue to be so. "Five more months and two more weeks." He shook his head sadly, finally feeling the effects of the whiskey. "Miss Murphy follows me everywhere, too, boys. I need some sympathy here."

"Hell, Jess, how could you need sympathy? Like you said, you aren't even married to her yet," Nicholson said. "Tie the knot forever; then we'll give you sympathy."

Jonathan Freeman, the black man, grinned at them and bet a nickel. "Hard havin' yo every move watched, ain't it fellas?"

"Damnably," Jesse agreed. "But having to sneak away isn't the worst."

"Especially since ya ain't been that *sneaky*," Thurgood said, laughing. "We know all about your dinner with the schoolmarm."

Jesse scowled. "What's there to know?"

"The after-dinner part," Nicholson said. "From what we've heard, between Maggie Worrell and Cassie Jo, you've been painting the town red!"

Everyone was laughing as if they'd heard the stories, too, so Jesse let them go, although he had no idea where the one with Miss Worrell would have started. "Yeah, well, a man has to get his comfort where he can find it, you know?" he said, taking another sip of his drink while they all nodded in agreement. "You don't know what I'm going through back at the ranch."

"How's that?" Freeman asked.

"Miss Murphy makes *lists*. I come back from riding fences all day, and there's a list of things I have to do. A list of things to fix at the house. A list of things I should be doing with Theodora. Lists of the church's activities for the month so I make damn sure I take Theodora to one of the Sunday socials for the town ladies to see that Theodora has a proper father figure. Lists of things I didn't get to the day before."

The four men around the table shared looks of horror as though they'd never heard of such a thing as a woman giving a man lists of things to do.

"You'd better get some control, Jess," Thurgood advised.

Jesse threw up his hands. "When I argued, she told me there's so much she can't expect me to keep track of it all and she's trying to help me out."

"It sounds like misery," Nicholson said in complete commiseration. "A man should be master in his own home, even if you do have to take care of outsiders."

"The hell of it really is, it's not my home." To the startled men, he explained, "Rainbow's End is *her* ranch until I earn it by being a good father to the kid." Instead of gulping his whiskey, Jesse only sipped on his refilled glass, determined to slow down so he'd be sober enough to enjoy Evaleen's face when he showed up to lay down the law.

"Her ranch? Is that what Reynard did in his will?" Thurgood asked.

Since Jesse had lived with Reynard's stipulations in his mind for so long now, he'd forgotten that hardly anyone else knew about them. And he decided that he was just drunk enough to tell them what exactly was going on. Besides, they needed to know if they were going to help him by keeping his Saturday night fun secret from their wives. Because with the way women stuck together, as evidenced by Evaleen and her aunt Victoria, he was going to need all the help he could find to get back the ranch and at the same time maintain his freedom. He didn't need a bunch of women helping Evaleen figure out some way out of the trouble he was going to present to her—*tonight.*

"Evaleen! Oh, my Evaleen!"

Lulled from a deep sleep, Evaleen opened her eyes. The masculine voice singing her name seemed close, as did the equally deep masculine laughter that followed it. She heard shushing, as though the men were trying to be quiet but not truly caring if they were or not, and she stared around her at the shadows in her bedroom, trying to wake up so she could get her bearings.

The gentle glow of moonlight was flowing through the parted lace curtains at the window, so it was still night.

With the silence she heard now, she gazed around and wondered if she'd been imagining things.

"Evaleen . . ." the masculine voice came again, only to be once more shushed with great gusto.

The window. Hoisting herself out of bed, Evaleen pulled on the plain brown Mother Hubbard over her white linen nightgown and hurried to the window to look out into the front yard.

From what she could make out, one man was holding the reins of Jesse's mount, and Jesse was leaning into the other man, who was holding him up. Behind them were three horses, so apparently the men had all arrived together. Frightened, at first Evaleen thought Jesse had been hurt or shot, but then from the way he warbled her name again, she knew.

Yanking her window open all the way, she leaned out. "Jesse Stockton, you're drunk!"

He appeared to raise his face to stare up at her. "No sirree."

One of the two men elbowed him.

"Er, that's no sirree, *ma'am.*"

The three of them laughed. Evaleen's body went rigid. Jesse was making fun of her. How stupid she'd been for pining over him! Why would she want *him*?

"Jesse," she yelled, her temper getting the best of her, "you are nothing but a low-down, cavorting, drunken scoundrel!"

"She sounds like a wife, Jess," one of the other two men said, and they all began laughing again. Her cheeks flaming, Evaleen pulled back from the window until she could barely see him.

"Shhh! Let me handle her," Jesse said. Evaleen stifled the urge to yell at him again. Then he called up to her, "Naw, Evie, I'm not drunk. What happened was a bunch of wild train robbers ambushed me on my way back from picking up the mail in Raton last night. They hit me over the head." He rubbed the top of his head for emphasis. "If it hadn't been for Thurgood and Nicholson here, I'd still be out cold alongside the Santa Fe tracks."

Evaleen slammed the window shut.

"Oh, boy, yer in trouble now," Thurgood told him, slurring his words. "I told ya she wouldn't believe that yarn."

"She's from Kansas, Seth. How would she know there isn't a brutal gang of train robbers around here?"

"Tarnation, Jess. All she's got to do is get close enough to smell the whiskey on you and she'll know exactly what hit you in the head—a bottle of good whiskey." The three of them shared another belly laugh until the second Evaleen opened the front door.

"Oh, boy!" Nicholson warned with a whistle. "Trouble, she's acomin'!"

Evaleen was holding a lantern, and as she stepped out on the porch with the light, Jesse swayed on his feet and raised an arm to shield his eyes. Evaleen's face was drawn in anger, but her cheeks were flushed and her eyes were afire, speckled by gold flames from the lantern. She'd never looked prettier. Jesse wished he could get her alone, tell her how beautiful he thought she looked, and coax that smile back to her lips, but that would be impossible now. Suddenly, he wished he'd never started this plan of his to exert his own power, because he had a feeling he had only ended up hurting himself.

She was going to hate him now, and that hadn't been what he'd intended. Not at all. All he'd wanted was to reassert his command over the household and his life, the command he'd lost the second Evaleen Murphy had almost run him over on the road.

But now, even with the ace in the hole he had to hold over her pretty head, he wasn't sure he was going to get his life back, because every time he looked at Evaleen he wanted her. Desperately. Beyond reason. Because if he were reasoning, he wouldn't want her.

He wouldn't because all the little woman in front of him wanted was to take his ranch. She'd already admitted that. He could have any woman he wanted, yet he wanted none except for her. She was driving him loco. No, he thought, feeling liquor-wise. She had driven him *to drink*.

Her jaw trembling with irritation, Evaleen looked directly at him. "Do you know what time it is?"

Jesse grinned and patted his pocket. "Of course I do. I've got a watch. Don't you know what time it is?"

Trying to ignore the guffaws of laughter, Evaleen turned toward the other two men. "I suppose you both support Mr. Stockton's story?"

"Yeah. We found him out cold, all right," Thurgood said, shooting a smirk at Nicholson.

"And he *was* ambushed," Nicholson said.

"I'll just bet he was," Evaleen said, her voice strong. "Somewhere in the vicinity of your saloon, by whiskey."

Nicholson suddenly looked uncomfortable. "Uh, I think I have a prior engagement," he said, hurrying to mount his horse without answering her.

Thurgood tipped his hat and likewise jumped ship, leaving Jesse to face Evaleen's anger as he rode away.

"Didn't you ever stop to think what might happen if Theodora woke up and saw you?" she asked. "How the child would feel?"

"Uh, no." He hadn't. Now he kind of wished he had.

"Do you wish to run another tall tale by me before I record this incident in my journal?" she asked, one hand on her hip. "Or will my guess at what really happened suffice?"

Jesse couldn't help but remember what she had guessed about him at the train depot a couple of weeks ago, and the corners of his lips lifted in a smirk, which only made her harrumph with anger. He grinned wider.

"So what's your guess?" he asked.

"It's four in the morning, Jesse. *Sunday* morning. I would lay a bet that you sneaked out of here when we were all asleep, at around ten, if not earlier, and then went to a poker game, it having been Saturday night." She sniffed and then hurriedly fanned away the smell of liquor and a soft wisp of a flowery perfume. "Then you probably had some fun at the saloon, judging by the smell of you."

She fastened her glare on him. "Well, I've had enough. I hope all this is worth losing the ranch. I'm going to Calloway Nesmith tomorrow and telling him that you are absolutely flaunting what Reynard wanted, that you aren't even trying—"

"No, ma'am." Jesse shook his head. "No, you are not going to Calloway tomorrow, and I'm not going to lose the ranch. You aren't even going to write this incident down in your book, or anything else that I might do in the future that annoys you for that matter."

Jesse's face was triumphant, and suddenly afraid of just how much emotion was boiling up inside her, all because of this one man, Evaleen stepped back, feeling uncertain. "You *aren't* going to tell Calloway about what happened in the study?"

The smirk left his face. "I wouldn't do something like that, Evaleen."

"Then what on earth are you talking about? Why shouldn't I write down that you played cards, got drunk, and went to see a . . . a . . ." She couldn't say the word. She didn't want to envision Jesse with some woman who didn't care about him. Not that she did. Much.

"You shouldn't write down any more about me because I've started a journal of my own." He flashed her a cockeyed grin.

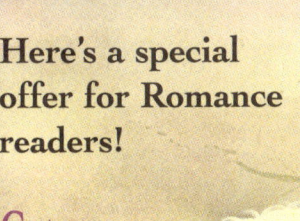

Here's a special offer for Romance readers!

Get
**4 FREE**
Zebra
Splendor
Historical
Romance
Novels!

*A $19.96 value absolutely FREE!*

Take a trip back in time and experience the passion, adventure and excitement of a Splendor Romance... delivered right to your doorstep!

Take advantage of this offer to enjoy Zebra's newest line of historical romance novels....Splendor Romances (formerly Lovegrams Historical Romances)- Take our introductory shipment of 4 romance novels **-Absolutely Free!** (a $19.96 value)

Now you'll be able to savor today's best romance novels without even leaving your home with our convenient and inexpensive home subscription service. Here's what you get for joining:

- 4 BRAND NEW bestselling Splendor Romances delivered to your doorstep every month
- 20% off every title (or almost $4.00 off) with your home subscription
- A FREE monthly newsletter, *Zebra/Pinnacle Romance News* filled with author interviews, member benefits, book previews and more!
- No risks or obligations...you're free to cancel whenever you wish...no questions asked

To get started with your own home subscription, simply complete and return the card provided. You'll receive your FREE introductory shipment of 4 Splendor Romances and then you'll begin to receive monthly shipments of new Zebra Splendor titles. Each shipment will be yours to examine for 10 days and then if you decide to keep the books, you'll pay the preferred home subscriber's price of just $4.00 per title plus $1.50 shipping and handling. That's $16 for all 4 books plus $1.50 for home delivery! And if you want us to stop sending books, just say the word...it's that simple.

Check out our website at www.kensingtonbooks.com.

## 4 FREE books are waiting for you!
## Just mail in the certificate below!

If the certificate is missing below, write to:
Splendor Romances, Zebra Home Subscription Service, Inc.,
P.O. Box 5214, Clifton, New Jersey 07015-5214
or call TOLL-FREE 1-888-345-BOOK

# FREE BOOK CERTIFICATE

**Yes!** Please send me 4 Splendor Romances (formerly Zebra Lovegram Historical Romances), ABSOLUTELY FREE! After my introductory shipment, I will be able to preview 4 new Splendor Romances each month FREE for 10 days. Then if I decide to keep them, I will pay the money-saving preferred publisher's price of just $4.00 each... a total of $16.00 plus $1.50 shipping and handling. That's 20% off the regular publisher's price plus $1.50 for shipping and handling. I may return any shipment within 10 days and owe nothing, and I may cancel my subscription at any time. The 4 FREE books will be mine to keep in any case.

Name _____

Address _____ Apt. _____

City _____ State _____ Zip _____

Telephone ( ) _____

Signature _____
(If under 18, parent or guardian must sign.)

Terms and prices subject to change. Orders subject to acceptance by Zebra Home Subscription Service, Inc. . Zebra Home Subscription Service, Inc. reserves the right to reject or cancel any subscription.
Offer valid in U.S. only.

SN020A

# Get 4 Zebra Historical Romance Novels FREE!

A $19.96 value.
**FREE!**
No obligation to buy anything, ever.

**SPLENDOR ROMANCES**
**ZEBRA HOME SUBSCRIPTION SERVICE, INC.**
120 BRIGHTON ROAD
P.O. BOX 5214
CLIFTON, NEW JERSEY 07015-5214

AFFIX STAMP HERE

"I'm not impressed." What journal?

"You should be. It's about you."

"Me?" Since he had just said he wasn't saying anything about the kisses and the other, Evaleen couldn't imagine what on earth he could write about her.

"In this journal," he said slowly, his eyes capturing hers, "I have put down that you have refused to come with me to check the fences. I have written that you had no interest in checking on the mare that foaled, nor did you want to even reconcile the ledgers for your ranch."

She stared at him, confused.

"Reynard wrote you were supposed to learn about the ranch, and you aren't upholding your end of the bargain, sweetheart. I've recorded your refusals. Tit for tat," he said.

"You didn't really expect me to do all that," she protested, putting down the lantern that had grown heavy as she'd stood there. Her insides filled with dread as she remembered that at least two times, she'd turned down his request to go with him because she hadn't been able to bear being close to him. Because she desired him. This was awful! Again her inability to control herself was ruining all the good she was trying to do for Theodora.

"Can't help it." Jesse shrugged. "Reynard decreed that you are supposed to learn how to manage the ranch, and Calloway informed you. Sorry if you don't like the idea. Neither do I like being told what to do every minute that I'm not out taking care of Rainbow's End. And I don't much like my freedom being taken away from me so I can hold on to what should rightfully be mine anyway. And I'm not a woman, so I don't much like playing mommy to Theodora. Daddy would be just fine, but you keep insisting on the other."

Despite the liquor he'd imbibed, his eyes were sincere.

Evaleen couldn't protest. Put from that perspective, he was right.

She groaned low in her throat. What on earth was she going to do? She was supposed to help Jesse change, and now she was going to have to choose between doing what she knew was right and being Theodora's mother. This wasn't right.

Worse, he was going to be loose in town, doing whatever he wanted, seeing women whenever he wanted ... and a small part of her hurt inside at the thought. Suddenly, without even knowing why, she had to ask.

"Did you stay with a saloon girl tonight, Jess?"

Liquored up or not, Jesse didn't miss the wistfulness in Evaleen's voice. Suddenly he was quite happy about what had irritated him all to hell earlier, he *had* gone upstairs with Cassie Jo again, and once again, the closer he'd gotten to Cassie, the more he'd remembered the desire in Evaleen's eyes when she'd first looked at him the other night, before they'd gotten "carried away." Then he'd remembered the way Evaleen had cared enough to leave a hot meal for him even though he'd gotten in three hours after dinner had been served and he wasn't even talking to her. And then he remembered how good it felt to come home to a house full of noise and laughter, a place that Evaleen was making into a home. He even recalled, with some fondness, the way Evaleen had harped that she was going to send one of the hands to check on him if he'd been much later.

All those things had made him feel boxed in when he'd actually been living through them earlier, but at Nicholson's saloon, up in Cassie's room, he could only think of how good it had felt that someone cared if he came home at night—or if he lived or died. Evaleen didn't have to do all she did for him. But she did, and it confused the hell out of him to the point where he couldn't even touch Cassie, much less do anything else.

After that, all the goings-on in the saloon and the liquor wasn't much fun, and so he'd left the saloon and, as prearranged, found Thurgood and Nicholson, and come back to Rainbow's End.

"Nope. I didn't stay with any saloon girls," he told Evaleen. Was that a pleased look in her eyes or a trick of the flickering lantern light? He cursed himself for the sudden glad feeling that he'd pleased her.

Her lips opened, and a delicate sigh escaped. His gaze fastened on her mouth. It was perfectly shaped. He'd always been so busy concentrating on the rest of her before he'd never really noticed her lips, but tonight, all his senses seemed sharpened. Picking up the scent of her rose toilet water on the breeze, he breathed in deeply.

"So are we agreed?" he asked. "I come and go as I please, and I leave you alone when it comes to learning how to manage the ranch?"

Her eyes looked confused, bewildered, as though she couldn't believe this was happening to her. She stood there for a full minute with the lantern in her hand, studying him, caught in indecision.

"I agree only to starting over from scratch," she said finally. "If you don't write down that I was uncooperative about learning about the ranch, I'll ignore everything you've done—or that I've suspected you've done—up to now. But tomorrow we begin again."

He shook his head. "Nope. Not agreed. We do it my way or not at all."

They stood staring at each other, the tension thick between them. Evaleen wanted to reach out and touch him, let him touch her, make the irritation in the air fade like the sunlight going into night... peacefully. Sweetly. But after the other night, she knew better.

Jesse wanted to touch her, change everything between them, but there was no way he was compromising what he believed in. And what he believed in was his right to do as he pleased at twenty-nine years of age, not have a ghost dictate his activities from the grave through the woman in front of him. Evaleen's being in charge was making him resentful as hell, and he didn't want to resent her. Resentment was the last thing he wanted to feel with her.

Reaching out, he pulled her into his arms, fully aware that he'd awakened her when he'd come home, and that she couldn't have had time to fully dress. Her soft, large breasts were bare underneath the two layers of material. He held her tightly against his hardness, and lowered his face to kiss her.

"Jesse, don't," she said, a tinge of fear in her voice.

Her words had the same effect as a bucket of cold water on his hazy, liquored brain. Stepping back, his arms out at his sides, he watched her pick up the lantern and put a few feet between them.

"We'll talk in the morning," she said, her words definite. Turning, she walked back toward the porch.

"No, Evaleen," he said. "I'll sleep on this and we'll talk around noon, when I get up."

She whirled around.

"Sunday is my morning to sleep late, remember?" he said. "We'll talk when I'm ready."

With a tiny sound of frustration, she hurried back toward the porch, giving him a pretty good view of her in the light of the lantern she carried. He'd never seen her hair loose and flowing down her back like that, and the sight impacted his loins like a gunshot. Her wavy hair bounced as she climbed the porch steps, and the light from the lantern she held out carefully to her side glinted off it, giving the illusion of gold.

Fool's gold that he'd never possess, but nevertheless, he

couldn't keep himself from wanting to run his fingers through it, from wishing he could hold it up in the air and let it drift softly down onto his skin.

No, he wanted more. He wanted Evaleen. He wanted to lie down beside her, run his hands through her hair and over her voluptuous hips and breasts, and feel her softness against him, and have her be gentle and warm and giving in his arms. He wanted all that.

Frowning, he shook his head in disgust. She didn't want any part of him, and he was dreaming. She didn't trust him. All that worry in her eyes about him coming home safely had been concern that she would lose Theodora if something happened to him. She'd purposely, with no thought to his feelings, made him look like a fool in front of the men in Nicholson's. What really made him think they would ever be compatible? She put too many stipulations on him, and he wouldn't have a relationship with a woman who couldn't love him unconditionally. He knew that from all the years of trying to meet his father's demands. That kind of love was worse than none at all.

Love? What the hell was he doing thinking about love? He had a ranch to run.

Sighing, Jesse picked up the reins of his mount and tsked, and together, they walked toward the stable. He'd have to wake up Denton to take care of his horse; he was too damned tired. And as for Evaleen—well, he could stop dreaming, face reality, and damned well get it up and running for Cassie Jo.

# Chapter Eleven

"But he's always grumpy if he gets up too early on Sunday mornings," Theodora said, staring up at Evaleen as though she'd gone crazy. They were standing in the hallway outside of Jesse's closed bedroom door, and Evaleen was about to go inside, something she'd never dared do before.

"He has to get up, Dorie." After his remark last night, that they would talk when *he* was ready, Evaleen wasn't particularly concerned if Jesse was grumpy when she woke him up. She had a job to do, an understanding to come to. "Jesse is going to church, whether he likes it or not."

Pursing her lips, she hesitated with her hand on the doorknob. Despite the conviction of her words, she wrestled with grave doubts that going in was a good, or sane, idea. But pounding on his door hadn't budged him out of bed. Now she wanted to resort to stronger tactics, and for those, she needed to go inside his room and be right beside his bed.

She took a deep breath, her heart pounding. A bachelor's bedroom was the most dangerous territory of all for an unmarried woman, worse even than a study with a closed door. The very thought of being next to a bed with Jesse in it made her stomach flip-flop. Sternly, she reminded herself that after seeing him all liquored up earlier that morning and having him attempt to kiss her like he didn't respect her at all, he wasn't all that likable.

But that was fibbing, as Theodora would say.

She glanced quickly behind her. The child was shaking her head grimly. "Suit yourself, Aunt Evaleen, but he's gonna be awfully mad."

"I told you, it's necessary," Evaleen replied, wishing she hadn't included the child in this. But she hadn't wanted to enter Jesse's room with no one else around. Even if Theodora remained in the hallway, she would prove an effective buffer against any revenge Jesse might wish to take against her. "Jesse has been acting like a fool," she continued. "He needs to go to church to learn some morals and manners."

"I don't think God's gonna do any better than you, Aunt Evaleen," Theodora said.

The possibility of that was not especially comforting, Evaleen thought. Just then they heard rapping on the front door down the stairs, and Theodora raised her eyebrows. "Maybe I'd better get that. Aunt Victoria was eating breakfast when we came up here. She may not want to roll all the way to the front door."

"Go ahead." Evaleen nodded, telling herself it was just as well. On second thought, she figured the child would be better off not hearing if Jesse let out a string of curses upon awakening.

Waiting until Dorie disappeared down the stairs, Evaleen turned the knob and pushed open Jesse's door.

And stopped.

Even with half his body under a sheet, Jesse was a sight

to behold. Evaleen's gaze settled first upon the rise and fall of his naked chest, with its rippling muscles and soft curls of dark hair. Then, damning herself, she followed the small hills and valleys the sheet made until she reached the part of the coverlet that masked his hardened privates. Her mouth fell open, her breath caught in her throat, and something deep inside her clenched and pulled with a delicious swell of desire. She hurriedly forced her gaze back to his face.

An invisible ribbon reached out to wrap around her insides and tug her toward the bed, step by step, until she was standing over him. She had to fight the urge to stretch out next to him. The temptation was so strong that she hurried on with her chore before she could give in.

"Jesse Stockton, wake up now. It's time for church!" she called in a loud voice. Nothing but a soft snore.

Reaching down, she grabbed his hard shoulder and ignored the electrifying sensations cascading into her caused by touching his bare flesh. Giving him a hard shake, she told herself it was the exertion making her breathe faster and harder, and not the way his work-hewn muscles felt under her fingers. Again she called his name and again she pushed on him, and then, at last, she knew she had no choice.

"Jesse, I'm sorry, but you *are* getting up for church." Taking the pitcher of water on the nightstand, she stood back and poured it over his head. It fell in a stream, puddling in his mouth and eyes and cascading over his neck.

Jesse's eyes flew open, and he lurched up to a sitting position, muttering an oath that brought blood flowing directly to Evaleen's cheeks. She stepped back as he pushed himself up and half-fell out of the bed, still partly asleep, apparently trying to escape the source of whatever had shocked him awake.

"The devil!" he said, shaking off the water like a dog caught in a torrential downpour.

Evaleen had already stepped backward, but then, when she saw that the sheet had fallen completely away from his body, she froze in place, shocked. He was tanned to the waist, and magnificent. His chest hair extended down past his waist to where it tapered on untanned skin and branched out again, surrounding his manhood.

"You're huge," she breathed, unable to move. A deep yearning flooded every part of her body as Jesse mopped himself off with the sheet and looked up at her with incredulous eyes.

"Why in the hell did you try to drown me?" he exploded.

"So you would get out of bed for church," she whispered, barely getting the words out, so mesmerized was she by the sight in front of her.

At that second, when both of them were intent on each other, a woman screamed from the doorway, "Oh, my stars, he's naked!"

It was the beginning, Evaleen knew then, of the end.

Everyone went into action at once. Having seen the best Jesse had to offer, Mrs. Grover, wife of the owner of the general store, fainted dead away. She was caught by the tall, big-boned Mrs. Thurgood, who uttered, "Oh, my."

Swiftly, Jesse wound the sheet he'd been using as a towel around his waist. Evaleen, mortified, backed up and ran toward the door, and Mrs. Thurgood, the tiniest of grins on her face, grabbed Mrs. Grover under the arms and began to haul her out of the room. Once in the hallway, Evaleen shut the door behind her and faced not only the two grown women but Theodora, who was looking from woman to woman in bewilderment.

"I tried to make them stay downstairs, Aunt Evaleen," Theodora said, "but when they heard the yelling up here,

Mrs. Grover told me they wanted a tour of the house. What was all the commotion about?"

Evaleen couldn't speak. She knew what was coming. She would be ostracized from the town now. Her reputation was ruined, absolutely ruined, just as Cynthia's had been. This was by far the worst thing that could ever happen to her, being caught in a bedroom with a naked man who wasn't her husband. Oh, my. Oh, misery.

Tears began to stream down her cheeks. Busy reviving the unconscious Mrs. Grover, Mrs. Thurgood didn't notice. But Theodora did. Walking over, the child tugged on her skirt, her eyes big with concern. "Aunt Evaleen, did Uncle Jesse hurt you?"

"Everything's going to be fine, dear," Mrs. Thurgood said, brushing back some wisps of blond hair that had fallen loose from her bun after she'd finally patted Mrs. Grover's cheeks enough to bring her back to consciousness. She added with just a trace of a German accent, "Run along downstairs and tell your aunt Victoria that for me. Dear lady that she is, she'll be vorried."

When Theodora saw Evaleen nod, she took off down the stairs, looking relieved to have escaped.

Mrs. Grover pushed herself to her feet and looked to Mrs. Thurgood. "You know this is terrible, just terrible."

"Vell," Mrs. Thurgood said softly, "Miss Murphy is young and single, and it's really none of our business."

"Yes, it is," Mrs. Grover, a petite woman in her forties, insisted. "You know Victoria has already told us how far things have gotten here."

Evaleen took a deep, shuddering breath. She should defend herself. But she couldn't. She had kissed Jesse, and her aunt had happened upon them. Even worse, she had let Jesse see her bosom in the study. What if Theodora had remained in the hall up here and seen the naked Jesse getting out of bed with her in the room? The poor child had enough to contend with.

Evaleen began to tremble. She had made one poor decision after another since she'd arrived here, and they all seemed to tie directly in to Jesse.

Jesse's door opened, and reflexively, Evaleen jumped away from it, covering her face with her hands.

"I think it's a little late for hiding your eyes," Mrs. Grover said stiffly. Slowly, Evaleen lowered her arms. Out of her peripheral vision she could see Jesse, who was leaning against the hallway wall, fully clothed in a blue work shirt and black pants. Despite his wet hair, he still looked every bit as desirable as he had minutes before.

She was going to be damned eternally to Hell.

"Would either of you care to tell us what on earth was going on here?" Mrs. Grover asked.

Evaleen glanced at Jesse, hoping he would come up with something believable to get them both out of this. But he merely shrugged. "You're so good at talking, Miss Murphy, you can go ahead and tell them what you were doing in my room this morning. You have my permission."

"I wanted Mr. Stockton to go to church. I had no idea of how he slept, since I've never been in his room before."

"You did that to get him to *church?*" Mrs. Thurgood let out a peal of laughter that came from the bottom of her lungs. "That's a good von. *Ja,* it is."

Mrs. Grover stared from her to Evaleen and back again and shook her head. Keeping her eyes carefully off of Jesse, she said, "I believe I'll have a word or two with Miss Victoria, and then I'll be waiting for you out in the wagon, Ingrid."

Once she was out from under Mrs. Grover's harsh, judgmental stare, Evaleen brushed away her tears and met Mrs. Thurgood's eyes. "You're so understanding."

"Vell, you told us the truth, didn't you?"

Evaleen nodded her head emphatically.

"Then the rumors are true? You have to get him to church and to the school board meetings, and the town council? You have to reform him?"

Evaleen moaned. "Does the whole town know?"

Ingrid Thurgood was trying hard not to smile as she looked at Jesse. "Since last night, probably, *ja.*"

"It's true," Jesse said.

"Then you did vat you needed to do." Ingrid's blue eyes twinkled. "I've accidentally viewed a couple of unclothed bodies myself in the line of Mr. Thurgood's undertaking vork—dead of course." She smiled at them. "I cannot say that this experience was quite as bad. How Mrs. Grover did go on." She shook her head in dismay and added, in a voice that held a hint of frivolity, "Perhaps you vere too much for her, Mr. Stockton."

"I guess that depends on how you look at it," Jesse said.

"And I'm sure she did," Ingrid replied, biting back her laughter.

Even though Evaleen felt no inclination to grin as Mrs. Thurgood and Jesse were doing, she did feel a glimmer of hope. Mrs. Thurgood seemed to have a sense of humor about all of this. But the kind woman's next words put out her hope as effectively as a bucket of water dousing a lit match.

"Of course, I do not have the final vord in town. For some reason, even though Mrs. Grover has not been here that long, the other vomen tend to listen to her."

Evaleen sighed. "I'm ruined."

"Vell, I must go. The last time Mr. Nesmith brought your aunt to town, Victoria asked us to pick her up for church this morning, and ve must hurry her there before it begins. *Guten Morgen,*" she bid them, and then her eyes twinkled again. "Very *gut* morning, I think." Twirling, she headed toward the stairs.

Evaleen started down the hall too, not wanting to be up there alone with Jesse while the two ladies were still in the house. No, that wasn't being exact enough. After this, she never wanted to be alone with Jesse again. He'd messed up her well-ordered life, rocked it to the foundations, and made her think about nothing but him and his damned "allure." She hugged herself as she walked. If he touched her again, she would scream. If she had to see him again, she would—

Jesse caught her arm firmly enough so that she couldn't keep walking away. The memory of him naked took over her mind again, and she batted against his rock-hard chest, gasping for air, her bitterness breaking loose in a torrent.

"All I wanted, Jesse Stockton," she said breathlessly, "was for you to become a good man so I could get Theodora and maintain my reputation. But you couldn't let that happen, could you? You had to bring me down to your level, ruin everything good I tried to make for myself and my life!" She dragged in a long breath, feeling as though she were drowning as his fingertips dug into her shoulders. "And furthermore, I don't care what the will said. I'm taking Theodora and leaving!"

"Damn it, Evaleen, no you won't. I'll hunt you down and bring you back. I didn't do anything on purpose. All I wanted was to get my ranch back!"

His ranch. Freezing, she searched his face—and then she knew. The kisses they'd shared had meant nothing to him; she could see it in his shaded eyes and in the hardness of his jaw. And his touching her ... Her heart sank and turned to ice. She wanted to turn to ice too, so she wouldn't care, but she couldn't. Wounded by his words, she was filling up with self-disgust and hurt.

Exhausted and still half-asleep, Jesse let go of her shoulders. Evaleen lurched away until her back was against the wall. She hated him for his power, for the mental control he had over her. After all this, her body still cried out for Jesse's caresses, her lips for his kisses. And her heart . . . her heart cried out for Jesse's sense of fun and his smiles that warmed her to her toes, something she knew she now would never have. Not her. Not sensible Evaleen with Raton's notorious rake. She knew better than to laugh at life. Only sometimes . . .

Running away, she hurried down the hall and out of his sight. She didn't know what she was going to do now; she just knew that since she'd chosen the wrong way to carry out Reynard's final wishes, she was in more trouble than she'd ever been in her entire life.

Jesse didn't end up going to church, but at four o'clock that afternoon, the church, in the bodies of the five most upstanding citizens of the community—the minister, the mayor, Calloway Nesmith, Vince Grover, and Seth Thurgood—came to him with a command. Pacing the length of his study as they gave their reasons for this demand, Jesse only half-listened to them. He needed to sort out what *he* wanted, which, as usual, no one was considering.

He'd been badly jolted when Evaleen had declared she was taking Theodora and leaving, and not for the reasons she had assumed, either. Well, not entirely. Yeah, it would be damned hard for him to get the ranch if she disappeared with Theodora, but at the thought of the empty house that would result if she wasn't in it, a surge of loneliness and bleakness had rushed through him.

Evaleen had filled the house with laughter and her love for Theodora and her aunt. The house was now a home for him; he hadn't felt that way since his mother had passed away. He still thought, no matter how stupidly, that home was sacred, and he didn't want things at Rainbow's End to change back to what they'd been before Evaleen had come. He didn't want her to leave.

And Theodora, he couldn't let her go either. The child reminded him of the days when he'd been young and doted on his father's every word. Just like him at that age, she could ride like she'd been born to the saddle, and she had a seriousness to her that made her seem more mature than her years. Best of all, whenever she could, the child followed him around as if he really was her prince, and he'd been teaching her little things about the ranch as they'd traveled over it. Unlike it had been in his childhood, Theodora had no rival for his attention. Jesse answered her every question and treated her as if she were important. In exchange, he was feeling like he was the center of her universe.

Unlike Evaleen. He sighed. If only the woman hadn't been so damned intent on following Reynard's dictates in the will, she would never have come into his room. But then again, hadn't he half-expected, half-hoped that she would? Wasn't that really why he'd neglected to put on even a nightshirt when he was sleeping in a houseful of females where anything could happen?

A rush of disgusted voices reminded him of where he was and that he'd better listen to the men discussing him and his future, or he could end up in jail over this incident and not even know how it happened.

"Gentlemen, gentlemen," Calloway was saying placatingly to the others. "I do blame myself for this horrible situation. Victoria tried to warn me trouble was brewing, but I thought with Miss Murphy being so upstanding, there wasn't any danger of anything bad happening."

"Nothing bad did happen," Jesse growled.

"I'm glad to hear you're finally venturing an opinion over this, Mr. Stockton," Reverend Mortenson interjected.

"What's there to say?" Jesse shook his head at the man

he'd never liked and then regarded Calloway impatiently. "I suppose you agree with the others? Miss Murphy and I have to get married?"

"Heck, Jess," Thurgood broke in, "Calloway was the one who suggested marriage in the first place as the only possible solution to keeping Miss Murphy's reputation intact."

Jesse decided not to remind them that two other women had caught a glimpse of him naked, and they weren't going to be forced to marry him. He supposed Evaleen's reputation being ruined was bad enough.

"I can do the ceremony right now," the minister said. He shifted uncomfortably at noting the cynical look that came into Jesse's eyes. "Are you willing or not?" he asked.

"What's my alternative?" Jesse asked.

Calloway answered that with a wave of his hand through the air and a firm resolute look. There was no alternative, Jesse read on his ruddy cheeks. The lawyer affirmed that guess with his next words.

"Since," Calloway said, "it will be absolutely obvious that you have failed to become the upstanding citizen your father stipulated you must become, I would say that any judge will decide you've lost the ranch at this point. You might as well pack your bags and leave Rainbow's End."

"What happens to Evaleen?" Jesse asked the half-circle of men.

Calloway took a deep breath. "Since Miss Murphy was a part of this, she will be deemed unfit to be Theodora's guardian and therefore will also be unable to carry out the terms in Reynard's will. Theodora thereby becomes my ward, and will go, by Reynard's decree, to a boarding school in the East until she is of age."

"No," Jesse said.

"As her blood aunt, Miss Murphy will be free to visit

her if she chooses. With no official ties to the child, you will not."

*Evaleen could visit Theodora if she had the cash, or if she was able to leave Victoria.* Which meant that Theodora would probably spend most of the next few years alone. Jesse's jaw jutted out squarely at the thought. He refused to give up the ranch. Something way down inside him said that he couldn't stand to lose Evaleen either, but he pushed that thought aside for now. No matter whose fault this whole episode was, he wasn't giving up this ranch without a fight. "Evaleen will never agree to marriage," he warned them, without saying yes or no.

"My Ingrid is working on her right now," Seth Thurgood said.

*Marry Jesse?* Evaleen's breath caught in her throat. Since the two women had left with her aunt for church, she'd holed herself up in her room and tried to cry her way into some sort of solution to this mess she'd gotten herself into. Theodora had knocked tentatively and left lunch, a sandwich the dear child had made herself, by her door on a silver tray. One look at that Stockton family heirloom, an obvious reminder of Jesse, and Evaleen had closed the door, unable to touch the tray or the food on it.

Finally, she'd cried herself to sleep. And then Theodora had come up the stairs and said three of the ladies from the church were there, demanding to see her. She'd almost pled illness, but no one would have been fooled, and her agony would only have been prolonged.

One of the ladies had turned out to be Mrs. Thurgood, so she'd thought the others wouldn't overwhelm her. But she'd been wrong. Mrs. Mortenson, the minister's wife, might look like someone's grandmother, but she came on like charging cavalry. Evaleen had sunk down on a chair in the parlor and taken a deep breath, continuously forcing back the tears that were threatening to come again.

Where was the backbone that had kept her going all these years? she asked herself. Her whole life, she'd never broken down before, not once, no matter how bad things had gotten, not even when Reynard had won custody of Theodora.

But then nothing had ever so thoroughly ruined her reputation before.

And now these women of the community were telling her she would have to marry Jesse. If she didn't, people would look at her askance whenever she went in Raton, as though she were dirty. She'd be an object of scorn in town, and she wouldn't be able to hold her head up high. Just like Cynthia.

But she'd done nothing wrong! For a few seconds she wondered if she could get by without paying any attention to the townsfolk, but all of a sudden, an incident she'd buried deep into her mind came back to her like it was yesterday.

She'd been about fourteen, out walking with Cynthia on one of her sister's infrequent visits home, and a man had come up to them. He'd said he remembered Cynthia from Kansas City. With a leer that had frightened Evaleen, he'd told Cynthia if she'd dropped the man she'd been staying with, his friend, he was available. Cynthia had pushed her along the street at breakneck speed to get away from him, but he'd called after them, laughing, saying that if Cynthia wasn't available, he'd be happy to have a go-round with her friend.

He'd meant Evaleen.

She shuddered now. Only indecent women got accosted in that manner. If Cynthia hadn't chosen to live with a man openly, if she'd been a properly married woman, the man's friend never would have approached them like that.

And if she didn't marry Jesse, she would be looked at by people in the same way Cynthia had been viewed.

More sickening to Evaleen was the memory that she had let Jesse take liberties with her without being married to him. The women would be right to treat her like dirt.

Through her lowered lashes, Evaleen stared at Victoria, who was sitting across the room and watching her niece's every move. Victoria had been Cynthia's most vehement critic, and Evaleen had come to realize her aunt had been frightened to death that her other niece was falling into the same trap while living here and being around Jesse. As if it ran in the blood. That was why she'd alerted the good women with them now that she'd seen Jesse and Evaleen in a torrid kiss, and that was why she had urged the two up the stairs that morning to make sure Evaleen was all right.

As the minister's wife droned on about proper behavior, Evaleen closed her eyes, feeling faint. Her poor sister was dead now; she could forgive her. But not a hint of bad behavior must be allowed to be tagged to the Murphy name ever again, not if Evaleen was to live with her conscience. She wasn't only thinking of herself, either. When word of this got to Theodora's friends and classmates, and Evaleen couldn't assure it wouldn't, how on earth could the child survive the stigma?

"So what have you decided, Miss Murphy?"

The sudden silence as Mrs. Mortenson stopped speaking was deafening to her ears, and Evaleen raised her head and looked at each of them in turn, letting her eyes rest last on Mrs. Thurgood. The sweet woman had tried to soften the whole incident by pointing out that she, too, had seen Mr. Stockton in the altogether, as had Mrs. Grover. But that hadn't been enough to take the pressure off Evaleen, and now they were all waiting for her decision.

But what would she do? Calloway had already relayed

through her aunt that since neither Evaleen nor Jesse would be deemed fit to continue as guardians after this type of behavior had been observed, Jesse would lose the ranch, and Theodora would go to a boarding school in the East, with Calloway as her guardian. Like it or not, Evaleen had no choice. She was not losing Theodora.

"Yes," she said slowly, "I will marry Jesse Stockton."

# Chapter Twelve

Pulling the proper collar of his stiff white dress shirt outward with one finger, Jesse walked into the study. The men had all left him alone when the women had come in and announced Evaleen's decision. Out of respect for Evaleen, Jesse had gone upstairs and changed. When he'd returned to the main floor, he'd found the women had all gathered in Victoria's room. The men were outside, smoking and discussing how much Reynard would have liked what they'd managed to accomplish for his rakish son that afternoon. Eavesdropping on a few words of that conversation had been all Jesse could take, so he'd decided to go someplace where he could be alone.

He spotted Theodora in the big armchair by the open window. Wanting to keep his conversation with the girl private, Jesse leaned out to see if he could hear the men situated on the other side of the porch. He couldn't, except when they suddenly laughed.

*Yeah, this has all been real funny,* he thought sardonically.

"Are you hiding too, Jess?" Theodora asked.

"Yeah, I guess I am." Moving away from the window, he settled in a chair and offered the child a tight smile, unable to muster much else in the way of encouragement when he felt none himself. "What are you hiding from?"

Lifting her head and twisting in the chair, Theodora peered between the brown drapes out the window, and then she resettled in her chair and frowned at Jesse. "I'm hiding from the evil knight because I'm not going to be your princess anymore."

His mouth arched downward in concern. "Who on earth told you that?"

"Nobody had to." She huffed out a breath that was a girlish version of a sigh. "You're getting married to Aunt Evaleen. When the prince gets married, all the other maidens in the kingdom have to go back to their houses and weep."

He held back the wide grin that dearly wanted to pop out onto his mouth. She sounded so resigned. "I'm not leaving you, Dorie darlin'. I told you, no matter what happens, I'm not letting that evil knight get you."

She brightened, tossing back her brown-red curls. "Why is the town mad at you, Jess? Because you're marrying Aunt Evaleen?"

"Nothing quite so simple, I'm afraid."

"Why are you getting married all of a sudden?" she asked.

He had to think a minute for an acceptable answer. "Because everyone in town believes it would be best if your aunt and I got hitched, since we have to stay here in this house together. You don't mind, do you?"

"I guess not." She shook her head solemnly. "Because I'm too little to get married. Besides, if you're married to Aunt Evaleen, then you'll have to leave the ranch when she takes me back to Kansas, and stay with us to protect me, 'cause husbands and wives stay together. I wouldn't want us to go without you, Jesse. I'd miss you."

"I'd miss you, too," Jesse said over the sudden lump in his throat. Her simple loyalty moved him in a way nothing else had. He'd never felt needed by anyone in his entire life, and now that he did, the feeling was precious to him.

It was also bittersweet. Theodora had just reminded him that, married or not, Evaleen would leave him at the end of their time together to return to Kansas. And Theodora would go with her. He winced at the inward pain the lack of both of these females in his life would cause. He'd have the ranch house, but once again, he'd cease to have a home.

Rising and hunkering down in front of her, Jesse took her hands. "I'm glad you're here, Theodora."

She grinned at him, showing her missing tooth. "I hope you get married soon, 'cause I want to go outside and play, and I can't in these clothes." She looked woefully down at her dress, a frothy yellow creation with lace and frills that any woman would go gaga over.

"You look like a princess," he said.

She looked down scornfully. "Aunt Victoria made it for me. Can you keep a secret?"

He nodded.

"I don't even like it. It's usually for church, but Aunt Victoria said I had to put it on for the wedding."

Jesse almost laughed. She sounded so grown-up, so womanly, and she was only eight. But he was Theodora's guardian, not Victoria, and if the child wasn't comfortable in the dress, he couldn't see sentencing her to an afternoon of a tight collar. Bad enough he had to wear one.

"You can change into your calico dress if you want," he said. "You have my permission."

"But you're getting married," Theodora protested. "I've got to stay dressed up."

"Honey, it's bad enough that adults have to follow propriety. You go ahead and get comfortable." Jesse pulled at his collar again. "But you'd better hurry. I think the shotgun is going to come out real soon now."

Her face wrinkled in confusion.

"That's a fancy way of saying the wedding's going to be starting shortly."

"Oh." Rising, she walked to the door, but then she turned around before she opened it. "Are you happy you're marrying Aunt Evaleen?"

"What do you think?" he asked, wiggling his eyebrows in an attempt to make her laugh. She did. "Now get on and change your duds, before the wedding starts."

She closed the door behind her, leaving him alone to ponder her question. *Was* he happy to be marrying Evaleen? He supposed he shouldn't be. But, and it was a big but, he craved her body like a man craves drink to send him into sweet oblivion. And that was agony, the wanting but never getting. Married, he was sure Evaleen would give in—eventually.

Then there was the fact that every once in a while a soft look popped out on Evaleen's face, and when it was directed at him, he thought about what could be in his life if things were different between them. If she didn't have her crusade to change him into a different person and deny him his right to exist as he was.

He rubbed his head where remnants of a hangover from last night's drinking still throbbed gently, reminding him that maybe the carefree existence he wanted wasn't a good one after all. The ache in his head also made him recall how much happier he was looking at Theodora's smile than he'd ever been staring into a whiskey glass.

So much happier, if the truth be known, that he whimsically wished Evaleen would look at him the way the child had. With admiration, with love . . .

He pushed that thought to one side as another, more enticing one took over. Within an hour, he would be Evaleen's husband. He was willing to accept the responsibility. Yes, he enjoyed himself to the fullest when it was time, but no matter what his father had thought of him, he always took his responsibilities very seriously.

And showing Evaleen just how seriously he was going to take her was going to be a pleasure.

The minister intoned the last of the vows. Even though Theodora had tried to brighten the occasion by picking a bunch of bright yellow wildflowers and handing them to her as she entered the room, Evaleen couldn't stop the tears from forming in her eyes. Jesse had no ring. That was an indication of how loveless her marriage was. And her tears—they were the sign of how deep her misery ran at entering into a marriage that would, by mutual agreement, end up voided in a few months. This wasn't what she had planned for herself, and it was definitely the darkest day of her life.

"You may kiss the bride."

Not caring who might hear, Evaleen turned to Jesse to warn him not to touch her, but she didn't have a chance to open her mouth. He pulled her to him, his hard arms encircling her waist, his muscles flexing to stop her brief struggle as his mouth went over hers. A second later she forgot to fight him as the heat of the man's mouth made her ooze with a molasses-thick desire for him. Her arms crept up until the fingertips of one hand hooked gently on his collarbone, and the other hand pressed her bright yellow flowers against his black suit. The kiss he gave her was a gentle one, once she settled into his arms. It was a kiss filled with warmth and a tender kind of longing....

No, the longing, and all the other feelings she was sensing, were originating from her. She was only imagining that Jesse was showing her any emotion at all. This was all wrong. This wasn't what she had so carefully planned for herself, for her future. She was marrying a man who didn't really want her, and it was turning into the saddest day in her life.

Despite what she knew she had to do, she was still breathless with wanting Jesse. Pulling away, she walked out of the study full of the self-righteous townsfolk, her bouquet of bright yellow wildflowers falling unheeded on the carpet. She got all the way outside and behind the stables, out to the copse of trees that bordered the edge of a small stream before she stopped, safe from being viewed from the house. As she gazed at the high, blue, breathtakingly magnificent mountains in the distance, she bit her bottom lip, trying to cause herself enough pain to forget Jesse's touch and his lack of love.

"Theodora thinks you didn't like her flowers," Jesse said from behind her.

"What?" She hadn't thought about anyone following her, and his presence was a shock. She stared at him uncomprehendingly, then down at the wildflowers in his hand. Their brilliant yellow color represented the happiness she should be feeling, mocking her.

Jerking her gaze away from the flowers, she stared at Jesse's well-cut jacket, opened to reveal the fancy white shirt underneath. During the walk down, he must have unbuttoned the shirt at the top. She could now see the skin at his throat and some of the hair. . . .

With a deep shuddering sigh, she looked directly at the face of the man who was now her husband. His eyes examined her as thoroughly as she'd been studying him. Thickly lashed, spellbinding, they held her in a trance that she couldn't seem to break free of, until he moved forward and opened her fingers, then closed them over the ribbon-tied stems.

"I dropped them," she said softly, staring at the bouquet in her hand. "Not on purpose ..."

"I told Dorie that you weren't having a real good day. She understands now."

The knowledge that she'd hurt Theodora, who'd been sweet enough to bring her a bridal bouquet, stung Evaleen to the core. Couldn't she do anything right? She didn't even try to hide her trembling shoulders from Jesse. She no longer cared. Let him see her at her worst.

"Aw, Evie," he said, pulling her to him. For a few minutes, he let her rest her head on his broad chest and cry, sobbing softly. Why she was turning to the very cause of her inner pain for comfort, she didn't know, but he was there, and he was strong, and he was willing to hold her.

A fresh onslaught of tears rolled down her cheeks. She felt Jesse move and then was aware of soft cotton against her exposed cheek. A handkerchief. He was wiping away her tears.

"Evaleen, being married to me won't be that bad," he said quietly. He handed her the handkerchief, and she held it against her closed eyes, letting his shirt soak up the rest of her tears.

"Yes, it will!" she protested, breaking away from him, his handkerchief in one hand and the bouquet in the other. "You're a rogue, the talk of the town. All my life I thought I would marry an older, scholarly type who would respect my intelligence and my desire for independence."

"I do respect your intelligence."

"But you're a rogue. You want other women."

"I haven't been with another woman since I met you," he told her. "I haven't wanted anyone else but you."

Her mouth fell open. He was telling her the truth, she could read it in his eyes. Too swiftly, she remembered his lovemaking on the study's sofa, and she was filled with confusion.

"You hate propriety," she said.

"I married you because it was the proper thing to do. I didn't have to."

"You only did that because you want Rainbow's End."

"I won't lie to you—I didn't want to lose this ranch. But, honey, I assure you, no woman could ever drag a man like me into marriage against my will—not for a ranch, not for any reason. Surely you realize that about me."

Reason broke through the muddle of her confusion. That was true. Jesse was no hypocrite. It would have been so easy for him to pretend to be a reformed man for six months and be handed the ranch on a silver platter. But he'd fought her all the way, publicly, even at the risk at losing the ranch.

"But you don't want a wife. You aren't the type."

Jesse whooshed out some air. "Maybe I like having a home instead of a house for the first time in years. Is that so unbelievable?"

"You do?"

He nodded solemnly. "Since my ma died, I never had much in the way of what you and Dorie have brought to Rainbow's End. I kind of like it."

Evaleen's heart went out to Jesse, but she didn't know what to think. She stared helplessly at him. "But you don't want to change."

"Maybe I'm not so bad as I am. Did you ever give that some thought?"

The sides of her mouth curved upward as she remembered him drunk in the front yard. "I'd say you were pretty bad last night."

He grinned back, a slow, shy grin that started her heart pounding. "Yeah, I guess I was. But how about giving me another chance? All I want is a home, Evie. That's all I ever wanted. And you're about the only person who's ever come close to giving me that. How about if you let me show you how seriously I take marriage?"

Slowly, because she wanted to believe this could work out between them, to believe she hadn't made the biggest mistake of her life, she nodded. Just as cautiously, she stepped back into his arms, and lifted her face to his.

Wrapping his arms around her waist, he parted her lips with his and moved his tongue deep inside her mouth, sending waves of pleasure through her. She slipped her arms around his neck and tilted her head backward, urging him to take his kisses further, as he'd done in the study. He moved his mouth to her cheek and then down to the throbbing pulse of her throat, and for the few seconds before she closed her eyes, she saw a patch of blue sky through the tree branches, going red with the sunset.

His hands moved down her back to cup her buttocks and push her against the hardness of his manhood. Inside she melted. Her breath quickened, and she opened her eyes. Almost without thinking, she began to pull open the buttons of his shirt. Once his skin was bared, she gripped his muscular shoulders and ran her fingers down the hills and valleys of his chest as she sought his lips on hers again.

Their mouths locked together in a hot kiss, she sank with Jesse to the ground, landing in his arms on top of him and casting her bouquet of flowers to one side. It seemed she couldn't get enough of the man captured in her embrace. Inside, she felt feverish, almost faint with the need to have Jesse touch her all over.

They continued to kiss. Time seemed to stand still, and she couldn't concentrate on anything except the feel of his hands. They were shifting her skirt and petticoat to her waist so that her stomach, clad now only in her drawers, rested fully against the bulge inside his trousers. She shifted her hips restlessly as they continued to kiss, subconsciously seeking the connection that would quench this desire for him. His fingers worked at her waist, squeezed the flesh of her buttocks again, and went back to her ribbons.

"Just a bit longer, darlin'," he said, his voice tense, forced. Then, suddenly, he was pulling her drawers down off her hips and his hands were all over the bare skin of her backside. Throbbing started deep down inside her, and as though he sensed that, his fingers slipped between her legs and began to stroke.

Breathing hard, she pulled upward, realizing that he was close to her most inner feminine place and suddenly becoming worried as to what he planned to do. She thought she knew, but she didn't know enough. "Jess, is this how a woman gets ruined?"

He groaned, lifted his hands to her waist, and pulled her back for another kiss.

"I need to know, Jess."

"You're married to me, Evie," he said throatily. "You can't be ruined."

"But how does a woman get ruined?"

Taking a deep breath of exasperation, he opened his eyes. "No one ever told you?"

She shook her head, and her hair, falling from its soft bun, toppled down onto his chest. Jesse thought he was going to die. He'd never met a woman he'd had to stop everything for just to explain what he was about to do. But knowing Evaleen, perhaps he should have expected this. He decided to keep the explanation simple, so maybe they could get back to the good part.

"I take this"—he put her hand down on his manhood, and she gasped—"and I slide it into *there*." He slipped his hand gently between their bodies until his fingers reached the core of her femininity.

She gasped again at the way his fingertips lingered on

her sensitive part, gently stroking. "It won't go," she said swiftly, breathlessly. "It feels like it's too big."

"Sometimes there's a little pain the first time."

"For whom?"

"You, I'm afraid," he said.

"Why did I know that?" she murmured.

"And after that, yours stretches," he explained. "That's the extent of what I know. The rest of my expertise comes in the doing. Now can we get back to it?"

It *was* the way women got ruined. "But what if you can't change, and our marriage doesn't work out?" she asked. She was hoping he would reassure her that everything was going to be fine. Maybe even tell her he was going to do his best to take on the responsibility of making sure their marriage succeeded.

Maybe even whisper something about love.

"If it doesn't work out," Jesse told her, his blue-gray eyes half-closed, "I'll give you a divorce. It'll be that easy, I promise you."

She froze. Easy for *him*. Shifting back out of his arms, she rose to her knees, her cheeks flaming as she hiked up her drawers.

"Oh, Evie, what are you doing?"

"Saving myself." Rising to her feet, she smoothed down her skirts and tucked her bodice back into her skirt. How could she have been so stupid? Pain. Ruination. Easy for him to say. A lifetime of being cautious reared up, and she knew she couldn't go through with it. Trusting Jesse was too new, and she couldn't manage it, she realized, not without any mention of the most important factor of all.

Love.

"Saving yourself for marriage?" Jesse threw his arm over his face and groaned. "You don't trust me to be a good husband forever, do you?"

"Should I?"

"Of course you should," he muttered. "I won't see other women. I won't get drunk and beat you, I promise."

"Beat me ..." Her voice caught, and she sputtered in indignation. "If you even try such a thing, I'll make sure you never use that weapon you're so proud of!"

Weapon? His manhood? Was she referring to the pain he'd mentioned some women having the first time they were with a man? Hearing her exasperation, Jesse figured maybe he'd better get up and quit letting his private parts be such a good target. He didn't think Evaleen would resort to violence, but then again, maybe he didn't trust her so much either.

She watched Jesse rise to his feet, irritation whirling through her that he would even mention beating her. "Just because I don't choose to continue our lovemaking, that doesn't give you any right to imply you might lay a hand on me in violence."

"Some men *would*, you know," he pointed out drily. "Men own their wives when they marry, and many don't like being denied." He'd never beaten any woman, but he couldn't resist telling her a few of the facts of life to keep her on her toes. After all, she *had* left him aching inside for her, and she deserved some kind of punishment.

"You'll never own me!" she said, trying to fix her hair.

"Someday, sweetheart, you'll want me to own you, body and soul." He crossed his arms and smiled. "But maybe by then I'll be sick of getting denied and deny you."

"I don't want to talk about this anymore." Feeling sick, Evaleen scooped up her bouquet of flowers, just so that Theodora wouldn't get upset if they disappeared, and walked up the hillside, heading back toward the ranch house. She didn't want him to own her, she realized as she hurried away.

She wanted Jesse to love her.

But it wasn't going to happen. So when they reached

the area behind the stables, she turned again to address him.

"Just to make things perfectly clear before we're back in front of people, keep your hands off me for the next five months," she said, unable to meet his gaze. "Totally. Not even a touch as we cross paths. Do you understand?"

"Sure, darlin'. Are you going to keep your hands off me in return?" he asked, chuckling. "Judging from how far you let me take things just now, I have my doubts. Let's just see what happens, shall we?" He moved around her and headed toward the house.

"Not so fast, Jesse."

He halted his steps, but did not turn.

"You think I'm joking, but I'm not. When the five months are through, I couldn't stand living as a divorced woman." She added, a little desperately, "If you don't ruin me, I can get an annulment when the time is up."

He did turn then, his gaze startling her with its intensity. There was a firestorm in his eyes, and she knew she was going to hate what he was going to say.

"An annulment? Are you positive you can take five months of having me around you and stick to that wish, sweetheart?"

No, she wasn't. She was only certain she had to try. "Of course. It shouldn't be that difficult," she said.

"Yeah, it shouldn't. Except that I kind of think it's a lot harder for you to resist me than you're letting on. Every second of the day, you could be a nun, Evaleen, until that one second you go into my arms. And then you want me as much as I want you."

"That's not true. I don't want you." Not unless he loved her.

"Huh!" His chuckle was disbelieving. "And I've suddenly become a fine upstanding citizen because I'm married to the most virtuous, upright woman in the territory of New Mexico." He paused for a second. "If you believe that, honey, I'll believe you don't lust for me in your heart."

She threw her bouquet of flowers at him. They landed square on his chest and then dropped onto the trampled ground at his feet.

He stared down at the buds and blossoms in the dust.

"I guess that about represents the beginning of our marriage," he said sadly, and then he looked up at her. "It's up to you if the flowers die, Evaleen."

Turning, he strode away toward the house, leaving her to stare down as the dust from his retreating footsteps billowed over the blooms.

# Chapter Thirteen

The sign in the window of Calloway Nesmith's small office said that he would return at one, and it was almost that as Evaleen paced up and down his small expanse of boardwalk, her black Harvey Girl skirt blowing in the wind that was whipping up.

It had been two weeks since her marriage to Jesse. There was a little under five months to go until she could get her annulment, custody of Theodora, and a ticket out of Raton. She wished it were tomorrow.

Oh, on the surface, everything had been fine since her confrontation with Jesse—if you didn't count that she ached with desire for him. Aunt Victoria was talking to her again as though the distance between them had never existed. Jesse was making every effort to be polite, and he hadn't disappeared last Saturday night. Theodora was happy, bubbling over even, since her precious Jesse was married to her Aunt Evaleen, which meant he was now really her uncle.

Yes, everyone around her seemed very content. Inside, Evaleen's own emotions were like a runaway wagon, careening and out of control even though Jesse was doing his best to keep things on an even keel between them. She could see he was. Marriage had changed him; he was suddenly taking it—and her—seriously. Instead of coming up with ways to outwit her, the ranch had become his main concern, and he was buying stock and building and accomplishing all kinds of things—taking pains, he said, to expand their holdings.

Her new husband was working hard, and she admired him for it. But every time lately when she turned her head, she caught him staring at her in a speculative way that she'd finally understood. He still wanted to make love to her. And God help her, she wanted to make love to him with every fiber of her being—only she didn't have his heart, might never have it, and that was holding her back.

But that was not why she was in town waiting for Mr. Nesmith. What had sent her running to town for advice was that two hours ago, Jesse had told her he would be going to church tomorrow morning, and she could either ride with him and Theodora, or she could hitch herself up another buggy, now that Waco had taught her how. Her eyes widening in shock, she'd said she'd go with him.

He'd then invited her to go with him to round up some strays, but she'd told him, fully remembering that she had to learn something about ranching during her time there but wanting to buy time, that would have to wait until she learned to ride better. Waiting until he'd left, she'd hightailed it to town. Calloway Nesmith had been one of the men holed up with her new husband the day they'd been coerced into getting married, and she wanted to know a few things from him about this change in Jesse—which she still wasn't sure was real, but so much wanted to believe was.

Reynard Stockton's solicitor finally came out of the Raton Harvey Hotel a couple of buildings away. Lifting her skirts, Evaleen rushed down the street toward him.

"Miss Murphy!" he said congenially, although he appeared startled to see her. "What can I do for you?"

*Miss Murphy?* How quickly he'd forgotten, she thought, giving him a wry smile. "It's Mrs. Stockton now, Mr. Nesmith, remember? Or was there something illegal about the marriage, something I should know about?"

"No, no, not at all," Calloway assured her, waving his arms expansively. "Of course, you're correct. I should have said Mrs. Stockton. Many pardons." He beamed at her. "So what brings you to Raton, madam?"

"I needed to speak with you. Do you have a few minutes?"

"Certainly." He offered her his arm, and she rested her fingers on it as they climbed back onto the boardwalk.

"You were in the room when the question of marriage between Jesse and me was brought up. Why did he agree?"

Mr. Nesmith gave her a sheepish grin. "We didn't have to hold a gun to his head, if that's what you're worried about."

Jesse hadn't lied to her then. He hadn't protested the marriage. Evaleen let herself be thrilled for a few seconds, but then an inner part of her told her to be cautious. She was certain Cynthia had thought each of her men different, too.

"Perhaps," Nesmith continued, "Jesse decided if he didn't settle down, he was in grave danger of losing his ranch. What better way to prove he was getting serious about his life than taking on the responsibility of a wife?"

"I don't think of myself as Jesse's responsibility," Evaleen said quickly, and then, at the sight of his surprised face, reconsidered her reply. "I'm sorry, Mr. Nesmith. I realize none of this is your fault. It's just that Jesse is being so circumspect around me lately, it's hard for me to believe he isn't up to something."

"I can understand that, my dear," Calloway said sympathetically. "After all, he does have a past, doesn't he?"

That he did. They reached the front of his office, and she let her hand fall to her side as Calloway reached into his pocket for the key.

"But perhaps he just felt sorry for having put you into the position of seeming compromised."

"Jesse never struck me as being the type who would particularly care about a woman's reputation," she said drily as she walked behind him into the front room of his office. "Least of all mine."

"On the contrary—" Nesmith said, and then he clamped his mouth shut. As Evaleen was wondering what he'd been about to say, he spoke again. "Try not to look for trouble, Mrs. Stockton. If Jesse is going to fulfill the terms of the will without any further prodding on your part, then sit back and count your blessings."

Evaleen wanted to, but somehow she couldn't believe her life had suddenly become that easy. She felt that Jesse had to be planning something, and she needed to be fully on her guard or she was going to lose out. Cynthia's tragic ending had been too great a warning about how vastly different men could be than what they seemed, and besides, Mr. Nesmith had said it himself: Jesse had a past.

Across the street and a block down, finished with ordering supplies from Grover's, Jesse spotted Evaleen standing in front of Calloway's office with the lawyer. He had to get back to gather strays, just as he'd told Evaleen, but seeing his wife with Reynard's lawyer made him pause. Evaleen had not said a whole lot to him since their confrontation after the ceremony, and Jesse knew she was unhappy with the whole situation. Now she was talking to Calloway. Was she unhappy enough to make arrangements with the solicitor to give up Theodora and leave him? To ask for an annulment? He had to know.

As the pair went into Calloway's office, Jesse strode across and down the street, hopping silently up on the boardwalk. He stopped when he got to the side of Calloway's building. Evaleen and the lawyer were just inside the door near the window, and he could hear almost every word they said. He leaned back against the wall to listen.

What he heard he found very interesting. So his little wife was worried that he was up to something. He hadn't been, but he could understand her not trusting him. He hadn't exactly been a pillar of society and graciousness since she'd arrived.

He'd learned something from getting married. Doing what he wanted was his right, sure, but his going to town that Saturday night had set off the chain of events that had led to Evaleen's being compromised and had almost caused him to lose the ranch. His fault, not Evaleen's. She hadn't been doing a damned thing to cause him to lose the ranch—he had. It was time for him to change.

So, during the past two weeks, he hadn't been "up to" anything except doing his best to hold on to Rainbow's End and fulfill the terms of the contract. Only he'd felt like she was ignoring him, so he'd decided to go to church and shake her up. He obviously had gotten her attention, or she wouldn't be worried enough to go to Calloway now.

Grinning, Jesse pulled back on the far side of the building as Evaleen came out, thanked Calloway for his time, and got onto her buggy. Well, if his telling her he was going to church had thrown her for a loop, he couldn't wait till after church tomorrow when he sprang his other surprise on her.

* * *

Evaleen smoothed the dark blue silk of her dress and folded her hands over the Bible on her lap as Reverend Mortenson finished his lively sermon about helping thy neighbor. She wondered if any of the others in the congregation had listened to it. Not two minutes had passed during the address in which someone hadn't turned to grin in her direction—at Jesse.

Perhaps, she speculated, they were thinking about God's miracle that had brought the sinner to repent, or maybe they were wondering if the devil himself had chosen to appear in their church.

Jesse sat next to her, close enough to make her totally aware of his clean soap scent, his muscular arm pressed against her softer one, his every breath. All yesterday after talking with Calloway, she had still doubted he would get up and come to church in the morning. But when he'd first entered the kitchen while she'd been making breakfast, dressed in his black suit, his hair clipped so nicely the waves fell away from his face, he'd stolen her breath away. That feeling had yet to cease.

Giving him a sideways glance, Evaleen reminded herself that it could be Jesse was changing his ways only to save his ranch. He'd grown tired of fighting her, so he'd reversed his tactics and was doing everything his father had wanted. Still, a tiny part of her was beginning to hope his behavior was for real. Because if it was, maybe she could trust him enough to begin to change, too.

Halfway into the closing hymn, Evaleen was astonished when she noticed Jesse wasn't looking down at the hymnal, he was quietly singing the words by heart. The second the music stopped she asked, "This isn't your first time in church?"

He leaned down to whisper in her ear, "Now what would

have given you that idea? I went all the time when I was a kid. I even used to like it."

"What happened?"

His mouth lost its teasing lift, and he sat back down in the pew. Still on her feet, Evaleen glanced around the sanctuary for a few seconds. The service was over. Theodora and most of the parishioners were heading outside, and Calloway Nesmith was carrying her aunt Victoria to the wheelchair waiting in front of the church. They'd be all right for a couple of minutes without her presence. She wanted to seize this opportunity to talk to Jesse in a place where neither of them would be inclined to pick a fight.

She hoped.

She sat down—too close. Her breast touched his upper arm as she turned to look at him for his answer, and for a second, they stared at each other in blazing awareness. Remembering her admonition to Jesse not to touch her, she scooted sideways to put some distance between them.

"You were going to tell me why you stopped attending church," she prodded gently.

"I stopped going because I was kicked out for a time," Jesse admitted. "Somebody stole the offering, and the theft got blamed on me. The good folks of this town"—he turned his head and glanced briefly to the main door where people were still filing out and shaking Reverend Mortenson's hand—"wouldn't let me back in until the real thief happened to be discovered. By then, I was a bitter twelve-year-old and didn't want anything to do with any of them."

She frowned at him. "Who really stole the money?"

Jesse offered her one of his lackadaisical smiles that hid what he was really thinking and made her insides twist with sympathy over his hurt. "My brother, Patrick, and one of his cronies," he told her. "But his friend ended up getting the blame; Patrick got off scot-free. Reynard told the good reverend that Patrick had been with him, even though he hadn't been. My father never could stand the taint of sin on his firstborn's name." He chuckled and added, "Not even back then."

"Your brother got away with it?"

Jesse shrugged his shoulders. "Reynard considered it a boyish prank and upped his contribution until the amount was paid back."

Only no one had ever paid Jesse back for the respect he'd lost, Evaleen thought. His hand was resting on the seat next to him, and reaching out, she covered it with her own. "I'm sorry, Jesse."

"Thanks." He turned his hand and intertwined his fingers with hers, and for a few seconds, Evaleen felt their hearts connect.

"Pa never believed Patrick could have instigated the theft, just like he never believed Patrick could have left me to die." His eyebrows narrowed as he stared intently at her. "But if Patrick comes around the ranch, sweetheart, don't you be as hardheaded. If he is Theodora's evil knight, as I suspect, he's perfectly capable of carrying her away to get this ranch or money, whatever he currently needs."

A chill went through Evaleen at his words. Half of her still believed that the evil knight was Theodora's invention, but the other half was starting to believe Jesse. And to believe in Jesse, too.

"I consider myself warned," she said softly.

"Good." He glanced around the almost empty church, taking in the pews and the stained-glass window Nicholson had ordered to be sent in along with his bar and had donated to the church. The glass with its multicolored panes depicted the form of Jesus, and looking at it now brought Jesse the strangest sense of peace. He glanced sideways. Or maybe he just felt peaceful because he was sitting next to Evaleen with her warm hand in his, he wasn't certain. Either way, being here this morning with Evaleen and Theodora had felt wonderful, like he was part of a family.

"Shall we go?" he asked, rising.

"One question," she added, rising with him but not letting go of his hand. Her eyes met his, clear, lime green eyes that touched something deep within his soul. He held his breath.

"What's changed with you, Jesse? Why did you stop fighting me?" She blinked. "I mean . . . why did you stop fighting the will?"

"I want the ranch, Evaleen." He reached up and touched her cheek. He couldn't remember touching anything softer. Her skin was like a rose petal underneath his fingers. "It's all I ever wanted in my whole life."

*Until I met you* drifted into his thoughts, and Jesse let go of her hand and stepped back, confused. He'd known he wanted her body, but just now he'd had the overwhelming feeling that he wanted her to stay. To love him.

Was that what he really wanted? He couldn't hope for that, could he? Come the end of a few more months, Evaleen was leaving. Sure, he had the capability of making the rest of their time together smooth and maybe even pleasant, but could he expect love from her? If she loved him, she would have to love him the way he was, as a man who directed his own life. Could she agree to that, what with the way she was?

And could he love her back? Evaleen tended toward tyranny and had an independent streak she didn't bother to hide. She might leave him when she finally had custody of Theodora, and he didn't think he could stand that any more than he could stand losing the ranch. Was she a woman who would love him and remain utterly devoted no matter what? That was the only kind of love he wanted.

He couldn't risk loving her back if it ended up she couldn't love him like he needed her to.

He sighed. If he had to choose between the woman and the ranch, he guessed he would have to choose land. It was solid, dependable, and would always be there. He wasn't so positive about Evaleen.

While Jesse had been lost in his thoughts, Evaleen had been considering what he'd just said. Land. He loved Rainbow's End so much he was willing to give up his freedom for it. Would she ever inspire such devotion? She feared the answer.

"I quit fighting the will because I realized I almost lost the ranch with my bullheadedness," he was saying, "and I realized how stupid that would be. So I'm doing what I have to do to keep it."

"Including being married to me?"

"Yes." He took a deep breath. "Although I must say, being married to you is easier than I thought it would be."

Her steady green eyes wouldn't let loose of him, and she smiled. Her pearly teeth traveled once lightly across her bottom lip. "Shall we start with a clean slate then, Jess? I'd like to."

"Agreed." With half a bow, he held out his arm to her.

Evaleen gazed at it for what seemed like a long time, and finally, with a smile that hid her worry that she was getting in way over her head, she rested her hand upon his arm. His responding grin told her the small gesture meant more to him than he could say, even if no one noticed.

At the door of the church, Evaleen watched as Jesse stepped up to Reverend Mortenson. The preacher pumped Jesse's hand as though they were old friends, but Jesse's face shadowed and closed off some of the openness he'd shown with her. Apparently, enough of the hurt boy was left in him to keep him from entirely trusting the preacher now. Well, she could understand that. She could even sympathize.

She passed Reverend Mortenson with a short smile of greeting. Outside, while Jesse paused to talk to Mr. Nicholson, Evaleen searched the yard out front for Ingrid Thurgood, the one woman in town she considered a real friend. Although Mr. Thurgood was present, the tall mortician's wife was nowhere to be seen, so Evaleen walked back to her buggy where Theodora was prancing around Calloway and Victoria. Her aunt had already told her she planned to ride back to Rainbow's End with Calloway, so Evaleen didn't understand why the two were waiting by her buggy.

Theodora's silky brown curls bounced over her shoulders as the child ran to greet Evaleen. "Guess what? We're going to a—"

"Shush, child," Victoria said from her wheelchair. "I want to talk to your aunt Evaleen a minute. Run along and visit with Missy Harper."

"What was she going to tell me?" Evaleen asked.

Victoria shook her head as though she didn't know, and absently, Evaleen glanced back to see what was keeping Jesse. She spotted him in the midst of three of his friends, two of whom had been the men who'd brought him home that night he'd been "ambushed." She smiled briefly at the memory. He'd really thought she would fall for that hokey bit of blarney, had he? She ought to set him up. . . .

"Evaleen, where are your thoughts?" Victoria asked, waving her fingers to get her niece's attention back.

Evaleen focused on Calloway. The solicitor stood quietly behind Victoria, gazing fondly at the older woman, which drew Evaleen's eyes downward.

"I'm sorry, Aunt Victoria. I guess I wasn't listening."

"Calloway has proposed marriage to me this very day, and I've agreed."

Marriage? Her maiden aunt, who had lived with one or

another of the Murphys since she'd had her accident and lost the ability to walk, married? A wife, meant to keep house and take care of a husband? Aunt Victoria was the one who needed care. She couldn't possibly handle a household. Frowning, Evaleen continued to stare at Victoria as though the older woman had lost her senses.

"Oh, please don't tell me you're shocked," Victoria said. "Couldn't you see it coming?"

Evaleen shook her head. Apparently she'd been so busy worrying about Jesse she'd been blind to everything else.

"Why, Calloway has visited so often, and we've been spending hours together in the parlor. Don't tell me you didn't even have a clue!"

Victoria was smiling like a schoolgirl with her first beau, and Evaleen suddenly realized why. The fifty-year-old woman was in *love*. "B-but," Evaleen sputtered, "you need someone to take care of you."

"Calloway can do that."

"Excuse me," the stocky, ruddy-faced solicitor interrupted. "I believe you two ladies need to talk." He strode away, walking toward Jesse and his friends. As soon as he was far enough away, Evaleen leaned down close to her aunt so no one would overhear.

"In all the years you've lived with me, you've told me you believe men are nothing but trouble," she swiftly whispered, feeling like she was in shock. "I thought you'd never—"

"Pshaw." Victoria waved her lace handkerchief in the air, dismissing hundreds of lectures and talks the two of them had had in one graceful movement. "I just said those things because you were young and I was afraid you'd get all starry-eyed, just like your sister did, over the first thing in pants who came along. You proved it, too, with your canoodling with Stockton there."

"We weren't doing anything!"

"You weren't? I saw you kiss, and there was the day you came out of the study with him, your lips swollen and your buttons undone. It didn't take a genius to figure out what you'd been doing in there." Her aunt narrowed her eyes. "Kissing like that heads right toward trouble. I know of what I speak, Evaleen. Hot bloodedness is the Murphy way." Her voice softening, she continued, "I couldn't stop Cynthia from doing what I did, but I thought I could darn well stop you."

Evaleen's mouth dropped open. Stooping on one knee so she could speak face to face with her aunt, she held the arms of the chair for balance. "What did you do?"

Victoria gazed around to make sure no one could overhear. "The day I was in the stage accident?"

Evaleen nodded.

"I was on my way to meet my own Jesse." When Evaleen's face wrinkled in confusion, she added, "Oh, Evaleen, grow up. I was on my way to meet my lover."

Lover? Evaleen shook her head. "Jesse and I aren't lovers."

"Perhaps not, but if we hadn't forced you to marry, can you really say you wouldn't have been, and soon? You can truly tell me the man wasn't in the process of overwhelming you with charm?"

"I don't think charm is quite the word for what Jesse Stockton has," Evaleen said with great surety.

"Oh, pshaw! Then his allure. His attractiveness. And don't tell me you don't find him attractive, Evaleen."

Her niece clamped her lips shut.

"I thought so." Victoria nodded sagely. "And there was something else about me. Something no one ever knew except my doctor. I was expecting a little one by this man, but the accident ended that."

"Oh, Aunt Victoria," she whispered.

"I was so in pain over that loss," the older woman said

softly, a faraway look in her eyes, "that I couldn't bear the thought of another man touching me for the longest time; although with my being in a wheelchair, I assure you, not many came to try. After that, the doctor said I should never even attempt to have a child, so I avoided men."

"Does Calloway know?"

"Everything." Victoria nodded, her eyes once again concentrating solely on Evaleen over her wire-rim spectacles. "Calloway is mature and can handle something like that. Most men could not."

"Yet he was in an all-fired hurry to get Jesse and me to the altar, and the two of us are of age."

"I'm afraid it was I who was in a hurry and pushed him. This way, with you taken care of, I'm free to leave your home for Calloway's. He's already hired a housekeeper to give me what help and company I'll need while he's working."

Evaleen pushed herself to her feet. Soon, Victoria would be marrying and moving, and she would be left alone in the house with Jesse. With no one watching over them save an eight-year-old child. This was going to be interesting. She and Jesse might have just declared an official truce, but it was a mite early to start testing it.

Victoria stared up at her from her wheelchair. Around them, people were walking to their buggies. Over their heads, the sky was blue. Everything seemed so normal—only it really wasn't. She was married to Jesse and had to deal with that, and her aunt was getting married. Evaleen's whole world was changing.

Suddenly she got the urge to lean down and hug her aunt with all her strength. "All the best to you, Aunt Victoria. At least one of us will be happy now."

Victoria smiled as Evaleen straightened. "Your time is coming, Evaleen, I promise you. Give him a chance."

If her aunt could find the courage to let a man into her

life, Evaleen thought, she would have to give a whole lot more serious thought to not being so afraid herself. "When are you marrying?"

"The sooner the better," Victoria said. "After all, neither of us is getting any younger." Pushing her wheelchair into a forward motion, she warbled, "Cal-lo-way!"

"I think it's time we were going," Jesse said from behind Evaleen.

Startled, she turned and gazed into his blue-gray eyes, which seemed to be twinkling. Flustered that he'd been so close by while all her thoughts had been about him, she barely found the voice to ask, "You knew?"

"I thought it was a secret," Jesse said, shaking his head and looking disappointed, as though his biggest secret was now out in the open. Evaleen barely had time to consider that when Jesse asked, "Who told you?"

"Aunt Victoria."

"Well, now that you know, I guess that wrecks my surprise," Jesse said.

"*Your* surprise? Really, Jesse, you had nothing to do with Aunt Victoria getting married." Her feet went into motion as she turned to seek out Theodora.

Jesse trailed her. "Victoria's getting married? To whom?"

"Calloway." Stopping short, Evaleen met his eyes. They were filled with confusion, but they also held her in a dazzling grip. A surge of longing went through her. "But I thought you said you knew, you did say you had a surprise." Her own eyes widened questionly. "So what were you referring to?"

"Nothing, really." Grinning at her, he pushed his reddish brown hair off his forehead with his hand. "Don't you think we ought to find Theodora and get back to the house?"

"No." She hated surprises, she really did. Surprises

messed up her orderly life and caught her off-guard; she didn't like anything that put her off-guard . . . except Jesse.

Maybe.

He was looking at her now like a boy with a secret, and she couldn't help but smile back, knowing he was up to *something*, but totally unable to guess what it could be. As she smiled at him, his eyes shone all blue-gray heat, catching her up with their power.

She almost groaned. Aunt Victoria had been right after all. If she thought to resist Jesse's charm, she was going to be in for an uphill battle all the way.

Placing her hands on her hips, she kept herself from smiling at his grin. "I think you ought to tell me what surprise you have planned, Jesse Stockton."

"Nope. You have to wait."

"Fine. Don't tell me. I'm not in the least bit curious."

"Heck, Evie. You expect me to believe that?" he asked. "A woman who isn't curious?"

"Believe as you will," she said, her mouth melting into a smile. He was teasing her, and he'd called her Evie, treating her fondly as a husband would a wife. No man had ever cared about her enough before to tease her. Maybe she was wrong and Jesse was different from other men. . . .

"Jesse!" Theodora said breathlessly, running up past her to look up at him. "Is it—?"

Her words stopped abruptly, and Evaleen jerked her head up just in time to see Jesse's finger against his mouth and his eyes filled with a roguish light.

"What is going on?" she asked.

"I thought you weren't the least bit curious," he said seriously, but the teasing look never faded from his blue-gray eyes. "Sorry I can't accommodate you."

Evaleen grinned back at him; her eyes challenging his.

"Theodora, will you please tell Jesse that when he decides to be accommodating, so will I?"

His face lit up. "Theodora, please tell your aunt that I'd love to know exactly just how accommodating she's willing to get."

"Aunt Evaleen, Jesse said—"

"Yes, dear, I know. I heard him."

Not comprehending what was going on between the two adults, Theodora shook her head in exasperation. "I'm waiting in the buggy."

Evaleen nodded. There was no mistaking the suggestion in Jesse's words, and in his eyes. Her insides flushed with heat, even as her brain was telling her not to pursue the subject. But finally, the desire to keep him looking at her in precisely the same way won out.

"Wouldn't you just love to learn the answer to that, to how accommodating I can get?" she asked him directly, her voice low.

He reached out and skimmed her cheek with his thumb, ever so gently, his hand gone before she could voice a protest. "Yeah, I think I would," he said. "Do you want to tell me—or show me?"

"Oh, Jesse." His proximity was doing strange things to her equilibrium, and she pulled back from him, her heart thumping in her chest. "And here I thought you might be changing," she chided teasingly, her eyes shining. "I should have known better. You still believe every woman in Raton is pining after you."

"Not every woman, darlin'," he said, shaking his head. "Just one now that I'm married. You."

"Well, Jess, now that you've discovered I'm not infallible, I think you should know something else."

"What?"

She leaned more closely to him so they wouldn't be overheard by the few people still milling about. "If what

I'm reading in your eyes is the truth," she said softly, "I believe perhaps I'm not the only one who's pining." Turning and striding away toward the buggy, Evaleen forced back her smile. As much as she liked the attention Jesse was paying her, she had to admit he was right; she *couldn't* get his body off her mind. But the simple fact remained: this was her life she was thinking about changing, and in a major way. She had to be certain she was doing the right thing if she let her heart become involved with Jesse.

She had to be relatively certain the man had changed as she was starting to believe he had. Because if she believed in him and he failed her and went back to his womanizing ways, she'd be the laughingstock of the town.

Staring at the man approaching the buggy, she took a deep breath. She wanted to believe in him—she truly did. But did she dare?

# Chapter Fourteen

On the ride back to Rainbow's End, Jesse felt almost like a kid discovering the wonders of the world again. When Evaleen had risen to his bait and had actually flirted with him, he'd felt like someone had jerked the earth from beneath his feet. Sure, lots of women had flirted with him since he'd reached his full height, but Evaleen's flirting had been different. Her words had grabbed him in the gut and wouldn't let go.

During the church service, he'd kept remembering the way his mother had been with his father, how a real marriage was. When his father had looked at his mother, it had been with real love. From this vantage point, Jesse could even see how Reynard's marriage to Evaleen's sister had been doomed from the start. Cynthia had never made his father proud, nor had she put the glow in his eyes as his own mother had done.

Like Evie was starting to do to him.

Shotgun wedding or not, he never would have married

a good woman like Evaleen, Jesse reminded himself, had he not planned on taking their marriage very seriously. He might not have liked her at the start, but she'd proven to be more than enough of a challenge for him and the attraction was there. Lots of attraction. Lately, like this morning, it was overpowering. When Evaleen had used that suggestive, flirting tone with him, he'd known he'd done the right thing by planning a surprise for her. This afternoon would add to the harmony between them, which, if Victoria really was marrying Calloway and leaving, would be very important.

Needing to stretch the time out before they arrived back at Rainbow's End, Jesse drove slowly, passing the spot where, the first day he'd laid eyes on her, Evaleen had brushed close enough to him to leave him butt down in the dust. He glanced sideways at her, and she met his look with a delicately amused one of her own.

*You remembered,* he commented silently.

*I'll never forget,* she said with her eyes.

He grinned at the memory and then broke into laughter that mirrored the way he was feeling.

Sensing Jesse was laughing at himself, Evaleen couldn't help but laugh too, glancing at him. Their eyes locked, and she shared a special look with him that made her shiver with anticipation. What was their relationship turning into? Could it be that her future with Jesse was not so cut and dried as she'd believed?

At that thought, her laughter caught in her throat. But Jesse continued to grin, and finally she laughed again. She had to stop worrying, she told herself. Not worrying felt so good.

Alone on the rear seat, Theodora leaned forward between them. "What are you and Jesse laughing at?"

Not quite sure herself, Evaleen shrugged helplessly and

reached up to wipe the tears that had gathered in the corners of her eyes.

"You two have gotten really strange since you got married," Theodora said loudly, sitting back on the seat, crossing her arms, and wagging her head in disgust.

They both glanced backward at her, at each other, and then Jesse's masculine chuckle again chorused in the air and mingled with Evaleen's delicate laughter.

Minutes later, they were close enough to the ranch for Evaleen to see buggies and wagons clustered in the front yard. She looked at Jesse questioningly. "Your surprise?"

"My surprise." Jesse nodded.

"Everyone in Raton must be here. Are we celebrating Aunt Victoria's engagement?"

"Nope." He held the reins in his hands and gave her what she could only term a sheepish look. "We're celebrating our wedding. I've heard every woman should have a wedding party, and you never got one, so I thought you might have felt bad about that. With Mrs. Thurgood's help and your aunt's blessing, we planned this."

"Why, Jesse?" she asked, all traces of the earlier merriment fading away. "Why are you suddenly so worried about the way I'm feeling about this marriage?"

"Uh-oh," Theodora said. "If you two are going to start a fight, I'd rather walk."

"Theodora's right. We can wait and discuss this after we park the buggy," Jesse offered. Evaleen, glancing at Theodora, nodded in agreement. She hoped it was a discussion. Her only hot urge now where Jesse was concerned did not involve fighting.

When they were parked and Theodora had hopped down and run off, Jesse leaned forward and stretched his leg until his boot touched the top of the foot rest. "Okay, Evaleen, get whatever it is off your chest," he said carefully.

He would try to understand her and not get angry, he vowed.

"I'm afraid, Jess," she said carefully, and ever so softly, making sure not to let any of her usual take-charge attitude show through in her voice, "you never cared about my feelings until we got married, and now everything is so changed. Should I let myself believe you care now, or is this just some sort of game you're playing with my heart until the marriage can be annulled?"

Jesse looked off to the distant mountains. "I guess things have changed with me," he said finally. "I don't take marriage lightly, and I don't plan on this marriage ending." His eyes settled on her, all smoky blue. "I want to make you happy, Evie, so that you'll want to stay here on the ranch—with me."

"As in forever?"

"If I live that long," he said. "Of course, at the rate I seem to be irritating you, I think you're going to be chasing me with that skillet you once mentioned Victoria using and putting me into an early grave with a crack on the head way before the two of us see forever."

Struck herself, Evaleen took a few seconds to think as Jesse climbed off the buggy, came around to her side, and held up his arms to help her down. What he had said bore no resemblance to the repertoire of sweet things she'd understood men used to woo women they later tossed carelessly aside. He sounded as though he really needed her—and wanted her—in his life.

Climbing down, she slid right into his arms. Feeling the power in his shoulders as they flexed before he set her gently on the ground, she searched his eyes. The sweet, urgent feeling of desire for Jesse was growing stronger within her with every passing moment, pushing down the wall she'd built around herself to protect herself against men. Against Jesse. He no longer seemed like the threat she'd expected him to be.

"Thank you for the party," she said, wanting to show him she appreciated his trying. "It was a sweet thing to do."

"I know," he said, grinning down at her.

Her Jesse. Rolling her eyes, she smiled back. In response, he slipped his arm around her waist and walked with her around the house to the clearing where they'd set up the gathering.

Hours later, in Jesse's arms, Evaleen was aglow as she finished the polka and drew in a lungful of warm, clear air. As the afternoon had progressed, her relationship with Jesse had grown better and better. His crew had set up a place for dancing, and a couple of men had brought their fiddles. Albeit not as freely as the other couples because of his limp, Jesse had still managed to dance the last two sets, and Evaleen couldn't remember a time she'd felt happier.

They began the sweet strains of a slow waltz, and without asking, Jesse put his hand on the small of her back and swung her gently through the first swaying steps. Feeling his hand through the silk of her dress, his palm warm against her spine, Evaleen imagined it moving up her bare back and circling around to massage her breasts. Sighing, she leaned closer against him.

"Ah, sweetheart," Jesse murmured. "Eventually, you *are* going to have to give up and admit you like me."

"Never," she said. But a smile lifted the edges of her lips as she glanced up at him. "Or maybe five minutes from now. I'll let you know when I decide for sure."

He grinned. The music quickened its tempo, but the two of them stood where they were, almost oblivious to the other couples swirling around them. All she could think about was him, and he didn't seem that eager to leave her side, either. She tugged at his shoulder until he leaned down to where he could hear her.

"You can go talk to your friends now," she said into his ear.

"You want to get rid of me?"

She shook her head. "I just wanted to give you a way out of dancing with me—in case you were being too polite to tell me."

He raised his eyebrows. "Me? Too polite?"

"True." She tapped her forehead. "What could I have been thinking?"

"I'm making you lose your mind, huh?"

"Is that what's been happening to me today?"

He laughed loudly, and Evaleen thought maybe it was the best thing in the world, making Jesse laugh.

Making Jesse happy.

"I think my sense of humor has rubbed off on you," he said, hooking his arm around her waist and guiding her through the dancing couples to the relative calmness around the tables of food.

The fact that Jesse was not making a beeline for his friends now that he'd proven to the public he was an attentive husband was such a change, Evaleen had to ask. "Are you feeling all right, Jesse?"

"Funny, the way we've been getting along, I was about to ask you the same thing."

They laughed again, and Jesse got some lemonade for her. While she wanted to tell herself this change in Jesse was too sudden to be true, thinking back over the past few weeks, Evaleen had to admit the change hadn't been sudden at all. The signs that Jesse was a good man had always been there; she'd just been fighting him too hard to see them. When it came to giving of his heart and his time, he'd been like a father to Theodora from the beginning. That was something no one could have taught him. The same was true when it came to the ranch; no one cared about his home and his land more than Jesse.

And now he seemed totally serious about making her happy as well.

Jesse brought back two cups of lemonade for them, which, thirsty after the dancing, they swiftly downed. Then Jesse put her cup and his on the table, took her hand in his large, warm one, and lowered his head until his lips were tantalizingly close to her ear. "We have to talk."

Sensing the disapproving eyes on them as they walked away from the crowd, she protested. "It's not right of us to leave our own party."

"We'll only be gone for a few minutes," he said, continuing to tug her gently away. Not wanting to be the topic of people's gossip, but not wanting to lose the special rapport she'd been building with Jesse either, she went with him, laughing at the game he was playing.

"All right, but whatever this is, it had better be fast," she threatened lightly when they reached the front porch. "And it had better be worth it."

"I'll guarantee this will be more than worth putting up with a little gossip," Jesse replied, right before he stopped and turned to draw her into his arms. Before she knew what was happening, she found herself flat against his chest, so close she could feel his heartbeat. Her breath caught and blood began to hum in her ears, and as she gazed up into the gray-blue smokiness of his eyes, it seemed she was losing her ability to think and reason. All that was left was to feel.

He leaned down and met her lips with a tender kiss that warmed her insides with its seductiveness. When he finally drew his face back from hers, leaving her wanting more, she could only sigh.

"I am worth it, huh?" he asked, smiling.

"You put a very high value on yourself," she teased back. "Maybe I want more for my money."

"Oh, Evaleen," he said with mock regret. "No matter what we do, we still have to challenge each other, don't we?" Without giving her a chance to reply, he kissed her again, but this time was different. This time his lips were demanding, probing, and anything but gentle. This time he seemed to be responding to the need that had been building up inside both of them all day, or maybe ever since they'd met. He parted her mouth with gentle pressure from his own, and their tongues danced, making her knees go weak. He seemed to be touching her everywhere, and she forgot to care as her heart thumped against her ribs and her insides went hot with need.

This time she was the one who pulled back, and she brought a hand to cover her kiss-swollen mouth as her chest rose and fell with her rapid breathing. All she could do was stare at him.

"I wish this was for real, Jesse."

"What's between us *is* real, Evie," he said, his voice low and husky.

"I mean our marriage."

"So do I. In fact, I have something for you to prove it." Jesse pulled a small white box out of his pocket. "I want to give you this."

She smiled with pleasure as she took it and untied the ribbon. Taking off the lid, she revealed a lovely, shining gold band that caught the sun rays in an almost magical aura, and she raised her eyes to stare questioningly at Jesse.

"It was my mother's," he said quietly, and she could see the seriousness in his eyes. "I know it isn't real fancy, but she believed the love in the marriage would shine through the ring and make it beautiful." He took it out of the box, and Evaleen watched as, with his large hand, he slipped it on her ring finger. It fit well enough for it to stay on, almost as if it was meant to be on her finger.

"Oh, Jess," she whispered. He was making her feel so special, something she had wanted all her life to be but had never become. Special. To anyone. "Are you sure you want me to have this?"

"It was the only thing Mama left to me when she died. I wouldn't give it to anyone but the woman I planned to be married to forever."

"Forever," she whispered. Staring into his eyes, she shook her head in wistful denial. "I don't understand. You could have your pick of women, Jess. I'm plain and stubborn and argumentative, and we mostly get along like oil and water. What hope could I possibly have of keeping you happy?"

Jesse stared at her for what seemed like a long time. "You don't see it, do you?"

She shook her head.

"You've supported your aunt for years all by yourself. That alone is remarkable. But then you came here and put up with the worst I could possibly dish out and didn't turn tail and run, just so you could be sure to be the one to give Theodora a home with a family who loves her."

"I didn't have a choice," she said softly. "I still don't see—"

Reaching out, Jesse gently touched her lips with his finger. "Not only are you hardworking and brave, you've got more character in one fingernail than any of the other women I've ever met. Every step of the way, I've been fighting you, but you never gave up trying to help me get my ranch back. I've learned to admire and respect you, and I can't say the same for the other females I've ... known."

The meaning of his hesitation wasn't lost on her, but

he was paying her the highest of compliments, so she overlooked it and let him finish.

Maybe, she thought, she, like Jesse, was changing.

"Only since you moved in here have I realized how lonely I've been since my mother died," Jesse continued, staring beyond her off at the range. "She was the one who tied the four of us together. After she was gone, my brother got worse and worse, so I steered clear of him. I always suspected that to my father, I was little more than another hired hand."

"How horrible it must have been for you." With all her siblings, and then with working and having her aunt Victoria always around, loneliness was one thing Evaleen couldn't recall ever feeling. She wondered if that was why he'd started being the rogue. To get someone—anyone— to notice he was alive.

"Yeah, well," he said, turning back to her. "I've done some stupid things in my life, Evie, and probably will do a few more, but marrying you wasn't one of them. Your character alone would be enough to make me want you as a wife, but, Evie honey, you aren't plain. When you look at Theodora, your heart's in your smile and your love for her lights your eyes. I'd give anything for a woman like you to look at me like that."

Taken aback, she could only stare.

"When you're smiling, Evie, I think you're the prettiest woman I've ever laid eyes on."

Evaleen's heart melted. The moment was so tender, so right, that when he leaned down and kissed her lips, and then moved his mouth down to the side of her neck and farther, she couldn't say a word.

"I want to consummate our marriage, Evie," he whispered near her ear as his hand trailed a path up and down the small of her back. "Prove to you that it's real. Come upstairs with me, honey."

She drew a sharp breath. The very idea of making love with Jesse both thrilled and frightened her. Most of her wanted to, but . . .

"It's too soon," she said, scarcely breathing over the thumping of her heart. "I need some time to think about what you've said and how I feel, and . . ." Her voice trailed off, and she lifted tentative fingers to touch the side of his mouth. As she did, his mother's gold wedding ring glinted in the sun. "I'm sorry."

He groaned softly with disappointment, but she could tell he wasn't angry. "Maybe," he said, "you should stop thinking for once and just give in to your feelings."

Breaking into a smile, she lifted her eyebrows questioningly. "Does that order apply when I feel like braining you with a skillet?"

He shook his head negatively, also smiling. "If you need time, you need time. I'll be here if you change your mind." Planting a fast kiss on her cheek, he turned away and took the porch steps slowly.

"Is your leg bothering you?" she asked over the side of the porch.

"Nope," he said cheerfully, waving at her. "I'm favoring it for later—just in case." He gave her the most devilish wink she'd ever seen, and as he rounded the corner of the house and went out of sight, Evaleen could hear him start to whistle.

Alone, she leaned against the railing and looked out past the carriages over the acres of land that comprised Rainbow's End, her mind still racing and her lips warmed by the brand of his kiss. Jesse wanted *her*—he really did. By giving her his mother's wedding band and confessing his innermost thoughts to her, he'd proven that his feelings ran deep. She'd wanted to go upstairs with him the very second he'd asked.

So why hadn't she? Because of what had happened to

her sister, she thought immediately. Cynthia had not used her head when it came to men. They'd used her and she'd ended up paying. Evaleen had lived with that knowledge and had been afraid to give her heart to any man for so long, now she didn't know if she could.

But Jesse wasn't just any man; already he'd become special to her. She stared down at his mother's ring. He was also on his way to winning the respect of the town. Everything was so right now.

She pushed away from the rail and hurried down the steps to go find him. Jesse was changed to the point where he wanted a home and a family—and her. She finally had to let herself believe in him, trust in her ability to know when a man was for real. She wasn't her sister. She wouldn't be making a mistake in giving herself to Jesse.

He was a good man.

Staying married to Jesse just might work out for the best all around, she told herself. Theodora would have a bona fide father who loved her, Jesse would have the home and family he wanted, and she ... well, she would have someone to love—and someone who could love her in return.

She couldn't wait to tell him she was ready to love him after all.

Jesse knew without saying that Evaleen wasn't going to like this. How in the hell he had gotten himself cornered in a tiny supply shed by a *female*, he couldn't begin to say. It had all started when Miss Worrell, Theodora's schoolteacher, had asked him if Theodora was supposed to be playing out by the storage shed, so far away from the party. The shed was a couple of hundred yards behind the barn, too far away for Theodora to be playing alone with his brother still on the loose and watching her. Cursing himself for not making arrangements for someone to watch the child while he'd been talking to Evaleen, he'd hurried to check on her.

Seeing the shed door wide open, he'd called for Theodora to come out, but no one had answered. There was no sign of her anywhere, so Jesse had stuck his head inside the dark area, called her name, and heard a scratching sound. The second he'd gotten to the far end of the tool shed, the door had been shut behind him.

Trapped.

Whirling around and drawing his pistol, he'd fully expected to find a smirking Patrick. Instead, what he saw in the dim light streaming in from the holes in the roof was Miss Worrell, the schoolmarm. She was smiling at him, like the cat who'd caught the canary. He recalled the times he'd let her think he was interested in her to get her to help him with Dorie, and he knew he was in trouble.

It wasn't as though this type of thing hadn't happened to him before—it had. Pretty women cornering him in interesting places with offers. But that was then, and now he had Evaleen to think about. Now he minded.

Where Miss Worrell was concerned, he should have expected a trap, too. She'd been sending him moonfaced looks since he'd arrived with Evaleen.

"I decided this might be the only way for us to have a serious . . . talk," Miss Worrell told him. Her hand went to her throat, and she unbuttoned the first button of her high collar as she stepped forward.

Jesse didn't quite think talking was what she had in mind. It was time to show how much he'd changed. He couldn't resort to glibness as he once would have. This was serious. "I know what I implied the couple of times we've spoken, but, Miss Worrell, surely you can see that with my marriage, things have changed."

"I can't see any reason for you to withdraw your offer.

In fact, I've been waiting a while for you to come around, and I thought you might need some prompting."

This was Evaleen's fault, Jesse thought. If she had just said yes to making love earlier, he'd be cozy with her instead of in this trap.

"The rumor, Mr. Stockton," Maggie added, "is that you were forced into marrying Miss Murphy."

"Now who would spread a rumor like that?" He gave her his boldest grin. "Me? Forced into intimacy with a woman?"

"Not intimacy." Miss Worrell stepped closer and reached out to touch Jesse's shirt, her fingers gliding down the front of it until Jesse stopped her by gently pushing her hand away. But that didn't seem to stop her.

"Rumor also has it, Mr. Stockton, that you and Miss Murphy don't share a marital bed."

"Now that's a nasty rumor. I'm surprised you ladies don't have anything more constructive to talk about." He frowned at her. "Are you going to let me get back to my wife, Miss Worrell?"

"Maggie." She smiled at him again and moved back until her hips hid the door handle. "Aren't you in the least bit curious as to what I'm wearing under this skirt?"

"No," he said lowly.

"Nothing. And I don't care about your wife."

"I do." Jesse could feel anger start to heat up deep inside him, and he purposely worked to control his temper. He had a feeling it wouldn't pay to get angry with the schoolmarm. Physical, that she'd probably enjoy. But angry, no. He was starting to get the impression from her cat-eyed gaze and manner that she had a nasty streak and would do what she damned well pleased to get her way.

He wondered if he should approach the school board about her unsuitability to teach the children in Raton.

"I'm getting out of here, Miss Worrell, one way or

another. Am I going to have to pick you up and move you?"

"I'll scream and tell everyone you tricked me into coming here so you could enjoy yourself," she threatened.

"Come now, Miss Worrell, you're forgetting my reputation. Everyone knows I don't have to trick women into anything. They come willingly."

"I'll tell your wife you've been carrying on with me ever since our first meeting," she said, her voice even.

Now that Evaleen might believe; their relationship was just that tenuous. He tensed and then scowled when he saw Maggie Worrell smile. She'd sucker punched him, and now she was sure of his weakness—Evaleen. He didn't want his wife getting hurt, not by him, not by rumor, not by *anything*, but the worst thing he could have done was let his enemy know his Achilles heel.

And there was now no doubt about it. If he didn't show Miss Worrell a good time, he was going to have one formidable opponent to his future happiness. Standing there, wishing for a miracle, he cursed his rakish past.

# Chapter Fifteen

Evaleen told Theodora to stay with Victoria, then hurried away from the happy crowd of townspeople and the gay music, a sinking feeling in the pit of her stomach. Jesse had last been seen speaking with Maggie Worrell, and now she couldn't find him.

Her feet went into frenzied motion as her heart clenched. Why had her life suddenly grown so complicated? Jesse wanted her. Miss Worrell, judging by the cow eyes she'd been making at Jesse all afternoon, wanted Jesse, apparently badly enough to lure him away from the party. And Evaleen herself? All she'd ever wanted was to be happy.

But right now, she definitely was not.

Rounding the barn, she walked a hundred yards down the path, and a few feet from the closed storage shed, she quickly saw that no one was around it. Inside the shed, however, was a different matter. She could hear Jesse's voice, cajoling and reasonable.

"Now, Maggie, you know I find you very attractive. But whatever I implied before, I can't follow through on now. I'm married."

Whatever Miss Worrell replied was too low to hear, but after a few seconds, Jesse added, "I've got to leave, now. People will miss us."

"I guess it probably would be better if we practice discretion," Miss Worrell answered. "I want to make sure there's a next time."

"There won't be."

Red-hot anger flushed Evaleen's face as she yanked open the door. The first things she saw, over Maggie Worrell's shoulder, were Jesse's startled eyes. His look changed into one of gratefulness that held nothing of the self-satisfaction and devil-may-care attitude he'd displayed when she'd confronted him about his womanizing with the headmistress of Theodora's school. Instead, he was imploring her with his smoky-sky gaze to understand that things weren't as they appeared to be. There was a softening in his eyes that said he was actually glad she was there.

Miss Worrell turned, and then, slowly, a faint smile crossed her lips. "A little late, Mrs. Stockton," she said, taking great pains to button up the top of her bodice before brushing past Evaleen and walking away.

Evaleen didn't want to think about her. At the moment, she cared only about Jesse and what he was trying to tell her with his eyes. His serious gaze seemed glued to her face, and for a few seconds, the two of them stared at each other.

"What just happened?" Evaleen asked softly.

His look was one of pure innocence. "Danged if I know."

The two of them heard a barely disguised harrumph of displeasure behind them, which finally broke Jesse's concentration as he looked up to see who had made the sound. Mrs. Grover was walking away at breakneck speed, apparently to spread the gossip of what she'd just seen—the schoolmarm having an assignation with the town's bad boy.

"There goes my reputation," Jesse said idly, but his face never lost its worried look. Compelled to turn around herself to see who was leaving, Evaleen crossed her arms over her chest and sighed.

"I didn't plan to meet Maggie," Jesse said before she could ask. "You believe that, don't you?"

Did she? Gazing into the depths of his eyes, Evaleen searched for the truth, and in the span of the next silent moment, she remembered a lot of things.

Jesse's devotion to Theodora, for one. For another, how he had married her to save her reputation even though he didn't have to and hadn't even liked her, and also how he had been behaving himself since the marriage so that she wouldn't be the subject of ridicule in town for having married the town's rogue.

And she remembered the wedding band on her finger. He'd planned this party for her, complete with the wedding cake and his mother's ring, because he'd wanted to make her happy. Would he really have given away something that had meant so much to his mother, and thus to him, if he hadn't planned on their marriage lasting?

She didn't think so.

In that second, Evaleen came to the decision that, just as Jesse seemed to be, she was in this for the long haul, whether there ever was a ribbon of love between them or not. Blinking, she gazed back into his eyes.

"I believe you," she said simply.

A rush of sheer bliss overcame Jesse. With the possible exception of Waco, who had a dubious past himself, no one had taken him at his word in a long, long time. Evaleen, with all her character, believing in him meant more than anything to him at that moment.

He held out his arms to her. Without a second's hesitation, she flew into his embrace and rested her cheek against his broad shoulder.

"Your faith in me means more than I can say, Evie," he told her in barely a whisper. "I'm going to do everything in my power to make sure you're never sorry for that trust."

She tilted her head up to gaze at him. "Can we make this marriage work, Jess? Can we really?"

"We can try." He angled his head down until his lips met hers, and then he was kissing her and she forgot her doubts, her fears, and her anger at Maggie Worrell for disturbing the precarious balance of her life. Evaleen forgot everything but the tenderness of the moment, and the gentleness of Jesse's lips on hers.

For a long moment they kissed each other with that same sweetness, and then Jesse clenched his arm more tightly around her waist, clutching her against his rock-solid form, evoking a sigh of contentment from deep inside of her. She was finally in the right place, she told herself, Jesse's arms. She wasn't sure that her sister had been entirely wrong about men—the Lord knew Jesse had his moments—but right here, right now, she was sure she didn't want him to go away.

Jesse deepened his kiss, and the most beguiling of urges drifted up through her like smoke from a fire. She lifted her arms to circle his neck and let herself be engulfed in the pleasure of his kiss. Despite her lack of experience with men, the intensity of the way he was holding her told her that Jesse could not possibly want her this much if he really desired Miss Worrell. The womanly side of Evaleen reveled in the newfound realization of her power.

She parted her lips when his tongue prodded and went weak kneed with the pleasure of it darting and dancing with hers. Jesse pulled her backward until his back was against the shed, kissing her all the while. Finally, breathless and hot with desire from his pressing against her, she had to pull away.

"The party, Jesse," she uttered. "We have guests."

"Hang the guests." His hand cupped her cheek. "I've wanted you for so long, Evie, and I know you want me. Do you really want to wait?"

"No," she whispered. She was married to Jesse, but the marriage would never work without lovemaking, even she knew that. And without a doubt, with all her heart, she wanted it to work. She wanted Jesse, and she wanted to be his—all his.

"But where, Jess?" she asked. She could feel the heat from his open hands on her back through her Sunday best, urging her closer to him.

"Down by the water?" he suggested. When she nodded, he took her hand. Together they rushed farther away from the party and the real world that awaited them, closer to their future.

Minutes later, down at the same knoll where they'd once fought, Jesse spread his jacket on the ground. Then, still desperate to have the love they'd been denied for so long, Evaleen and Jesse went into each other's arms and sank onto the cloth-covered grass.

Reaching forward, Jesse pulled pins out of her hair, which tumbled in waves around her shoulders. Then he unbuttoned the tiny pearl buttons of her blue silk dress, one by one, gradually exposing first her cleavage and then her chemise to his hungry gaze. Slipping her silk dress off her shoulders, he leaned down to kiss each expanse of flesh next to the lace straps of her chemise.

As she watched, he deftly removed both the dress and her corset and laid them down at his side. After that, he stared at the rose nipples straining against the batiste of her chemise. Watching him look at her took Evaleen's breath away. Suddenly, with an urgency that didn't know reason, she wanted to feel his lips, there, on her now-sensitive bosom. Slipping her hands below her breasts, she tilted them upward and whispered his name.

It was all the invitation he needed. Covering one of the peaks with his mouth, he sucked and licked through the thin material until the pleasure bubbling deep within her became unbearable. Together, they fell backward onto their bed of grass.

Reaching up, Evaleen looped her arms around his neck and met his lips with her own. The muscles of his shoulders hardened under her fingers and in an age-old response, her lower regions began to grow soft and wet with need. His mouth played with hers, coaxing her into sweet oblivion. She ran her fingers up and down his muscular arms and then reached for the buttons of his shirt, pulling them open as he untied her petticoat and pushed it free of her legs.

Kissing him with an urgency stemming from her need, Evaleen pushed all thoughts of her sister's tragic end aside and slipped his shirt off his shoulders. Being here like this with Jesse felt so good that she was filled with joy. The townspeople, Reynard Stockton, Mrs. Grover—they were all wrong about Jesse. He'd changed. She'd never been so sure about anything in her life, just as she was positive that nothing bad was going to come of her loving him. She just knew it.

His hands cupped her bottom, and mindlessly yearning for fulfillment, she shifted her hips upward against the hardness of his manhood. Her tongue danced with his as she rubbed the taut, warm skin of his shoulders. But then his lips moved down her sensitive skin as he sampled the delights of her other breast, and the heat within her blazed.

Evaleen moaned low in her throat. There was something driving her she could not fight and did not understand. She didn't want him to stop touching her—ever.

Almost mindless with need, Jesse reached for the ribbon of her drawers and undid the bow with one hand. She stopped him long enough for them to kick off their shoes. Then he peeled the drawers off her legs, revealing her sheer stockings with lace-covered garters and the vee of dark hair leading to her femininity.

Jesse's insides clenched.

He cast her underwear aside. Beneath his hands her skin was now bare, smooth, and well rounded, and he rubbed his palms over her buttocks, kissing the tops of her breasts. She was all womanly curves and flesh, and he groaned under his breath with his need to possess her. Leaving her chemise on, he gently rolled her onto her side and slipped his fingers between her thighs.

Evaleen gasped with pleasure. An inkling of fear passed through her, but she let that trepidation pass to some distant region of her mind. For now, she just let herself respond to the bliss wrought by Jesse's fingers.

Her lips went wild on his neck, gently sucking and pulling at his taut skin until Jesse thought he was going to explode. Sensing her urgency, he reached down for the buttons on his trousers, but then he remembered how she'd stopped him the last time. How she'd been too frightened to go on. "Are you sure?" he whispered.

She met his gaze, and Jesse thought the irises of her eyes had never been so huge, so vivid green, and so filled with desire. "Yes," she said, her voice downy soft. Certain. Trusting.

He would not betray that trust, he vowed. Ever.

Jesse shed his trousers and underwear as Evaleen watched, the throbbing in her feminine regions increasing as she witnessed his nakedness once more. Not wanting to take the time to think, and trusting the man next to her with her life and her heart, she threw her body against his, put her arms around his neck, and started kissing him again with abandonment.

She barely felt his hands slipping into her abundance of hair as he rolled her onto her back. Her thighs parted for him in direct reaction to her desire to have his body closer to hers and his manhood hot and throbbing against her wetness. He covered her mouth once more, shifted his hips, and gently began to push her into full womanhood.

Evaleen could feel the tearing and the stinging, and she uttered a startled gasp as some of her pleasure cooled. But Jesse went so slowly, not hurting her more, and kissed her so fully that she was soon arching toward him in another surge of passion.

His tongue probed and his lips kissed, and soon the pleasurable sensations warmed her to her toes. There was nothing like this, nothing that could compare to his lovemaking. Caressing his buttocks, Evaleen pushed him farther into her, until the heated desire mounted and surged and mounted again, and she didn't even notice the leaves waving gently in the breeze above her head or hear that the faint strains of music from the party had abruptly stopped. She didn't sense anything except the exquisiteness of being there with Jesse. Just when she thought the pleasure could not possibly be greater, stars shone behind her closed eyelids and she reached the brink of fulfillment. She fell still as her body flooded with a peacefulness unlike any she'd ever known.

Sensing Evaleen was satisfied, Jesse let himself go. Seconds later, his need for her at least momentarily satiated, he nestled himself against the comfort of her body. She was his. He wasn't going to let her go anywhere at the end of six months. For all her stubbornness, Evaleen was the first woman he'd ever met who had the passion and the fight and the drive to match his.

At this moment of absolute clarity about his life, Jesse

realized that his lack of commitment to women in the past had been due to his waiting for a woman like Evaleen to fill the aching void in his life with the strength and caring that only a woman like her could give him. The other ladies had all needed him to be the leader, the teaser, so they would never have to take the responsibility for what they wanted from him—which in most of the cases had been only sex. He never got their attention unless he played the role of charmer. They'd wanted him only because he made them feel desirable as women.

But not Evaleen. She was smart enough to know exactly what she was getting in him, but she seemed to want him anyway. God knew he hadn't been charming her—anything but. But she was still willing to take him as he was, flaws and all, and that meant more to him than she could ever know.

What had happened to her? Evaleen sighed underneath Jesse, not even feeling his weight. Desire and the need to be loved were such powerful things she had ceased being rational. All she'd known was the aching desire to have him fill her body and her heart in ways she'd only suspected, but wasn't sure about.

Now that she knew the strong lure of lovemaking, she marveled at Jesse's previous ability to stop the other two times when she'd pulled away. That made her even more aware of how much integrity he had. The only thing she wasn't sure about was what would come next in their relationship. Now that they had crossed over, she didn't really know what to say to Jesse, or how to act.

He kissed her cheek and rolled onto his side. For a few seconds he watched her, and then he smiled. "I guess we should get back to the party, see how much damage Mrs. Grover has done."

The party! Evaleen's eyes widened in horror. She'd been so totally wrapped up in Jesse she'd forgotten the yard was filled with their guests. "We do have to get back there, Jesse," she said, grabbing her underthings and yanking them back on. "No doubt by now that woman has told them the whole story about how you were caught in the storage shed with their exalted schoolmarm and they're forming a lynch party."

"What a way to go!" Jesse paused in his dressing to put a hand on his neck. "You won't let them hang me, will you, darlin'?"

"No," she said, smiling sweetly. "Because even if you *had* been up to something with Miss Worrell, hanging you would be *my* prerogative, not theirs."

He chuckled low in his throat. "That'll be a comforting thought in the dead of night when we're sharing a bed."

The idea that they actually had a future together made Evaleen smile for all of three seconds, until she remembered the sobering thought that she would have to deal with the people of the town way before any future came. From what she'd heard, Miss Worrell was much admired and well respected. And to be sure, with Jesse's roguish reputation, what Mrs. Grover had heard was sure to come out against him, no matter what the truth was.

By promising to love, honor, and keep Jesse Stockton, she thought, bemused, she had sure bitten off a lot to chew.

On his feet, Patrick Stockton shifted from his spot, angled across the lake from where his brother had just been snaking around in the grass with Evaleen. His plan to snatch the kid wasn't working; Theodora was too well watched. If the old lady wasn't right with her, or his brother's wife, then that bastard hand Waco was never out of shouting distance from the kid. The only real chance he'd had to take her was outside the school grounds in Raton, but then one of the town biddies had happened along, and he'd had to run before someone recognized him and discovered he wasn't really dead like the old man had said he was.

He'd been camped out here—after all, it was Stockton land—when he'd woken up to see his brother and his wife rising up from the ground buck naked. Figuring exactly what they'd been doing and that he'd missed the whole show had put him in a cussed mood. From the time his father had declared him dead and told him not to come back, his damned brother had gotten everything—the ranch, Theodora, and now a wife he wouldn't mind humping himself.

He let out a slow breath. He'd stayed away as long as his father was alive, but now he was back to get what was rightfully his. As first son, he should have been the one to inherit Rainbow's End. Theodora was his daughter by anyone's standards; Cynthia might have spread her legs for any man that walked by, but not while she was living with him. He'd knocked all that lustful thinking out of her. And she had been all his before she went crying to his father, thinking that Reynard would have the power to protect her. That was right, because he couldn't return to the ranch to get her off.

So that made two out of three. With eyes that were reddened from too much liquor and smoke and too many late nights, Patrick stared at Evaleen Murphy Stockton as she hurried up the hill, with Jesse following her like a worshipful puppy. She was buttoning her blue dress over tits like he'd never seen. Sweat began to trickle down his back just at the thought of having her himself.

But it wouldn't be rape—oh, no. Eventually, he'd have everything Jesse had, including his curvaceous wife.

Hell. Now he was gonna have to break out of hiding one more time and get him some of his own.

And after that, he was going to find some way to rid himself of Jesse and get everything he deserved. It shouldn't be too hard. From what he'd just seen, he thought he knew where his brother's Achilles heel was. . . .

His new wife.

# Chapter Sixteen

The first thing Evaleen noticed before they even drew close to the party was that the music had stopped. She let go of Jesse's hand and swept slightly nervous fingers over her bodice and hair, checking for anything out of place that might announce what they'd just been doing to the world.

Jesse reached up and let two gossamer-soft locks fall across his fingers, just to remind himself of how good they'd felt to his touch when they'd been back by the river.

How good she'd felt.

"You're still a little disheveled," he told her. "Want some help?"

Nodding, she cast another glance toward the barn. "Hurry though. The music has stopped, and I have a feeling that means they're waiting for us to return."

Jesse's fingers were once again touching her, diverting her attention for a moment. He was surprisingly skillful, picking one of her hairpins out of a hastily woven braid, winding her loose locks around the bun, and tucking and pinning it in place.

"You did that like you've done it a hundred times," she had to say, her lips poised on the edge of a smile.

"Never with hair as beautiful as yours," he said easily, patting the bun he'd just fixed.

"What blarney comes out of you, Jesse," she told him, grinning.

He faked a hurt look. "Other ladies always called it charm."

She laughed nervously, Jesse noticed, glancing and then glancing again over her shoulder toward the barn. They knew their guests were on the other side of it. "I hate it when people gossip," she told him when he took her hand.

"I won't let them hurt you."

"I don't think it can be stopped." She shook her head sadly and walked with him. "That's why Cynthia killed herself, you know. She couldn't stand the gossip any longer."

That took Jesse by surprise. His former stepmother had seemed too full of herself and her own desires to ever sink that low. Stopping abruptly, he faced her. "I had no idea. How?"

"Poison." Evaleen pressed her lips together to force back the sadness that threatened to overwhelm her every time she thought of the tragedy her sister's life had become. "Men pushed her over the edge, Jesse. They always demanded of her, never gave back. She wrote me everything in a note." This last she said so softly he wouldn't have heard her had he not been right in front of her. "I found her body."

"That must have been horrible," Jesse said gently, taking both her hands in his. He was starting to understand a little better why it had been so hard to reach Evaleen. Now he could see the hurt and the vulnerability in her eyes, so he decided it was not the time to tell her that from what he'd seen, Cynthia had gotten back from people about as much as she gave, which was little to nothing.

Having a wife who didn't care a lick about him sounded like a pretty good bet for what could have helped turn his father so bitter, Jesse realized now—too late. Had he thought about it earlier, maybe he could have been more understanding.

His thoughts turned back to Cynthia. Somehow, the ivory princess, as he'd overheard the cowhands calling her one time, killing herself still didn't seem right to him. Jesse had a feeling there was more to the story.

A lot more.

They rounded the corner of the barn. Out of the three dozen people who had attended the party, only the minister and his wife, Grover and his missus, and Victoria and Calloway remained. They were gathered in a line as though they'd been waiting for Evaleen and Jesse to show up. Their lips were pursed, their eyes condemning.

Jesse let out a long, irreverent whistle. "Looks like the party's over, Evie."

She seemed to want to smile, but didn't, because that wouldn't be Evaleen. But neither, Jesse thought, did she give him a lecture on his deportment, which he supposed reflected the improved state in their relationship. He squeezed her hand and let it go, looking for Theodora.

The child had retired—or had been sent—to the porch, where she sat with a doll, silently observing the grown-ups as though she knew something was wrong. Miss Worrell, Jesse noticed with a great surge of relief, didn't appear to be in evidence.

Inwardly, he had to grin. He'd never thought he'd see the day when he preferred not to see an attractive female chasing after him, but darn it anyway, the day had come.

Heading straight for the porch, Jesse said to a worried-looking Theodora, "I think you'd better go inside, Dorie."

"Are you in trouble again, Uncle Jesse?"

Despite the gravity of the situation, Jesse shot her a cockeyed grin. "Would you worry if I was?"

Standing, Theodora regarded him gravely. "No, because you have a talent for getting yourself out of miserable situations."

He laughed aloud this time, ignoring the disgruntled sounds that came from the minister and his wife. "How do you know that?"

"It's what Aunt Victoria always tells Mr. Nesmith." She grinned and gave him a quick kiss on the cheek. "Checkers after you're done arguing, Uncle Jess?"

"If they don't give me a necktie party out here first."

"Oh, goodie, another party!" Theodora skipped to the door and went inside, leaving Jesse to his fate.

He turned to find Evaleen right behind him, her eyebrows raised in mock chagrin. "You're spoiling her, Jess."

He grinned. "I plan to spoil you, too, if you'd just let me."

Once Theodora was gone, Reverend Mortenson could wait no longer. "As you probably know, Jesse, Miss Worrell isn't very happy right now."

"Well, neither am I," Evaleen broke in softly. "Miss Worrell purposely tricked my husband to lure him away from me—at my own wedding party. I don't think she needs to be teaching children, do you?"

The reverend look flustered, but then quickly recovered. "That wasn't what Miss Worrell told us."

Evaleen gazed at them all, totally aware of Jesse by her side. "I'm sure Miss Worrell would like to believe my husband wants her, but I assure you, she has read more into words he spoke in the past than he intended." Jesse was gently squeezing her hand and reminding her that she was not alone as she faced the judgmental group in front of them and, with any luck, would never be alone again. Evaleen experienced another surge of happiness, until she viewed the skepticism on everyone's faces.

With her inner need for acceptance—Cynthia's ostracism was hard for her to forget—their doubts about Jesse's innocence lay heavy on her heart, because a short while ago, she would have been the first to believe he had wangled a clandestine meeting with Miss Worrell, married man or not. But now she knew another side of Jesse, and it was up to her to make them see it too.

She returned each of their looks with a censuring one of her own. "You all surely aren't giving me much credit for keeping my marriage happy if you're thinking Jesse's already running to other women."

"Mrs. Stockton..." Calloway stepped forward, rubbing his chin, looking chagrined. "We know how hard you've tried to make a solid citizen out of Jesse. We also know how much you've suffered from being forced into marriage with him. Reverend Mortenson and I have discussed this, and we believe, after what was seen today, that we owe you our apologies and, of course, the offer to annul your marriage and still let you keep custody of Theodora."

Evaleen gasped with indignation. From the smug look on the face of the reverend's wife, she had the feeling the idea of the offer had probably stemmed from her. The sanctimonious so-and-sos! There had to be some way to prove to them she believed Jesse had changed....

She had it. Turning to face Jesse, she looped her arms around his neck and gave him a kiss. Her point proven, she would have stopped and stepped back, but Jesse hung on to her and deepened the kiss until her heart was racing. Finally, she pulled away, and shot Jesse a narrow-eyed stare of disapproval that she wasn't at all certain she meant before turning back to the man who'd spoken.

"Did that look like I'm suffering, Solicitor?"

"My word, you poor dear!" Mrs. Grover said, waving her fan quickly near her bright red cheeks. Evaleen wondered if she was so embarrassed because she was remembering the sight of Jesse, naked. "He's gone and used his charm to totally fool you, too."

Evaleen watched all of them nod in agreement, like a line of puppets on a string in a marionette show. Her eyes rested on her aunt Victoria, who wore a very worried expression. "I thought you, at least, were finally for our marriage."

"I was, Evaleen." Victoria gave Jesse another long look. "Until Jesse was caught behind closed doors with Miss Worrell. I'm surprised you're taking that so well."

"Nothing at all happened," Jesse swore. "I was looking for Dorie and then, suddenly, Miss Worrell showed up."

"That wasn't the version we received from Margaret," the minister's wife said. "And, of course, with her fine standing in the community, we must regard her version with a bit more weight than yours, Mr. Stockton."

"Not to mention you didn't deny a thing when someone at the poker game mentioned you painting the town red with Miss Worrell," Grover added. "Or so I heard."

Jesse's eyes narrowed. The rumor. He should have stopped it then. Obviously Maggie had been planning on trapping him for a while. He just had to wonder what the hell had taken her so long to make her move.

"I never touched Maggie Worrell, Evie," Jesse swore to her in a low voice.

"I believe you, Jess." And she did. She wanted to shake all of the people standing around in her yard, one by one, until their teeth fell out. But with Jesse's arm wrapped around her waist, she was forced to stay where she was. "Doesn't my belief in Jesse mean anything?"

"Evaleen, we are all forced to admit there are certain

factors about your husband which might tend to sway an inexperienced woman's better sense to the wrong side of thinking about things," Calloway said. Reaching into his pocket, he pulled out a handkerchief and wiped at the sweat beading on his brow. "That is to say, we suspect he's had enough time to woo you over to his way of thinking. Remember, he gave you no end of trouble in the first few weeks you were here, sneaking around and doing exactly what he pleased."

"We're married now. He's settled down. Changed."

"Humph!" Mrs. Mortenson said.

Something inside Evaleen clenched. She could read the look on Mrs. Grover's face; she instinctively knew what was coming.

"Leopards don't change their spots," the woman sniffed. "And if you insist on standing behind a man who has such a depraved character, Mrs. Stockton, don't think you'll get such a wonderful reception in town at my store as heretofore."

The woman's haughty tone reminded Evaleen of when Cynthia had taken her out to the market in the old neighborhood after her sister's reputation had gone bad.

Glancing at Jesse, she was surprised to find him staring at her with those intense blue-gray eyes of his. Caught up at once in his stare, she knew what she would have to do—prove to them all, somehow, that Jesse was now a man of integrity.

Reynard's will had come full circle.

Silently, she turned to Jesse and gave him a look that she hoped told him he was not to worry, and then she pivoted and walked into the house without saying anything to the townsfolk. Let them worry about what someone else thought for a change. They'd be sorry when she proved Jesse was a good man.

Assuming she could. She stopped and leaned her forehead against the door jamb. Jesse *was* a good man, but how on earth was she going to prove it to everyone else when they were ready to condemn him with every intake of breath?

It was something she couldn't get off her mind as she spent the rest of the day with Jesse, cleaning up the party mess and assuring him that she *had* chosen him, she just didn't know what on earth she was going to do about the closed-minded town. Her conviction that she had to do something increased during the following week as some of the people in town started taking pains to avoid her. And her joy at really finding love in Jesse's arms finally made her certain—she had to do something to make sure everyone else knew that Jesse Stockton was a good man, a strong man, who deserved their respect.

Finally, that evening after her aunt had retired for the night, she formulated a plan as she watched Jesse and a tired Theodora finishing up a last game of checkers. A little while later, as she slipped into bed with Jesse, she told him the first part of what she wanted to do and why.

As he pulled off her gown and tossed it over the side of the bed, he told her that although he understood why she wanted the town to believe him, he was worried about what she was planning.

"But it's a good idea," Evaleen insisted, rolling over on top of him. Her hair fell in long waves around his shoulders, and Jesse thought he'd never felt better than when her naked body was against his, her soft hair was tickling his skin, and her smile was warming his formerly lonely heart. He'd been with other women, but before Evaleen, he'd always been alone. Evaleen had made him part of a family again, had filled his empty places, had made him whole.

And he loved her for it.

"Let me make sure I have this straight," he said. "You will go to Miss Worrell, tell her that her campaign to win me will wreck our marriage, and plead with her to give up on me and go after some other man."

"Preferably unattached—like maybe Waco."

"I'm sure he'll appreciate that to no end," Jesse said drily, but he didn't smile.

The corners of her mouth lifted. "I'm glad you're taking this so seriously, Jess."

"Maggie Worrell is serious. I think she's determined to ruin me if I don't cave in to her wishes."

"Hmmm." She gazed at him thoughtfully. "Isn't that the same thing you said about me?"

"You were different. You were frustrating—irritating—and from the minute we met, I didn't desire anyone but you."

Warmth flooded through Evaleen as she felt the sudden evidence of that desire against her bare abdomen. She nuzzled her face in his neck, then went back up on her forearms. "Then how come you gave me so much trouble?"

"Because I didn't want to admit that after all his preaching Reynard could finally have been right—that I needed to change my ways." He ran his hands up and down the length of her body, stopping long enough to savor the soft curves of her breasts and to circle her nipples with his thumbs.

She shivered softly with anticipation. "Reynard wasn't one hundred percent right, Jess," she said. "Some of your old ways are just fine."

"Want me to show you another one of them?" he asked, lifting his head and running his lips along the curve of her neck.

"In a minute. We need to get the plan settled first."

Closing her eyes for a second, she mustered all the willpower she could and rolled away from him. She heard a rough sound deep in his throat.

"You can groan all you want," she said, "but we have to get part two of my plan settled first, and I don't think we can do that if we're all cuddled up together."

"Leave it to me to marry a woman who needs to be in charge," he muttered.

"After we discuss my plan to get Miss Worrell to leave you be and have everything back exactly the way Reynard envisioned it with you and the town; then I promise"—she circled her fingers along the broad expanse of his chest, started trailing them downward—"I'll let you be in charge."

"Forever?" he asked unbelievingly, his gaze riveted on her fingers and the extra surge of desire he was feeling for her.

"For a while," she amended.

"In charge of everything?"

Her fingers reached an especially sensitive spot of his anatomy. "Everything important," she said sweetly. "I know you still have a lot you can teach *me.*"

He caught her fingers and stopped their meanderings. "Tell me part two—and make it damned quick."

"After I leave her, somehow we rig it so you bump into Miss Worrell with Mr. Nesmith and me watching," she suggested. "With any luck, she'll show her true colors without you saying much of anything."

His blue-gray eyes stared doubtfully back at her.

"You look like you don't think it will work."

"I'm not sure." He hesitated, then pressed her hand against his chest. "I don't want this all to blow up in our faces."

"I don't believe things could get any worse," Evaleen

said assuredly, rolling back on top of him. "Now that you have the plan, what do you think?"

He thought things probably could get a lot worse, considering human nature and the probability that what could go wrong most likely would. But instead of voicing his doubts and jinxing his newfound happiness, Jesse pulled Evaleen to him for a long kiss. If Miss Worrell suspected something was up and never said a word or, worse yet, started acting like she had in the shed, hinting that he'd had a hand in some imagined seduction at another place and time, Evaleen might just begin to have the slightest of doubts.

He couldn't stand that. He would do anything to keep her happy.

What that anything might end up being, he didn't want to consider.

Evaleen pulled away. "Then you'll do it?" she asked, her lips swollen with his kiss, her voice thick with desire.

"You really care about belonging, don't you?"

"I really care about belonging to you," she corrected. That part was true, Evaleen swore. But what she cared about more was the town knowing what a fine man Jesse really was. He deserved the respect of the townspeople, and deep down, she knew he must feel the pain of their rejection, just as she had in her hometown. It hurt not to belong.

She wanted to do this for Jesse, because he'd been alone so long. And also, because deep in her heart, she suspected she loved him.

She shivered just a bit, and Jesse pulled her tightly against him, knowing he would give her the world if he could. She'd certainly given it to him when she'd let him into her heart. Since she did have just about the best character of anyone he'd ever met, that meant the world to him.

And so did she.

"Okay, then. I'll do it." And, he thought, pulling her down for another kiss, he'd pray like hell that everything turned out exactly the way she wanted it to.

Even so, he couldn't kill the nagging suspicion that he was overlooking some point, and it would be a very dangerous point to overlook. But he couldn't tell her that.

"When?" she asked breathlessly, caught up in his kiss.

"Tomorrow."

# Chapter Seventeen

Evaleen stomped up the boardwalk toward where she could see Jesse leaning against the front of Calloway's office building. She could hear her footsteps and knew she wasn't walking like a lady should, but at the moment, she didn't care. She had just finished the first part of her plan by speaking with the schoolmarm. Now anger was churning around inside her like a cataclysmic whirlwind, and she felt ready to explode from the pressure.

All it took was the sight of Jesse's eyebrows raised questioningly.

"I had to leave before I strangled that woman!" she said in a low voice between clenched teeth when she finally stopped in front of him. "I have never met a more stubborn, aggravating, unprincipled fabricator in all my days on this earth than Maggie Worrell!"

"Does that include myself?" Jesse asked.

Evaleen stopped ranting, drew a deep breath, and finally focused her dark lime eyes on him. "True, you did have evasion and irritation down to an art form. But you somehow made it charming."

Not seeming to care a lick that they were on a public thoroughfare, Jesse slipped both his arms around her waist and drew her close for a quick kiss.

"Well, thank you, darlin'," he said, giving her a smile that lasted no more than a few seconds, like a leaf riding on the wind.

"I just cannot help but wonder what you ever saw in her," Evaleen said.

He leaned down and brushed a lock of her hair behind her ear, his finger tracing an earlobe enhanced by a dangling jet earring. "Nothing, Evie. I may have flirted with danger, but the closest I ever got to it was you."

The last week since Evaleen had first gone to Jesse, heart and soul, it had been wonderful, but she had lived too long with the feeling that she was just plain, unappealing Evaleen Murphy and that she would never know this kind of love and devotion from a man. She had to understand what it was that set her apart in his eyes.

"Truly. Why settle down with me, Jesse? Why not her?"

"My house became a place worth coming home to again when you settled into it, Evie," he said softly. "I have never liked living as much as I have since I met you. And when you smile, your heart's in your eyes. I picked you, Evie, because there's no other woman like you."

"I don't know what to say," she whispered, in awe of his words.

Leaning downward, he kissed her again. Forgetting where they were as people passed by them, she encircled his neck with her arms and held him to her, kissing him back. Finally, he pulled away.

"That's all right, Evaleen. Your lips said it all."

She smiled up at him, then pointed to the law office behind her. "Shall we get this over with?"

"The sooner we do and get back to the ranch, the better. I want to see if I can strike you speechless again."

Despite his teasing, Evaleen's face went pensive as Jesse opened the door to Calloway's office building for her. The rest of the plan called for her and Calloway to hurry over to the Harvey Hotel restaurant, where one of the waitresses, her friend Kitty, was holding a table nearby the one that was practically reserved for Margaret Worrell at suppertime each evening. The solicitor and Evaleen would be on the opposite side of an ornamental paper divider, but with luck, they would be able to hear everything when Jesse "happened" upon Margaret. Once Maggie Worrell saw him, Jesse was certain that she would invite him to join her, and then, hopefully, she would bury herself with whatever she said.

A wonderful plan, Evaleen had called it almost a half-hour before, right before she'd taken Jesse's hand, squeezed it for luck, and gone off to see the schoolmarm. But after listening to the schoolteacher's accusations that Jesse truly didn't love Evaleen and her lies about Jesse visiting her late at night before their marriage, Evaleen was beginning to wonder if their plan was only a recipe for disaster. Jesse swore he'd never slept with the woman, and she believed him. But would the town?

Calloway's clerk came out of a back office, spotted them, and turned back to tell the solicitor they were there. Evaleen began to pace the length of the empty waiting room.

"Are you sure you want to continue on with this, Evie?" Jesse asked, thereby stopping her pacing. "It might be a lot simpler to accept their offer of an annulment and to take Theodora back to Kansas with you."

"And have you live the rest of your life without me, Jesse Stockton, unattached, with no one to keep you on the straight and narrow?" she asked sweetly, walking right back up to him. She would have been angry that he'd suggested such a thing, but she had heard the fear in his voice, even if he didn't know it was there himself. She knew why he was asking. He was making sure she had no plans to leave him. "You should be so lucky as to get off so easily."

"At least then you wouldn't have to join me every time I get dragged through the mud," he reminded her, his blue-gray eyes narrowed and filled with some emotion—worry? Sadness for her? She wasn't sure.

"Perhaps, but then where would I find my excitement in life, Jess? I can safely say that each day with you turns into quite an adventure." She'd been right. Jesse was concerned only about her in this, and he feared she would grow to hate him if she didn't have the position in the community she wanted. She attempted to reassure him that she wasn't about to leave him. Slipping her arms around his waist, she lay her head against his hard chest, savoring the comfort of having his arms around her.

Behind them, Calloway cleared his throat, and she reluctantly pulled away. "It's time to bury Miss Worrell, Jess," she said, full of faith that everything was going to turn out right.

She just wished Jesse looked as certain as she was.

Maggie Worrell's eyes got sultry when she saw him, and Jesse wished he could scowl and bring her down a peg or two. But he couldn't. He was going through with Evie's plan because, despite what he'd suggested to Evaleen about her going back to Kansas, he couldn't imagine his life without her. He didn't want her to go. But he was all too aware that if they didn't get this problem ironed out soon, Evaleen would end up despised by the town, soon after, despising him for it, she might leave anyway. So, hoping he could do something—anything—to fix his reputation for Evaleen's sake, he adjusted his collar and stopped in response to the invitation in the schoolteacher's eyes.

"Miss Worrell," he said, standing by her table and tipping his hat.

"You were calling me Maggie before," she said, then patted the chair next to her. "Were you joining someone?"

"Just waiting for my wife to arrive. I believe she went shopping."

Maggie's dark brown eyes suddenly had a harsh light in them, but she said nothing about the visit she'd had with Evaleen just prior to dinner. "Then do sit. I'm sure we'll have a while."

Jesse glanced around, wanting to appear nervous so that Maggie wouldn't get suspicious, even though he'd never felt more coldly calculating in his life. Then he settled his eyes on her. "I don't believe that would be a good idea."

"Is there someplace else you prefer to meet?" Taking his hand, she pulled him toward her a bit. He stiffened and then took a step closer. "Somewhere cozier, perhaps?" she asked. "Like last time?"

Jesse wanted to turn to see if Evaleen was taking this all right, but he knew he had to play his part. "Last time? I don't know what you're talking about."

"That night you spent in Raton not too long ago, Jesse?" she said, her voice holding a wisp of impatience. "Surely you remember where we were before you went back to the saloon and your friends? Us, together, in the privacy of my home?"

Despite what she was implying, Jesse didn't have to search his mind to know that even drunk, he hadn't been able to perform for another woman since he'd met Evaleen, even assuming the remote possibility that he had visited the schoolmarm's small home that night, which he couldn't recall having done.

"I can't believe you don't remember what happened!"

Maggie said in a voice that was louder than she really needed to use.

"I can't remember it because I was never with you in private anywhere." Jesse shifted uncomfortably. She hadn't even come close to mentioning anything like this while they'd been in the shed, and he wondered what she was up to now. Unless . . . His eyes narrowed as he gazed down at her. Could she have guessed that this was a trap?

Her eyes were still harsh as she met his, but then, as if on cue, they softened and tears began falling down her cheeks.

At almost the same instant, Jesse felt movement to his right. The waitress had arrived with a bowl of soup.

That explained the show, he thought.

The waitress, Evaleen's friend, paused at the unexpected show of tears and looked with concern from Jesse to Margaret Worrell. Maggie rose, shaking her head. "I'm too distraught to eat. I can't believe any of this is happening! You don't remember?"

Gloves in hand, she brushed by him, and growing more angry by the second, he followed her to the front door, where he finally caught her by her sleeve.

"What's with the act, Maggie?" His low voice didn't hide his fury. "You're dead set on ruining me in this town and with my wife. Why?"

She turned her tear-streaked face up toward him, and he could see how empty her eyes were. "I dreamed about you when you said we might have a good time together, thought about you almost every second of every day. I came by the house as we agreed, but you were never there. No man breaks a promise to me like that." Her eyes darkened until they were almost unreadable. "And no one tries to set me up as a liar, either."

"You knew Evaleen was at the next table." He spoke the thought aloud.

"Someone sent me a note to warn me," she said, just loudly enough for him to hear. "I hope this destroys you. I hope you really suffer now!"

She started to turn, and he reached out, his hand catching her arm before she could leave. "If I lose Evaleen over this," he said in a forceful, grim voice that was meant to worry her, "I swear, you'll be the one who suffers."

"Don't threaten me!" she said. "You were the one at fault!" Her formerly elegant air had become a pitiful look that Jesse knew was put on for the benefit of the restaurant patrons. By now, most of the diners in the vicinity had grown silent and watchful, and as usual where he was concerned, condemning. Even before Maggie turned and stomped away, Jesse realized the end to his short-lived, dream-come-true was coming.

When he turned and saw, at their table, Calloway was scowling at him and Evaleen had her face in her hands, he knew he'd gotten that wrong.

The end was already here.

"Just where does Jesse believe he is going?" Calloway asked, sounding irritated and angry.

Her hands over her eyes, Evaleen took a deep breath and just barely stopped herself from rising to go find Margaret Worrell and slap her silly. But at Calloway's question, she had to look toward the front of the restaurant. It did indeed appear that Jesse was following the schoolmarm outside.

For a few seconds she wondered if she ought to go after him and make him explain, but then she realized she was falling into the trap Miss Worrell was setting for them. Margaret apparently wanted her to question Jesse and his feelings for her. She didn't have to. She knew he loved her.

"Now will you get the annulment?" Calloway asked her.

Slowly, she shook her head. Heaven help her, no matter where Jesse was headed now, or what he was going to do, she believed in her husband. She trusted him and would stand by him—she gazed defiantly at the pitying looks aimed at her—even if no one else would.

Resolutely, she rose to her feet and picked up her reticule.

"Now, where are *you* going?" Calloway asked worriedly, rising and following her out toward the cashier. "To follow him?"

"No," she said over her shoulder, and not caring if anyone heard, she added, "I'm going home—to wait for my husband." Whirling around, she walked outside and started the short walk to her buggy, praying that Jesse would be somewhere nearby, just waiting for her to come out of the restaurant, that he'd be joining her at any minute.

But he didn't. And much later, as she drove to the ranch house at Rainbow's End, she looked hopefully on the porch for him; he wasn't there either. All her old insecurities started bubbling to the surface, but she shoved them down. Jesse would be home just as soon as he could make it, she knew he would.

She was so certain of this that, after checking on Theodora and her aunt and changing into her nightclothes, she walked out and sat on the front porch swing to wait for him. But as the minutes passed into an hour and more, the one thought that kept crossing her mind, over and over, was . . . *where is Jesse?*

From the clenching in his gut as he spotted Evaleen in the dark on the porch swing, Jesse knew, for the first time in his life that he was truly scared. He'd been afraid since he'd seen Evaleen cover her face in reaction to Margaret Worrell's lies, frightened that Evaleen was going to turn like the tide, pack up everything, and leave him alone.

He didn't think that he could stand that, so he'd stayed away a bit longer than he should have, sitting in the back room of the saloon with a bottle he'd never even emptied by a quarter, wanting to be by himself with the misery he was feeling. His father had been correct in his judgment. He wasn't good enough. Not for the town, not for his father, and certainly not good enough for a fine, wonderful, sweetheart of a woman like Evaleen. She didn't deserve this kind of scandal, with the town looking down upon him and hence her. All the way home, he'd been certain she would have been packing.

But she was still here. He dismounted a few yards away from the porch steps, half-expecting something to come flying at him from Evaleen's hand. But she didn't move. Leading his horse, he walked to the bottom of the porch steps.

"This is all my fault," he said.

Her eyes widened in shock, their green catching the flickering gold of the lantern light. "She was telling the truth?"

"Hell, no!" he said, but then he saw the gentle, mocking lift of her eyebrows and realized that, despite the seriousness of the situation, she was teasing him.

*Teasing* him.

Taking the steps two at a time, he stopped in front of her and drank in the sight of her sitting in her calico robe, hair flowing down her back, looking tired but still beautiful nonetheless.

"I thought you hated me," he said, his throat thick with anxiety. "Hated me, realized what a mistake you'd made and had taken my family back to Kansas."

"I couldn't hate you." She shook her head, her hair glistening as it moved around her shoulders. "And I wouldn't ever do that to you, Jess."

"You ought to hate me," he said, watching every movement she made, every breath she took, as though he were seeing her for the last time. "If I hadn't been the person I was around Maggie Worrell, none of this stupidity would have happened. The town would still be tolerating me, and you wouldn't have to worry about being shunned at church next Sunday."

"If you hadn't been the person you were," she said softly, rising to face him, "I wouldn't have fallen in love with you."

"Oh, God, Evaleen," he groaned, pulling her to him tightly as his lips went down on hers with an urgent need to make damned certain everything was settled and fine between them. It was like a reprieve right before a hanging.

Her lips kissed him back, and then moved hungrily to his cheek, down his jaw, and back to his mouth, before she finally rested her head against his shoulder. "I was so worried about you," she said, her breasts heaving against him as she drew in air.

"I followed Maggie out to get her to tell you the truth—but she refused."

"I know the truth."

"After that, I went over to the saloon for a few drinks in the back room. I couldn't bear the thought of coming home and finding no one here."

"I'm not the town, Jesse," she whispered against his chest. "I don't run hot and cold with my loyalty."

"I remember. When you didn't like me, you sure didn't like me."

"And then you gave me reason to change my mind," she said softly.

"Then you believe me?"

"Of course." She gazed into his blue-gray eyes, so dark when the only light around them came from the shimmering lamp. "I saw you up on the hill when you put flowers on your mother's grave. You honor her memory so much, I can't see you purposely bringing shame down on her by lying to the woman you gave her ring to."

He didn't know what to say. So instead, he just kissed her, and she looped her arms around his neck and kissed him back. Finally, they sank down into the porch swing, so tightly wound in each other's arms they sat as one.

"What are we going to do about the townspeople now, Evie?" he asked.

"If you're starting to worry about things like that," she said, smiling up at him teasingly, "then I'm going to tell you I want my Jesse back."

He had to smile back then; still, he knew what the townspeople thought of Evaleen did matter to her. It mattered a lot.

"You shouldn't have to suffer through their remarks and what they're thinking," he told her, running his thumb across her cheek.

"Neither should you, since you did nothing wrong." She shrugged. "I don't like it, Jess. But after a while, when Margaret Worrell realizes you aren't changing your mind, then I do believe everything will settle down and get back to normal."

"You think so, huh?"

"If we're wrong," she said, sitting back against his arm, "there's really only one thing left to do."

"What's that?"

"Hurry up and marry her off to somebody so she leaves you alone."

He smirked. "Got any victims in mind?"

She shook her head. "But I must say, I sure wish the reverend wasn't already married. Maybe someone like Margaret would loosen the old fuddy-duddy up. Plus it would serve him right to have to deal with her."

"Maybe the good Lord has already given him his just due with Mrs. Mortenson," Jesse commented drily.

Evaleen's laughter rang out through the darkness, but Jesse couldn't bring himself to laugh. Evaleen didn't deserve the chastisement of the townsfolk.

"I just wish I knew what else I could do to prove to those people that you aren't as bad as you seem," she said musingly.

Jesse shot her a wicked look.

"Oh, you know what I mean. After changing you, influencing the town ought to have been simple." She rolled her eyes. "Believe me."

"I know I gave you a hard time. But I'm glad you like me now, Evie." He stroked her cheek with the side of his hand as he gazed out into the darkness. "It was too hard having you as an enemy. Every time I wanted to have some fun, I kept seeing you." He waved his hand in the air, just as she had a minute before. "Oh, you know what I mean."

She laughed as she shook her head in mock despair. "I guess we almost deserve each other."

"So what do we do now, Evie? Leave well enough alone?" Jesse didn't want to leave things the way they were, but he didn't know what else to do.

"I think so." Evaleen nodded. "Today's plan only made things worse. I'm all for just staying out of everyone's way until the talk dies down."

"Do you think it will be that easy?"

Grasping her hand in his, she pressed her lips to his palm. "Yes, I do. I'm out here with you on Rainbow's End. Nothing can touch us here, Jess. Nothing."

Feeling the warm breezes caressing them, knowing that he had everything he'd ever wanted at that very moment, Jesse wished he could say he agreed with her. But he couldn't. He kept feeling he didn't deserve what he was now holding in the palm of his hand, that something was about to go very wrong and his whole life was going to be snatched away from him.

"Let's go upstairs," he whispered in her ear.

Wanting to feel the reassurance of Jesse's arms around her, Evaleen wasn't surprised that he felt the same way. Silently she rose, letting him follow behind her and pausing as he locked the front door. It was very late; her aunt and Theodora had long since gone to bed. It was time to forget about Margaret Worrell and everything that had happened and to remember that she and Jesse were as one.

United in everything.

Once in their bedroom that had been Jesse's own, the urgency to be together grew in Evaleen with every passing second. She pulled off her robe as he took off his shirt, her body so close to Jesse's that every move he made sent tiny lightning bolts through her.

Jesse lowered his mouth to hers, giving her whisper-soft kisses that made her forget he was the town's eternal bad boy and remember only that she was with the man with whom she had fallen in love.

One of his hands slipped down and pulled off her nightgown. Barely feeling it falling down to her ankles, she knew only that Jesse's mouth was now at the vulnerable spot between her breasts. He bent, freed them, and took one of her nipples in his mouth, sucking on it hard enough to make some inner muscle deep inside her pull sensuously. The throbbing in her femininity increased in tempo and intensity, and her breathing came more rapidly.

Her hands fell on his hard shoulders, and she realized that he must be filled with the same kind of desperation that she was experiencing, because, in seconds, he cupped her breasts with his warm hands. As she caught her breath from the surge of excitement that went through her, he knelt and wet the skin on her bare stomach with his tongue, licking its softness. Then his mouth began to taste the skin right above the waistband of her drawers, enticing her into sweet oblivion. He increased the pressure against her body, and the two of them fell sideways and backward onto the bed.

She began to touch him back with the same fevered fervor, and heard a groan come from deep in his throat. His fingers hitched the sides of her drawers and slid them off her in one smooth movement, leaving her exposed to his touch and gaze. Her legs opened of their own will as he lowered his mouth toward the curls covering her femininity.

He buried his lips down there, where she was already wet and hot, and she gasped. For a few seconds she tried to pull away, but he held on to her, and then she wanted—no, *had*—to give in to her body's reaction to his lovemaking. Her hips began to convulse, and she wrapped her legs around his shoulders, deepening the exquisite feeling.

He left her lower regions to position his thighs on either side of her so that she could feel their hard muscles against her fleshier hips and his manhood pressing against her stomach, tantalizing her. Then she closed her eyes and knew only sensations, such as when his mouth came back up over a breast, teasing and wetting it to an even tauter peak than before. More sensations, such as when he lowered his body and pressed against her, his manhood throbbing against the still damp skin of her stomach, but not pushing into her core, where she wanted it to be.

"Jess, now ... please," she asked from deep in her throat.

"No. It's my turn," he said, rolling her over on top of him and then pushing her up so that she was almost sitting on her bent knees with her femininity arched over his manhood, her wetness mingling with his heat. Her mouth dropped open with the pure sensuality of it all, and then he was urging her upward. Finally understanding, she reached down and positioned him so that he entered and slid deep inside of her.

She moaned with utter pleasure and then began to move from side to side.

"Hurry, Evie," he said, barely getting the words out. "Hurry."

Her heart thumping, she began to raise and lower herself, up and down his shaft, until she fell into a natural rhythm that sent her blood humming. To balance, she arched her back. The curve lifted her breasts outward, and they rose and fell, bouncing wantonly. She saw he was watching them, his eyes hooded, his expression dazed, his mouth half-open.

That only made her want him more.

What she was doing was so abandoned that she tightened inside, and her throbbing increased to an almost unbearable level as she pressed on to obtain her release.

"Darling Evie," Jesse uttered, as off-balance, she fell forward onto him. He caught her with his strong arms, bending upward so that her luscious breasts covered his face, and as they continued to move together, he knew he couldn't last for much longer. Wanting this to be perfect for her, he placed a hand on each of her buttocks, pulled her into him, and, with a smooth movement, rolled her over onto her back.

He made love to her then with his heart and soul, strumming her body into the same passionate heights that he reached. At last, when he thought he could take no more, he felt her convulsing and heard her soft moans of pleasure, so he plunged into her one last time and reached his own release.

Every inch of Evaleen was filled with delight and contentment as he toppled down over her. Right now, everything was so perfect she could barely remember why she'd been worried. The townspeople would realize the error of their ways when Margaret Worrell found someone else to badger or love. It was as simple as that. When they did, she and Jesse would live happily ever after.

All she had wanted, Margaret Worrell thought as she stumbled forward toward the building she was seeking, had been Jesse's love. Her head hurt. Her face hurt. She thought the bastard might have broken her ribs. Everything inside her told her that Jesse Stockton could not possibly have beaten her up like this, that it wasn't in the roguish charmer to really hurt a woman, but she had seen the man's features. And she had his note that told her to meet him in the backroom of the saloon and enter by way of the alley. She'd had just enough wine after she'd gone home to be insanely self-assured. Evaleen had left him, he'd written, and he'd finally come to his senses. She'd left her home and come to the saloon filled with hope.

Stupid. How could she have been so stupid? He'd sworn to get her if she'd cost him Evaleen, and she must have, so he'd certainly gotten her.

Dizzy again as she finally reached a wall, Margaret hung on and slid down until she was on her knees, her hands leaving a trail of blood down the wood. She should have suspected something was very wrong when she'd seen Jesse, bottle in hand, sitting in the veil of darkness relieved only by a couple of small candles on the sideboard and a small light in the hallway, only enough light for her to barely make out his features.

But then he'd risen, closed the door, come to her, and pulled her into his arms, holding her so roughly yet so tightly that she'd felt an odd thrill inside her which quickly turned into a throbbing need. Wanting to savor every moment of her victory, she'd told Jesse to slow down, that the night was young and she was willing to be his.

He hadn't replied, had just shoved her against the wall,

and that was when she'd grown frightened of him and had opened her mouth to scream, but he'd placed a hand over her lips and held her pinned where she was. His free hand ripped open her blouse and made the precious pearl buttons go flying everywhere.

Furious at the waste, she'd bitten his hand. He'd laughed and hit her in the face, hard enough to make her see tiny pinpoints of light in the darkness. Stunned, she'd been almost limp as he'd ripped open her chemise and then crudely fondled her breasts while whispering lewd remarks in her ears.

Long seconds passed before she'd recovered enough to realize he was yanking up her skirts and that he was half-naked and was about to violate her, right there, without waiting for her to be ready, after hurting her, and she'd opened her mouth to scream, but then he'd punched her in her middle. She'd felt something inside of her crack— a rib?—and then she'd been pushed down to the floor and she'd smacked her cheek on something; that was when she'd started crying. She'd kept on crying, because then he was having his way with her, and *that* hurt like it had never hurt before.

She had to stop thinking about it, she told herself, her tears mingling with the blood on her hands from where he'd punched her in the mouth because she'd been moaning from the pain and he didn't want to hear it. Then he'd yanked her up off the floor and thrown her back into the alley like so much trash. She'd fallen against something and her rib had moved and she'd felt such pain she'd passed out.

From somewhere—where?—she could hear the chime of a clock and men's laughter, and she knew if she could just get inside the saloon, someone would help her. Rising to her feet caused horrendous stabbing pain with every breath she took. She stumbled around to the front of the building, and teetered up the two steps of the boardwalk, calling weakly for help, not being heard over the piano and the laughter inside the building. In only a few feet she would reach the door and someone would see her, only she didn't think she could make it, because she was seeing stars again. . . .

"Oh, gawddamn!" some deep voice said fairly near to her, right as she stumbled forward toward the town's grizzled old drunk, whom she would never have given the time of day under any other circumstances, let alone allowed to touch her.

"Hey, w-w-what's happened to you?" the miner asked her, and then, as her legs finally gave out from under her, he caught her before she fell to the ground and yelled toward the saloon for someone to come help.

Margaret wanted to protest, ask him to be gentle, but his arms slammed around her like a vise as he tried to keep himself from falling. The pressure from his innocently reaching out to help her was enough to drive her broken rib into something inside her, and she knew all her troubles were ending. She forgave the man in an instant—he reeked of liquor and probably wasn't smart enough to guess he could kill her with his touch—but she wasn't letting her real murderer off so easily.

"Jesse did it!" she murmured on her last breath, right before she became a dead weight in the miner's arms.

Ezekial Tanner frowned as he heard the name the schoolmarm muttered. Now, he couldn't believe Jesse would kill anyone; he surely couldn't. Yeah, he'd heard the gossip all right, but every time Jesse saw him in the streets, he flipped him a dollar for dinner. He couldn't let a savage murderer walk free, no sirree, but neither could he believe a kind man like Jesse would do something like this to the woman in his arms.

Then he felt eyes upon him, and perplexed, he glanced

up through the haze of liquor and saw a man standing in the dim shadows at the mouth of the alley. Jesse. It had to be. The man's hand dropped to his gun, and Zeke took a faulty step backward, still holding the girl up.

"You ain't gonna kill me, are you?" Zeke asked him. It didn't make any sense. Jesse liked him, and wasn't a vicious type.

The man pulled his gun out. Zeke could feel sweat pouring down his forehead, into his eyes. "C'mon, now. Think of what yer doin', Jesse."

The man froze; then, ever so slowly, he pushed the gun back into its holster. To Zeke's amazement, he thought he saw a grin pass over Jesse's face, right before he turned and started walking swiftly away from the scene.

Blessing his narrow escape and turning back toward the saloon, Zeke yelled again for help, this time loudly enough for someone to come see what all the shouting was about.

Seconds later, as someone did, all hell broke loose.

# Chapter Eighteen

Evaleen wasn't certain what woke her up; it could have been the sharp intake of breath that made Jesse's chest rise and fall where her arm lay across it. It might have been the feel of the cold steel muzzle of the shotgun pointed at Jesse's chest; it had barely brushed her fingertips before she'd withdrawn her hand. She just knew that she was awake, and her heart was pounding so hard she thought she was going to faint, because the man holding the gun against Jesse's chest was the sheriff, two of the other men standing with him were Calloway and Reverend Mortenson, and the last, the other one with his gun out, was the owner of the saloon—Jesse's friend.

"Never thought it would quite come to this, Jesse," Calloway said from off to the side.

"You'd better have a damned good reason for why you're here," Jesse muttered, not moving a muscle. "And an even better one for coming into my bedroom without knocking first."

"Maggie Worrell's been raped and murdered," the sheriff told him shortly, not looking at all worried about Jesse's ominously darkening features. "And she said you did it—right before she died. Plus, we have a witness who said he saw you leaving the area, and that you almost shot him, but changed your mind."

All the breath seemed to leave Evaleen, and she clutched the sheets to her and slumped back against the pillows. Jesse's roguish ways had snowballed from one problem right into another, until the trouble had finally rolled back to hit them like an avalanche. She saw Jesse barely turn his head until he was looking at her, his eyes questioning, but before she could gather enough breath to say a word to him, the sheriff picked up Jesse's pants and threw them on top of him.

"Get dressed. We're here to take you in."

"I didn't kill anyone," Jesse said, but it was more to Evaleen than to the sheriff.

She tried to tell him she knew that, but Sheriff Dunahy flipped back the blanket and gestured with his gun, diverting Jesse's attention from her.

"It's all over town how you threatened the woman at the restaurant," Dunahy said. "Nicholson says you spent over three hours drinking in the rear room of his saloon. That puts you in the right place at the right time, with a reason to do it. You got any other likely suspects?"

"My brother," Jesse said. If Patrick had been capable of leaving him to die when they were young, he'd be capable of killing someone now. "I think he's been following Theodora around ever since we got her from her school, so there's a good chance he's in Raton."

"Now, you know your brother's dead, Jesse," Calloway said, sounding disappointed. "Your father told everybody that years back."

"Reynard lied," Jesse said, his eyes going back to Evaleen. She nodded to show she believed him. "Patrick fought with him, and Reynard told him as far as he was concerned, he was dead. Patrick stole our payroll when he left, and after that, Reynard told the town he'd died."

Reverend Mortenson's face suddenly looked as if it was threatening to explode. "Now he's blaspheming his own father. If there was one thing you could count on with Reynard Stockton, it was the man's word. If you don't take him to jail, Sheriff, I swear I'll string him up here myself without a trial."

"But it's true!" Evaleen said, her eyes darting from one member of the posse to the next. "Jesse told me he thought Patrick was still alive a long while ago; he didn't just make it up."

"There's just no proof of it," Sheriff Dunahy said, watching Jesse carefully as the other man sat up and yanked on his pants. "What we do have are the witnesses who saw your husband threaten the schoolmarm, and we've got the witness who saw him walking away, as well as the victim's dying statement to that witness."

Evaleen didn't know what to say. It seemed their minds were made up. Her hands clenching around the sheet drawn up to her chin, she uttered a curse low in her throat.

The sheriff shook his head, then turned his attention back to Jesse. "Now, are you coming, or do we have to haul you to Raton?"

Dumbfounded, Evaleen stared from one man to the other as Jesse finished dressing. Because she was naked, propriety demanded she stay exactly where she was, buried under the bedclothes, but propriety couldn't stop her from showing her fury. "Take him and get out of my home," she said, and then, in a softer voice, she added, "Jess, don't worry. I'll get you out of this. Somehow."

Jesse's eyes flew to her, but they were barren, lifeless. "Go back to Kansas, Evie."

She frowned. "Jess . . . It's going to be all right."

He didn't answer as he walked out of the room. The rest of the men trailed after him, looking somewhat sheepish at having seen the exchange between them.

He couldn't have meant that, Evaleen decided. He was just worried that she wouldn't be able to take the townsfolk ostracizing her as the wife of a prisoner. But she could. For Jesse, she could take anything. She would simply have to find a way to prove his innocence, probably by finding Patrick, and then Jesse would realize he didn't really want her to go anywhere.

Filled with renewed determination, she pushed up and out of bed and began to dress. Nothing was as important to her as saving Jesse.

Nothing.

At noon, Waco—at his insistence—drove her to town so she could make sure Jesse had a decent meal. While thinking that morning, she'd made him a peach pie from canned peaches, fried chicken, and the big flaky biscuits that Jesse loved. With the town's current opinion of her husband, she couldn't trust anyone to feed him.

The problem was, she still didn't know the best way to go about finding Patrick. But she wanted to see Jesse alone so she could tell him that she loved him more than anything.

Declining Waco's offer to go inside the jailhouse with her, she rustled through the front door with her basket, and was greeted by a long, hard look of speculation from the deputy.

She tilted her chin up. "I want to see my husband."

The deputy only raised his eyebrows and indicated that she should put her basket down on his desk. She watched, fuming, as he rifled through the food. That she was thought of as someone who was less than upstanding and who therefore needed to be searched should have embarrassed her, she thought, but it didn't. It just made her more angry than she could ever remember being before.

"I'll have to bring the prisoner the food and ask him if he wants to see you," the deputy told her finally.

"Of course he wants to see me!" Evaleen snapped, unwilling to relinquish her basket when she wasn't at all certain Jesse was going to receive its contents.

"I specifically heard him say no visitors when he was locked up." The deputy raised his eyebrows. "Now, do you want me to bring him that food and ask him, or not?"

Tightly pursing her mouth to keep from giving him a chafing retort, Evaleen handed the basket over. She was about at her wit's end due to the fine citizens of Raton. Jesse was not guilty, which meant whoever had murdered Miss Worrell was running around loose. Every woman in town was in danger. If it was Theodora's black knight who was doing this, she wasn't so positive that Theodora was safe, which was why she'd had Waco order a couple of the cowhands to watch the house until they returned.

The deputy opened a door that led, she saw, to three cells. He walked straight back less than a dozen yards and stopped. On tiptoe, she angled herself and tried to see over the man's shoulder, but Jesse had to be sitting down.

"Jesse," she called, "tell him you want to see me."

"Tell my wife to forget about me and get a divorce," he replied loudly enough for her to hear.

"I have never heard anything so stupid in all my born days, Jesse Stockton! I doubt if you'd say that to my face!"

"Tell her," Jesse's voice replied, "to go back to Rainbow's End and tell Waco I said to please take care of the ranch until she finds herself another husband."

Evaleen pursed her mouth in frustration. "When I get you out of this, Jesse Stockton, you are going to be the sorriest husband who ever walked the Earth. I'm going to give you such a piece of my mind your ears are going to ring for days! Not only that ..." She searched her mind for something worse to threaten him with. "Not only that," she added triumphantly, "I'm going to start wearing that hat again!"

Whirling around, she smashed the front door shut behind her and marched to the buggy, climbing on without waiting for Waco's help. He jumped back into the driver's seat and shook the reins as she stared straight ahead, shaking with righteous anger at her husband.

"Jesse Stockton is the most stubborn, idiotic man to ever walk the face of this Earth," she said before they'd rolled a dozen feet.

"If you say so, ma'am."

"Aren't you going to ask what happened?"

"Don't have to," he said. "I could prit' near hear every word."

"I suppose you agree with him!" she exploded.

Waco finally pushed up his hat and gave her a hard look. "Don't yell at me," he said in his low, husky voice. "I'm not your husband, and I'm not one of these stupid townspeople." He then added like it was an afterthought, "Ma'am."

Immediately, she felt a stab of guilt. Waco *had* stood by the ranch for a lot of years. He'd kept everything running smoothly after Jesse's father had died, and he was right here by her side, being a friend now. "I apologize," she said, never more contrite in her life.

"Okay." He brought the buggy to a stop in a cloud of dust at the side of the road leading out of Raton. Turning to her and keeping his voice low so no one could overhear, he said, "I don't agree with Jesse about you getting a divorce. Hell, you wouldn't be much of a wife if you caved in when he needs you the most. But he must really think he's not going to get out of this."

"I don't know what to do, then," she said softly. The last time she'd felt this helpless—and sad—had been when she'd found her sister dead.

"Right now, I think it might be best if we got back to the ranch and made certain everything's all right."

"You're worried about Theodora?"

He shrugged, but then he did lift the reins and shake them back into motion. The sense of urgency she was getting from the usually cautious, slow-moving man made Evaleen think that he was concerned about Theodora's safety, which set her heart into a faster pace all over again.

"You think this black knight of Dorie's could be the same man who killed Maggie Worrell?"

She sensed Waco was on the verge of answering, but just as they entered the trees, he did the last thing she was expecting. Touching her arm, he handed her the reins almost nonchalantly, but she could see his body was now taut and one of his hands was resting on the barrel of his pistol.

"I saw something out there. When I tell you, pull the horse to a stop, get down on the ground on your side, and stay behind the buggy for cover."

She didn't ask questions; Waco wasn't the type who would stand for them anyway. As soon as he muttered, "Now," she halted the buggy and slid down to the road. Simultaneously, Waco pitched himself off and ran toward the trees, kicking up dirt behind him. Slipping to the rear of the vehicle, she peeked out to watch the cowhand slip behind a tree for cover, crouching low, his gun drawn.

"Get out in the open where I can see you!" he yelled to someone—who it was, she didn't know. Afraid the man Waco sought was going to come from behind and ambush him, Evaleen could not tear her eyes away. What if Waco got cornered? Hurt? How was she supposed to help him with no weapon?

"D-don't shoot, Waco!" It was the voice of a frightened, old man. "I've been waitin' to talk to ya. It's important!"

"Zeke?" Waco called.

"Yeah, it's me." A graying, wild-haired man appeared from behind one of the trees, his hands high above his head.

"Dammit, Zeke, why the hell didn't you just stay out in the open?" Waco asked, putting his gun back in its holster and motioning for the older man to join him.

Now that it was over and nothing at all was going to happen, Evaleen sank back against the buggy and took a long breath. Nothing was going right today. Nothing at all. Waco could have killed someone who was obviously a friend of his, for nothing; Jesse was locked up for a horrible crime he didn't commit, and she didn't know how she was going to survive without him. She felt like crying, only that would be a terrible waste of time, wouldn't it, what with a murderer to be found.

The fact that there was still a murderer out there made her brush her sleeve across almost teary eyes, square her shoulders, and go to join Waco. She couldn't fall apart. Jesse needed her.

"I had to hide." Zeke nodded his head, then tipped his tattered, dusty hat when he saw Evaleen. "I got a good reason. I didn't want anyone seeing me talk to you because you're on his side, too."

Waco glanced at Evaleen. It was obvious, she thought, that he was as confused as she was. "Whose side?" he asked.

"Why, Jesse's, of course. He didn't kill that girl. He couldn't have. I don't know why she woulda said that he did, but the man I saw couldn't have been Jesse. I figured that out right away when I sobered up this morning. I told the sheriff what the man had done, but Dunahy said that only proved Jesse had done it."

"You're the witness?" A surge of hope went through Evaleen when Zeke nodded. "What had you seen the man who looked like Jesse do, Zeke?"

Zeke looked from Evaleen to Waco and back again. "Why, he stared at me and had his hand on his gun—he was gonna shoot me, I know it—right until the second I called him Jesse. Then he did the strangest thing. He grinned and walked away, as fast as he could. Jesse wouldn't have done that."

"What, tried to kill you?"

"Yeah, that." Zeke nodded his head. "And he wouldn't have passed by old Zeke without throwing him a dollar for dinner and a bottle. He just never has. So it couldn't have been Jesse."

"But that won't hold up in court, Zeke," Evaleen said disappointedly.

"Well, there was the matter of this." Zeke took something out of his pocket and handed it to Waco. "It was in the schoolmarm's hand when she died, and I think when I caught her it must have slid into my pocket. I noticed it this morning, too, but I didn't bother giving it to the sheriff. I decided to bring it to Miz Stockton instead—because the sheriff didn't want to hear anything I said."

Waco didn't comment on that, Evaleen noticed, as she saw what the item was. A gold pocket watch.

"It's Jesse's," she said, having seen him take it out of his pocket any number of times. She wanted to shrivel up and die. How on earth had Miss Worrell gotten Jesse's pocket watch? She didn't doubt Jesse, but the evidence was so overwhelming against him, she knew for certain her husband was going to hang. "Somebody's got to do something," she said worriedly, walking toward the buggy.

"Yeah," Waco said in agreement. "But the question is, what?"

Worried about Patrick changing his mind about murdering Zeke, the only witness who could positively identify him, they decided to take the miner back to Rainbow's End with them for the time being. He kept Waco busy talking for the next three miles while Evaleen remained silent, thinking over Waco's question. What could anyone do to save Jesse?

It wasn't until Waco pulled the buggy up to the stable area that the answer, so clear it was frightening, occurred to her. Could she do it? That she would be giving up everything she'd ever craved—a good life of plenty and the respect of the people in the community—she didn't care about, not if she saved Jesse. But could she actually, physically, pull off what she had planned?

She had no choice.

For a few seconds, she sat still in front of Rainbow's End, looking at Waco and Zeke as they climbed down off the wagon. Dare she tell Waco? She would have to, she decided, before he decided he was going to hunt down Patrick himself. He was that kind of man, she knew. But she needed him here to take care of things.

Waco appeared at her side to help her off the wagon, and she turned to him, not moving. She had to tell him. Now.

"I'm going to break Jesse out of jail," she said, looking into his eyes to gauge his reaction.

She heard Waco's sharp intake of air, but his face was guarded rather than surprised. "Now why on earth would we want to do that?"

"Not we. *Me.* So Jesse can hunt down his brother and bring him to justice."

"I can do that," Waco said guardedly.

"I don't want you getting involved or being in trouble

with the law. I have a feeling you don't want that either, am I right?"

He gave her a nonchalant lift of his dark eyebrows. "I'm destined toward hell already, Miz Stockton. A little more trouble in my life won't make a difference one way or the other."

She wasn't buying that. "Yes, and that's why you've remained totally trouble free for the last ten years or so on this ranch, right?"

"I'm not the issue here."

"That's right," she said, not wanting to argue. She had to save her strength and gumption for what was to come. "Jesse's the issue. He's everything to me, Waco; that's why I'm willing to do this. Besides," she said, her voice softening, "you might think you aren't worth anything to anyone, but you're needed here. Someone brave and capable has to watch over Theodora in case Patrick doubles back. And there has to be someone here Jesse can trust to keep this ranch going for us in case it takes a while to find Patrick."

Waco was scowling. "You'll be here with Theodora, and you'll have the hired hands to help you."

She shook her head. "I'm going with Jesse."

"The hell you say." Waco shook his head. "I've known Jesse a long time, Miz Stockton. He'll never stand for you ruining your life, especially not for his sake."

"He won't have a choice," she said resolutely.

"Why don't you just leave this to me?" Waco asked her, a note of pleading in his voice that she was amazed to hear coming from a man like him.

"I can't." She had no choice. When she broke Jesse out, she was going to make darned sure he knew that she'd sworn for better or worse. . . .

And she would damned well give up everything to keep her vow—for his sake. He'd been alone for too long. If they were both wanted and had to take Theodora and live the rest of their lives in hiding, well, then, that was the way it was going to have to be. She would do it for Jesse.

For love.


However much she might want to break Jesse out, Waco had other ideas. With his flat refusal to let her go anywhere, Evaleen had to wait two nights before he relaxed his vigil enough to leave the ranch. But, ever wakeful and a bundle of nerves since Jesse's imprisonment, she'd seen him ride out late in the evening when he'd probably assumed she was in bed. She'd waited over an hour to see if he returned before asking one of the hands where he'd gone. When told Waco had left to check on a reported rustler out on the south pasture, she'd known the time would never be better. Calloway Nesmith was coming by early the next morning to take her aunt shopping in town, and he could see to Victoria's and Theodora's needs. It was now or never.

Less than another hour later, armed with a pistol, her horse and a spare mount saddled and waiting for her in the back, on them packs loaded with supplies and blankets, Evaleen stopped by Theodora's room and kissed the sleeping child good-bye, unable to keep a couple of tears from falling onto the pillow beside her head. Then she went to the kitchen and left a brief note on the table, imploring her aunt to believe the best of her and to mother Theodora until she was able to return or send for her. Evaleen had every hope she would be able to—eventually.

Finally, she slipped through the back door and into the darkness. It occurred to her ever so briefly that Jesse might be angry that she was putting both their lives in jeopardy, but she'd have to deal with that when it happened. She had no choice. It was as though everything in her life had been destined for this moment, and even though nothing she had done in the past had frightened her so much, and the good Lord knew she didn't want to leave Theodora behind, she was ready to face the next phase of her life, so she walked steadfastly to where she'd left her horses.

They weren't there.

Frustration filled her, to be quickly followed by fury. Had Waco ordered someone else to spy on her and keep her from leaving, no matter what? Well, as of this moment, with Jesse in jail, she had the power on this ranch, and she would damned well leave if she wanted to.

Pivoting on her booted foot, she headed toward the bunkhouse where a light still gleamed, fully intending to get her horses resaddled and back under her control. Before she'd gone three feet, a hand came out of the darkness and over her mouth, and she was slammed up against a body and captured by an arm that held her in place despite her clawing at it with all her strength.

Patrick? Could it be?

It had been this moment she'd been dreading, but instead of screaming with fright, she went deadly cold inside and quit fighting. Patrick had made her lose her husband, the only real friend she'd ever had and the only man she'd ever loved.

Patrick had taken away her Jesse.

Her hands were still free, so she reached under her jacket into her waistband and pulled out the small pistol she'd gotten from Reynard's gun cabinet to use to get Jesse out. They might both wind up in hell, but she wasn't letting him do to her what he'd done to Maggie Worrell.

She'd shoot him where it would do the most harm first.

# Chapter Nineteen

"I thought you had more sense, Evie," Jesse said, his voice gravelly in her ear.

"Jess!" With a rush of relief, Evaleen gave him the pistol, which he pocketed, and then twisted in his arms to give him a long kiss. But he only brushed his lips across hers, lingering a little but not nearly long enough before letting her go.

She stepped back. He was barely visible in the dark, but then, she didn't have to see his features to know he was still withdrawn. She had heard it in his voice, felt it in the way he'd kissed her—as though he cared, but didn't want to show it. "How did you get out, Jesse?"

"Waco worried that you were going to get yourself involved in this mess, and he decided to save you the trouble by getting me out."

"And you came here for me, right?" She nodded without waiting for him to answer. "I knew you were only trying to drive me away from the jail to protect me, to keep them from suspecting I might try to help you."

"Evie—"

"We have to hurry if we're to get away." She strode away from him toward the stable. "I had two horses all ready, and I don't know what happened to them."

"Evie, listen to me!" Jesse caught her arm and made her face him. "We have the horses."

"We?"

He nodded. "You aren't coming with me. Waco is."

That stopped her as quickly as a slap in the face would have. "To find your brother, right?"

He nodded.

"Then you'll be back as soon as you do?" Her body began to relax a little, until she realized he wasn't answering. "Jess?" she asked, uncertainty, concern, and fear edging her voice.

"I'm not coming back."

"Of course you are. If you find your brother, then you can make him tell the truth and bring him in so the townsfolk will know who really killed Maggie Worrell."

"Do you really believe it will be that easy?" Jesse asked gruffly. His hands gripped her upper arms tightly. "Patrick despises me. If I'm lucky enough to find him and get him to admit to killing Maggie, he's not going to confess. Besides, if he does admit it, a man who could do that to a woman can't be allowed to get away with it and run free."

In horror, she realized what his words meant. Jesse was going to kill his brother. "There must be another way to see justice done. The people in the town—"

"I can't chance the townsfolk doing what's right. You think I want him coming back here to get you?" He paused, his teeth gritted. "He would, Evie. He wants to take my happiness away from me. He's stolen my freedom. Don't think for one minute he won't try to take away the only other thing in my life that means anything at all to me—you. The only chance I have of saving you is to find him and keep him on the run."

"Or make him think you don't care about me."

"It will keep Patrick away from you," Jesse told her, taking her hand in his. It was hot against the coolness of her skin. He'd been riding hard to get away from the jail, and Evaleen knew she was only holding him up. But she loved him, so how could she let him go? If she didn't, the law would catch him and put him back in jail—or worse. So she couldn't let him stay, either. That left her only one choice.

"Take me with you," she whispered.

"I can't."

"I can help you."

Jesse shook his head. "You're the most amazing woman I know, Evie, but even you can't fix this."

"Jesse," Waco said from somewhere off in the shadows near the stable, startling Evaleen. "We've got to hurry."

Jesse's hand came up to cup the side of her face, and he felt the sudden tears trickling down her cheeks. "We've both got to face this, Evie; I'm no good for you. Hell, I probably never was. A woman like you deserves someone upstanding that'll never cause her a moment's pain. You deserve someone wonderful."

Evaleen took a deep breath. Jesse wanted to give up everything to keep her safe, including having the family and the love she guessed he'd probably not had in a long, long time. Evaleen reached for his hand and gripped it between her own. She couldn't let him do this alone. "I've got someone wonderful already, Jess. Let me come with you."

Jesse pulled his hand away. He knew he had to. If he continued to feel the warmth of her skin against his, he would go mad. "I left instructions on the deputy's desk when we tied him up. He'll open them and have to bring them to Calloway. The ranch is yours Sell it, take the money, and start over with Dorie somewhere."

"I can't do that, Jess," she said, shaking her head "Rainbow's End is yours. It's all you've ever wanted."

"Wrong," he said softly, his heart melting away and leaving only a cold, lonely emptiness behind in its place. "I know now that you were all I ever wanted. But some things, darlin', just aren't meant to be."

"If I was all you ever wanted, then why are you giving up on us?" Evaleen asked, unable to believe that everything really wasn't going to work out for them after all. "What about our marriage?"

"Get a divorce."

"Jess—"

"Forget you were ever married to me, Evie. Leave the state and start again. It's the best thing you could do for yourself, and for Dorie. After we take care of Patrick, Waco and I are going to split up and go our separate ways, so neither of us will ever return to New Mexico anyway."

To her. He'd never return to her. "You can't mean that," she said, her voice choking on the words.

"I wouldn't say that if I didn't."

"I'll go with you. Aunt Victoria and Calloway can take care of Dorie for a while, and we'll settle someplace, then send for her. You won't have to be alone."

"I refuse to ruin your life any more than I already have." He grated out the words. Even if Evaleen didn't realize it—or wouldn't—Jesse knew her whole future was at stake. He couldn't have her along, growing to hate him when she had no life save that of a fugitive, watching for the law around every corner. "Besides, having you along will only prove to Patrick how much . . ."

*How much you mean to me,* Jesse thought, stopping himself from saying the words. If she knew how much he wanted her along, she would follow him anyway. He couldn't drag her down any farther into the mud with him. "Forget it," he said. He could hear Waco muttering and asking himself why he had ever gotten into this, because they were going to get caught and wind up in jail after all. Jesse knew he had to wind this up. "You can't go, Evie. I don't want you with me, and that's that."

Turning away, he left the air filled with only the lies he'd just uttered and the soft sounds of her crying. Cursing himself for hurting her, but not knowing any other way, he strode back into the shadows toward where he knew Waco was waiting.

Evaleen stood amazingly still, feeling as though her entire body—especially her heart—was turning into stone. He didn't want her to come with him.

And he wasn't coming back.

She heard the whinny of horses as he and Waco mounted, and suddenly she realized she hadn't told Jesse how much she loved him. Surely that would have to make a difference. It had to.

Blindly, she ran around the side of the stables toward where she believed they were. At the sight of their silhouettes riding off, she ran harder, but she couldn't catch up, and stumbled down to her knees.

"Jess, I love you!" she cried at the top of her lungs. But neither man turned, and neither came back. She couldn't even tell if they'd heard her.

Jesse heard Evaleen call out to him. His gut heard her, every nerve in his body heard her. His world was collapsing. The worst part of all of this was that he knew he'd brought this moment, and his and Evie's pain, on himself.

"I'm still willing to let her come along." Waco's low voice rumbled through the darkness.

"I'm not."

"Maybe it's for the best," Waco agreed.

From what his friend had said earlier, Jesse knew damned well Waco didn't think that at all, and was trying to goad him into agreeing to go back for her. Already knowing what he had to do, he was just plain not in the mood for a second person to talk reason to him. "Drop it, Waco, or I'll forget how highly I regard you and knock you off that high horse."

"So much for eternal gratitude," Waco said in an easy voice. "All I did was save your neck from a rope and try to talk you out of leaving behind the best thing that ever happened to you, and you want to make an enemy out of me." He paused. "Why is that, do you suppose?"

"How come you're so talkative all of a sudden?"

"Nerves," Waco said. "This is the first time I've gotten myself in a precarious position in . . . in a hell of a lot of years. I always talk when my nerves get rattled."

"That trait, given the mood I'm currently in, could be dangerous," Jesse said.

"I'll take my chances." Waco gave him a small grin that Jesse could see in the eerie moonlight's glow. "Are you sure about going north so close to Raton?"

"They'll expect us to go to Mexico," Jesse said. "I'm guessing Patrick will be sticking around town and looking for an opportunity to score big before he makes any other moves."

"You mean like rob a bank when the sheriff and deputy are gone?"

"That could be." In reality, Jesse didn't know what the hell Patrick thought he was doing. He could only hope he was right. Rubbing the weariness from his eyes, he cut across the road leading to Raton and led them into the cover of the wooded hillside so they could thread their way back toward town unnoticed.

"Well, Zeke will be a help." On his way to Raton earlier, before breaking Jesse out, Waco had paid for a room on the top floor of the saloon where Zeke could stay until Patrick was caught. Zeke had agreed to be their lookout, which meant staying up in that room and watching for Patrick to meander down the street in the evening.

"You think he'll stay sober?" Jesse asked.

"Sure. I promised him a reward if he helped me catch Patrick."

"A bottle?"

"Hell if I'm going to contribute to the man's debauchery. Nope, I promised him papers to his own patch of land."

Caught by total surprise, Jesse gazed at him. "You have land?"

"Some." He waved his hand in the air. "Not that it matters. You can have all the land you want, and it doesn't mean a damn thing."

"Ain't that the truth," Jesse said. The emptiness increased. But he did have one thing left to say to Waco.

"Thank you."

Waco shrugged. As they got deeper into the cover of the woods, he quit talking, apparently not so nervous now that they were no longer in the open. The silence, Jesse thought, was worse, for now he could hear the echo of Evaleen's words in his mind.

She loved him. He thought of the way his father and mother had loved each other, of the way his father had never gone far from the ranch and her memory, and of the way he was going to spend the next sixty years without his wife. Even if she divorced him, he would consider her to be his wife. A cold, empty feeling filled him, and he wondered if the emptiness was what a man felt when he went insane. His life was spinning out of his control, had been ever since he had turned his back on Evaleen's love.

God, he'd wanted to take her with him.

But to do so would have been purely selfish, condemning her to a life on the run, a life during which she wouldn't be the fine, respected citizen she'd always been. He couldn't go back to get her. He loved her too much to condemn her to his sentence.

As they rode, the emptiness Jesse was feeling ate at him, bit by bit, and he began to wish Waco would talk again to keep him from having to think about Evaleen. For the first time, he could finally understand what his father must have felt like when his mother had died. Like nothing else on the earth really held any meaning for him any longer. What had kept his father going, Jesse didn't know, but he did know what was going to drive him until the end of his days.

Destroying his brother.

By the time he and Waco finally settled on their blankets deep in the woods outside of Raton, all Jesse could think about was that he would now have to survive a life without Evaleen's love. From the pain inside him, he knew what he would have to do. Not care. Somehow he was going to have to make himself not care, convince himself that he was better off alone.

Like Waco was.

He had never bothered Waco for information about himself, about what the man was hiding from, but now he wondered. How could he have done it all these years, being alone? By not caring about anyone, or anything? But there was then one thing that didn't make sense....

"Why did you yank me out of jail, Waco?" he asked.

Lightly touching the gun at his side, Waco leaned toward Jesse. "Your father took me in, and both of you gave me a home for ten years," he said. "When a man's been treated so squarely for all that time, it's damned hard to sit back and watch one of his benefactors get hanged for something he didn't do."

Waco might have been running from something, Jesse thought, staring at the man, but he hadn't shed his ability, or maybe his need, to care about people. He probably wouldn't be able to either, which meant the rest of his life was going to be agony without Evaleen.

Agony, nothing. It was going to be sheer hell.

"You do realize that if the deputy ever figures out who hit him from behind and broke me out, that'll make you wanted too," Jesse pointed out.

"I just wish I could say that bothered me"—Waco pulled his dark hat over his eyes and settled back against his bedroll—"but it doesn't. I figured two heads will get your brother found and this mess straightened out better than one would. When we do that, I'll let you take all the credit, and you can come back as king of the town."

"That's awfully kind of you, Waco," Jesse said.

"Yeah, well, I'm not as fond of notoriety as you seem to be."

"I meant about putting yourself in jeopardy to help me."

Waco didn't move a muscle as he stared off into the forest in front of them. "You've got a pretty decent little family here who needs you, and family's worth riskin' a lot over. Besides, I'm not holier than thou like you're starting to think."

"Don't confess anything you don't want to," Jesse said.

"Naw. At the very least, you have the right to know. I've been keeping a secret about your brother. Now I guess I should have told you a while ago." He fell silent.

"Hell, don't stop now," Jesse said. Most of Waco's face was hidden under his hat, so Jesse couldn't tell why he was no longer talking. "If the posse shows up, we might just run out of time."

"You're a man of little faith." Waco pushed his hat up, and Jesse barely made out his grin in the moonlight. "I'm not certain," he continued, "that you're gonna even want to hear this. But judging from the circumstances we currently find ourselves in, I think you ought to know the worst."

"Spit it out," Jesse said, hoping whatever it was would take his mind off losing Evaleen. When he heard what Waco had to tell him, for a few long minutes, the shock of it actually did.

Still dressed in the riding clothes she'd been wearing when she'd thought to break Jesse out of jail, Evaleen sat in the large chair in the study, her hands resting on each arm, unmoving. In the hours since Jesse had ridden off, she'd felt like a china doll broken into a thousand pieces. She'd been sitting in the study since she'd picked herself up off the ground and come inside, unable to summon up the will to do much of anything except help Victoria get dressed and into her chair when morning had come. She'd been waiting, she realized now.

Waiting for all hell to break loose.

Just as she'd expected, a furious Sheriff Dunahy had shown up with Calloway Nesmith. Both of them paced in front of her now as her aunt sat near the doorway.

"I'll ask you again, Mrs. Stockton, have you seen your husband since he escaped?" Dunahy asked.

"I don't know where he is, Sheriff." She barely recognized her own weary voice. Upstairs, two of the fine members of the town were searching the rooms for Jesse, and she winced at every thump they made, wondering what kind of mess they were creating in Jesse's home. *Their* home.

"Then you did see him."

She met Dunahy's eyes. "Long enough for him to tell me to sell this ranch, get a divorce, and start over."

That stopped the man's anxious pacing, and he gave her a long look. "He had help getting out of jail."

"It wasn't me," she said emotionlessly. "I was going to, but someone beat me to it."

"Evaleen, that couldn't be true!" a shocked Victoria admonished. "You couldn't possibly have considered breaking a suspected murderer out of jail!"

Some sort of energy coursed through Evaleen's veins, and she pushed up out of her chair. "Of course it's true. My husband did not murder that unfortunate woman, and if you would all look past your judgmental noses for the truth, you would see that, too! Jesse loved Rainbow's End. There hasn't been anyone who has tried harder to keep a ranch going in this county. He wouldn't sacrifice everything he's been working for since his father's death to murder anyone."

"He threatened Miss Worrell!" the sheriff reminded her. "Many people heard him, including yourself."

"He told her that if she wrecked his marriage, she'd regret it. But what you all seemed to have forgotten in your haste to condemn the man is that I love Jesse Stockton, I will love him until the day I die, and he knows it. I've made no secret of it. He also loves me. There was no wrecked marriage here, gentlemen, and therefore, no motive for him to kill Miss Worrell. There was nothing between the two of them anyway except for her tortured imaginings of wooing Jesse away from me."

"If that is so, Mrs. Stockton," the sheriff said, his eyes narrowing, "then who on earth did kill her, and why would Miss Worrell accuse Jesse?"

"There's only one answer to that: Jesse's brother Patrick is still alive." She walked over to the fireplace mantel and picked up a small framed photograph that showed the two brothers together with Reynard Stockton some ten years before. According to Jesse, his brother had been twenty-four in the picture to Jesse's twenty, and the resemblance was so close they could have been twins—if you could dismiss the fact that even in the photo, Patrick's head was turned slightly askew, as though he didn't want anyone looking him in the eyes, not even in a likeness. At his worst, Jesse had never failed to look anyone in the eyes.

Evaleen handed the picture to the sheriff. Surprised by the sudden life flowing through her, she opened her arms to implore them to consider what she was saying. "If Patrick had caught her by surprise in the dark, then she may have really believed it was Jesse. Either that, or she was so furious at my husband for ignoring her overtures that she was purposely trying to condemn him to die with her. I don't know."

"But Reynard said a long time ago that Patrick was dead," Calloway reminded her. "And Jesse's reputation—"

"Oh, for heaven's sake!" Evaleen wanted to stomp her foot. "Reputation be damned! Sheriff, the day I went into that saloon, there was a saloon girl sitting on the lap of one of your neighbors. Does that make him a possible killer? I saw three men sitting in front of the general store a couple of Sundays ago instead of being in church. Does that make them killers? No one doubts my reputation, but I would have broken Jesse out of jail and helped him bring his brother to justice, if I could have. Does that mean I helped Miss Worrell to her death? If it does, why didn't she name any of us?"

Silence filled the room. The sheriff put the picture down on the table to the side of the sofa.

Calloway had been staring down at the envelopes he'd brought with him. Now he ventured to speak. "Why wouldn't Jesse take you along with him if he loves you so much, Evaleen?"

Her eyes teared up, and she blinked furiously, vowing not to let them see her weak. "I'm sure it's because he doesn't want my life ruined along with his. If that isn't true love, gentlemen, I truly don't know what is."

"Love or not, the best thing you could do for yourself is get a divorce," Victoria said sternly.

Evaleen stared directly into her aunt's challenging eyes. "Not even at the threat of death would I deny my love for Jesse Stockton, let alone divorce the man. It is my sincere hope that this mess gets cleared up and he's allowed to come home."

In the end, all her valiant pleading did little to change the sheriff's mind about finding Jesse, although apparently Dunahy thought her innocent enough of any complicity that he didn't take her to jail. He merely reminded her that if Jesse showed up again, she was honor bound to report it to him or the deputy, who, fortunately, had not been hurt too badly.

Before he walked out of the room, Calloway left her the envelope with the deed to the ranch in it, just as the letter from Jesse that the deputy had found had instructed. He'd also told her that due to the circumstances, he was going to take Victoria with him to stay in town, and that he'd be marrying her aunt within the week.

Victoria offered to take Theodora for company, and Evaleen accepted. The two would be staying at Calloway's large home with his hired help while he stayed at a hotel. Calloway had assured Evaleen she still had custody of Theodora, and the child would only be away from her a little while, until she figured out what she was going to do with the ranch, so she let Dorie go.

The arrangement, Evaleen thought once the house was empty, would probably be for the best for the time being, since her earlier inertia seemed to have been replaced with the energy of anger. Walking back into the study, she glanced down at the picture the sheriff had left behind on the table. Picking it up, she carried it back to the mantelpiece, but lingered there to stare at the three Stockton men for a while longer, especially at Patrick.

Abruptly, Evaleen turned, walked out of the study, and headed for her own bedroom. There was something she could do to help get the real killer. She could try to trap him. Jesse had indicated as much when he'd said that Patrick wanted to destroy him and get everything he had. If Patrick thought there was an iota of a chance that he could get Rainbow's End—lock, stock, and barrel—or perhaps her, it might be enough to entice him out of hiding, wherever he was.

So she would offer the ranch up to him on a silver platter—and make sure she had one of the noteworthy upstanding citizens of Raton listening as a witness when he came out of hiding. She'd made a stand in the study today for her husband, but she was going to have to do a lot better to fight for the man she loved to be able to return to her.

If he even would . . .

"Oh, no, Jesse." She swore under her breath, taking the gold watch Zeke had found from her skirt pocket and cradling it in her hand, along with his mother's wedding ring, next to her heart. "You aren't getting away with one more day of the bachelor life if I can help it. I don't want you to start liking it again."

Somewhere, she could picture Jesse grinning back at her, and she got busy making her plans, refusing to believe, for one second, that love wouldn't get Jesse back to her where he belonged.

# Chapter Twenty

It took Evaleen a whole day to get the items she needed made, but then, the next morning, she was able to seek out and have a talk with the manager at the Harvey Hotel, Mr. Hackensfield. After discovering that she was a longtime and honored employee of the line of restaurants and had a letter of recommendation from Mr. Harvey's top manager in Kansas himself, Mr. Hackensfield was happy to agree to let her see prospective buyers of her ranch in his hotel lobby, where she'd be safely chaperoned by the many people in and out all day.

After that it was a matter of tacking up the ranch-for-sale posters she'd had printed up all over Raton. It was possible, she thought as she did so, that Patrick could have gone to Mexico. Or East. Or to hell. The point being, he might not have remained around Raton. But she hung on to the hope that if he was anywhere about, her signs with the squared letters, RAINBOW'S END RANCH FOR

SALE—Inquire at Harvey Hotel Lobby, were sure to attract his attention.

Finished, she returned to the hotel, went to the spacious, comfortable lobby sofa with a book, and waited. Her mind was so busy focusing on how she would handle Patrick should he show up, that the words on the page blurred together. She was frightened—she'd be a fool not to be, she guessed—but if she could pull this off, she would have her beloved Jesse back again.

On the other hand, if she couldn't pull this off, Patrick might end up killing her, too. But that wouldn't matter, she supposed. For if she failed at getting Jesse back, what hope for happiness did she have anyway?

"You ain't going to like this, Jesse," Waco said flatly, dismounting at his and Jesse's camp after a surreptitious trip to Raton late in the evening. Behind him on a second mount was Zeke. "Everything's gone to hell."

"One could definitely say that," Jesse said. He ached from missing Evie; the sky was threatening rain with bright flashes of white, and he was close to crazy from waiting for Waco to get back with some kind of news about whether or not Zeke had seen Patrick in town. Yes, his life had gone to hell. "But why in particular are you philosophizing?"

"Evaleen's in town," Waco told him. "She's put posters up all over to sell Rainbow's End."

Hell, Jesse thought, had just gotten hotter.

"But the thing is," Zeke said, "she's stalled two bona fide offers. Good offers. It's like she ain't plannin' on sellin' at all."

Jesse scowled. "How do you know she turned down offers?"

Pulling his hat down further over his wild gray hair, Zeke

leaned down to help himself to a cup of coffee. "News is all over the saloon. Nobody can figure it out."

Jesse turned to stare at Waco for over a full minute. By the way his friend was staring back, Jesse could tell Waco had already figured it out and was just waiting for him to say he did. "Damn it all to hell, she's trying to lure Patrick out of hiding."

"It'd appear so." Waco's dark eyes never left him. "Told you to bring her with us. Leastways we could have kept her from doing something stupid if she'd been here."

"You could get annoying." Jesse scooped up his hat. Even though going into Raton could get him killed—he hoped not, but he had to face facts—he never considered any alternative. He couldn't let Evie go up against Patrick. She didn't stand a chance. "And since I don't feel like getting any more annoyed than my wife has already made me, you'd better stay here while I go get her."

"Not hardly," Waco replied, the words slipping smoothly off his tongue. "You'll need someone to play guard dog while you sneak in there and get her out of her room."

"At this point, nobody except Zeke knows you're helping me. You could still have a life. You aren't wanted."

"Not in Raton, anyway." Waco gave a dry chuckle. "Don't worry about it, Jess. I'm coming. You need me. I know Evaleen's room number."

"I give up." Jesse pointed to Zeke's mount. "Where did you get that?"

"Rented from the stables, fair and square," Zeke assured him. "I'll ride back with ya, and start watchin' again from the saloon. And I'll see to payin' the rental. That way you can keep the horse for Miz Stockton."

Jesse stared down at the grizzled old man. "Thanks, Zeke. I don't know why you're doing this, but I surely do appreciate it."

Zeke's pale cheeks turned bright red in the firelight. "Well, hell, Jess, I guess there's still a few of us left in town that figured you weren't so bad to begin with, and we think this is all a damned shame. No matter how it all turns out, I hope you don't forget that."

Zeke's earnest words left Jesse all choked up. He had at least two friends in Raton who cared enough to chance hanging along with him, and maybe a couple of others he didn't know about, and he had a woman who loved him enough to go up against his murdering brother. Ranch or no ranch, he was truly rich, and it was time he started understanding that.

All he had to do was get to Evaleen before Patrick did, and he'd be a damned lucky man, assuming he didn't get killed by the posse after him.

Almost ready to leave, he stowed the last of his bedroll under a lean-to he and Waco had made, then straightened to look at the two men who mirrored what he was feeling. The atmosphere felt charged. Jesse almost hoped he didn't spot his brother on this trip. Everything about the night seemed to be rushing pell-mell toward disaster, and he was beginning to feel like tonight was going to be the penultimate: either he or his brother was going to die.

It sure would be nice, though, if it wasn't him.

Shortly after the clock struck eleven that evening, Evaleen heard a faint clap of thunder. A storm. The perfect addition to a miserable day, which, at this point, seemed never ending.

Standing, she crossed the floor of her hotel room and, with a long sigh, put her unread book back in her valise. Still wearing the white bodice and skirt she'd had on all day, she found herself continually postponing bedtime, trying to avoid a repeat of the previous night, when, alone in bed, she'd kept remembering Jesse's lean, warm masculine length pulling her up against him. That memory and the thought of Jesse sleeping on the hard ground, living life as a fugitive, had made sleep elusive, as she was afraid it was going to be this night. He deserved so much more than to be outside and without a home—or a bed—especially on this night with rain pelting down on him. He deserved to have love in his life.

Walking over to the vanity chair, she sat down and stared into the mirror at her red-rimmed eyes and the bitter smile on her lips. At one time, she would have thought being struck by lightning would have served Jesse right. How things had changed. How *she* had changed, once Jesse had made her understand how much she needed love—and him—in her life.

Picking up the hairbrush she'd brought from home, she pulled it through her tousled hair. Her frustration stemmed mainly from not having Jesse's arms around her, yes, but also from the fact that her great plan was failing damnably, even though, ironically, it seemed she could sell Rainbow's End anytime she had a mind to.

She'd gotten four offers total, two by townspeople, which she'd promptly stalled, saying she would let them know. The third offer had come by messenger from a well-known, nearby rancher who'd gotten wind of her offer to sell. Since it, too, had been a bona fide bid, she'd sent a message back that she'd let him know. All that was left was this out-of-town man, who was supposed to have arrived on the seven-o'clock train. But if the inquiry had been for real, she hadn't found any strangers at the depot. If it had been set up by Patrick, neither had she seen anyone who even faintly resembled his picture or Jesse.

At the knock on her door, her eyes widened. It was after eleven. Who on earth . . . ?

"Yes?" she called through the still-locked door.

"It's Samuel, ma'am. You've a gentleman at the desk named George Avery, inquiring after buying the ranch. Should I tell him to call back in the morning?"

George Avery was the rancher with whom she'd corresponded by messenger. Why he had come to the hotel this late she had no idea, but it was possible he'd just finished his work and it was the first he could get away. Remembering the long hours Jesse had put in at the ranch before all the trouble, it sounded logical to her. And she had written on her posters that interested buyers should inquire at any time, wanting to leave the evening hours open in case Patrick came under cover of darkness.

Telling the doorman she'd be down directly, she pinned up her hair and splashed cold water on her eyes. But when she arrived down in the spacious lobby, the soft glow of the lamplight lit only the figures of the doorman, Samuel, and the manager, Mr. Hackensfield, bent over some paperwork on the counter. They lifted their heads when they heard her.

"Mrs. Stockton. Still up, I see," Hackensfield said with a smile. "The gentleman who wants to see you is having a smoke right out by the front door."

"Oh." Smiling briefly at them, she walked the few feet to the double doors. Through one of the glass panes set in both doors, she could see Mr. Avery's back and his arm straightening as he flicked away the small golden fire from a cigar onto the ground.

She opened the door and stepped outside under the canopy that kept the rain from soaking the two of them. "Mr. Avery," she greeted. "Do come in before the rain starts getting heavy."

"I believe I would rather talk out here." The man ground out the tiny fire with his boot and turned. Seeing him in the light coming from behind her, Evaleen gasped.

It was Patrick. It had to be. The resemblance was uncanny, except for his eyes, which were treacherous.

Jesse's brother smiled. "You recognize me, I see. Taking a big chance coming out here alone with a stranger, aren't you, what with the fact that there's a murderer on the loose?" His shrug was nonchalant, but it made Evaleen shiver.

"I know you don't believe your brother did it," she said, even though she knew the answer to that.

"No," he said, giving her a cold smile. "And I'd be willing to bet real money, Mrs. Stockton, you don't believe Jesse did it either."

The snake. She found it hard to believe he and Jesse shared the same upbringing. She'd left Jesse's watch in her pocket, and reaching inside, she gripped it for courage. She had to keep her wits about her and get Patrick inside where Mr. Hackensfield could overhear their conversation.

"The lightning will be starting soon," she said softly, surprised that she could still find her voice with her throat so tight. *Jesse,* she reminded herself. *Dealing with Patrick will be the only way Jesse—and our love—can be saved.* "We should go inside. Since Sam and Mr. Hackensfield didn't recognize you earlier, you'll be safe enough."

"By all means," he told her. "I'd love to go back inside. I want to hear the plans you have for the ranch."

Not wanting to turn her back to him, but having no choice, Evaleen reentered the lobby. The store manager glanced up and nodded at them, and she shot him what she hoped was a look that would show him she wanted him to listen. But her eyes were the only thing she dared let speak, since Patrick was close enough to her that he could hear a whisper. Remembering Maggie Worrell's grisly fate, the last thing she wanted to do was to make Patrick angry.

She walked over to the far side of the foyer, trying to

remain close enough to the two Harvey employees for them to bear witness to whatever Jesse's brother might say. Turning to face Patrick, she took another deep breath.

"I've been delaying buyers and turning down offers, hoping you'd appear."

Patrick's eyebrows rose in interest. "You don't say."

"I wanted to make you an offer."

"This should be interesting." Patrick leaned back against the wall and crossed his arms over his chest. In those few seconds, he did remind her of Jesse, and her heart gave a little thump at the painful reminder. "What's your offer, Evaleen?"

"I'm going to sell the ranch, and I'll give you all the proceeds, every cent, for a new life in Mexico or Europe or wherever, if you will write on a sheet of paper that you were the one who really killed Margaret Worrell."

Patrick's lips rose at the sides in a slow smile. "Now why would I want to do something crazy like that?"

"I'll keep the paper to myself for a week," she said, swallowing to keep her voice from shaking. "That will give you the chance to get so far away you'd never get caught. Jesse might be free, but you'll have gotten your revenge or whatever it is you want from your brother. Even if Jesse would want to buy the ranch back, he wouldn't be able to, with no money. He will have lost the only thing he ever cared about."

"I don't believe that," Patrick said, his mouth—so like Jesse's—still smiling at her. "He cares about you."

She shook her head, an overwhelming surge of sadness running through her. "If he cared about me, Patrick, he would have taken me with him while he hunted you down. I offered to give up everything for him, but he didn't want me. He's too eaten up with his fury over losing the ranch because of you."

"What makes you think a piece of paper will make anyone believe I did it?" Patrick asked easily. Although he would appear unconcerned to the casual observer, Evaleen noticed his eyes shift occasionally toward the two men at the counter, as though he was watching them, speculating . . . about what, she didn't know. "As far as this town is concerned, they all think I'm dead, remember?"

The last remark was wrapped up in bitterness, catching Evaleen off kilter. She had to think for a few seconds to remember the answer to his question. Why would anyone in Raton believe Patrick had come out of the blue and murdered Miss Worrell? She couldn't mention that the other two men would witness his confession and put them in danger if Patrick decided he didn't want witnesses.

The watch. It was Jesse's watch, but Evaleen would bet her life that Patrick had stolen it from the ranch at some time and had possessed it the night of the murder. Margaret had apparently grabbed it during the struggle and had dropped it when she'd died. It would implicate Jesse more than Patrick, but maybe he wouldn't realize that—if he didn't know what it was.

She covered it with her hand and pulled it out of her pocket, taking care not to let him see anything other than a tiny dot of gold and not to tell him how she'd really gotten it. "I found this where Miss Worrell died after they put Jesse in jail."

She was about to add some tomfoolery about how this evidence along with his letter would prove his guilt, but she didn't have to say another word. Patrick's face changed from a look of cold serenity into one of pure evil. In a split second as he took a step closer to her, she understood exactly what Margaret had faced in her last few moments of life. The devil himself.

"Oh, my Lord," she whispered, wondering if the man were indeed capable of tearing her apart limb from limb right there. "I lied, Patrick. It's only Jesse's watch."

"Give it to me, Evaleen," he said, taking a couple more steps toward her, "or you will be very, very sorry."

She stood unmoving, thinking that he wouldn't do anything with two men so close by—and praying she was right. Both her hands tightly grasped her only remaining connection to the love she would never see again, if she couldn't succeed at proving Jesse's innocence. Jesse had always worn the watch in his vest pocket next to his heart, and even though she might have lost him, she wasn't giving up this connection to him.

Patrick's fingers were suddenly gripping her hands so tightly she knew she would see bruises on them the next day. Then, as he yanked her fingers open with brute strength, she realized that she had better get away from this man, or she might not have to worry about bruises the next morning. She might not have to worry about anything.

Even though he still had one of his hands wrapped with brutal tightness around her wrist, he had the watch now. With that link to Jesse gone, her fight was over.

"You win," she said, trying to pull free from him. But he wouldn't let her loose.

"Not that easily." He gave her a long, slow look that made her want to kick him someplace where it would hurt him badly. "You know, I'm surprised. I knew your sister wouldn't fight me, but after watching you with my brother, I really had been looking forward to more of a battle."

Her sister ... With the knowledge of what Patrick was capable of still fresh in her mind, a sickening feeling flooded through her. She had to swallow to wet her throat before she could speak. "What do you know about Cynthia?"

"The same thing you do." He grinned. "Your sister wasn't the suicidal type, was she?"

"Oh, my Lord," she breathed, nerves prickling her face and neck.

"She told me she wanted some money for Theodora, or she would tell Reynard the truth—that Dorie's daddy wasn't some cowpoke passing through town, but his own no-good son. That she'd only come to him because she'd known he had money, and it was only right he should help support his grandchild. I couldn't let her ruin Reynard. He wouldn't have been able to hold his head up in town ever again."

She was talking to a murderer. She had no reason to believe that Patrick was telling her the truth, yet everything fit—Patrick's reasons for talking to Dorie, his daughter. . . . Theodora was Patrick's daughter.

"Till the day she left him, my father never suspected that Cynthia had been using him. She deserved what she got. Walking out on him like that damned near killed him. So I slipped her something to make sure she never hurt him again."

Cynthia hadn't committed suicide. Patrick had murdered her. Evaleen pulled against his grasp again, to no avail. Even though she'd lost Jesse, and she shouldn't care about anything anymore, she had to get free—she had to! Without any proof that Patrick had murdered Maggie, he'd be free to take his daughter, and she couldn't let that happen.

Using her free arm to slap him, Evaleen kicked the side of his leg as hard as she could. In her peripheral vision, she could see that Hackensfield was staring at them, and Samuel had started for the door.

"Shit, you've done it now," Patrick muttered, pulling his gun out and waving it toward the men as he jerked her around and up against him with his other arm. "Don't think about getting help," he told Samuel.

Her heart sank.

The indignant manager had been heading toward her, but stopped when he saw Patrick's gun. "What the hell?"

"You don't have to do this, Patrick," Evaleen said, her conscience throbbing miserably with the realization that she'd put two men at risk. She hadn't even thought that might happen. It was supposed to have been so simple— a written confession and Mr. Hackensfield overhearing Patrick admit who he was and that he existed.

"It's only Jesse's watch that was found as evidence," she hastened to tell Patrick so that he would let them go. "That would incriminate him in the murder, not you."

"Tell me another tale." Patrick released her. Since he still had the pistol aimed directly at her, she moved a foot or so away and turned toward him, just in time to see him flick open the watch. He then held it out toward her so she could read the inscription inside the front cover. When she did, the room began to spin.

To Patrick, Christmas, 1886, Love, Father, it read. When Reynard had given Jesse his watch, he'd apparently also sent Patrick one. Just two short years ago, and many years after Reynard had declared Patrick dead to the town. Evaleen felt sick. If she'd only opened the watch, she would have seen the year on it and could have used it to convince the sheriff to search for Patrick himself.

But now all she could do was stare at Patrick.

He grinned. "Yeah, the schoolmarm was holding my watch. I murdered her. My brother had everything all his life, including our father's respect. But Jesse wasn't happy, so I could let him be—then." He paused for a brief second or two. "But when I came back here, just to take a few things I could sell now that Reynard was gone, I watched Jess for a while. He was happy. You could see it in his face. He was married to you, he was taking care of Theodora, who worshiped him. . . ." His voice dropped off, and Evaleen thought she saw a trace of hurt in his eyes. "I'm the kid's father. She should have been worshiping me."

"Oh, my Lord," Evaleen said, feeling her knees go weak and the room start to spin at the very notion.

Ignoring Hackensfield's protest, Patrick stepped forward and once more pulled her against him with his free arm. "Now that the lady is a bit more cooperative," he said, the evil back in his eyes, "it's time I took what I wanted—which is all the money in your safe." He gestured at Hackensfield. "And don't bother lying about not having money. I know for a fact that you won't make a deposit until tomorrow, and there's three days' worth of receipts. Cough them up, and then I'll tell you what I have planned for the four of us."

Agreeing it would give everyone the best possible odds, Waco and Zeke parted from Jesse at the edge of town and rode toward the back entrance to the saloon, meaning to keep a low profile as Zeke returned to his room on the upper floor. Jesse hobbled his mount near some trees and, avoiding any light from homes along the way, headed on foot through the two side streets leading to the Harvey Hotel.

After Waco dropped off Zeke safely, his friend was going to come with the horses to the west side of the train depot close to the hotel and wait there until Jesse arrived with Evaleen. They'd split up, and Waco would retrieve Jesse's horse and join them at the original campsite they'd just left.

That was the plan. What would happen, Jesse knew, was anyone's guess, especially with Evaleen possibly angry at him and his dragging her two miles in the rain.

Drops of rain ran down his shoulders and the sleeves of his shirt as he limped quickly nearer to the hotel. There was no sign of activity anywhere under the canopy or around the front entrance, which would figure, since the last train of the evening came in at eight.

He stood there a minute. He supposed he could just walk in with his hat pulled low over his eyes like he had a room there and head toward the stairwell, but he ran the risk of being recognized. Still, he couldn't not get Evaleen. Hoping his luck would hold, he tugged his hat low over his eyes—hell, it always seemed to work for Waco—approached the door, and put his hand on the knob.

And stopped himself from entering, just in time.

In front of him, at an angle, he could see Evie was in trouble. A tall man had his back to the door, and he was waving a gun at two other men who stood near the counter.

Patrick. Jesse knew it was. Everything inside him went cold, and he lifted his gun out of its holster. From the looks of things, Patrick was robbing the place, but worse, his brother was holding Evie around the waist and had her pulled up against him.

That son of a bitch. He was going to have to kill him.

Inside, a well-dressed man was handing his brother a large canvas bag, and from the woebegone look on his face, Jesse guessed it was filled with money.

Patrick let loose of Evaleen and took the money in hand. Pointing his gun at her, he backed up, growing close enough for Jesse to hear his voice.

"I'm taking Evaleen here with me. Give me at least twenty-four hours to get away before you send the law after me," Patrick said, "and I'll let her live. Agreed?"

He paused, but no one answered.

"Oh, hell, then, I'll shoot you two here and take her anyway. They'll just think my brother did it, and his little wifey here helped."

Jesse swore under his breath. The two other men, afraid for their lives, nodded at Patrick, but then the man Jesse guessed ran the hotel turned his head. He and Jesse made eye contact, and the hotel manager acknowledged Jesse with a slight lift of his fingers.

His gun still on Evaleen, Patrick backed up one more step. "Open the door for me, sister-in-law."

Since Patrick kept his gun pointed at her head, Evaleen didn't try to run as she pushed the door open. Certain she was not going to get out of this alive, she was trembling so hard she thought she would fall down if she had to walk three more steps.

A bolt of lightning blinded her, and she moved her head involuntarily against the sudden brightness and the clap of thunder that followed. That was when she saw him.

Jesse.

Unsure if he knew what was going on, she opened her mouth to call out a warning, knowing that Patrick was capable of killing him if he saw he was there. Jesse clamped his finger to his lips to keep her quiet, and she shut her mouth—but too late. Patrick sensed her hesitation and looked in the same direction she had.

He pointed his gun directly at Jesse.

"No!" Evaleen yelled, throwing herself full force against Patrick's arm at the same time Jesse launched himself at Patrick. The three of them rolled in the wet grass to the side of the walk as the gun went off.

Almost deafened by the shot so close to her ear, Evaleen lay where she landed. To her side she could feel the thumps against the earth as Jesse and Patrick fought, fists smacking against flesh. Knowing she was powerless to help Jesse, she tried to get up and out of the way, but then Patrick managed to get up and step backward, and his boot heel came down on her outstretched arm. She cried out in pain.

Patrick was jerked away by Jesse, freeing her, and then suddenly, out of nowhere, Waco was lifting her off the ground and carrying her away from the hotel, shielding her body as best he could from the pelting rain.

"Let me down! You have to help Jesse!" she cried over the thunder, batting at his chest.

"I've got to get you to a safe place first. Jesse told me whatever happens, to make certain you were safe."

"You don't understand, Waco!" she said, her voice filling with desperation. He had to get back to help Jesse. "Patrick confessed the truth in front of witnesses. Jesse's going to be free. You've got to go help him. Don't let him kill Patrick! If he kills Patrick, he'll never be free!"

Waco stopped. As Evaleen stared at him, she could see in his eyes that he agreed with her. Then within seconds, Waco went into action, swiftly putting her on her feet and hurrying back to the two brothers.

Evaleen lifted her skirts and ran after him. Jesse had Patrick down on the ground and was pounding a fist into his brother's face, over and over. Waco pulled at him, but filled with fury as he was, Jesse pushed him away and lifted his fist to hit his brother again.

"Jess, no!" Evaleen screamed, catching his arm herself. "It's over. He confessed!"

Jesse's arm stopped in midair, and he looked over his shoulder at her. The mass of confusion in his eyes slowly melted away. Letting Patrick drop to the ground, he rose to his feet, and she slipped into his arms. He held her tightly, the heat of his fury warming her even with the rain pelting down on their heads, soaking them both as they listened to the commotion around them. They stood, holding each other, until Carter Hackensfield approached.

"I've sent someone for the doctor and to find the sheriff," he said. "You and Mrs. Stockton need to come inside and wait."

Jesse lifted his hands to her shoulders and pulled away from her. His eyes were shaded in the next streak of lightning. "I ought to turn you over my knee for this one, Evie. I told you my brother was dangerous."

"Not as dangerous as standing in the rain drawing lightning is," she said, giving him a tiny little smirk in return. She would have been worried about his tone, but his thumbs were slipping under the neckline of her blouse and caressing the tender skin there.

"I'm serious."

"Let's discuss this inside," Evaleen said, capturing one of his hands in hers and pulling him toward the door. But Jesse hesitated. Next to the entrance, Samuel had a gun and was guarding the moaning Patrick. He wanted to ask his brother why he hated him so much, but somehow it didn't matter. It was over. Patrick was finished....

And he had Evaleen.

Evaleen gave Patrick a sideways glance filled with hurt. "He killed Cynthia," she said, feeling the pain flowing through her. Then she remembered and met Jesse's eyes. "Oh, Lord, Jess. Patrick is Dorie's father."

Jesse nodded. "Waco suspected as much when your sister was here. He spotted her meeting Patrick a couple of times out in the hills, and finally warned your sister to leave Reynard or he would tell."

Closing her eyes, Evaleen tried to banish the image from her mind and let her sister rest at peace.

"Mr. Stockton," the Harvey manager urged, appearing before them. "Please come inside. Consider yourself a guest of the hotel. We have towels and hot coffee ready."

Jesse faced the grateful man. "Did you hear Patrick confess to the murders?"

Carter Hackensfield nodded affirmatively. "And we saw the evidence Mrs. Stockton had for him. You're free. What's more, you're a hero for saving half a week's worth of Harvey Hotel income. I wouldn't be surprised if Fred Harvey came to Raton to thank you personally."

"Right now, I'll settle for the sheriff," Jesse said grimly. "I can't wait to see the look on his face when he sees my brother back from the dead."

As Mr. Hackensfield went inside, Patrick moaned and muttered something that sounded like a curse under his breath, and Jesse turned to him. But when Evaleen gently squeezed his arm, he turned away. It was over. He started to follow his wife into the hotel, then stopped and turned.

"Waco?" he called, but save for Samuel and his brother, there was no one else out there in the rain.

"It seems like he's gone," Evaleen whispered.

Jesse nodded solemnly. "He said he would stick around long enough to see me free, and when the time came, he'd let me have the glory."

"Do you think he'll return to the ranch?"

"I don't know. We'll talk about him later. Right now, before the sheriff gets here, you and I have a few things to discuss."

The two of them slipped through the doorway to the lobby, where a maid had left towels and coffee, courtesy of the hotel. Still standing, Evaleen took the towel and wiped the blood at the side of his mouth. She looked ready to pretend the whole evening had never happened, Jesse thought—but he wasn't.

"I have never been so scared in my life," he said. "If I hadn't been there, Patrick could have taken you off and done horrible things to you. If you had just stayed at the ranch, none of this would have ever happened."

Her eyebrows lifting, she lowered the towel and backed up a step. "If I had stayed at the ranch, Jesse Stockton, no, none of this would have happened. We wouldn't be here right now. I would still be all alone, Patrick would have succeeded in robbing the hotel, and you would still be running from the law, curled up on some rock in the rain, alone with your own personal misery. I suppose that's what you still want, from the look on your face right now."

"Hell no, I don't want that," he told her. "I've never wanted that."

"Well, that's good." Her lips parted in a smile again. "Because for some silly reason, I happen to love you."

Jesse couldn't help it, he began to chuckle. Leaning down, he brushed his lips across her neck. "I'm one hell of a lucky man."

"Yes, you are," she said softly, tingling at the feel of his mouth against her wet flesh. Dropping the towel she was holding, she slipped her arms around him to give him a long kiss.

He finally pulled away, but only a little. "We're both dripping wet."

"I know," she murmured, and kissed him again.

"The sheriff just walked in."

"I know," she said, and kissed him again.

"But what about appearances?" he muttered low in his throat, his hands warming her back as they caressed her.

"If caring about them means losing you, I don't give a hang about appearances," she said earnestly.

Jesse kissed her this time, his tongue dancing around with hers before he pulled away. "The whole time I thought we'd never be together again," he told her, "I kept dreaming of the way you were when I fell in love with you. The hat, the remarks, and that twinkle you got in your eye whenever you got something over on me."

"You saw a lot of that twinkle, didn't you?" she asked, leaving her arms looped around his neck. "But not enough, or you wouldn't have risked your life coming back to get me." She tilted her head sideways in question. "That was why you came back, wasn't it? To get me?"

"I wasn't standing out there with an offer to buy the place back from you, sweetheart," he teased. She tried to step on his toe in retaliation, but he circled her waist and lifted her off her feet for another kiss that got her sidetracked again.

When he pulled away, he added, "When I heard from Zeke that you were selling the ranch but had turned down good offers, I knew what you were doing—and that I'd have to come get you so you'd be safe. The whole way here, I promised myself once I had you again, I was going to make sure you knew how much I love you and that I was miserable without you."

She smiled up at him, her eyes bright. "After we make sure everything is settled with the sheriff, we'll go to my room and you can show me exactly how much you love me." She turned and walked a step, then said over her shoulder, "By the way, now that I know you're really fond of the hat, I'll start wearing it again."

"I'm not that fond . . ."

She purposely ignored him as she walked over to the sheriff, leaving Jesse with a huge grin on his face. How quickly his Evie could turn the tables on him. He adored her.

The hat, on the other hand, was history.

# Epilogue

*One year later*

"I've gotten a letter from Waco," Jesse said, entering the study and walking over to where Evaleen was feeding their two-month-old son, Josh. He held the letter in his hand and skimmed the first page. "It seems he heard about the winter we had and was worried about us. He wants to know if we need any money."

"How sweet of him," Evaleen said, watching Jesse as he continued to read the letter. It *had* been a long, hard winter. Patrick had been hanged for the murder of Margaret Worrell, but with his death had come a blessing: Theodora was officially their daughter now, and no one could ever take her away. The town had accepted the three of them fully. Several men had apologized to Jesse for doubting him. She herself had had a difficult pregnancy in the midst of everything, but baby Josh had been born healthy and was now thriving. And the snows ...

The snows had come in the worst blizzards that anyone thereabouts could remember, and cattle had perished everywhere, including on their ranch. But they had survived the winter better than most because Jesse had heeded warnings from their new foreman Zeke, who had sobered up and come to live on the ranch with them, saying he was too old to move far away to the land Waco had deeded him. They'd discovered the older man had a real feel for ranching, and he'd known a few tricks which had enabled them to save some of the cattle, including their best breeding stock.

No, they didn't need any money, but it was kind of Waco to worry, Evaleen thought. It made her just that much more curious about him.

"Where do you suppose he came into enough money to offer any to us?" she asked Jesse. "And where is he?"

Jesse flattened out the pages. "He says he's headed to Colorado; he's always had a whole lot of money, and for the last ten years, it's been sitting in a bank in San Francisco. He's left most of it in there, and says it's available anytime we need it. He thanked us for naming him Josh's godfather, but says it's an honor he'll probably never get back here to accept."

"What does *that* mean?"

"With Waco, who knows?" Jesse shrugged. Although inwardly he felt a sense of foreboding, he didn't want to alarm Evaleen. She'd been through enough since she'd met him. "In case you're curious, he also wrote that his real name is Ethan Waco Steele. I never knew that, either. He wishes us all the best, and adds if we ever need help, we're to contact his banker in San Francisco. We're his only heirs." He gave her an ironic grin. "Damn, but I wish people would stop putting us in their wills."

"I don't think it worked out all that badly before," Evaleen said, her eyes twinkling. But then she added wistfully,

"When you write him, tell him he always has a home here." She waited for Jesse's nod, and then continued, "I wish he'd find someone and settle down so we could be sure he's all right."

"You think marriage would make him happy?" Jesse asked, sticking the folded letter back in his pocket. Kneeling down in front of her, he leaned forward and ran his finger slowly along her cheek, but his gaze wandered down to where she was feeding the baby.

"I don't know," she admitted, adjusting the baby's blanket to cover up her breast. "After all, he's been footloose for a long time. I don't know that he could change just for a woman like you did."

"I did not change," Jesse said, moving the edge of the blanket back down and grinning. "At heart, I'm still the same rogue you fell in love with."

"You are?" she asked innocently. "I've forgotten in the last couple of months since the baby." She met his gaze with a naughty grin. "As soon as Joshy falls asleep, I guess you'll have to show me all over again and prove it."

Leaning over and kissing the top of his baby's head and then her breast, Jesse looked up and brushed his lips across her mouth. "Upstairs, ten minutes?"

"I'll be there."

He walked back out of the room, whistling.

"And I'm bringing my hat!"